DRAKE MCCREIESS SOCIETY

BELFORD SCOTT

authorHOUSE®

AuthorHouse™
1663 Liberty Drive
Bloomington, IN 47403
www.authorhouse.com
Phone: 1-800-839-8640

All characters appearing in this work, Drake McCreiess Society, are fictitious.
Any resemblance to real persons, living or dead, is purely coincidental.

Published by AuthorHouse   12/15/2014

ISBN: 978-1-4969-1016-5 (sc)
ISBN: 978-1-4969-1015-8 (e)

Library of Congress Control Number: 2014908201

Any people depicted in stock imagery provided by Thinkstock are models,
and such images are being used for illustrative purposes only.
Certain stock imagery © Thinkstock.

This book is printed on acid-free paper.

DRAKE McCREIESS SOCIETY is a fast paced novel about love, war, friends, powerful people, and betrayal. Drake McCreiess is a flawed protagonist coming to grips with right and wrong. Questions of God, sin, and redemption weigh heavy on his mind. He is a man that realizes there is more to him than what others need and believe. His wartime experiences haunt him and his search for a new beginning drains the life from him.

It's a work that cuts with a double-edged sword and will always be relevant – good versus evil – flawed man coming to grips with right and wrong. The story is a sequence of events that will softly touch the reader's heart, have the reader cringing, make the reader laugh, and create an inner debate for the reader throughout the story.

The war is over but it lingers for many. The human cost of war is enormous. People are killed, wounded, and lives are forever changed. The scenes of evil, carnage, blood and despair is something that many soldiers deal with on the battlefield as well as at home. On the battlefield it is dealt with by having the simple human instinct of just wanting to make it to the next day. At home it is a constant struggle for Drake McCreiess to keep his war experience and personal tragedies in perspective.

Drake McCreiess is trapped by societal regulations and he knows he is better than those that created the rules. He is a good man who has the capability to be violent. His captors will use his violent capabilities to carry out a professed justice for those they feel walk the streets with impunity after creating so much criminal mischief. McCreiess will set himself free, but first he will have to confront the demons created by war, and then the friends and powerful people that ensnared him in such a secret and wicked association.

PART 1

Sucker...

October 04, 1983 – US Marines and Beirut, Lebanon

Corporal Drake McCreiess peered through his Leatherwood ART riflescope at his potential target. The target was a young man flirting with the two hundred meter perimeter the Marine platoon had established with the use of barbed wire. The young man never touched the barbed wire, but he got real close on a few different occasions. McCreiess placed the cross hairs of his scope on the young man's forehead and took a deep breath and held. The young man bent over to pick up a soft drink can; he shook it and then swallowed the remainder of the drink.

McCreiess placed the M21 rifle he held on safe, let out his breath, and placed the rifle on the sand bags near him. The young man turned out not to be a threat. McCreiess allowed the tune "*Trouble*," from an Elvis Presley movie, to enter his thoughts as he continued to monitor the young man and the area he was tasked with securing. He lightly sang to himself.

"Marine, many of man has died for less around here."

"Sir?" McCreiess jerked from his concentration on the young man and whirled to find that Captain Grant was standing behind him.

"Especially around here." Grant paused and then smirked. "Drinking from the cans that third platoon discarded should not be tolerated." He chuckled to himself.

"Sir." McCreiess tried to interject but didn't know what he wanted to say.

"You have every right to kill that man." Captain Grant looked through his binoculars. "Yep. That man is too close to our yard." He smiled. "And I enjoy the Elvis song. That movie, King Cre..."

"Sir. He has not crossed the barbed wire. Nor has he attempted..."

"Isn't that just splitting hairs?" The Captain grinned and chuckled as he placed the binoculars on the bags next to the rifle. "No one would say a thing if you split that Jihadist's head like a cantaloupe."

"I don't know that he is a Jihadist..."

"Aren't they all?" The Captain dusted himself off. "This is Beirut, Lebanon, son."

McCreiess stood silent, unsure how to respond.

"McCreiess, I know you have the gift for killin'. Everyone in the division has heard the story about how you took out the three Jihads near the French compound."

"Yes Sir. It was actual..."

"Why'd you become a Marine son?" The captain interrupted McCreiess as he wiped the perspiration from his chin. It was a balmy 102 degrees, and with little shade Grant worked up a sweat as he moved from one guard post to another.

"To serve and protect my country, Sir." McCreiess quickly answered.

"To serve who and protect them from what?" The captain drilled. "Hell, the homeland hasn't been attacked in..."

"To protect the freedoms our forefathers..."

"You see anyone in this country trying to take freedoms from anyone in the United States?" Captain Grant frowned as he became more serious. "Politicians in your own country will shit-can more freedoms than anyone around here ever will."

"Sir..."

"Everything you believe is propaganda that someone has pumped into you and you believe every word of it." The Captain pushed his canteen toward McCreiess, offering him a drink.

McCreiess declined with a hand gesture.

"We're here to defend the Christians who can't defend themselves. We're not here to protect the red, white, and blue." The Captain took a drink. "Every one of these Christians could be slaughtered and the flags in the US would keep flyn' high." Grant nodded at the young man near the barbed wire. "We're here because some evangelical lobby group says we should be here, and they donate a lot of money to politicians who want to keep their cushy jobs."

"I just thought."

"Marine, don't buy into the shit pumped into your head by the people who want you to keep doing their dirty work. We are not the best and the brightest. We have no higher form of citizenship and no one is in debt to us because we wear these uniforms." Captain Grant smiled and finished off the canteen. "You didn't have to volunteer for this shit and just because someone else decides not to join doesn't make them any less a person." He slowly twisted the cap back onto his canteen. "We fight wars to keep others fat, happy, and wealthy. And they tell you stupid shit because they don't want to pay you to do it."

"You speak of General Smedley Butler, Sir." McCreiess looked toward the barbed wire fence and saw the young man he earlier pointed a weapon at pick up more soft drink cans, shake them and either toss them or drink from them.

"General Smedley Butler was a fine Marine. And he was right about the 'sucker class' of which you are now a part." Grant placed the canteen in its belt holder and secured it by snapping it closed. "Smedley spoke out about the 'sucker class' and against deployments like this. What he considered adventurism and interventionism."

McCreiess remained silent as he kept a watchful eye over the barbed wire area he was responsible for securing.

"Don't be a sucker all your life McCreiess because you will only have yourself to blame when you wake one day to realize that you are a poor and stupid person who did so much to keep others in suits and champagne."

McCreiess took a deep breath and let it out. He wasn't sure what to think about the captain's words of wisdom.

"That young man and his family appreciate the fact that you are on duty." Captain Grant smiled as he watched the young man fiddle with cans. "Many a Marine would have split that young man's head wide open." He paused. "I appreciate you as well, Corporal McCreiess. Real discipline is a rare gift."

The Captain turned to walk away.

"Why do you do it, Sir?" McCreiess asked before the captain could get away.

"Every life I've lived on this earth has been as a warrior, so why would this life be any different?" The Captain glanced at the young man near the barbed wire fence. "Go ahead and kill him if he messes with that wire. If only to set an example."

"Yes, Sir. I will." McCreiess remained on watch.

"I know you Drake McCreiess. You and I have served in many of battle together." Grant removed his steel pot helmet and squinted as he looked into the sun. "Shit son, we fought in battles people read about in history books. Some battles we fought never made it to a book."

Grant turned and walked away as McCreiess sat silent, reflecting upon the Captains cryptic remarks.

McCreiess watched as Captain Grant faded away. He turned his attention to the young man who was now looking at him and holding a can to his mouth. The young man tilted the can back, sipping its content until it was finished and then tossed it to the ground. McCreiess waved at the young man, smiling when he waved back.

The young man finished sifting through all of the cans that lay in front of him. He looked back at McCreiess and gave him a smile and wave before running away; probably to find more half empty cans other Marines ditched, McCreiess wondered.

***

McCreiess never saw Captain Grant again. The next morning the Captain and two hundred and nineteen other Marines perished after suicide bombers detonated truck bombs inside the lobby of the Marine barracks. He lost several friends in Beirut, most in the barracks bombing, some to engagements with the enemy, a couple to suicide. Many of the Marines killed in Beirut were young men he attended boot camp with, trained with while serving the 1st Battalion 8th Marines, and eventually fought alongside. The only reason McCreiess' life was spared from the barracks bombing was because the Marine tasked with relieving him from his guard post over slept and was killed by the collapsing and crushing rubble.

McCreiess was in Beirut for another four months after that and eventually made Sergeant before leaving for the States. He like many of the other Marines who remained in Beirut after the bombing wanted revenge for the deaths of their friends, but the order for the Marines to pull out of Lebanon came instead. The withdrawal seemed more like a retreat for many of the Marines and that combined with the deaths of his brothers in arms only made McCreiess realize that life was cheap to politicians who ventured without knowledge and conviction. He arrived in Beirut a tough naive young person who wanted nothing more than to serve his country on the battlefield. He departed Beirut with the knowledge of who he really was.

The System

Max Merrell looked over the room he and Drake McCreiess had shared for the last forty-eight hours. The room was part of a field barn that had been in the Merrell family for more than a half century. The barn set on a large secluded fold of private property adjoining the Ocala National forest. Merrell's great, great, grandparents specifically selected the site because it was far away from roads, traffic, and other homes. The site was a place the family would gather to relax, rejoice, and recharge. Since the passing of the old folks, the land and barn was used as a weapons range and place for accomplishing missions, such as the one they were currently planning.

The walls of the barn were covered with relevant pictures that had to do with the upcoming mission such as aerial photos of the estate and the adjoining national forest McCreiess would be maneuvering over. One picture of the actual house on the estate caught Merrell's attention. He studied it more closely.

McCreiess remained in the corner of the room checking the personal equipment that would accompany him on the mission. The van they would use for the insertion, monitoring, and extraction part of the mission was parked near the large wooden door.

Isolation is what they called it. It was the invaluable time and tool to be used prior to mission kickoff. It was the time prior to the operation when everything from mission statement, equipment, and task assignments, were laid out. It allowed the two men to separate themselves from anything and everything unrelated to the mission.

McCreiess pulled a picture from the wall and studied it. He placed it back on the wall. He pulled another picture from the wall and walked to the sand table in the middle of the room. The sand table was a detailed model of constrained sand used to represent the area the two men would be operating in. Merrell was able to get aerial photos of the area of operation but McCreiess got more out of creating the area as a model than he did from the photos. He looked at the aerial photos and military style topographical maps to create the table. He could visualize every piece of the area. He would think up different potential obstacles and scenarios. From insertion to extraction, every potential step or task was envisioned and taken into account.

"Drake, it's important that you get across this creek before sunrise." Merrell pointed to the representation of the creek on the sand table. "Tomorrow is our window of opportunity and if, for some reason, you can't make it... we may have to scrub and push it back a couple days."

"I know. Forty-eight hours here." McCreiess nodded in understanding as he gazed at the table. "I'll get across the creek bed before sunrise, Max, and hit you with comms when I'm there." McCreiess interrupted and made eye contact with Merrell. "The vegetation shouldn't be..."

"The creek is your first hard commo and by then we should know what we're looking at." Merrell walked around the table to face McCreiess after interrupting him.

It was important that McCreiess reached the creek before sunrise because water was something that attracted all sorts of things, from animal to human, and if McCreiess was going to be compromised during the upcoming mission it would most probably be around water.

"If for some reason you can't make it...we may have to ..."

"I'll make it across the creek." McCreiess was irritated that getting across the creek bed was even being questioned. In his mind, Merrell should not even be inquiring about the issue.

"We may have to scrub and push it back a few days is all I'm saying." Merrell was irritated.

Merrell was always irritated at the end of isolation and planning. He and McCreiess had been cooped up in a barn miles away from everything for the last few days. He was always relieved when the plan became more action oriented.

"We'll know more then what we're looking at," Merrell said before he paused to look around the wall for a specific picture.

"Is this the one you're looking for?" McCreiess asked as he pulled a picture from his pocket and unfolded it. He held up a picture of the ex-congressmen and now banking executive, Michael Henshaw. The picture was a typical business picture that would hang in the hallways of office buildings to show patrons who they're dealing with.

"Second hard commo is day break and you should be here." Merrell pointed at a ridgeline on the detailed sand table. Ridgelines were something aerial photos could not be specific about, but topographic maps and sand tables provided a better understanding of what a ridgeline actually was. "At that point you should know exactly what we're looking at. It should provide a good visual of the pasture, house, and stables."

"The congressman should be having his coffee." McCreiess turned from the table and walked toward the wall. He hung the picture on the wall. The knowledge that the congressman had coffee at a specific time and place was common knowledge since the congressman himself spoke about it often during campaign stumps. The congressman enjoyed speaking about sitting on his porch overlooking his property each day, thinking about the issues of the day; how relaxing it was to have coffee before enjoying a ride on top his favorite horse, Slider.

"Listen, Max, I'll get across the creek bed before sunrise. I'll hit you with comms. I have enough food to last a few days and I have the creek for water resupply if needed."

"I don't..."

"I'll be on the 'X' on time and ready to go," McCreiess said with a hint of anger to his tone before Merrell could finish his thought. He took a deep breath and let it out.

Merrell felt the tension. It was tension that had been building since their good friend Kevin Halcot had been killed in Iraq. The tension got worse when McCreiess' wife, Abby, finally succumbed to breast cancer. Both deaths happened within a year of each other and took a toll on both men. The deaths were hard on Merrell but McCreiess was closer to both so his anguish was severe and constant.

The plan McCreiess and Merrell were cooking up had sinful intentions and McCreiess felt he was exposing himself to Abby. McCreiess knew Abby suspected nothing in regards to him creating evil when she was alive. He believed she knew everything now that she had passed over to the other side.

"Tomorrow is his guaranteed ride day." Merrell sighed. "Saturday would be his next guaranteed day, but I don't know if I want you out there that long." Merrell walked from the table and started removing things from the wall. "If for some reason we lose comms. Route alpha is the no comms corridor, final destination old lookout tower. I'll be there at zero five every day until you make it." Merrell paused to make eye contact with McCreiess. "If technology goes to shit, we can always go back to the basics."

"Yeah, basics." McCreiess stepped back and pointed at the topographic map stationed next to the table. "And

I choose between Alpha, Bravo, or Charlie, for evac. All decisions based on situation. Bravo preferred, Charlie only if necessary."

"From the flight and map recon route Charlie looks to be a bitch." Merrell groaned.

Merrell had maneuvered through his share of dense forest so he understood the need of concealment, which dense forest provided, but he also understood how density of vegetation slowed movement. A dense area of forest, such as route Charlie, could be used as security but both Merrell and McCreiess considered speed to be a form of security in the right circumstances.

McCreiess planned the corridors of land he would potentially traverse. Each corridor offered something different from the other. Alpha offered mostly flat and open terrain and would only be traveled at night. Bravo offered the perfect mixture of vegetation and flat terrain and was the most preferred route. Charlie was dense terrain filled with steep hills, wetland, and rocks, and would only be used if he was compromised and needed to disappear.

"Get some rest, Drake. We got a few more hours before we insert. It will be good to get out of here." Merrell paused to look over the room. "You get rest and I'll bag and burn pictures, maps, and anything else operation specific."

McCreiess moved to the sand table and smoothed it out. Leaving no trace of the description of land he would move about. He no longer needed maps, pictures, or sand tables. Everything about the mission was memorized so if he were ever compromised he carried nothing that could be traced back to Merrell.

***

Tad Faris stepped from the County Council's office. The large oak doors swooshed and banged as they closed behind him. He was immediately identified and rushed by journalists who pursued his client, retired congressman and banking executive, Michael Henshaw.

"Gentlemen. Gentlemen! Please understand that Congressman Henshaw will not be making a statement this evening." Faris was irritated at how close the journalists got to him. He actually had to place his hands on one individual to prevent being shoved into the oak doors.

"Will the Congressman be stepping down from his executive position with National Bank?" The question was shouted.

"Neither the Congressman, nor I, will be making a statement this evening about the position the Congressman has with National Bank, or any other position the Congressman holds professionally or personally."

"Will the Congressman be coming out from behind the doors anytime soon," was a question shouted over many others.

"Congressman Henshaw has important business with the County Council that cannot be interrupted at this time. A press conference will be scheduled when something needs to be conveyed to you by the Congressman."

"A young man is dead, Tad. We need..."

"You need to move to a different story." Faris cut the journalist off. "That story has played out. There is nothing more to be said other than the Congressman is very sorry. He has expressed his sorrow to the young man's family long ago and all involved have moved on."

"That's the problem! People have moved on." One angry journalist shouted.

Faris stepped back, turned, and moved toward the oak doors.

"What do you have to say about yesterday's article in the Star that a large sum of money was transferred to the young man's family?" The question was shouted.

"Yeah, Tad, What do you have to say about..."

"Check your source. The Star has had it out for the Congressman." Faris stopped for a moment and paused before he quickly opened the large oak door and disappeared behind it.

* * *

McCreiess fell asleep in his ghillie suit, which allowed Merrell a chance to admire the detail and craftsmanship that McCreiess put into building such an outfit. He awoke to Merrell opening the door to the van. Merrell was putting communications equipment into place. McCreiess stood, yawned, and stretched before he moved to the van. He noticed that the room was sterile accept a hay bale with a target hanging from it. He noticed his reflection in the tinted glass window of the van. Until this moment he never thought much about how some of the black hairs were now becoming grey on his rugged jaw line. His steely narrow eyes seemed to be steelier if that were possible. He looked down and thought about being naked and what he might see if he were. The "ten pack abs" that were there in his youth now floated between six and eight, depending on the amount of energy he put in during workouts or how much beer he consumed. Workouts seemed to be getting farther apart and nights drinking beers seemed to be getting closer together. Aches and pains that use to come and go seemed to linger for him. He thought about the small tattoo he had etched on his back. Only those that could read kanji would know its meaning - Ichigo-Ichie, or a meeting that takes place only once in a lifetime. Both he and his wife Abby had the tattoo placed on their backs only days after they first met. The tattoos were small and would never be seen by anyone else unless either of them broke from their usual modest behavior. He broke from his moment of self-pity as Merrell pulled a black weapons bag from the van and handed it to him. A sigh of relief came over him because he realized Merrell's movement allowed him to break away from any thought of his wife, a thought process that could take him away from his current task.

McCreiess unzipped the bag and pulled a Barnett Ghost 400 Carbonlite Crossbow with scope and quiver from the carrier. He pulled one of the eighteen-inch aluminum arrows from the quiver and mounted it to the bow. Raising the bow he took aim at the target mounted on the hay bail. He took a deep breath, exhaled completely, and held his next breath. He gently squeezed the trigger. The arrow left the bow and struck the target, embedding more than half the arrow into the bail and into the 8x8 wooden posts behind it. The arrow hit the center of the target at a speed of over three hundred feet per second. The bowstring, cables, limbs, and cams moving at a high speed came to a sudden stop. The energy produced by the sudden stop created a vibration, which translated to noise no one would hear if they were not in the immediate area. He started to breath normally again.

"That should do it," Merrell handed another arrow to McCreiess to put into the quiver. "Would you want to check grouping with a couple more?"

"Nope, it's a real smooth piece." McCreiess approved of the 180-grain traditional broad head tip of the arrow before placing it in the quiver. "Little loud, but can't do anything about that." McCreiess shrugged. "Not as loud as a bullet though." He bagged the bow and arrows.

"Regardless of what you use, one shot, one kill." Merrell handed McCreiess a holstered Tactical Kimber .45 caliber pistol. "Here, there's one in the pipe." He looked toward the gun box. "Would you prefer the H&K?"

"Always need one of these just in case one shot won't do." McCreiess pulled the weapon from the holster, pulled the slide back just enough to see brass, to ensure there actually was a bullet in the chamber. It's not that he didn't trust Merrell, it's just that he would be the one using the weapon if needed and he felt it his responsibility to guarantee such things. He slowly slid the pistol back into the holster, then put the thigh holster on and looked over his rucksack laying in the van. "Everything should be good. The Kimber is what I want. It's all been checked, checked, and rechecked."

"We'll be getting out of here in about ten minutes." Merrell switched on the mounted Motorola radio and police scanner he would monitor while in the van. He handed McCreiess a Motorola portable radio. "Let's get a quick comms check." Merrell picked up the microphone and spoke into it. "Check, check, check. How copy?"

"Read you loud and clear," McCreiess spoke into the hands free Motorola headset attached to the two-way radio.

McCreiess was looking forward to getting out of isolation. The thought of the operation and what it meant to accomplish the mission started to weigh heavy on his mind.

"Programmed in the radio are specific times I will monitor the different frequencies. If for some reason we lose commo for more than four hours. Go to no comms plan." Merrell looked McCreiess over for anything that might be a cause for concern, such as anything shiny, or anything that did not blend with his suit.

"No comms plan. Continue mission and meet you at the old fire tower, corridor Bravo." McCreiess looked over his gear and jumped up and down a few times to ensure nothing was loose or made any unusual metallic sounds that someone other than himself would be able to hear. He was satisfied nothing was loose or noisy.

"Yep, you got it." Merrell sighed. "Fundamentals, technique, and assignments." Merrell hopped from the van. "We are fundamentally sound, the technique is tried and true, and our assignments are clear."

McCreiess took a deep breath, let it out, and jumped into the back of the van. The distance he would have to cover over the next couple days was nothing that concerned him, forty miles, forty-five tops, if no comms plan goes into effect. It was the mission itself that weighed heavily on him.

***

Ex-congressman and banking executive, Michael Henshaw, looked out over the stables where his favorite horse Slider resided. The room he stood in was a magnificent part of the house. It was large and elaborate. The focal point of the room was the sizeable oak framed bed. Henshaw opened the sliding glass door that led to a comfortable porch. He loved the scenery from the porch and the smells that the wooded area and gardens around the estate provided.

"Are my boots ready?" Henshaw questioned. He wore horse-riding apparel. His breeches were too snug and made his belly hang over his belt line, but the shirt he wore covered that, he thought.

"Are my boots ready?" Henshaw yelled angrily, turning toward the large bed.

"Boots. Boots. Yes! Boots are ready...shined," a young, thin, naked man said as he rose from the bed, rubbing sleep from his eyes.

"I want more than just the toe shined. They're calf length boots. Expensive leather boots," Henshaw snarled.

"Yes the whole boot is shined." The young naked man lay back down. "The expensive, leather, boots, are shined," he yawned and fell asleep.

Henshaw poured a cup of coffee from the solid silver container on the hearth of the fireplace. He walked onto the porch to enjoy the morning.

***

McCreiess lay motionless in the tree line. The ghillie suit was a perfect match for the forest. He blended in seamlessly. He slowly lifted his head and peered through his binoculars. From his position he could see a gradually drawn out pasture. The pasture expanded to a spacious, plush, and well manicured-lawn to a Victorian-style mansion. Flower gardens blended nicely throughout the lawn. *Nice fuckin' place*, He thought as he slowly pulled back from the tree line. Once off the tree line he maneuvered to a position that allowed him to view a heavy iron gate that stretched over a paved driveway that winded through an orchard, past the main house to a barn with attached stables.

"Stables, 'X' marks the spot," McCreiess whispered to himself.

McCreiess followed the paved driveway back to the house with his eyes. He reached into his rucksack and pulled out binoculars. Using the binoculars he could get a better view of a man who was sitting on a porch and wearing breech pants and sipping from a coffee cup. McCreiess remained still as he monitored the situation. He was meticulous and careful. He understood that the wrong move would bring interest from anyone who saw movement around the estate.

Crossing the creek was not a problem for McCreiess and he was able to make good communication with Merrell who was stationed a good twenty miles from the Henshaw estate. He understood that his friend, Max Merrell, only worried about the creek crossing because that was his nature. The creek water was low and he was able to cross at a point that enabled him to not leave a trace of his existence. Using a filter he was ensured the creek water he filled his canteens and camelbak with were potable. He had enough water to last him a couple days and he knew he would need it all. He took the last bite from the energy bar he pulled from the cargo pocket of his pants. He savored the taste of peanut butter and chocolate while he repacked the packaging of the bar in his pocket.

Henshaw rose from his seat and stretched.

McCreiess looked at his watch (0745). He pulled a drink from his camelbak, packed the binoculars and picked up the crossbow. He removed the cover from the mounted scope and peered through it.

"Got a visual," McCreiess spoke into the radio, keeping his voice low.

"Roger. You have visual." Merrell's voice could be heard coming through the Motorola's earpiece McCreiess was wearing.

McCreiess adjusted his earpiece.

"I have Mike Hotel." McCreiess spoke the phonetic alphabet for Michael Henshaw.

"Roger. Mike Hotel," Merrell's voice cracked again in the earpiece.

"I'm moving in. Out." McCreiess closed the scope cover, slowly rose from the ground and stealthily moved to a position that gave him a clear view of anyone who approached the stable doors. The view was one that allowed him to look from the rear of the stables to the front of the stables. Anyone who approached the stable doors would be facing him and all vitals would be exposed. To help him relax he lightly sang the old Elvis song *"Heartbreak Hotel."*

* * *

Henshaw took the last sip of coffee and placed his cup on the table in front of him. Leaning forward he cut an enormous fart. He chuckled to himself, wishing he could have shared that one with some of his old colleagues in the capital building. He use to enjoy cutting loud farts as soon as the elevator doors closed. It would bring loud shrieks and laughter from most who knew him.

He rose from the chair and straightened the cushion. The boots he inquired about were waiting for him by the fireplace. The young man who shined them was making the bed.

"I will be riding Slider." Henshaw picked up his boots, sat down, and started putting them on.

"Will you need help?"

"Why would I need help," Henshaw said angrily.

"I...I...I don't know. I don't know why I asked that question."

"You probably asked the question because you want something. You feel that if you help in some way that I will owe you something."

"No. No."

"It's alright. Most everyone wants something from me. At least that is what I have found." Henshaw sighed as he zipped and then tied his boots. "I just can't understand why people can't ask me. Why do I have to be played like a little boy?"

The young naked man knew better than to continue the conversation so he quickly draped himself with a robe and hurried away.

***

McCreiess was finally positioned. The tree line he sat in and the ghillie suit gave him ample concealment. The thought of cover never crossed his mind because there would be no one firing at him so nothing between him and his target needed to stop a bullet. In front of him lay an open field of fire, a perfect ambush for anything that walked through. McCreiess lay in the prone position with his crossbow propped on a bipod in front of him. He opened the scope cover and peered through it. Using the distance finder, he made note of the distance from where he was compared to the front of the stables. It was 30 feet. The large oak tree directly in front of the stable was 48 feet. He pulled the crossbow string back, mounted an arrow, and waited.

***

Henshaw moved through the living room toward the foyer door. He stopped by a small chest to retrieve the stable keys but before he could open the drawer to the chest the home phone rang. He debated on whether he should answer it. Answering the phone usually meant bad news. It was either someone wanting something or someone providing news he didn't want. He decided against answering the phone and continued on to his meeting with Slider.

***

McCreiess first caught a glimpse of Henshaw moving around the house. The paved road from the stables to the house was winding so it was impossible to keep a visual of something on the road from where McCreiess was laying. Looking past the large oak tree he was able to see Henshaw walking the paved road that led to the stable.

"Deer approaching salt block," McCreiess whispered into the Motorola.

"Roger. Deer approaching salt block," Merrell cracked back. "Green light on this end." Merrell's voice came across the radio again.

Henshaw was in plain view as he rounded a bend in the road. There was now nothing between McCreiess and Henshaw. Henshaw was whistling as he approached the stable doors. *He's whistling the tune from the movie Bridge Over River Kwi*, McCreiess thought as he settled into the ground.

Henshaw was halfway between the large oak tree and the front of the stable. The scope distance finder read 39 feet when Henshaw stopped and started feeling his pockets.

Perfect, McCreiess thought to himself as he drew a deep breath, let it out, and held before taking another. His aim was steady, the cross hairs of the scope aligned with Henshaw's lower left breast. There was no breeze to take into account. McCreiess noticed Henshaw mouth the words, God damn it.

Dumb fucker forgot his keys, McCreiess thought to himself when he pulled the trigger, sending the arrow toward Henshaw.

Henshaw hit the ground face first. His heart and mind turned off so quickly that he didn't have time to even think about putting his hands out to prevent his face from striking the hard pavement.

McCreiess first noticed the arrow sticking in the large oak tree. The arrow passed completely through Henshaw, blowing a hole through his heart on its way out his backside and into the tree. McCreiess remained still. He was calm as he watched blood pool around the body. Henshaw's body made a few involuntary muscle twitches and spasms. He looked for movement past the body of Henshaw and saw none. He listened for any sounds that might indicate someone would be interested in the area he was operating in, but heard none. He fought the sudden urge of collecting his arrow from the tree, understanding the arrow could never be traced back to him or Merrell. He remained vigilante, understanding any movement he made would attract anything that heard the vibration of the bow turn to sound. He breathed normally again. If his heart rate were taken it would register the normal forty-two beats at a resting position.

"Lights are out. Extraction Bravo," McCreiess spoke softly into the mouthpiece of the radio. He was certain no one was around, but doctrine dictated that he remain as quiet and still as possible immediately after such a mission.

"Roger that. Lights out, and extraction Bravo," Merrell responded.

McCreiess took a deep breath and let it out. After a few minutes had passed and he was sure no one was moving in his direction, he closed the scope cover and looked over his immediate area to make sure he would leave nothing behind. He looked toward the house and wondered how long it would be before anyone would notice the body of a large man laying dead and in a pool of blood.

"Nothing personal. I'm just part of a system. The System," McCreiess whispered to himself as he rose to his feet and moved away from the stable. It was easy to say something like that. It was easy to pull the trigger of an instrument that would leave a man like former congressman, now former banking executive, Michael

Henshaw crumpled in a pool of his own blood. He hated what he had become, a tool for someone else, but he understood it was the price he and Henshaw had to pay for their actions. Henshaw's payment was death and it was quick, simple, and painless. McCreiess' payment was being the grim reaper to anyone The System, a secret society, deemed worthy of death.

How is Drake McCreiess?

Doom is what Judge Stephan Carson felt as he sat in his judge's chamber. The black leather chair he sat in and ottoman he propped his feet on were comfortable. He felt the chair could swallow him. He enjoyed sitting in the chair that was a gift from the students of a constitutional law class he taught many years before. It was the portable oxygen concentrator that accompanied him everywhere he went that brought on the feeling of doom. He was eighty-three years old. Much too young for feeling like he did, he thought.

Judge Ron Ellenberg, Carson's protégé, sat next to him in a smaller less comfortable chair. A briefcase on top of a small table sat between them. Ellenberg was fifty-two years of age and in great shape. He was deep into thought as he read over a briefing that was provided to him by his law clerk prior to his meeting with Carson.

"You have good news for me, Ron?" Carson asked.

"Yes sir. I'm sure you will be pleased."

"What's the source?"

"Max Merrell called last night and the Morning Star confirms." Ellenberg placed the briefing on the table and reached into the briefcase and retrieved a newspaper.

"Please read it to me, Ron."

Ellenberg scanned the paper quickly and picked up halfway through an article.

"Former Congressman and banking executive, Michael Henshaw, was found dead at his home last night in what sources inside the local police department say could only be described as murder." Ellenberg continued to scan the paper. "Six years ago the powerful congressman was forced to leave the legislature in disgrace when he was charged with the murder of a twenty year old male college student. Henshaw admitted to having an affair with the student but denied having anything to do with his murder. The nation was stunned when two witnesses for the prosecution changed their stories and subsequently fled the country." Ellenberg handed Carson the newspaper.

A picture of Michael Henshaw accompanied the article.

"The article does a good job of explaining our side." Ellenberg smiled.

"Good people at the Star." Carson smiled in agreement with Ellenberg's statement. "We do pay them well, you know."

Ellenberg received the paper from Carson and placed it back in the case.

"Merrell and McCreiess?" Carson's smile faded.

"Sir, I guess..."

"How are Max Merrell and Drake McCreiess?" Carson questioned.

"All's fine. McCreiess pulled the trigger. Extraction went as planned and they are both leaving the country soon. Merrell is heading up a ninety day National Guard security detail for the department of state somewhere in Iraq." Ellenberg stood. "That should get them..."

"How is Drake McCreiess?" Carson interrupted Ellenberg and motioned for him to sit back down.

"Drake is doing well." Ellenberg caught Carson roll his eyes so he paused for a moment. He knew he should have used his last name. He didn't know McCreiess or Merrell well enough to call them by their first names.

"Mr. Merrell said his wounds have healed and..."

"Wounds caused by metal and lead will heal." Carson cut Ellenberg off again. "It's not those wounds that concern me."

"Yes sir. You would know." Ellenberg sheepishly smiled.

"It's all yours now, Ron. Please inform the other members that my obligations have been fulfilled." Carson paused and looked directly into the eyes of Ellenberg. "We are defined by how well we fulfill our obligations." Carson paused again to put emphasis on his last statement and the upcoming question. "Don't you think?"

"I will meet with the other members soon." Ellenberg took a deep breath and let it out.

"Remember, Ron. Your presence is needed now more than ever." Carson leaned back in his chair, knowing he did not receive an answer to his question.

***

Sitting quietly behind his desk at home, his head down and eyes glazed over, Ellenberg acted as if he was hard at work as he scanned a brief that he had no interest in. *The guy's guilty as hell*, he thought as he tossed the brief aside.

He explained to his wife that he hated working briefs at home but felt that things at work needed special attention. In reality he just wanted to think. The desk at home provided him some comfort. It told others to stay away someone is busy here. His wife knew better than to drift in the office while he was behind his desk, but his children would sometimes press their luck and get a good scolding for wandering too far down the hall.

Ellenberg stopped pretending as if he cared about some so-called anguished man who was so tormented that he strangled the next-door neighbor and his children. The defense forgot to mention the so-called tormented person and the neighbor's wife enjoyed living off the dead man's disability payments.

Ellenberg took a deep breath, lifted his head and sighed out loud. He could still fill his lungs with air, so the feeling of air leaving his lungs brought him comfort. The documents he read on a daily basis gave him little comfort in his fellow man so he had to seek it out in the little things. He looked at the desk drawer and hesitated before opening it. The letter that sat in the drawer seemed to be there for troubling times. The man who sent the letter provided him comfort and seemed to always be there for him. Carson always seemed to be the mentor he needed. The man who sent the letter was the father figure who had no problems providing needed discipline or love, depending on the circumstance. A quick thought about a time when he was giving a speech to a veterans group flashed in his mind. The speech was about veterans who were in trouble with the law. He mentioned, off the cuff, that he felt the veterans should be provided more educational benefits. Carson chided him, explaining that speeches to such organizations needed to be specific. "You're not some whore politician! Spouting some feel good at the moment shit," Carson sternly explained after hearing the speech. Ellenberg could make the correlation between education, or lack of, and trouble with law. To Carson, veterans should have been instilled with enough discipline to stay out of trouble with the law.

Ellenberg let his mind drift to a meeting that had taken place earlier.

:-

Ellenberg gave himself a once over as he followed the walkway to the front door of Judge Carson's home. He knew the Judge wasn't feeling well but he had an understanding that the Judge wouldn't tolerate an appearance that could be seen at the local sports pub. The visit was a formal one of sorts and he would be in the presence of Harriet, the Judge's wife. "Act like you have met her before," Judge Carson would say when Harriet would be around.

Ellenberg knocked on the door and waited for Harriet to answer. He knew she was catching one of her favorite talk shows, but she would be quick to a door knock.

"Ron. It is so good to see you," Harriet enthusiastically answered the knock like she always did. "Stephen said you would be coming. Please come in."

Ellenberg stepped in the foyer and wiped his feet. He knew the Judge would not be greeting him at the door. In times past the Judge would usually greet him in the bar area in the basement. The Judge would meet him with a smile and offer him a drink. He would usually pass. "Connecting with souls past," The Judge would explain the drink away.

"Stephen is outside enjoying the sun. He has a pitcher of tea and a glass already on your side of the table."

"Good. I've been looking forward to your sweet tea, Harriet." Ellenberg moved toward the porch and stopped because he felt Harriet's hand on his arm.

"I want you to know that your visit today has really lifted his spirits." Harriet smiled as she directed Ellenberg to the porch. "He has been really down lately, but your coming today is as if a large rock has been lifted from his shoulders."

Ellenberg cautiously smiled at Harriet, nodded, and continued to the porch.

Walking out on the porch Ellenberg was happy to see the Judge looking so well. The Judge was sitting up and he had color to him. The last time he saw the Judge, the Judge was laying in bed and pale. Now the Judge was sitting up with a glass in his hand, looking out over the beach. Ellenberg wondered if it contained vodka.

"Ron! Thanks so much for coming, Ron." Carson smiled and held his glass up. "Your reply to my letter brings me great relief."

"It's the right thing to do, Sir." Ellenberg had an uncomfortable moment so he looked quickly behind him to make sure the door closed.

"In the letter I mentioned a team you would be responsible for, but I didn't tell you who is on that team." Carson paused and poured Ellenberg a glass of tea. "You know these men. These dedicated men."

Carson stared into Ellenberg's eyes as he handed him the glass. "Max Merrell is leading the team."

"Max Merrell? From..."

"Yes, that Max Merrell." Carson interrupted Ellenberg.

"Let me guess, Drake McCreiess and Kevin Halcot are along for the ride."

"Drake McCreiess, Yes. Kevin Halcot was killed in Iraq about a year ago. He worked as an Army Special Forces operator and he was killed when an I.E.D exploded by his vehicle."

"I.E..."

"It stands for improvised explosive device." Carson explained.

Carson broke eye contact and turned to look out over the Gulf. "Those men did more to choke the drug trade in this State than any government agency or force. I needed them more than they needed the prison system."

"So that's why you wanted me to drop the Merrell investigation?"

"These are fine men we are talking about," Carson became unyielding. "Principled, honorable, and trustworthy men who pride themselves on doing something instead of being a somebody." Carson brought the stern stare as he made eye contact once again. "As you know, that is hard to find these days."

"Yes, Sir. It is." Ellenberg cowed.

"We are all on one team, Ron." Carson softened a bit. "Working together to provide that oversight they always talk about in Washington...as they raid the coffer." He hardened again after his last statement. "We decided to practice law because we believe in the protection of innocent people. But the truth is, that law has sadly become a business, a contest of egos and money, that in no way reflects justice in our society." He leaned across the table to emphasize his point. "Remember, Ron, there are two basic types of people, the Apollonian's, who follow reason, science and logic. And then there are the Dionysian's, who the vast majority of people in our world are. And the people most selected to sit on our juries are..."

"Dionysian." Ellenberg answered.

"That's right. So we are forced to contest with those who readily toss out the facts, simply because they feel some emotional connection to a defendant." Carson sipped from his glass of tea. "Or they are so easily swayed by the personality of a witty attorney."

"Yes. I agree, Sir."

"Sometime long ago. We believe as far back as the Revolution. A group of judges decided that a jury

would often mistake the facts and rule on emotion."
Carson took a long sip from his tea. "Those men had
the courage to rival the English courts, and take
matters into their own hands." He held up his hands
for theatrics. "When a man who is truly guilty escapes
justice in our courts of law, and is free to enjoy the
fruits of his evil deeds." He let his last few words
hang for a moment. "We have an obligation to see that
justice is met."

"Yes, Sir."

"We believe the spirit of the law makes our nation
strong, but the letter of the law has contaminated it."

"I agree with everything you have said, Sir."
Ellenberg paused to consider what he was saying.
He didn't know if he agreed with his last statement
or not. He would have to ponder and pontificate to
himself about what was being told him. "And I look
forward to providing the needed service you just
talked about."

Ellenberg was confused with what he was thinking
and what was coming out of his mouth. What he said
seemed so right. He didn't want to disappoint the father
figure of a man in front of him.

"A few more things," Carson said as he took one last
big drink of tea. "You will meet the other members soon.
I won't go into great detail about who they are but rest
assured most have backgrounds similar to ours."

"I am sure they are all fine people and I look forward
to working with them." Ellenberg sipped from his glass
of tea.

"I received…" Carson stopped for a moment because he was hesitant to say what he was thinking. "I received a message from a dear friend of mine before he passed away."

Ellenberg leaned forward in his chair as if he couldn't hear what was being said.

"His name was George Mader and his honor, loyalty, and duty to his country and fellow citizens was special by even our standards." Carson took a softer tone with his voice. "My dear friend was concerned that a member, or members, may have personal ambitions that could bring scrutiny from the outside."

"Scrutiny?" Ellenberg asked.

"Yes. Scrutiny from the outside." Carson's face turned red with anger, but he kept his voice low. "A scum sucking politician…I can't believe a politician…a twenty dollar whore has more honor. More character."

"Twenty dollars was big money in your day." Ellenberg attempted humor to settle Carson down.

"I'm sorry, Ron. I digress. My point is that we can't tolerate any of our members being scrutinized from the outside. There are so many different media sources out there today…once they start digging…you never know what they will find."

"Yes, Sir."

"Like many, my friend had a weakness for family. His daughter, Cynthia, has different motives. My friend either overlooked it or didn't see it?" Carson let out a sigh. "Regardless, I fear feelings…emotion…may have clouded decision making ability and…"

"Her?" Ellenberg was curious to know more about the female member. It never crossed his mind that a female would be involved.

"We can talk more about her later and you will understand when you meet her." Carson paused to look out over the Gulf. "The other thing you need to know is that justice will be served soon for two men. I have been working with Merrell on this matter, but I need to step aside now and get you involved." Carson chuckled. "My youthful experiences are now meeting up with my old age."

"Lots of metal flying around Saint Mere and Inchon." Ellenberg knew all about his mentor's war experiences. His mentor parachuted into Saint Mere, France during WWII as a young paratrooper with the 82nd Airborne, and battled the North Koreans for the ground of Inchon during the Korean War. He was injured in both wars.

"Harriet would say too much beer, whiskey, and cigar flying around everywhere I seem to show up." Carson held his empty glass of tea up and looked disparagingly at it. "I hate an empty glass." He shook his disapprovingly.

"Do you want me to get a hold of Merrell?" Ellenberg questioned hesitantly.

"He will contact you." Carson poured another glass of tea. "He is working on a case right now and he understands you are taking over for me. Like me, you don't need to know all the details of his plans. As you know, he is a very thorough man."

"Meticulous." Ellenberg had firsthand knowledge about how detailed Merrell could be when it came to planning.

"Needs more vodka. Don't you think?" Carson smiled as he rose from his seat and moved toward the bar.

Ellenberg opened the drawer and stared at the letter. He looked away. His eyes drifted to one of many pictures on the wall. A picture of him with three other friends from law school, arms around each other as they stood wearing graduation gowns and caps. It was a picture that represented a moment in his life when he was most proud. He remembered how tough that first year of law school was and how often he thought about just doing something else. The letter in the drawer stood for confusion. He closed the drawer, placed his elbows on the desk, and then placed his head in his hands. He was confused. He contemplated the reasons why he would be involved in an organization that would have people like Merrell and McCreiess working with them. He asked himself many times over why Judge Carson would ask him to get involved in such a secret organization. He wondered why he jumped at the chance. Was it because he felt some sort of loyalty for the judge, or was it away to impress the man he respected so much? He looked at another picture on the wall; a picture of him as a young Marine lieutenant. He had mixed feelings about his service because he was never tested in battle like Judge Carson had been. He always wondered how he would have fared in combat. He always felt the need to impress those that that did witness the horrors of battle. He did know that being accepted by men like Carson, Merrell, and McCreiess made him feel worthy.

***

Ellenberg stood on the rooftop of the 28-story office building overlooking Tampa Bay. The skyline shined on the Florida west coast during the day, but in the evening the cool breeze was comforting at 600 feet above the ground. The building was part of a tower system office complex built on two square blocks of the downtown area. Each building was tall and thin and housed anything from law firms to airline companies. The buildings provided an awesome view of the Gulf and they harmonized with the rest of the city skyline. The buildings were striking and blended nicely with the other signature architectures aligned on the coast.

"Thanks for coming." Merrell extended his hand to Ellenberg for a handshake.

"I've been looking forward to meeting you." Ellenberg was surprised at the strength in Merrell's grasp. "Judge Carson told me..."

"You're in now." Merrell looked at his own hand as he pulled it away and rolled his eyes.

Both men stared at each other during an awkward pause.

"I want you to know that I don't look back. I trust Judge Carson as I would my own father and he said your skills are needed out here more than they are in prison." Ellenberg paused, noticing Merrell checking a

42

text message. "How was Africa?" Ellenberg's question was off beat.

"We're caught up now. We got back earlier than expected so we moved on the enviro-radical."

"What! When?" Ellenberg was shocked at the news presented him. "You never asked about tickets."

"Late last night." Merrell handed Ellenberg a piece of paper. "Printed it off less than an hour ago." He paused as Ellenberg scanned it. "McCreiess was able to get into his basement. And Africa is still ten minutes outside of the stone-age."

"C.C.N.S. reports that Ross Evans, the radical environmentalist, was killed." Ellenberg continued to scan. "An accidental explosion in his basement? Why didn't you inform me about this?"

"I just did." Merrell stepped closer to the edge of the building and leaned against the safety wall as he looked out over the Gulf. "You will be meeting with the members soon."

"Yes. Soon."

"Cynthia Mader called me. She was pushing me about the enviro-nut. Did Judge Carson talk to you about her?" Merrell waited for a response. "I don't want her calling me. I go through you."

"Yes." Ellenberg was shocked by the news he received.

"Only you!" Merrell demanded.

"He has talked to me about her." Ellenberg was stunned by the outburst.

"Now that the 'Old Man' is out, the last link to the past. Well, I fear..."

"Your fears have been noted." Ellenberg tried to get some kind of control.

"Get control of her! Or this thing will spin out of control."

"I...I..."

"The 'Old Men' could put their thumbs on her, and those like her. Her father, Judge Mader is dead, and I don't think Carson has long," Merrell said as he looked out over the skyline.

Ellenberg was stunned by the use of the Judge's name. He had never heard of anyone talk about Judge Carson in such away, so informal. He was shocked to hear that Merrell felt things could possibly get out of control. The questions of what he had gotten himself involved in flooded his thought process. His stomach seemed to twist in knots as he watched Merrell turn from the skyline and head for the door before giving any sign that the conversation they were involved in was over.

I am sure he is.

Judge Cynthia Mader and her law clerk Andrew looked over her chambers. She was impressed with the changes she had just made. The wainscot was premium grade mahogany that she personally picked out and she was especially proud of the high back mahogany chairs with leather seating. The wood came from her late father's wooded property. She spent many days overseeing the cutting of the trees and then the millwork. The white walls above the wainscot were filled with pictures, awards, and mementos. All picture frames matched the wooden wainscot, chairs, and desk. The piece she was most proud of was the large swivel chair she sat in. It was different from everything else. The chair was made from the oak tree that was once the centerpiece of her father's estate. The tree was over four hundred years old when it was struck by lightning. Most of the tree burned, but what was left was a very large stump that she visited often to pay homage to her father, and exactly enough wood to make the chair. Wood shavings and saw dust created from making the chair were placed in jars and stored in her basement. Her hope was to one day spread them over her father's gravesite.

Cynthia picked up a file in front of her. "Do you agree with the changes I have made?"

"I do. Yes. Very much." Andrew continued to look over the chambers while Cynthia scanned the file. "I can't believe you actually had all of this done. And the expense of..."

"That's not your concern, Andrew. I will only say that federal funds were used wisely." She tossed the file in front of Andrew.

"Yeah. Nunez." Andrew leaned back in his chair.

"Mr. Nunez argues that insufficient evidence supports both his convictions for conspiracy and possession with intent to distribute." Cynthia leaned back in her chair. "Why are we hearing this case?"

Andrew sat forward. "Mr. Nunez believes that his jury engaged in a degree of speculation and conjecture. He also believes that the jury's finding was only a guess, and..."

Cynthia held up her hand to silence her clerk. She became stern.

"Yes, Andrew. I know why." She leaned back in her chair. "Whatever." She paused. "I know why his council is appealing. I was really hoping not to hear from you. Please get a grasp on when I do want to hear from you and when I don't"

"Yes, Judge Mader." Andrew cowed.

"The defense believes conspiring to smuggle narcotics and aiding and abetting the distribution of narcotics must be overturned when there is substantial evidence that the defendant drove a scout vehicle for a drug smuggler but where there is only circumstantial evidence that he knew the specific contents of the smuggler's van." Cynthia looked toward the ceiling.

"Yes, your honor." Andrew puffed out his chest. "The defendant is saying that the evidence does not reasonably support the jury's finding of guilt."

Cynthia provided Andrew with a sharp look. "Yeah, well, he better keep a tight grip on his bar of soap because he is staying in prison."

"Do they still use bar soap?"

"Andrew." Cynthia acted annoyed. "You will probably need to read US versus Crater, versus Jones, and versus Wilson."

"Yes, your honor."

"We consider only whether, taking the evidence both direct and circumstantial, together with the reasonable inferences to be drawn there from in the light most favorable to the government, a reasonable jury could find the defendant guilty beyond a reasonable doubt." Cynthia leaned back, turned in her seat, and looked out the window.

Andrew grabbed a pen and pad of paper from the desk and started to jot down notes.

"A conviction should be reversed only if no reasonable juror could have reached the disputed verdict." Cynthia continued. "The evidence necessary to support a verdict need not conclusively exclude every other reasonable hypothesis and need not negate all possibilities except guilt."

Andrew continued to write notes and make eye contact as needed.

"Instead!" Cynthia emphasized the word. "The evidence only has to reasonably support the jury's finding of guilt beyond a reasonable doubt." Cynthia turned and looked toward Andrew. "However! A jury will not be allowed to engage in a degree of speculation and conjecture that renders its finding a guess or mere possibility."

Andrew moved to sit on the edge of his seat and continued with his notes.

"To obtain a conviction for conspiracy in violation of twenty one U.S. Code eight forty six," Cynthia raised her voice, "the government must establish beyond a reasonable doubt that there was an agreement to violate the law, the defendant knew the essential objectives of the conspiracy, the defendant knowingly and voluntarily took part in the conspiracy and the co-conspirators were interdependent."

"You're just thinking out loud?" Andrew questioned and shrugged his shoulders.

"Do you see how this law stuff can be so trying at times?" Cynthia smiled.

There was a knock on the Chambers door and a young female administrative assistant peeked in the chambers.

"Judge Mader, a Judge Michael Stallings is on the phone." The assistant tried not to make eye contact with anyone.

"I will take that," Cynthia said as the assistant closed the door. "Andrew, look those cases over. Mr. Nunez is staying in prison, but look them over anyway."

Cynthia pointed at the door to help Andrew get the point that she needed privacy. The young clerk hustled out the door.

***

Once Cynthia was assured she was alone, she took a deep breath and let it out. She pushed a button on the phone.

"Michael." Cynthia wanted to sound happy. "It is so nice to hear from you. I hope all is well in your circuit."

"All is well, Cynthia." Judge Stallings always sounded enthused. He was a man who prided himself on how well he kept himself. A man who always found time to workout at least once daily, and never shied away from a mirror or camera. "Have you heard about the late congressman slash banker? And the enviro..."

"Yes. Yes. That is great news isn't it? Judge Carson has fulfilled his obligations and we will meet his successor, Mr. Ellenberg, soon." Cynthia chimed in.

"I am sure Mr. Ellenberg will do fine. The 'Old Man' has vouched for him. Enough said." Stallings laughed.

"I agree. If Judge Carson vouches for you...enough said." Cynthia paused. "Any word on the meeting?" She quickly questioned. "Has General Hathaway and Mayor Porter Okayed the time frame?"

"They have." Stallings answered. "Everything is a go and Judge Carson has said that Mr. Ellenberg is looking forward to meeting us. Says he is excited about getting started."

"I am sure he is." Cynthia leaned back in the chair and was now prepared to steer the conversation away from business. She placed the phone on speaker.

Lot like her Old Man.

Senior Agent Ben Kelly was a gigantic man with a deep voice who was more known for being mild mannered than anything else. All who came in contact with him enjoyed his presence. He was a capable person when it came to his position of authority but he was never one to flaunt his position within or outside the FCICU, a small detachment of the FBI. Kelly sat in his office with Special Agent Carl Brenner, an unassuming individual in his early fifties. Brenner was content with his position within the Bureau. He was shocked when he was asked to accept the position of Special Agent. Most knew he was handpicked because he would rarely question authority.

"We have four new people coming aboard, Ben." Brenner was looking through personnel files. "I already have each assigned to a task force but what..."

"Should be one in there that..." Kelly pointed at the files Brenner was thumbing through.

"Which one?"

"English."

"Oh yeah. English. I have her assigned to..."

"No worries about assigning her to anyone right now."

"But, Ben, I have her assigned to Miles because I really think she needs the supervision that Miles can provide." Brenner pulled the file of SueAnn English from the others he held. "From her file English seems to be a person who likes to..."

"Exactly." Kelly reached for the English file. "That's why I don't want her assigned to anyone right now. We'd only be setting Miles up to look like a bigger idiot than I think he already is." Kelly opened the file and scanned the front page. "No. I think we let her settle in. Maybe run some data. Keep an eye on her."

"Do you think..."

Kelly leaned back in his chair and clasped his large hands behind his head, which signaled to Brenner that the decision was firm.

"And the others?" Brenner moved away from conversation about English.

"The others need to stay away from Agent English. She will be my special project. I have a soft spot for people like Agent English." Kelly paused. His eye-to-eye contact remained with Brenner. "Lot you can learn."

"Sir?" Brenner sat with his mouth open.

"Lot like her Old Man. She is." Kelly paused. "We'll put her on some of the cold stuff. Stuff that never seems to get solved."

"Well we could..."

"From what I gather. She won't be insubordinate, and she won't create dissension. And she's not one to tolerate stupid shit either."

***

Agent Branch Stevens, known to be a charming young man by most at his FBI Academy class in Quantico, Virginia, also had a knack for getting under people's skin. To his Senior Agent, Ben Kelly, he was obnoxious and arrogant. Kelly considered Stevens as one of the individuals who were only in the FBI for a particular reason and time; enough time for others to think he did something special before he moved on to something larger, possibly political. Kelly could care less that he graduated from an Ivy League institution. He figured Stevens had no need to be arrogant because he ranked near the bottom of his Ivy League class as well as the FBI's academy. He presumed it all had to do with family, politics, and favors.

Stevens strutted into Kelly's office and the Senior Agent was sure Stevens would not be happy about a new agent with the background that SueAnn English had.

"I don't like it, Sir!" Stevens paced before Kelly, who was sitting at his desk. "She has been a pariah everywhere she ends up. Bank robberies, as well as political corruption. Both divisions sent her packing."

"Her daddy sure was a great man." Kelly pulled the English file from his desk, leaned back in his chair and thumbed through it. He may not have cared for Steven's opinion but why make the kid an enemy so soon? After all, Stevens was still a wet behind the ear kid who thought he was someone he wasn't. *Regular J. Edgar Hoover*, Kelly smiled as that thought crossed his mind.

"If you're going after a Senator with presidential aspirations," Brenner chimed in as he sat in one of the three chairs in front of Kelly's desk, "well, you might want to make sure his friend list doesn't include the director of the organization you work for."

"Her daddy wouldn't have cared." Kelly smiled. "Presidential aspirations or not, the man was steering contracts to pad his accounts. Word is...she had him on film sucking contractor dick as some sort of payment scheme." Kelly became less comfortable in his chair. He tossed the file to the desk and sat straight up.

"I guess the US dollar isn't worth as much these days." Stevens took a seat and smiled although no one else caught the humor in his last comment.

"I'm looking forward to meeting her. Carl, why don't you ask her to come in?"

Brenner started moving toward the door before Kelly could complete the command. "SueAnn English." Brenner waved for the newly assigned agent to join the meeting.

Brenner and Stevens stared at SueAnn as she entered the office wearing blue jeans and a t-shirt. Stevens rolled his eyes for all to see.

SueAnn English was tall and slender with an athletic build. To those that knew her she was an attractive, engaging, intelligent, and tactful woman. Most who knew her well knew she was an athlete with a very competitive spirit. She didn't mind losing a board game or a silly bet, but when it came to competing against herself, she could be relentless. She was at the time in her life when she realized the scoreboard was now the mirror.

"Agent English, come on in and have a seat. I've been looking forward to meeting you." Kelly stood and walked around the desk. His hand seemed to swallow hers, and he was not surprised by the firmness of her handshake.

"Yes, Sir. I have been looking forward to meeting you and I'm sorry about my attire. The person on the phone said you wanted to meet immediately." SueAnn glanced at Brenner and Stevens.

"No time to change?" Stevens sneered.

"Is there another definition for immediate?" SueAnn smiled.

"Don't you worry about it Agent English." Kelly's voice boomed. "I want you to meet your direct supervisor, Special Agent Carl Brenner, and the person you will be working closely with, Agent Branch Stevens."

"It's my pleasure." SueAnn provided a firm handshake to both Brenner and Stevens.

"Thanks for coming aboard. We have heard lots about you." Brenner smiled.

"Lots." Stevens turned to sit down. His sarcastic tone was not well hidden.

"Let's all just sit down. Let's talk a little. I know you're busy Agent English so I assure you, we won't drag this out." Kelly pointed to a seat for SueAnn to take.

The group began to sit as the Senior Agent Kelly suggested. "Let's start with why the Bureau would send you here. To this department." He smiled so that SueAnn would feel comfortable.

"Didn't you have to leave Bank...?"

"I did have to leave the division of Bank Robberies." SueAnn spoke up promptly and cut Stevens off. "I enjoyed working with most of the people there, but some would rather not have a person like me..."

"What. A woman?" Stevens pounced.

"No," SueAnn explained calmly, "well, maybe." She paused to think back. "It had a lot to do with actually doing something. Maybe a little to do with a woman doing something." She smiled. "Yeah, that's probably the best way to say it."

"Explain please." Kelly wanted to hear more about an event that happened six years earlier even though he had heard the story more than a few different times.

:-

FBI agents SueAnn English and her partner Brent Bear sat parked in a government owned vehicle as they monitored a radio. The parking lot, of a well-known home improvement store, gave them visual access to an intersection that was important to the surveillance part of the operation they had a role in. The lot was adjacent to Card Street and just south of Park Street. Just to the east of their position, at the end of Park Street, was Caldwell Bank. SueAnn and Bear could not see the bank but that wasn't their responsibility. They were two young agents tasked with keeping an eye on the corner of Park and Card Street. In the grand scheme of the operation they were two of ten, using four cars, roving FBI agents tasked with hunting two armed and dangerous bank robbers. The operation was called a rolling stakeout. Agents would maneuver their vehicles to preplanned spots and survey the area, hoping to get a glimpse of Marcwell and Turner, the two suspected criminals, known to be extremely dangerous. If the criminals didn't make themselves present the stakeout would be pulled and they would move to the next suspected area. The planned stakeout was based on nothing more than a hunch because Marcwell and Turner worked with no rhyme or rhythm. Their planning was sporadic and seemed to be timed with nothing. To find the two criminals would be based on surveillance training, skills, and luck. Their descriptions, backgrounds, and names were known; anything else was a guess. The two met each other while working good paying jobs as ironworkers. They both had families. Marcwell was married with three children and Turner was a divorced father of two children. Both were ex-military with no real bent toward extremism; probably taking banks and trucks for the thrill.

The bank robbers were suspected of many different bank and armored truck robberies and had no qualms with resorting to violence if they felt a need. They were suspected of killing two armored truck drivers and a bank security guard, and they used weapons to rescue themselves from two other occasions. Favorite weapons used by Marcwell and Turner were AK-47's and Glock pistols. Turner used a shotgun to stun customers at a bank once but he was never known to use it again. He fired buckshot into the ceiling; customers said they smelled alcohol on his breath.

SueAnn and Bear had only been at their location for less than ten minutes when Bear thought he got a look at Marcwell's distinct white hair. The two criminals were traveling north on Card Street.

"I think I got them!" Bear pronounced on the car's radio. "Suspects, Marcwell and Turner, heading north on Card."

"Roger that. Possible suspects heading north on Card Street." A voice over the radio sounded for all involved in the rolling stakeout.

"They passed our position and are now turning on Park Street." Bear was excited.

"Agent Bear hold your position. We have three teams in that area. We are moving in." The voice over the radio had a nervous crack to it.

The suspect's car made a right turn on Park Street and headed east. SueAnn and Bear lost site of the vehicle because of the different buildings of business between them and the suspects. It was explained in the after action report that two FBI teams trailed suspects after they turned onto Park Street. One FBI team heading west on Park Street from Caldwell Bank slowly moved head on toward suspects. The suspect's car was signaled to pullover by use of strobe light attached on top of the FBI team vehicle directly behind them. The suspect's car immediately stopped. Marcwell and Turner quickly exited their vehicle and a firefight ensued. Three FBI teams became engaged in a gun battle with Marcwell and Turner. Two FBI agents that signaled for suspects to pull over were killed within seconds of initial fight. Turner exited passenger side and sprayed a 30 round magazine into the front compartment of their car.

A few moments passed from being told to hold. SueAnn and Bear sat quiet, as they remained focused on the intersection. Suddenly gunshots could be heard coming from Park Street. The sounds of gunfire were sporadic at first and then it picked up into a steady roar. Cracks of high-powered rifles and thuds of lower caliber firearms were mixed and steady.

"Man down! We have men down! We need help! I... they..." The voice of some scared agent screamed over the radio before it fell silent.

"What the..." Bear sat stunned. "Oh my God."

"We have to get into it," SueAnn yelled. Her blood was pumping.

"We hold!" Bear was uneasy with her statement. "We were told to hold."

"Can't do that." SueAnn reached over Bears lap and popped the trunk of the vehicle. She opened her door and ran for the now opened trunk.

"Oh, no! We will hold. That was our orders. That is not our situation," Bear yelled as he exited the car.

SueAnn was now fixated on the sounds of a firefight and what she had in the trunk that could help the agents engaged in battle. Her and Bear were parked less than 200 yards from the action. She pulled an M4 carbine from the trunk and slapped a 30 round magazine into it. She charged the weapon and put it on safe. She grabbed four other fully loaded magazines and put them in her pant cargo pockets.

"We are not going to do this," Bear shouted as he grabbed her arm.

"Then stay. I'm not asking you for anything. I'm telling you that I'm going." SueAnn was calm and committed to what she knew had to be accomplished.

"Great! That's just great! I'll monitor the radio, I guess." Bear moved to the front seat.

The sounds of the firefight were no longer as steady. The agents and suspects had the "mad minute" of fire and then settled into cover, with each side maneuvering for position or holding their ground. Shots were traded and empty magazines were exchanged for full ones. Neither side was giving in. FBI agents were alive, wounded, and dead – two dead in the front seat of a car, one dead laying in the middle of park street, one wounded behind a car but remained engaged in battle, one wounded severely as she lay in Park Street and unable to stay engaged in battle. Three agents remained behind the engine compartments of their vehicles firing at anything that presented itself as a threat

Marcwell stationed himself behind the front of his car. The engine and his bulletproof vest blocked all bullets fired that had potential to take him down. Turner, hit a few different times, had a bullet in his thigh and was bleeding profusely. His bulletproof vest absorbed the slow moving .40 caliber bullets that hit him above the waist. He remained committed to the fight as he stuffed his wound with mud he found near a puddle of water on the side of the road.

SueAnn maneuvered around buildings as she closed in on the firefight. She had no idea what she would see when she came upon it. Shots were being fired so she knew bad guys still existed and agents were still dedicated. She was situated on the backside of a business. She hugged the wall and figured the fight was located directly in front of the strip of businesses she maneuvered behind. She wanted to hurry yet she understood the right or wrong move would make the difference between life and death.

Turner was pissed at himself for being in the situation he was now busy with. He had told Marcwell they should have moved north, to a different state, city, or area, and staked operations there. Marcwell felt invincible. He always felt that if things get bad they could always go to a level of violence others were not willing to go. He knew that those that thought they could go to another level would only pay a heavy price. Turner was now stuffing mud into a bleeding thigh and turning pale as he hobbled toward anything that could swallow him up for a moment.

"Move your dumbass behind that rock." Marcwell pointed to a large rock that hung a law firms shingle from it. It was large enough that Turner could lie behind and not worry about fire from the FBI agents in front of them.

Marcwell thought it odd for a large ass rock to be where no other rock existed.

"Yeah. Yeah. Cock suckers got lucky." Turner grimaced and limped toward the Rock.

"You need to stop! Now," An FBI agent yelled from behind the car he sought cover.

"Fuck You! You can stop! We got you fuckers!" Marcwell shot in the direction the voice came from. "Fuck..."

Marcwell caught a glimpse of Turner falling to the ground before he made it to the rock. It was a headshot. Turner lay face down with the right side of his head, above his eye, blown out; lying in blood and brain matter. Marcwell turned around quickly. He knew the fire had come from behind. *Took too fucking long*, He thought before two bullets slammed into his chest. The force of the bullets pushed him back against his car, but he remained standing. He raised his rifle and scanned the area, desperate to acquire a target. He dropped quickly to his knees as a bullet passed through the front of his neck and out the back. He was bleeding a great deal as he tried to catch or stop the blood with both hands before it left him. He felt the presence of someone near him but he didn't look. Instead he reached for his weapon lying in front of him with one hand. Blood sprayed to the ground as he pulled his hand from his neck. The last vision he had was the blood soaked dirt and weapon that lay in front of him. His last thought was, *kill the sons of bitches*.

SueAnn remained calm as she remained kneeling behind and beside the adjacent buildings HVAC unit. The unit provided ample cover and concealment. Both Turner and Marcwell lay dead in front of her. She wondered if

Marcwell ever saw who shot him. She could tell by the way he scanned the area that he was franticly trying to acquire a target. She dropped Turner and knew he was dead, never thought about putting another bullet in him. She turned to Marcwell and put two in his chest and was stunned that he remained standing. She was upset with herself that she was low with the third bullet, hitting him in the neck. She felt rushed, knowing that he would find where she was. It was only a matter of time. The third shot would have killed him; it would just take time for him to bleed out. She would have taken a fourth shot if one of the FBI agents engaged in the fight earlier wouldn't have gotten so close to him. Marcwell sat still for a moment and provided her a great opportunity for a headshot, but she didn't want to risk a stray bullet from her rifle hitting the FBI Agent standing next to him - regardless of how remote the possibility of her missing the target. The Agent finished Marcwell off with a point blank shot to his head as he reached for his weapon.

"Help us," the agent yelled at SueAnn as she moved toward the dead bodies.

SueAnn stared into the agent's wide eyes as sirens of law enforcement vehicles could be heard closing in on the area...

"Gosh damn." Kelly slid back in his seat after hearing SueAnn's detailed account of an event that took place six years earlier. "That was one day to be had from what I remember."

"That situation is still analyzed in Academy case studies." Brenner piped up as he stood and stretched, rolling his eyes as he looked at his boss as if to say, the woman is crazy.

"Yes it is studied at the Academy. And if I remember right, it was Agent Ferguson who was able to flank Marcwell and Turner with one other wounded Agent. While suppressive fire was being placed on the scumbags. Ferguson and the other Agent were able to put down Turner and, and... Hooch, or whatever the hell their names were." Stevens raised his voice.

"I'm sorry if that..."

"Agent Bear was a family friend of mine." Stevens cut SueAnn off before she could finish.

"Hold on their young Agent." Kelly chuckled as he put a stop to the conversation. He got up and walked around his desk, leading SueAnn to the door. "So the Agency put a boot in your ass." Kelly smiled. "If I recall. Your daddy had plenty of boot put in his ass."

SueAnn turned to look at Kelly as she walked toward the door. *He knew my father.*

"One more thing Agent English. The good Senator Winfield retired to spend more time with family?" Brenner questioned before SueAnn reached the door.

"Yes, Sir, he did."

"Lots of people thought he would have made a good President?" Kelly questioned.

"The honorable Senator has a better understanding of fellatio than he does public service."

SueAnn slightly smiled only because Kelly had such a huge smile on his face.

Senior Agent Kelly knew she was indifferent as to what one grown adult did to another as long as it was consensual. He also knew that political favors for public funds were illegal and if she was tasked with sniffing it out, she would bring corrupt people to justice.

"We'll see you in the morning Agent, English." Kelly's grin was as large as it could be.

Why death for everyone I love?

The ice in the highball glass was melting. Drake McCreiess poured scotch over the ice, knowing he would finish the drink before the ice melted completely. He tossed the empty bottle onto the couch as he walked to the wall where the picture of he and his wife hung. With the hope they would be together soon, he wiped the tears from his eyes. In the picture his wife was smiling. He remembered her being so happy in her wedding dress. He remembered her walking down the aisle as everyone stood in awe of her beauty. He remembered the stumble as her heel snagged the runner and how she laughed out loud so everyone else felt they could as well. He deeply missed his wife. The thought of him and her throwing a football into a tree several times so that they could knock the kite they had found loose, flashed into his thoughts. The kite eventually fell after more than a few hours of throwing the football into the tree. The kite symbolized their drive for each other and they flew it many times after its successful recovery.

McCreiess sipped the drink. His eyes drifted to another picture. It was of him and his very good friend Kevin

Halcot. In the picture, Kevin wore the Purple Heart medal for the wound he received In Afghanistan. Kevin was proud as he wore his dress green uniform. He was part of the 19th Special Forces who helped escort Afghan soldiers into their homeland to retake their country from the Taliban Emirate and Al Qaeda. As the Taliban fled Afghanistan they lobbed mortar rounds into the Special Forces teams. Kevin was one of the unlucky soldiers struck by shrapnel from one of the mortars. He was struck in the elbow and forearm. Although he was wounded, Kevin continued the fight until he was ordered by his commanding officer to seek medical attention. The elbow wound was turning and sure to be infected if medical attention was delayed much longer. McCreiess remembered receiving an email Kevin sent to him soon after the assault and the wound was never mentioned in the correspondence. The email spoke more about how his friend enjoyed spending time in a classroom with girls who were once forbidden classroom-learning opportunities. Kevin enjoyed teaching English to the children when he was not on a mission.

A tear slowly moved down McCreiess' cheek. He stopped bothering to wipe them away.

"Death. Why death for everyone I love." McCreiess' thoughts drifted to an event that took place six years earlier.

:-

"Shift right." Came the call from Sherman as he rode shotgun, or front passenger, in the lead vehicle of a 4 Humvee Special Forces Operational Detachment convoy traveling south on what the Americans called Highway Tampa. The call was made because debris was scattered on the left and center of the road.

Highway Tampa connected Baghdad with cities in Southern Iraq. Coalition forces that needed to conduct business in Baghdad and surrounding cities traveled Highway Tampa. The highway was not unlike many highway systems in the United States. It was four to eight lanes and prior to the war McCreiess was sure it was maintained.

Since McCreiess was in charge of the convoy, He rode shotgun in the third suburban. As the convoy leader, McCreiess said very little on the radio. Sherman, who sat in the front passenger seat of the lead vehicle, gave him a visual of what lay ahead. Convoys generally run as a snake, one behind the other, approximately 150 feet apart. As Sherman made the call to shift right, McCreiess saw the two vehicles ahead of his move right. He felt his vehicle make the right adjustment as well. He only felt the adjustment because He was mainly concerned with securing the right side of the convoy by looking out the front and passenger door window.

The first three convoy vehicles were "hard," or armored, vehicles. The fourth vehicle was "soft," or unarmored. The vehicles each held between two and five men. The fourth vehicle, called the "follow," carried five men and provided security if needed. The follow allowed the men inside to provide maximum fire support for the other convoy vehicles. The follows' windows were down and bristled with weapons ready to be deployed at any identified threat.

As McCreiess' vehicle moved past the debris, He waited for Kevin Halcot, the commander of the follow, to make the "clear through" call as he always did when the follow cleared a choke point. Kevin never made that call. Instead, McCreiess heard a large explosion behind him and Bauer's scream over the radio - "We're hit! We're hit!"

The force of the explosion, caused by an I.E.D., sent the follow into a clockwise spin and forced Bauer, who was sitting directly behind the driver, into the rear compartment with Cushly, the follows' rear gunner. Knight, the follows' driver, felt Kevin being forced out the passenger window and cranked the steering wheel against the spin with one hand and reached for Kevin with the other.

McCreiess looked in his rear view mirror and saw the follow spin, remarkably not flip over, and stay in line with the convoy. He watched as the follow came to a halt; the front of the vehicle rested up against a raised sidewalk on a bridge. It was surrounded by dust and debris kicked up by the spin. The entire convoy stopped.

McCreiess thought to himself, just for a moment, *they could survive that.* From his view, the follow had just come to a rest after a spin that could have been caused by driving fast on ice and losing control. It really did not register with him that the follow absorbed the full impact of an explosion.

McCreiess asked his driver, Booker, to turn their vehicle around and get behind the follow to pick up rear security. Booker quickly turned the vehicle around. McCreiess saw some of his men crawling out of the follow.

He told Booker to let him out and then finish picking up rear security. The men crawling out of the follow had just been through a violent experience and needed direction.

As McCreiess jumped out of his vehicle, He noticed a man lying on the highway in front of him, Elwood. When the explosion occurred, Elwood had been sitting directly behind Kevin and was ejected from the vehicle while it spun. McCreiess could tell by the baseball size hole in Elwood's forehead that he did not survive the explosion, so he continued past Elwood to reach the men bailing out of the follow. As He reached it, he saw men expressing different kinds of reactions.

Bauer noticed Elwood. "Oh my God, Elwood is hit," he yelled.

"Elwood is dead," McCreiess screamed, "Pick up a security position." He needed the men to think security. He was afraid that whoever caused the explosion would mount another assault.

"I have been hit," Cushly pronounced with shock, as he came out of the follow holding his neck. He had caught shrapnel from the explosion.

Knight, Kevin's Iraq buddy, was screaming, "Where's Kevin, Where's Kevin?"

McCreiess made it clear that security was priority one.

"Grab a weapon, and pull security," McCreiess hollered. Noticing that Cushly did not have a life threatening wound, but only a hole in his neck with little bleeding, he commanded, "Cushly, you are going to be fine. You will have to make your way to the lead vehicle and provide self aid."

Knight was still screaming for Kevin.

"I will find Kevin," McCreiess yelled so that the group around the follow could hear him.

While he was dealing with the follows' crew, his second in command, Ace, ensured that the two lead vehicles secured the stopped convoy's front and sides. He knew he could trust Ace and that he did not need directions to complete his job.

McCreiess thought he would run around the follow and find Kevin taking up a security position. Kevin did not need to be told how important it was to engage the enemy or provide security in the first few seconds of an ambush. However, Kevin was not engaging the enemy or taking up a security position. When McCreiess found him, he was pinned between the follows' front and the raised sidewalk. McCreiess could tell by his wounds, brain matter hanging out of his ears, and massive bleeding from his stomach area, that he had also succumbed to the explosion. Kevin's eyes were open but had no life in them.

"I'm so sorry Kevin." McCreiess spoke as if Kevin could hear him.

McCreiess left Kevin and took up a position at the follows' rear. He could see the convoy's entire length. Booker covered his back.

McCreiess murmured a quick prayer for Kevin and Elwood that asked God to have mercy on their souls. He might have said more, but a cry from Knight brought him back to the task at hand.

"Where's Kevin? We can't leave Kevin!" Knight cried. "He's my buddy."

"WE ARE NOT LEAVING ANYONE BEHIND!" McCreiess moved so everyone could see him. "Think Security," he yelled for all to hear.

"Fox," McCreiess yelled. Fox was a well-respected soldier who was in charge of communications, and the driver of the lead vehicle.

"Yeah." Fox's response was calm and collected.

McCreiess shouted for all to hear, "Get a hold of Merrell and let him know we have two KIA and one wounded. We are returning to BIAP Baghdad." Merrell was in charge of all Special Forces ODA operations in Al Hilla, Iraq and McCreiess' direct supervisor; he needed information on the current situation.

At that moment, the team fell silent. There was a new mission. No one doubted what each man had to do. They were no longer safely traveling from Baghdad to Al Hilla. They were now preparing for an enemy attack, eliminating the enemy threat, and moving their dead and wounded to safety.

McCreiess scanned the security line that was now in place. He saw Cushly holding a bandage to his neck with one hand and a weapon in the other. Bauer took up position and provided security. Ace, who had joined his team less than a week prior, knelt by the lead vehicle and secured the front position so others could perform their duties in the rear. Knight had a weapon and was ready to engage the enemy. The team had experienced such violence just minutes before. Now, they were doing all that was expected of them.

The enemy never showed up and anger swept over McCreiess. He, like the other men on the team, wanted more. He didn't know what he wanted more of, but it was hard to see two fallen comrades and no enemy to strike. In the distance, the team saw a group of people wearing burkas and assumed they were woman but could not be sure. They saw a vehicle parked on a nearby overpass.

"I'm going to take out the people in the burkas," one of the men yelled.

"We need to take out that vehicle on the overpass," another person screamed.

McCreiess thought, *What if the burkas were a disguise for the enemy? What if the enemy is using the vehicle? What if they were not?*

"We are not shooting at anything that is not an immediate threat! You will stand down," McCreiess shouted.

McCreiess did not order a strike against people wearing burkas or a vehicle on the side of the road. What if they were not the enemy? It would have been criminal to strike out against anyone or anything, unless he was sure it was the enemy. The men were acting on their emotions at that specific moment, anger. They wanted to lash out at something.

"I notified the boss that we have two KIA and one wounded." The voice of Fox cracked over the radio. "He wants to know if you want helo support."

"Negative. At this time there is no enemy threat," McCreiess said with a sigh...

McCreiess finished the glass of scotch with a few sips and one large swallow. He removed the pictures from the wall and stumbled before he reached the couch. He slowly sat down and placed the picture of Kevin and himself on the table in front of him. He leaned back in the couch, put his feet on the table, and held the picture of his wife closely to his chest. He cried. He reached for the bottle of scotch; it was empty. The bottle dropped to the floor and made a thud. He slowly slid down in the couch so that he could lay and look toward the ceiling, still clinching the picture tightly to his chest. The thought of his wife's worst days, two years earlier, crossed his mind; she was always the strong one...

McCreiess sat listening to his wife as she labored to breathe. He held Abby's hand as he laid his head on the bed. He snuggled his head as close to her as he could. He understood how uncomfortable she was, regardless of the amount of pain meds pumping through her system. Abby was pale and sweating profusely. In an attempt to be comfortable she rolled from one side to the other. The oxygen tube was doing little as it hung loosely from her nose. McCreiess knew that in very few minutes the oxygen tube wouldn't matter.

The bout with breast cancer had taken a healthy beautiful woman, and reduced her to 72 pounds of flesh and bone. She was once a vibrant person who lit up a room, a woman who was once a top track and field athlete for the University of Tennessee, a top accountant for one of the best and most well-known accounting firms in the country, before she moved on and became successful in private practice. She was accomplished. She looked forward to having babies with the love of her life, her husband. Their commitment for each other was intense and passionate. She now lay in her bed at home with no grand illusion of ever making it out of the predicament she was confronted with.

She fought hard at first for her life, then to be a proud woman and wife, and in the end, she just didn't want to be a bother.

It started with a lump she had found on her left breast. She asked the person she trusted most what his thoughts were. He could only suggest getting a doctor to provide the answer. They both knew it was more than nothing to worry about.

McCreiess accompanied his Abby to every visit with the doctor. He was there when they told her it was indeed cancer, it was small, and it will be fine. He was also there when they told her there was nothing else they could do and she should try and make herself as comfortable as possible.

They started with aggressive chemo treatment before a mastectomy, 8 different treatments in 18 weeks. The treatment drained her; anemia, loss of appetite, loss of hair, constipation, diarrhea, nausea, and bleeding were just some of the side effects she experienced. It was no wonder she seemed excited about the doctors offer of a mastectomy. The thought of going through anymore chemo treatment and the side effects that accompanied the treatment was something she wanted to avoid.

McCreiess and Abby talked about reconstruction of the breast, even before the mastectomy was performed. She desperately clutched to what she believed was wholeness; knowing that her husband would take her anyway she came. Even as the crying, bald, frail woman sat on the toilet, battling diarrhea, he professed his love for her. Telling her that, "if this cancer thing is a grand-plan to get me to run off, you have failed miserably." She hugged him as close as she could as he carried her from the bathroom to the bedroom. He lay with her that night as she shivered.

It was the day before reconstruction surgery was to begin that they were both notified that tests came back negative, the mastectomy did not get all the cancer. McCreiess wanted to fight. She wanted peace. It wasn't that she was giving up; she just understood the fight was over.

Abby gasped for her last breaths. He stood from his seat, still holding his wife's hand. She looked him in the eye. His eyes filled with tears that eventually dropped onto her face.

"Abby, you are beautiful. I love you more than life itself, Abby." He whispered.

Abby became still.

"One day. I promise. One day, Abby." McCreiess wept as Abigail Sue Ellen McCreiess' eyes went lifeless.

McCreiess tossed the picture onto the table in front of him and leaned forward. He was lonely and he knew it. He wished he could have told Kevin how much he loved him. He wished he had one more chance to hold his Abby and look into her eyes. He wished for one more kiss from her lips as he held her face in his hands. He prayed that he would meet them again. He knew his Abby would not approve of what he had become, a stone cold killer. He felt as if Kevin was looking down upon him with a look of disappointment and sadness. He just knew that both would want him to part ways from a society that only created more evil in a world that was already filled with wickedness. He came to realize that he hated what he had become.

The feeling of supremacy...

Setting just a few blocks away from the White House, the Willard Hotel gave some of its outside diners a feeling of supremacy. One could get a spectacular view of the Capitol Building and see the Washington Monument protruding from the skyline of the surrounding edifice. The hotel was situated in the heart of power. The hotel itself was a famous and favorite landmark, especially for those who knew its history. The original six structures were built in the year 1816. In its day the hotel was the place to stay for dignitaries from all over the world. Dukes and Emperors alike enjoyed its comforts. President Lincoln stayed in the Willard, before moving to the White House, after he snuck into Washington under the threat of assassination. General Grant coined the phrase "lobbyist" while staying at the Willard because everyone approached him in the lobby with all sorts of ideas that they wanted the government to spend money on. Martin Luther King wrote the famous "I have a dream" speech while staying in the beautiful hotel. It was no wonder why the hotel remained attractive for powerful people.

Cynthia enjoyed the feeling of supremacy as she walked the streets of Washington DC, understanding that decisions were often made inside of the powerful white buildings surrounding her. Her meeting with Senator Claire Miller was one of friendship but mostly business. Cynthia's goal was simple, promotion. She wanted to assure the Senator that she was not only interested in attaining the next level but wanted it more than anything, only she couldn't come across as being too willing. People in Washington enjoyed getting what they want without actually inquiring. Being reserved was an art form and those that played it best were usually at the top of the pyramids. Her late father, Judge George Mader, would tell her, "Get what you want. Just don't ask for it. That way, you will have earned it." Her father earned everything. He was modest, but never shy about anything. His understanding of the self-promotion that went on in the nation's capital was learned over many years.

"Cynthia! Cynthia!" Senator Miller waved her napkin as she noticed her friend entering the gate that separated the Willard hotel from the sidewalk.

Cynthia blushed. She was stunned at the thought of an influential senator who sits on the powerful judicial committee creating such a scene.

"Claire!" Cynthia hugged her friend as they greeted each other.

Both ladies gave each other a once over. Smiling as they each approved of what the other was wearing.

"I love your shoes. Let me guess." Cynthia paused for thought. "Giuseppe Zanotti."

"No. But I do like..."

"Gucci!"

"Yes. Yes."

"I love it." Cynthia enjoyed complementing her friend. She would often hone up on the different popular styles before meeting her. She knew Claire's fondness for fine wardrobe.

"Please sit, Cynthia." Claire motioned a waiter to come at once.

"Yes, Ms. Miller. I mean Senator." The waiter promptly responded.

"I would like a Bombay and Tonic with a lime and my friend would like..."

"I will have the same," Cynthia replied with a smile.

The waiter turned to walk away as both women made eye contact and then turned their heads to follow him as he walked to the bar.

"So early in the day, Senator?" Cynthia grinned.

"Girl, when you've been in this town as long as I have." Claire shook her head. "I have to drink so I can stomach most of the drivel that comes out of this town." She paused. "I remember your father telling me that he had to shower when he just thought about coming to this town."

Cynthia looked down the street at the Capitol Building. The thought of her father flashed in her mind but she quickly released it. Her father's passing was hard on her and she did not take it well, so any reflection of him was quickly forgotten.

"I was actually talking about the waiter, Claire."

"I wonder how many drinks he would have to have before I start looking good." Claire raised her eyebrows.

Senator Claire Miller was a well-known flirt and could care less what people thought. People who elected her didn't care about such behavior, or they cared more about low taxes and less business regulation. Regardless of what they cared about, she kept winning elections.

"Your drinks, ladies." The waiter placed the drinks on the table. "Is there anything else?"

"Not right now." Claire pulled her sunglasses down just enough to make eye contact with the young man.

***

"Cynthia, you are in the right position at the right time." Claire leaned forward, pushing her fourth Bombay and Tonic aside so that she could make an impression by tapping her finger on the table.

"I agree and I want to capitalize on it. What more do I need to do, and most important, what do I need not to do?" Cynthia was still nursing her first and only drink.

"You are on a very short list of candidates. A very short list." Claire sat back in her seat and sipped her drink. "Most would say it is yours to lose."

"Again, Claire! What is it I need to do or not do?" Cynthia kept her voice low, but her frustration with Claire's drunkenness showed.

"Don't do anything!" Claire removed her sunglasses. "Clear your calendar as much as possible and take it easy."

"That's easy for you to say." Cynthia sighed.

"Listen." Claire reached over to hold her friends hand. "The President has reviewed your file." Claire's speech was more slurred. "The judicial committee has reviewed your file. There is nothing in there that the other side can point at as out of the main stream."

Cynthia sighed again.

"Cynthia you are everything the President wants and needs. You are a strict Constructionalist when it comes to the Constitution and you stand strong for law and order. You are a woman!" Claire emphasized her last point by slapping her knee.

Cynthia leaned forward in her chair and smiled at her friend.

"The Supreme Court." Cynthia choked.

"What did you think..."

"I guess I wasn't thinking."

"Justice Aaron is expected to announce his retirement some time soon. He is old and ailing. Unless there is a ghost in your closet that hasn't seeped out yet...you will be the next nominee."

Cynthia sat up straight and paused to think.

"I have a meeting coming up with Senator Fellow. He is the President's go-to guy when it comes to finding a list of names. Potential Aaron replacement, such as yourself."

"I thought he was..."

"He is retired. But I don't think his book sold all that well so he needed something to do. I guess..." Claire laughed and then paused to cover her mouth to muffle a burp. "Cynthia, you are in the right place at the right time. You are on a very short list of candidates." She paused again to burp. "Have we already covered this?"

"I want to capitalize on the..."

"You forget...I'm the ranking member of the judicial committee. I have already submitted your name. And that, my very good friend, makes you a serious candidate... so clear your calendar and take it easy."

"I wish it were that easy." Cynthia was resigned to the fact her friend was drunk. She had been around Claire many times before when too much alcohol was used. She knew it was just best to nod, smile, and keep cerebral thoughts out of the conversation.

"No need for worry. Stop worr...unless you do something stupid ...like screwing an intern. You're not screwing interns are you?" Claire looked Cynthia in the eyes as if she was serious.

"No!"

"Good. Good. I would not like my name attached to such a person." Claire stirred her drink and looked at the waiter.

Cynthia tried not to roll her eyes as she sat looking at her inebriated friend.

"You're staying with me tonight!"

"I wish I could but I have to be in Richmond. I have a legal conference and I have to be getting on the road."

"Some other time. Soon," Claire said before she finished off her drink.

"Yes, some other time. Meetings like this are just too infrequent." Cynthia nodded and smiled.

"I should be going myself. I have to be in conference later today. We're discussing something about the Patriot Act or blah, blah, blah." Claire rolled her eyes. "It never ends."

***

Cynthia, had a spring to her step as she walked the Monument Avenue sidewalk, located in the uptown area of the Lower Fan district. She loved the red brick street and the many different monuments. As a child she spent plenty of time walking the city of Richmond with her father. Her father would provide lectures on the many different types of architecture. She would have to listen for hours, it seemed, as her father would explain the differences between Victorian style and Edwardian style buildings. When asked her favorite building she would point to St. Pete's Saloon. St. Pete's was a landmark of Richmond where local celebrities would unwind, politicians would strategize, and athletes would celebrate. It was also a favorite place of her father's. She knew he enjoyed a pint of his favorite beer at the saloon as he bellied up to the 32 foot tiger-oak bar and back-bar; she enjoyed the home cooked garlic fries sprinkled with onion salt. Her father couldn't resist when she pointed it out so they would go there for lunch and he would continue his lectures, inevitably leading to the American Civil War and how Richmond was involved. He would stand near the bar and rub his hand over the smooth top and describe how he and the owner personally picked the wood from his acreage. As a young girl at the age of ten or twelve her father's lectures on such subjects of battles and Generals, specifically General Lee, enthralled her. Her mind wondered as he spoke. She often put herself in place of General Lee or other great leaders of the brutal battles.

Cynthia now stood in front of St. Pete's as an accomplished person in her own right. In her mind she had become a leader, a person who was often on the field of battle, it's just that the battles raged behind closed doors and in smoke filled rooms, and the adversaries were often men. She took a deep breath. She gave herself a once over in the reflection of the large plate glass door. The last time she visited St. Pete's she received news of her father's impending death and his invitation and endorsement for her to join an elite society, The System. The news of his death and the link to the society were life altering. She often contemplated what it would be like to still remain in her father's shadow. In his shadow she was protected. Outside of her father's shadow she was free, but that often meant suffering the unintended consequences of her decisions.

She was now about to embark on another life altering experience. She straightened her blouse, nervously switched her briefcase from one hand to the other and opened the door. The chatter from the other patrons of St. Pete's calmed her and she gained confidence with each step as she moved past the bar her father adored.

***

Federal Judge Michael Stallings situated himself in his favorite corner booth. The booth was tucked away from other patrons and the waiters obliged him by removing the white cloth from his table before his arrival and had his favorite drink ready for him. His appearance at the saloon was nothing out of the ordinary because he frequented the establishment often. It was actually out of the ordinary if he did not show his face through the week at St. Pete's. The wait staff would question each other when he missed a Monday through Friday. The booth he favored allowed him to read over daily court material and have a few drinks to calm him before heading home to his wife and kids.

Stallings raised his head and reached for his favorite drink, a glass of Woodford over rocks. In doing so he was startled to see Cynthia Mader moving toward his table. His eyes met with hers. She smiled.

"Hello, Michael."

"Cynthia Mader. What are you doing in Richmond?" Stallings was surprised.

"I was in the area so I thought I would drop by and surprise you."

"Well it worked. How would you know I'm here? Here at St. Pete's."

"I know you come here after work and this is not your night to be with that young mistress of yours." Cynthia slightly grinned as she stared into Stallings' eyes.

Stallings knew Cynthia was looking for a blink or something that said he would lie.

"What are you getting at, Cynthia?" Stallings didn't blink and he didn't lie. He returned the eye contact with a stare. He understood that lies in such situations only made the condition worse. He understood a person such as Cynthia wouldn't make rash statements; after all, he did have a mistress.

"What are you getting at, Cynthia? What do you..."

"Let's just say the "i" has been dotted and now the "t" is being crossed."

"Well why don't you have a seat?" Stallings looked around and found that his booth was indeed snuggled away from the other patrons. "And why are we doing this here?"

A waiter approached the booth. "Can I get you any..."

"I would like a tonic on the rocks, with a lime. I feel a little spicy tonight." Cynthia grinned.

"I would like another Woodford on the rocks." Stallings spoke with a hesitation before the waiter hurried off. He actually thought about grabbing his things and hustling for the door, but he thought about the scene it might create.

"I'm here seeking your assistance and approval for my next case, the Tommy Mill case, and I feel safer doing it in a public place."

"Don't you think I should hear the case first?" Stallings rolled his eyes to show his disbelief and displeasure.

"No. No need really. You need only to present the case contained in this envelope and say aye when I ask for approval." Cynthia reached in her brief case and pulled a manila envelope from it. "There are some interesting visual aids in there as well." She smiled as she slid the envelope across the table.

"Blackmail, Cynthia?" Stallings held from touching the envelope. It was as if he touched it, he accepted it. "What do you have there?"

"You should look inside, Michael."

Stallings took a deep breath and let it out. The waiter brought the drinks and hurried away. The tension building at the booth could be felt by anyone within arm's length.

"Go ahead, Michael. Pick it up and look inside. There is nothing there that will shock you."

"I know what you have, Cynthia." Stallings sighed as thoughts of his wife and children rushed through his mind. "I'm sure it's compromising photos of my friend Carmen and me."

"If it were that simple, Michael. Michael, in that envelope is CD's, photos, and videos. My God, Michael, if Carmen was the only one I might just think, another slime ball doing slimy stuff. It's the orgies, ropes, leather, and young, young, girls." Cynthia spoke softly and giggled. "The only thing missing are the monkeys and midgets."

"I have never been with anyone that could be considered a minor."

"Probably true, Michael. But that's nothing an anonymous source to a journalist friend of mine couldn't take care of. He will cut you down to a damn pedophile if I tell him to. A pedophile! The only thing worse is a traitor to our country and that depends probably on the variables." Cynthia paused and looked around the room.

"Why, you would be old news before the truth ever came out...if it ever did."

"This is not funny, Cynthia. It's not funny one bit. I'm no sexual deviant. It's just that Carmen opened the door to..."

"Stop. Stop, Michael." Cynthia laughed out loud. "Michael I personally feel the fourth district is more enlightened for having someone like yourself on the bench. Not! But it's not me you will have to convince." She became stern. "Can you imagine, a federal judge, a respected family man, a father of two beautiful girls who attend the finest private schools in Virginia? Can you imagine such a person acting like those videos suggest he is acting? Shame, shame, shame."

"You wouldn't get your case through without me presenting it? Without blackmail?" Stallings was drained. He took a deep breath and let it out as he slumped in his seat. He grabbed his drink and took a gulp. The liquor perked him up for a moment, but he was resigned to knowing the ordinary facts would spoil any melodrama.

"If the videos only placed you in a position of playing footsy with a man in the next stall." Cynthia laughed. "Or texting a young male page. I think your wife is strong, but I don't see her being one of those pathetic wives who stands by her man when this stuff hits the fan." Cynthia paused. "The loss of community and political support will be overwhelming. Your so-called friends will collectively run for the hills. Oh, the humiliation." Cynthia sipped her drink. "That lime does do something."

Cynthia waved for the waiter to take an order. "Waiter, can you get my friend another drink?"

"Make that a double with no rocks." Stallings downed the rest of his Woodford with one long swig.

"Maybe you can pal around with Maury Povich?" Cynthia giggled.

"So let me get this straight," Stallings said as the waiter turned his back, "You want me to..."

"No, Michael." Cynthia started once the waiter was out of earshot. "Let me make this clear. I want no mistakes or misunderstanding. You will present and approve the case in that envelope."

"This is a big mistake, Cynthia." Stallings became firm in tone. "And it will create worries. This is the slippery slope our founders warned against." The waiter interrupted his thought as he placed the ordered drink on the table.

"Woodford double with no rocks." The waiter smiled.

"Put it on my tab, Brian. Nothing else right now." Stallings waved his hand, signaling the waiter to leave. "We are the check and balance." Stallings continued when he thought the waiter couldn't hear his conversation. "We are not vigila..."

"Don't you even start." Cynthia's face turned red. "My father brought me up in The System. He was talking to me about The System, this secret society, long before the hump chair was invented." Cynthia pulled a photo from the envelope. "Really, Michael, a hump chair, who knew such a thing, existed?" She looked over the photo as Stallings stared at the ceiling. "There's the midget!"

Cynthia pointed. "No. He's only on his knees. Carmen seems to be a very giving person."

"Your father would have never..."

"You have no idea what my father wanted. I remember as a little girl watching men gather once a year to sit at the pentagon shaped table. My father chose me. He warned against people like you."

"Cynthia, please don't do this."

"Three days and I want your answer. The envelope is yours. Familiarize yourself with the Tommy Mill case and look over the porn. I have plenty of copies."

"You will need another vote," Stallings said as he sipped the double of Woodford.

"Excuse me." Cynthia's mouth hung open.

"May I ask who else you are blackmailing?"

Cynthia looked around the room.

"Well, Mr. Ellenberg is new and he is a family man, and by all accounts he seems to be madly in love with his family. The general has a sister who is a communist." Cynthia sipped from her drink. "That would have been a big deal a couple decades ago. Does me no good now though. It seems you can't throw a dead cat anymore without hitting a communist."

"Porter."

"Mr. Porter is a politician, and most important, an out of work politician. He will kiss or kill babies depending on the support he needs." Cynthia sighed. "Politicians pick people like us to make decisions they don't have the guts to make. Porter epitomizes the scummy politician."

"Coattails?"

"Well, Michael. Some would say I'm a rising star. Mr. Porter would love to latch on to my coattails. Believe me."

"Porter is a huge zit who rears his ugly head when..."

"Yes, Michael. Regardless of what you might think of the man. And I do agree with you." Cynthia paused for a moment. She looked Stallings in the eye and made sure his eyes connected with hers. "I need the man."

"You need..."

"We were all aghast when a politician was nominated to our society." Cynthia interrupted. "Don't you remember, Michael? You vouched for him or did you forget?"

Stallings regretted vouching for the politician but it was his mentor who nominated him so he felt an obligation.

"No. I remember."

"I used to think political offices were filled with mostly honorable people with a few undesirables. Boy was I ever wrong." Cynthia laughed as Stallings swallowed the rest of his drink. "I could fill many more CDs of Porter shenanigans. I'll save them for later."

"What do you suppose..."

"We should clean it up, Michael. Starting with you." Cynthia answered before hearing the question.

"I'll do it. God damn it."

"Good." Cynthia rose from her seat and adjusted her skirt and blouse. "How do I look?" She didn't wait for an answer. She moved for the exit, but turned for one more quick parting gesture. "If you need help with presenting the case just call me. And thanks for the drink."

Stallings sat stunned. He was stunned by the strategy employed, the penalty of his actions, and the potential for disaster. *The woman must be mad*, he thought as he waved for the waiter to bring him another drink. He understood power and he understood how it corrupted. People who fell under the thumb of others were generally weak. They were easily destroyed by past wrongful ways. It was called character assassination; people were to be destroyed before they could become a future influence.

Stallings thought of his girlfriend Carmen. "Holy shit," He said to himself as the waiter delivered his double Woodford without the rocks.

PART 2

Mommy...

October, 1985 - Colorado State College

Gerald Cutter drove the 1972 Ford van as if its payload was nothing more than water. Turning curves he adjusted his speed very little, adjusting only when the large vehicle felt as if it would roll if he did not make adjustments. Coming out of a curve into a long straight stretch he floored the gas pedal, pushing the large cumbersome vehicle to max speed.

I can't be late. I won't be late, Cutter thought, trying to pump himself up for the early morning event.

"You better be ready Tommy!" Cutter shouted over the loud rock music coming from the maxed out speakers, and to no one but himself to hear. "If you're late I'm on my own." He kept the gas pedal to the floor.

Cutter, the head editorialist of *The Daily Goat*, was now fixated on time. He worried showing up late to pick up Tommy Mill would only give Mill an excuse to bail from the upcoming event. Seeing Mill standing by the phone booth located in front of the abandoned gas station Cutter started breaking, screeching the tires as he brought the van to a halt in front of the booth.

"Jesus, Gerald," Mill screamed as he jumped into the van and turned off the radio. "It's not fucking dirt you have in the back. It's enough nitrate and fuel to blow us into outer space if you're not careful." He slammed the door. "Now slow the fuck down, man."

"I don't want to be late, Tommy." Cutter reached out his hand to prevent his friend from entering his personal space. "You know how excited I am about this."

"We won't be. We are right on schedule." Mill looked at his watch. "It's almost midnight. We have almost four hours before we put it all in motion."

"Why in the hell did I have to pick you up way out here?"

"Do you not listen? Neither of us can be seen in the area today." Mill rolled his eyes. "We went over this a dozen times. Don't you remember anything about the job tonight?"

"Job, huh. That's one way to put it." Cutter paused for a moment of thought. "We are about to become legends, man, real heroes for the cause."

Mill stared at his friend. "I'm not looking for legend or hero status, Gerald." Mill opened the door that separated the driving compartment from the rear area of the van. "That's a shit load of explosives, man. I hope it works." He slid the door shut.

"You should trust Jimmy. He has it all set up for us." Cutter glanced at his skeptical friend. "What in the hell are you worried about, Tommy?"

"I'm not worried about this candle stick going up. I just don't trust any twenty-two year old man who still calls his mother 'mommy'." Mill rolled down his window, hoping to get some airflow in the stuffy van. "I could give a shit about the legendary status he promises. I just want the madness that takes place in that building to stop." Mill peeked again at the cargo they were hauling. "I could care less about moving up a chain that is linked by every nut case leftist group who has a bitch against capitalism."

"Oh the madness will stop." Cutter laughed out loud. "And I will be the hero then if you don't want to be."

Mill smiled at his friend. "I just want that momma's boy to pull off mommy's tit long enough to be there with the car."

"He will." Cutter reached into his pocket. "You got to admit, Tommy, those leftists sure do grow some good weed." Cutter grinned as he lit and smoked from his one hitter.

"They're losers with too much time on their hands." Mill crossed his arms and leaned his head back between the back of his seat and the door.

"Don't fall asleep Tommy. I will need your help with directions. I wouldn't want to wreck this thing."

**

Jimmy Mader paced the floor. He was waiting for his mommy to return from the store. His strides were small and quick as he continually walked back and forth

99

from the kitchen to the living room. He was excited and his hands waved in the air as he spoke to himself, practicing what he would say when his mother entered the apartment.

"Mommy this is big. What we will do tonight will make a difference. It is something you and the professor have wanted. A difference! Something we'll..."

Jimmy was interrupted by the sound of the door opening. He rushed to the door as his mother and Professor Shapiro entered the apartment. Jimmy's excitement plummeted. His pacing stopped and his hands fell to his side. A feeling of depression seemed to instantly overtake his mood.

Jimmy obediently grabbed a bag from his mother's arms as she walked to the kitchen.

"Thanks Jimmy. Please put that one next to the fruit bowl." Cynthia glanced at Jimmy. "I got your favorite cereal. Tony the Tiiiiiigerrrr."

"Mommy, what we are doing tonight..."

"We forgot the peanut butter." Cynthia's comment to the professor interrupted her son.

"A difference will be made. Hero's we all will..."

"I have the peanut butter. What do you want to do with..." A couple apples falling out of the bag Jimmy was holding interrupted Shapiro.

"Oh no," Jimmy placed the sack next to the fruit bowl and knelt to pick up the apples.

Jimmy started to weep. It was soft at first, his shoulders quivering slightly, and then it became uncontrollable, sobs shaking his whole body.

"Jimmy. Why are you crying? The apples will be fine. I will eat any that are bruised." Cynthia looked down on her son. "Are you off your meds again?"

Shapiro moved toward the door and made eye contact with Cynthia. He rolled his eyes.

"I'll leave this to the Mader family to hash out." Shapiro closed the door behind him as he left.

"Mommy, Mommy!" Jimmy was now on his knees and elbows, and clutching his face with his hands.

"What Jimmy? What is the matter?" Cynthia was annoyed by her son's behavior.

"Mommy, I think I've made a big mistake." Jimmy was sobbing.

"Jimmy! Jimmy! What have you done?" Cynthia's annoyance was replaced by anger.

Cynthia moved to stand over top her son.

***

The ROTC building at Colorado State College was centrally located on the campus. The college was situated on nearly 8,000 acres of land, located on the foothills of the Rocky Mountains, and its 14,000-foot peaks are visible to the residents, students, and those passing by on the local highways. Outside of agricultural research, the college was known for its ROTC program, which provided the U.S military with enthusiastic competent leaders.

Driving onto the campus, Cutter felt a rush of adrenalin. In his mind, what he was about to do was something many people would remember forever – the day the Reagan administration was stopped in their confrontation with the communist. The general population may not remember him personally, but the underground progressives would hold glasses high and salute him for years to come. He figured many in the media would spin the news as an inevitable and justified response to the Reagan Central American policy. But with no one to hold accountable, over the years, the story would eventually die down for anyone outside the cause.

Mill felt a rush of adrenalin, but for a different reason. He didn't want recognition from anyone or group. He wanted to stop the Reagan administration's fight against the "real people," or the Sandinistas of Nicaragua. Innocent lives being lost because of the bombs being designed in the ROTC building disturbed him. "Daniel Ortega was a real man of peace," he would preach to anyone who cared to listen. He knew bombs would continue to be built and dropped, but he felt what he was doing might save someone in South America and teach the ugly capitalist, Reagan, a lesson. He detested the wealthy and demanded more redistribution of their fortunes. His father taught him that work was for fools when "they" owed so much. Mill was a pacifist at heart, but he felt the need to accomplish one violent act before he could enjoy the illusion of a true pacifist. He identified with the communist party but he didn't want to be attached to any one group because he didn't want to be labeled or caught up in political drama.

Cutter made the left turn onto Main Street. Spotting the ROTC building he began to slow the vehicle. He stared at the five-story building that housed a military think-tank, the target of their mission. The van drifted and brushed the curve, jarring him back to his current task.

"Watch what you are doing, Gerald," Mill snapped, "Do the speed limit and stay on the fucking road."

"I'm sorry," Cutter snapped back, "It's just..."

"We'll be sorry if we get pulled over with a big ass bomb in the back of our van." Mill grabbed Cutter's arm, "We don't need to bring attention to ourselves, Gerald."

"In about twenty minutes we are going to bring some attention," Cutter giggled.

Cutter made the right turn onto Goat Ave, which placed the vehicle directly in front of the ROTC building. Making the right turn onto the building's service road, Cutter noticed the large gate leading to the underground entrance open, instead of chained like they expected.

"Look Tommy, it looks like you won't need the bolt cutters." Cutter was now more serious. "It looks like they are expecting us," He whispered.

"Keep going Gerald." Mill was spooked with the gate being opened but opted to stick with the plan. "Probably some stupid shit forgot to lock the gate." Mill justified the gate being opened.

"Point of no return, Tommy. Point of no return." Cutter steered the vehicle under the building and into the parking garage. He took a deep breath and gripped the steering wheel as if he were hanging on for life. He wasn't afraid. He just didn't want to be the person that prevented the mission from being a success.

"Over there, Gerald," Mill whispered with a hint of nervousness in his voice as he pointed toward the Northeast end of the building, directly under the think-tank. "Park over there."

Cutter parked the van as he was directed. Mill opened the door dividing the vehicle compartments. Pulling the trigger device connected to the detonation-cord he armed the explosive device. *Fifteen minutes,* He thought to himself. He was suddenly overwhelmed with the urge to defecate but he was able to control himself.

"There's plenty of time, Gerald." Mill looked around, looking for anything that might be out of place. "But there's no need to fuck around."

Mill opened the passenger door, jumped out and immediately walked toward the steps leading outside. Cutter caught up to him at the stairway. Pushing the door open to the outside Mill felt accomplished and free.

"Gerald. Gerald. What are you doing here?" Jamie Towns asked as she saw Gerald Cutter exit the parking garage.

"Ja...Ja...Jamie," Cutter stuttered as he made eye contact with her before rushing away. *Damn it,* He cried out in his mind. *Why would she have been here?*

"She knows me. She's an associate journalist at the *Goat.*" Cutter cried out as he caught up to Mill. "She is also part of the ROTC program." He wiped tears from his eyes and grabbed Mill's arm.

Mill took a moment to look around.

"Fuck it! She will have to go up with it." Mill was angry but controlled himself from yelling.

"We can go get her!" Cutter protested.

"That thing is coming down in a pile of rubble in less than ten minutes. Our asses need to be hooking up with Jimmy soon." Mill grabbed Cutter's arm and pulled him along.

Cutter stumbled as he looked in the direction of Jamie and the building, but he regained his footing and was able to keep stride with Mill.

* * *

Cynthia was stunned after hearing the plan her son and his friends hatched. She stood from her kneeling position and wiped the tears from her eyes. Turning from her son she walked toward the phone hanging on the kitchen wall. Bending over to pick up an apple she turned to her weeping son.

"Look at me, Jimmy," she said quietly.

Jimmy removed his hands from his face and raised his head. The apple slammed into his face before he had a chance to catch his mother's eye.

"Mommy, I'm so sorry, Mommy. I'm so sorry." Jimmy's body convulsed from crying so hard, covering up his face with his hands again.

"No Jimmy." Jimmy's mother removed the handset from the hook. "You are pathetic." She said as she dialed a number. "You don't know how hard it is to make this call," she scowled at her son who had crawled to her feet and curled around them.

* * *

Jamie Towns sighed. Looking at her watch (3:12 a.m.) she was not eager to put another all night study session in for the week. The thought of running into Gerald Cutter outside the ROTC building slipped her mind. She knew he was working on a piece that had to do with the think-tank. She thought about going home, but she promised a ROTC classmate she would hurry and get a seat at the local coffee shop. She was tired and wishing she wouldn't have made that promise, but the smell of the coffee shop around the corner perked her up. Within a block of the coffee shop she thought of her ROTC friend, she hoped all he wanted to do was study.

The explosion was powerful and loud. The ground Jamie stood on trembled. Buildings and windows near her shook. She turned around in time to see the East side of the ROTC building collapse, pancake, and crumple into rubble. Crump hall, located directly east of the ROTC building, had its West side collapse into ruins.

Jamie stood in shock. People rushed from the coffee shop and looked in horror at the rubble of the ROTC building. The huge cloud of dust and debris made it hard for anyone to recognize what was left of a beautiful building that had been constructed in 1889.

I entertain no other offers.

Present Day

The office walls were as bland as the rest of the walls in the prison. There was once a picture of the warden's mother on one of the walls, but it fell and broke. The warden asked the janitor to clean it up. The picture never made it on the wall again. "I asked you to clean the mess up. I didn't ask you to hang the damn thing again," the warden was heard yelling at the janitor.

The warden, Charles Goodnight Bean, had been in charge of the prison for over 30 years. He had seen many of people come and go from his prison. Some came and went a couple different times. Some went on to lead productive lives, never to be seen by him again. Some left in body bags, never to ever be seen again. Some went over the walls; most were captured within the same day. Only one had managed to escape capture completely but the warden knew that wouldn't last because he felt they always surface somewhere, somehow. "We'll get that pustule of a man," the warden explained to one group of concerned citizens.

The office he stood in was located in a prison so the possibility of injury was always there but it never really concerned him. Bean had been injured once. An inmate threw a piece of scrap metal at him. The metal hit him in the lower calf muscle. He received a few stitches. Warden Bean wouldn't tolerate such behavior from inmates. When he would talk to legislatures, citizen groups, and the media he raged about such surly behavior. The inmate who chucked the piece of metal that landed in the warden's leg received several broken ribs and a concussion. The concussion was so severe some called it brain damage. Warden Bean claimed the man was stupid when he arrived in prison. "Likely won't make too much difference if he leaves prison a tad bit more stupid than when he arrived," Warden Bean explained to a board that investigated abuse claims in his prison. The board wanted him drummed out for that comment, but outside influences were able to manipulate opinions otherwise.

Warden Bean had a sensitive situation he had to deal with. Tommy Mill and he were about to meet. Mill was a rare circumstance. Bean had provided favors before, but Mill's situation was rare by even his standards, and by most accounts he had few standards.

Bean paced the floor in front of his desk. The desk was the only thing in the office other than the chair that sat in front of the desk. Warden Bean was a person who stood most of the time because of a back injury he claimed to have. He lay in bed comfortably when he slept, but once he was up, he was up until he laid his head back down again that evening. He claimed to have been in a helicopter crash in Vietnam and his lower back has never been the same since. Prison guards have witnessed the warden partake in a few different bar fights over the last several years so they didn't know what to believe.

***

"Tommy, you have less than a week left. Any thought about what you're going to do when you get out from behind the iron bars and brick walls?" Bean paced in front of his desk. "Hell, I've been behind these walls so long myself." Bean shook his head as he glanced back over the years he spent behind the walls as a free man, who could come and go at will.

What type of person would choose to come to a place like this every day, Bean often pondered the question.

"I have a thought or two." Tommy Mill sat on the edge of his seat.

"Good! Because I think the easy part of your journey is over."

Mill sat in his chair as a person who had just been told he has less than a week to live. The thoughts of what he would or could do were something he contemplated constantly since receiving the news of his fast approaching release date. Over the many years his hair transitioned from long and black to short and peppered. His belly, which was once hard and shaped, was now soft and hanging. His appearance told those that looked at him that he was in his early fifties. He walked through the prison gates so long ago. He entered the prison a young naïve man. He would leave prison a once protected older naïve man.

"You know, protecting you wasn't always easy. Keeping you away from the general population for so many years has not always been easy. Not easy at all."

"Well I appreciate all you've done Warden Bean."

"Tommy, what you did is unforgivable in my eyes. I don't know what got in you and...and..."

"His name was Cutter. Gerald Cutter." Mill spoke up to help the warden remember.

"That's right. Gerald Cutter. I guess he didn't want to wait this long to be free. Although, I don't think suicide is setting oneself free." Warden Bean moved behind his desk to pull the window shades shut. It was the only window in the office. It gave him a view of the prison yard. "Damn shame."

"Damn Shame." Tommy frowned.

Tommy seemed to Warden Bean as if he was saddened by the thought of his old friend.

"Cutting your throat from ear to ear is no way to kill yourself," Mill wrote in a journal that Bean found soon after Cutter's death. "Suicide is something my friend would have never contemplated. Gerald's death was more of a threat to me than anything else." The writing continued. "Gerald had become religious since his incarceration, often talking about the beautiful gift of life and repentance for his sins."

Warden Bean never mentioned to Mill that he found the writing and never returned it to him. Mill never brought up a journal that went missing after a surprise inspection of his cell was conducted.

"I wish we could have gotten him some help, but he really never showed any signs of needing help." Bean sighed.

Warden Bean split the shade and looked down on the general prison population gathered in the large courtyard. He knew that Tommy Mill had it a lot better in his prison than the men smoking and joking down below.

"I'm just glad your daddy was able to help you Tommy." Bean turned to study Mill. "Glad I could be of service to you and your family during a time of need."

Warden Bean knew that Gerald's death was no suicide. It was confirmed when Mill's father confronted him with a security payment for his sons guaranteed safety the day after Gerald Cutter's death. Bean allowed his thoughts to drift back to a meeting he had with Tommy's father.

:-

Warden Bean entered the smoke filled boxcar establishment and stood as if he were the star of a western movie. He looked over the patrons standing at the bar and they returned his look and mumbled as he slowly moved to a table that allowed him to keep an eye on the entrance and keep his back to the wall. Bean made eye contact with the bartender.

"Whiskey. Neat." Bean removed his cowboy hat and placed it on the table in front of him.

The bartender reached below the bar.

"Top!" Bean got loud, stood up straight and raised his index finger. "Shelf." Bean closed his demand softly.

The bartender rolled his eyes, turned and pulled a bottle of Jack Daniels from the shelf. He poured the whiskey into a highball glass and pushed it forward on the bar.

"Four fingers." Bean demanded.

The bartender looked at a few patrons at the bar and smiled. He pulled the cork from the bottle and acted like he would pour more. He corked the bottle and pushed the glass forward. The patrons giggled.

Bean strolled to the bar, lifted the glass and looked at it. He quickly downed the whiskey and placed the glass on the bar.

"Four more fingers." Bean wiped his mouth with his fingers and tossed a few bills on the bar.

The bartender grunted and poured four more fingers worth of whiskey.

Bean picked up the glass and moved to his table. He made it to his table before noticing a fine dressed man enter the establishment. The fine dressed man looked over the bar and then made eye contact with Bean. Bean lifted his glass of whiskey as if to say, hello. The fine dressed man moved to meet Bean and sat at the table. Bean stood.

"I see you received my note, Warden Bean," the fine dressed man said as he leaned back in his creaky wooden chair. "Please sit?"

"Won't sit. I'm interested to hear what you have to say." Bean fiddled with his hat. "I'm not exactly sure as to what it is that you think I can do for your son, prisoner Mill, Mr. Mill." Bean sipped from his whiskey. "Would you like a drink?"

"No, thank you." Mr. Mill unbuttoned his coat to get comfortable. "What I want is simple. I want my son protected."

"Your son is in a prison. My prison. He is safe." Bean didn't like the insinuation that people behind the walls he was tasked with securing were anything but safe.

"Well, Warden. I guess I'm asking that he be kept a little safer than someone like Gerald Cutter." Mr. Mill stared up at Bean.

"It's hard to stop someone bent on killing themselves." Bean tried to lighten the mood with a smile.

"Yes. Suicide." Mr. Mill reached into his pocket and pulled out a piece of paper. He unfolded it, looked it over and placed it on the table in front of Bean. "That's how much I am willing to pay for my son's safety."

"Why do you think your son needs protected in a maximum security federal prison?" Bean picked up the paper and looked it over. "That is a rather large number, Mr. Mill. A large number."

"My son did a very stupid thing. I do not condone what..."

"Aren't you some big commie?" Bean sipped from his glass and continued to look over the paper. "Your grand daddy made a shit load of money in oil and you did the ol', exit, stage left, with his endowment."

"My grandfather was a very generous man, Mr...."

"Generosity is different from commie." Bean turned the paper over and pushed it toward Mr. Mill. "Your son is a murder..."

"My son was misguided. He got with the wrong people."

"Stupid friends are worse than enemies." Bean twisted the glass. "Anyway, don't you mean person? Cutter is dead and the only one left from that misfit team is your son, and he is tucked away from society just like a jury of his peers said he should be."

"Regardless, Warden Bean, I want my son pulled from the other prisoners. I want his safety guaranteed." Mr. Mill's voice cracked with emotion.

"Double." Bean sipped from his glass. "Double what is on the other side of that paper and I think I can help you."

"Think?" Mr. Mill became sterner.

"I can't stop him from cutting his own throat." Bean downed the rest of his whiskey.

"Tommy would never."

"Yeah. Well. Ten years down the road, if that long, after staring at nothing but prison walls and we'll see about that." Bean put his cowboy hat back on.

"Double it is, Warden Bean." Mr. Mill stood and walked toward the door. He turned back for a parting comment. "With that money, double and all, I would expect there would be more to look at than the walls. Maybe you could provide a little camaraderie."

"Oh, I'm sure I can rustle up some reading material for the starving soul." Bean smiled.

"And, Warden, if anyone approaches with a counter offer, an offer that is larger, and would tempt you to not be as protective..."

"Don't you worry, Sir." Bean chuckled. "I entertain no other offers."

"What did you do with all that money my father paid you for my protection?" Mill interrupted the warden's thought about a well-respected man who knew how to get things done, especially when it came to family.

"Well, the wife and I were able to provide the kids an education they otherwise wouldn't have gotten. And me and the wife, well the annual vacations, we sure do enjoy those." Bean tried to muster a smile as he turned to look at Mill. "I can't protect you outside these walls, Tommy."

"I know." Mill hung his head.

"I never asked your daddy why he felt the need to pay for your security. You are a smart kid who stays low. I don't know why anyone would want to harm you in here. It's probably best I don't know why someone would want to harm you out there." Warden Bean now looked beyond the walls of the prison.

"It's probably good that you don't know anything about my troubles Warden." Mill shrugged his shoulders, lay back in his chair and looked toward the ceiling.

"You've had your troubles haven't you Tommy?"

"That was such a radical time in my life. A time when I was influenced by a small radical element." Mill sat up in his seat. "Blowing up the ROTC building seemed right. A statement against Reagan's Central America policy was warranted. It was a statement that would save the lives of American soldiers who would surely be sent to fight was the reasoning." He laid back and sighed out loud. "We were just sure the building would be empty." He paused. "The gate was open. I didn't have to use the bolt cutters."

"American troops were never sent to fight in Central America, at least not in large numbers." Bean stared into Mill's eyes.

"I know." Mill nodded.

The two men broke from their stare and let silence over take the room for a moment.

"You ever think about those two boys and that young girl that were killed when that building collapsed on them." Bean looked into Mill's eyes. He looked for sympathy or anything that said Mill was something other than the person that walked into the prison.

"I think about them every day. Like I said we didn't think anyone would be in that building." His eyes showed a true sadness but as a moment passed they became steely and his face became red as if anger was building with in him. "I don't have time to think about past troubles." Mill cocked his head and looked away from Bean. "The thought of three cadets dying when the building collapsed saddens me and I pray each day for forgiveness. I truly wish I could have just walked away from that whole period in my life."

"That's probably why you're not spending the rest of your life in here. Believe me, your Daddy left plenty of security money for you. I just didn't think I would last that long." Warden Bean cracked a smile. "Your sins have been paid all up as far as the government is concerned. I have to let you out."

Bean paused for a moment, thinking about a man who may have gotten away from law enforcement's grasp. Mill had mentioned him once before when the alcohol got the best of him. Bean understood the steely eyes and red face Mill displayed moments earlier was because of the one who escaped.

"Blowing up an ROTC building in protest to Reagan's Central American policy. What in the hell were you boys thinking?" Bean shook his head. "What the hell were you thinking?"

"I guess we were not thinking." Tommy Mill slouched in his chair. "We were wrong."

It seemed to Bean as if Mill was filled with remorse for what he did so many years ago. Warden Bean knew Mill would have to put remorse and prayers in his past. The future and survival were the only things Tommy Mill should think about.

"To be honest. The parole board surprised me on this one. I thought they lost your name long ago." Bean shrugged his shoulders.

"You can't protect me out there," Mill said with a halfhearted smile.

"I can't protect you out there, Tommy." Bean stepped up to his desk and leaned on it. "The board may have forgiveness for your past wrongful ways. But I think someone beyond these walls has no such pity."

Bean was sad. He had gotten to be friends with Tommy Mill over the past many years. Football and baseball conversations would lead to bets and every now and again a few drinks. Tommy enjoyed drinking beer but not as much as the warden. He would always be gracious and accept when alcohol was offered.

"I appreciate all you've done for me in here, Warden. My father..."

"Your dad, God rest his old soul, was a straight up gentleman, Tommy." Bean interrupted Mill. "His word was always good."

"Yeah. He was always good." Mill's voice quivered. "I became such a disappointment to my family, but it was my father who stood steady with me. My mother left his side because of the shame of an only son who committed such a horrendous act came between them," he cried, "I'm not sure if she is still living or not."

"I wish I could help you, Tommy." Bean pulled a handkerchief from his pocket and handed it to Mill. "But the arrangement that good man and I..."

"No need to worry, Warden. Like I said, I appreciate all you've done for me. You filled your end of the bargain." Mill had a sudden surge of defiance with his tone of voice. "Above and beyond, and you owe me nothing outside these walls."

* * *

Warden Bean walked the long service road that runs through the prison compound. He stopped as he usually did to take in the view of the buildings and fences that housed and secured the inmates. On one side of the road was a large white concrete building that was approximately 500 yards in length and contained two stories of some of the most hardened, deviant, anti-social, and ignorant people the country produced. On the other side of the road was a smaller but similar building that housed the men who needed maximum security or segregation from all other inmates. The smaller building contained special control units or cells that were six by eight feet in width and length. Each cell was fitted with a solid door and small window, stainless steel lavatories and commodes, and concrete bed with mattress. Each prisoner housed in the special control units was guaranteed at least 22 ½ hours of hopeless confinement. The units were designed to minimize human connection and maximize sensory deprivation. Inmates received little face-to-face contact with others; guards monitored prisoners by round the clock electronic surveillance. Beyond the two white buildings and across another road lay a fenced in area with smaller white one-story buildings, and lined with tall concrete street lamps. The fenced in area, or the exercise zone, is where inmates received approximately one hour of outdoor activity, weather permitting.

Bean pulled his cell phone from his jacket and pushed a few buttons.

"Afternoon, Warden," the voice of a guard sounded on the other end of the call.

"Hey, I want Mill ready to go by four o'clock, understand?"

"Yes, Warden. Four o'clock. Mill...cell one-zero-twenty-three and pen number three, niner, five, x-ray, foxtrot, two, seven."

"I will be meeting him in building two at four o'clock sharp. Exercise area." Bean hung the phone up and continued walking the service road.

***

Tommy Mill sat on his bed in a soundproof cell eating his last meal as a federal prisoner. Other than the door window that allowed prison guards to look in, there was no window that provided a view. The walls were poured concrete and opaque. Mill knew he had it better than most everyone in the prison system, even some of the guards. Warden Bean and a few other guards in the know protected him. When he arrived in the federal prison system he was across the street in the larger building where general population lived. Across the street he feared for his life. He was different from most over there. He was a convicted felon, but he was not a predator. His chances of survival were nonexistent so when his father made a deal with Warden Bean for protection, he was happy to put on the shackles and move across the street to solitary confinement. He had no problem with being sealed away from the rest of the prison population. Solitary confinement was generally for the worst of the worst or those that needed protective custody. Some claimed the isolation of solitary confinement was a violation of the US Constitution, specifically the Eighth Amendment's cruel and unusual paragraph. Tommy Mill disagreed. His feeling was that it was cruel and unusual being housed with the degenerates across the street.

"You done, Mill," the voice sounded over the intercom.

"Yep."

"We'll be moving you soon. Place the food tray in the door slot when you're done. We'll be down with the shacks soon."

"Yeah, I'm finished. Come on down to get the meatloaf or whatever it is." Mill had no appetite. He barely touched the bland blast-chilled food. His thoughts were bouncing from one thing to another. He thought about the first Christmas he could remember and the G.I. Joe and G.I. Joe Jeep he received. He thought about the color of leaves during the months of fall in the Midwest. The thought of a building collapsing was always prevalent. He wished things were different.

Reagan was now long gone, so were the anti-nuke protests, even though plenty of nukes still remained in the world. His thoughts drifted to a meeting he had with the International Union of Students and Journalists in the early eighties. The unions spoke about the change they brought about during the Vietnam War, just two decades before, and how it stopped the killing of innocents. Mill bought into peace and how such movements could change the world. He watched as the unions, with help from the media, portrayed the Reagan administration as war mongrels that were building up to send young American troops into Latin America. He listened to left leaning politicians, media talking heads, and artists who aligned themselves with the World Peace Council talk about the evils of capitalism. He was able to romanticize the anti-war and nuke protests. In his mind, it was his time to make a statement. His mind was so polluted that he couldn't recognize the western comforts the artists and politicians surrounded themselves with as they condemned others for wanting them. In his mind, it was action that was needed, not words.

Over the many years of imprisonment he had an epiphany. He came to realize that he and many like him were used. He realized his movement wasn't about peace. It was more about one political movement maneuvering around another. No Soviet Union meant no anti-nuke and war protests. Was it just a coincidence, or was it that the money dried up after the demise of the communist power, he reflected. After so many years to sit and contemplate his actions, he realized he was nothing more than a pawn. Pro-communist groups who were determined to destroy the US by using rights guaranteed by the Constitution scammed him and so many others. Soviet Union backed US communist groups successfully used the 1st Amendment to sway public opinion during the Vietnam War.

"How could the young Americans of that era provide security for a small democracy when the communists released the fifth column, the useful idiots, in the streets of America," Bean would explain during his lectures. "Anti-nuke protests were nothing more than the communist using same techniques during a different era." Bean often went red with anger when he spoke about such things. "You dick heads are nothing but God damn cowards," Bean screamed once, as guards pulled him from Mill's space. "My brother Greg gave his life so idiots like you can say the stupid shit you say!"

At first Mill would get irate and argue his points as well. He would sometimes approach Beans' space, only to be cut off by guards who were accustomed to the bantering between the two men.

"The struggle materializes between the minority who own the means and the vast majority of the population who produce," Mill yelled. "Change occurs because of the struggle between the different classes within society who contradict..."

"Shut your pie hole and read meaningful shit written by people who make real common sense!" Bean would often say before he handed a book to Mill.

Warden Bean would allow Mill to read the writings of William Bradford, Ayn Rand, Milton Friedman, and Thomas Sowell. "That commie crap preached to you by lollygagging fools is going to eat your brain, Tommy. Somebody done went and opened your head and poured in commie, Tommy." Bean enjoyed the rhyme. "Your brain is still mushy son. I can mold it to right."

One particular book Mill enjoyed that Bean provided him was a book written by, Friedrich von Hayek. "*The Road to Serfdom*," provided Mill with courage to face his past. The theme of the writing that government control of economic decision-making through government planning would eventually lead to tyranny was like a dagger in his heart. He often wondered how many people needlessly suffered because of the supposed people who knew better implemented some type of scheme based on a central brain trust.

Mill had so many years to realize that those who feel guilty about their own success corrupted his mind. He was so distraught when he finally saw that those who protested the loudest were normally the ones who were affected very little, regardless of the outcome of events.

He was speechless when Bean provided him articles that explained how Reagan was now a hero in Eastern Europe and viewed as a man who helped set millions free. The article went on to explain how the Soviet Union spread its view of peace by using young naive students and journalists. It angered him that the well to do media, politicians, and artist types ran up more in utility bills in one month than most people did in two years. He felt dirty and betrayed. He lost all touch when he found that the man from Massachusetts, who he supported for President in the early eighties, wrote a letter to the leadership of the Soviet Union, offering support in their efforts to defeat Reagan. He threw a tantrum when he realized that Vietnamese were still very much oppressed and living in squalor, even though they lived within a strict communist economical system he once favored. He was dismayed when he found that countries such as Pakistan, Iran, and North Korea either had nuclear weapons or they were close to getting them, yet there were no protests outside of the relevant embassies against their getting them or having them. He was shocked when he finally realized that he was like so many of the wealthy people who never did anything to earn their riches other than being born within a family of "old money" or inherited fortune of an established upper-class. Like most who inherited "old money" he had done very little that truly meant anything, he created nothing, and he knew only what was lectured him by those that did very little themselves. Warden Bean would often say, "Son, you have done nothing and you know even less."

He caused so much destruction as a young and ignorant person. His thoughts drifted to his potential future. What lay ahead of him was not as certain as Warden Bean's protection. Gerald Cutter's death was part of the domino effect caused by his decisions as a young man. He wondered if there were still more dominos falling after so many years.

***

Tommy Mill looked over his orange prison jump suit hanging from the wall. He stood in the prison's pre-release unit wondering what would happen next. The orange suit he wore for so many years told all who placed their eyes on him that he was nothing but a prisoner. There was a lot of security in being a prisoner, especially an isolated prisoner. The whole release process had been a whirlwind experience up to that point. The clothes the warden provided were clothes that would not bring attention; jeans, t-shirt, tennis shoes. He was sure the bag in the corner was filled with similar clothing. The clothes other prisoners received on exit from prison were normally the ones they entered with. The bag in the corner was provided by the Warden and paid for by his father. The release process he was going through was anything but normal. He received none of the required classes provided by the federal government that he was required to receive prior to release, but he found the boxes for narcotics, alcohol, and anger management had already been checked on the release process sheet;

stating that he received the classes. The medical box was checked as well and the line where a physician was to sign had a signature. Accommodations, financial, employment, and legal matters were all checked and signed as if he went through the pain staking process of being counseled on such matters. What normally took a prisoner a few months to complete, Mill was moving through in minutes.

The idea of leaving the prison is something he really never contemplated. He never thought about escape because he was resigned to his fate. In his cell he had himself and the books the Warden provided him and that was enough as far as he was concerned. He could act out one of his favorite novels, *"Atlas Shrugged"*, playing the roles of Dagny Taggert and Hank Rearden until he had them completely memorized. The book was a large book with 1,168 pages; he memorized it from start to finish. When asked by the Warden about memorizing the Bible he said, "The New Testament should be enough."

"Atlas Shrugged and the New Testament! Son you are prepared. What more does a man need?" Bean smiled when Mill informed him of his accomplishment.

Bean took pride in his achievement of turning Tommy Mill from his earlier beliefs. The first few years of his imprisonment, Tommy Mill was a staunch communist who preached Marx, Alinsky, and Mao. He believed in the mantra, "it takes a village!" Which Bean would reply, "Have you seen who's in the villages, or who is running the God damn villages, the so-called pillars of society? It's a regular God damn Sodom and Gomorrah. You can't drive two miles in any direction of your home without crossing the path of a corrupt civil servant, a pedophile, an addict, a pusher, or some government teat sucking..."

"That is a subject mostly covered in Old Testament, book of Genesis," Mill said with conviction. "Vaguely touched in the New Testament, but you will find it noted in Mathew, Luke, Romans, Peter, Jude, and even Revelations."

"You say it so, I don't give a shit, man." Bean would get frustrated.

"I don't think the dinosaurs went extinct because one male Rex was screwing another male Rex. Nor do I think they died because a Rex went outside of his kind and screwed a Raptor. They went extinct because in due course things like meteors hit planets, and therefore make it hard for anything but cockroach type species to survive."

"My ex-wife would make it then." Bean would say in response to such comments.

"Well then what the hell you think about God then?" A guard once asked.

Bean rarely let guards get involved in such conversations with Mill, but he was interested in the answer that would be provided.

"I believe in a Creator!" Mill felt on the spot. "No. I am not a strict Biblicist. I appreciate the fact that someone put his life on the line for my sins. I do. I appreciate that. But I feel we are energy put in motion. In a human form that grows weaker by the second. The energy remains constant but..."

"Shut that Godless shit up right now you sloppy commie bastard," yelled a guard before Bean asked him to leave the room.

Mill once had a few guards so perplexed that they were almost in tears when he asked, "if the past is defined as any time prior to the time occurred'. And the future is defined as anytime that has yet to occur. You can only exist in the present so how much time do you really have to exist? Or, do you really exist at all?"

"Shit," one guard cried out. "Are you saying I just need to start smoking dope and singing James Taylor or Bob Fucking Dylan, songs to figure all this shit out? You creepy little weirdo!"

"It's that White Album bullshit if you ask me." Another guard was heard saying. "Just play it backwards, right?"

Mill was a protected man behind the walls, bars, and fences. He developed a relationship with the warden and that was it. The guards he used for occasional amusement. Most guards learned pretty quick not to converse over heavy studies with him. He understood Warden Bean would not be there forever, but his father had made arrangements for when Bean decided to retire or die. He never took into account that he would once again be a free man. The only person who he would even think to turn to would be his sister, but he had lost contact with her so many years before and for good reason. Most prisoners were excited about leaving behind the bars and walls. They were excited about a new start and seeing what had changed while they were incarcerated. He felt comfort with his books and walls. He knew there was something lurking beyond the walls and the chance of it forgetting him was zero.

***

Bean and Mill stood face to face in building two. Bean could tell that Mill was nervous. Mill stared at Bean but he only looked through him as if Bean was not standing there at all. Mill's thoughts were random and abundant, jumping from his first touch from a girl, other than his mother, to a train moving slowly down a track. The thought of the Johnny Cash tune, *Folsom Prison Blues*, ran through his mind. In the background one of the guards was shooting basketballs and missing way more than Mill thought possible at such close range.

"Tommy, your release happened a lot sooner than I ever expected. Hell...I...I never really thought you would be released." Bean pulled an envelope from his pocket. "There is eight thousand here. It is what your dad wanted. There is also banking info. Your dad set up an account for you. He left a lot of money just in case you ever did get out. All the information for a new start is there."

The men stood face-to-face and silent until Mill broke and looked away.

"Just as my dad said. You could have very easily..."

"Your daddy paid me plenty of money over the years, Tommy. I'm not a greedy man." Bean paused. "You never thought getting out would happen, but he hoped."

"Outside my father..." Mill looked toward the floor as he choked up.

"Tommy, you are on your own now. Things have changed out there, but you're smart. And I'm sure you will catch on."

"I'll do my best, Warden."

"I know you will. My personal driver will take you to a city park. The park will be busy. You get out of the car and you are on your own."

"Yes sir. On my own." Mill wiped his nose on his sleeve.

"I'm sorry we rushed you through, but when your name came down I was able to push things up a little. With your daddy's connections and all." Bean paused. "The man did have some connections."

"People owed him a lot." Mill became stern.

The father of Tommy Mill became a very kind hearted person as he got older and gave a great deal of his wealth away. His father was also a very shrewd and successful businessman who made many connections with highly influential people in many areas of expertise.

Bean looked at the guard shooting baskets. He shook his head in disbelief, as the man seemed to have very little coordination.

"Tommy, I don't know if the prison system really ever corrects a person. But I believe you have made amends for your moment of evil."

You are disgusting

"Fuck me," Benny Shills said to himself as he woke. His head seemed a little big from all the alcohol the night before. He glanced over toward the desk and got a glimpse of a half emptied tequila bottle. His head involuntarily shook, as he held back the urge to vomit. He did a quick mental count of drinks that he could remember - *nine stout beers, three glasses of wine, three shots of tequila.*

"Too much tequila," Benny said as he pushed the urge to vomit away again. "I'm late for something. God damn it. What the hell am I late for?"

The feeling of being late bothered him. The thought of his attorney, Ted Fienberg, crossed his mind. Money crossed his mind, attorney fees. *That fat ass always wants more money,* Benny thought as he scratched himself. *Cock sucker!*

Benny was half in and out of sleep. With every morning nature was calling and his bladder had to be emptied. He rolled to take pressure off his bladder, hoping to get more time in bed before he had to relieve himself. *Shit,* he thought as his leg rested against someone else's. His mind raced. Wondering who, what, when, where did he pick her up? It was the charity banquet he remembered. He couldn't really think what the charity event was for, but the thought of two large breasted blondes hanging from his arms flashed through his mind. He slowly turned his head to get a view of what followed him back to his hotel room. Her hair was blonde and it was all he could see of the woman, everything else lay under sheets. He looked toward the large window of his luxury hotel room. The shades were pulled shut but he could see the light shining through. He knew it was well past early morning.

Benny could hear the sound of his cell phone vibrating on the TV stand.

Ahhhh Shit. Has to be that money grubbing attorney of mine, Benny thought. Not knowing what time it was and knowing he had things to do and think about instead of lying next to a woman he met the night before, Benny moved slowly to the television stand. He scanned the room to see if he could find his underwear. Smiling as he realized that an adult film still remained on pause. *What in the hell did we do in hotel rooms before they made porn available*, was the thought that entered. Not finding his underwear or anything else to wear, he proceeded to make his way to the phone.

"Where the hell are my clothes?" He asked himself.

"Hello," was all Benny was able to get out before the voice on the other end interrupted. He noticed the time on his phone.

"Benny, you are late. You travel all the way from Europe to be late to see your children." Benny's ex-wife

Shelly started in. "You said you would be here at ten. It is now ten thirty, where are you?"

"Actually, it is ten thirty two." Benny moved to the master bathroom to relieve himself. "You didn't get my message? I said I would be there around noon."

"No. There was no message on my phone from you last night." Shelly paused. "Message my ass!"

"I sent an email or something." Benny gasped at the smell of his silent fart.

"Nope. Didn't get it. What's your excuse now? The pigeon had a heart attack!"

"What the fuck!" Benny preferred to sit on the toilet to relieve his bladder.

Benny's head fell forward and his eyes rolled back as the inevitable shiver ran down his spine. His body slightly convulsed before he gently tilted his head back and let out a thunderous burp.

"That's nice! You are disgusting," Shelly said.

Benny held the phone back from his ear as he stood and moved to the greeting room of the luxurious penthouse hotel room. The things Shelly would say was nothing he had not heard before.

"...And where the hell are you?"

"Ritz. Chicago." Benny sat down. "Quit yelling. God."

"Well, you're close. When are you coming?"

Benny now sat silently in the elegant black leather love seat. He threw one leg onto the seat. Now slowly massaging his penis while listening to his ex-wife rant about how he was the worse father to hit the world since Jo Jackson, Scott Peterson, and Arnold Schwarzenegger.

"What are you doing, Benny?"

"One guess. Say Schwarzenegger again." Benny giggled. "This time I want you to string it out a little more."

"You sicken me, Benny," Shelly screamed. "This thing we are going to do in the courtroom has nothing to do with our children. It has everything to do about winning something, and God only knows what victory is in your mind."

"Shelllllly," Benny moaned in a way that would have pleased his ex-wife 7 years ago.

Benny and Shelly's divorce had been finalized for more than five years, but he still couldn't pass on irritating her. Shelly left Benny after, in her mind, seven long brutal years. She divorced Benny for physical and mental abuse, and had plenty of evidence to support her claims. She was awarded the two children and hoped never to see her ex-husband again, hoping that he would slither away, or possibly get drunk while driving and hit a tree; a very large tree. After all, she really didn't want anyone else hurt when her ex-husband created his demise. In her mind, Hell would be a good place for his final destination, but Europe was fine until then. She only wished he would stay far away from her and the kids.

She was surprised when she got the notice in the mail that he wanted more parental rights than what was awarded him in the divorce settlement. He was awarded supervised visiting rights because Shelly was able to prove the years of abuse, but Benny was never able to muster up enough time to see his children. Money and time were never the issue, because he had plenty of both;

he just never thought much about being tied down to children.

"Don't start that Benny."

"Shelllly."

"You sick son of a greasy, carpet munching, bitch. You could care less about these children. It is all about getting a victory. Scamming twenty thousand of your employees and walking away with millions is not enough. You need to be able to put a chalk mark beside your name when it comes to our miserable relationship."

"You know I love it when you get this way." Benny was now slowly stroking himself. "That was a little rougher than usual in regards to my mother though." He paused to massage himself. "Tone that down a little will you?"

"Get here when you get here you sick twisted, little cockroach of a man, but know that supervision is still the deal."

Benny relished the fact that he still had some sort of control over his ex-wife's emotions. He turned off the phone and laid it on the couch. He had worked himself up.

"What do I do with this," Benny whispered to himself as he looked down and saw how excited he had become. He continued to stroke himself gently as he rose from the loveseat and walked to the bedroom. He caught a glimpse of himself in the large mirror mounted on the sliding closet door. He stopped to pose as if he were in a body building competition. "Oh Yeah," He grunted. *The penis enlargement pump seems to be working*, he grinned. At five percent body fat, he loved the way he looked.

There was a female in the bedroom, his penis was erect, and there was porn on the television.

What more can a woman want? Benny strolled into the bedroom.

We came to play.

Arnold Jillette sat behind his desk as his two clients, Carlos Buggy Brown and Alexi LeLaage, sat in front of him. Jillette was a small man in stature but his confidence seemed to make him look larger to most people. His clients were not people who noticed such things though. They needed help that not too many people, other than the Jillette Law office, could provide.

"The deal made with the Department of Justice was a gift from the judicial Gods. A deal that the Gods only make with a guy like me." Jillette leaned back in his chair and placed his feet on his desk.

"You saying we walk in there and say we're guilty." Alexi was miffed. She was a small woman who looked the age of someone in her late forties, but her age was actually thirty-three. The many years of drug and alcohol abuse had taken its toll.

"That is a bunch of bullshit if that is what you're sayin'!" Buggy was a large fat man who enjoyed showing his wealth by wearing large gold chains around his neck and diamond ear rings in both ears.

"I'm saying that the Justice Department is willing to let you walk the streets if you plead guilty and turn over information regarding international human trafficking."

"Can the judge dis...disre..."

"Disregard." Jillette took his feet from his desk and faced his clients.

"I know what the fuck I meant," Alexi shouted.

"I know you did." Jillette looked away.

"Can he do that?"

"What?" Jillette turned to face his clients again.

"Disregard! God damn," Alexi snarled and folded her arms. "Can he do that to the agreement we made?"

"We watch CSI," Buggy chimed in. "We came to play."

Jillette was confused at the last statement but he forged ahead. "Listen. They want the information you have more than they want you behind bars." Jillette shuffled through some papers on his desk and pulled one to look at. It was the agreement he signed with the Justice Department. "You two are special in the sense that you can provide information that very few people..."

"We don't know shit about any international human... what the fuck ever...ring. We get people young pussy at a fair price." Alexi sat back in her chair and flung her hair back out of her face.

"We went over this," Jillette said as he raised his voice.

"Ahh, Ahh..." Buggy tried to interject.

"We went over this. The tapes the Justice has suggested otherwise. They suggest you know a lot more." Jillette was uneasy. "And the tapes are hard to stomach."

"Well aint that some shit. A defense lawyer with a conscience?" Buggy leaned forward in his chair. "You're no better than us you pint sized little ass kisser. We pay lots of dollars so we don't have to be in this situation."

"Buggy. This is the situation. You are here." Jillette showed his disgust by leaning back in his chair and shaking his head. "Remember, if it wasn't for that dip shit of a prosecutor, I would have never been able to get you off these very same charges seven years ago."

"Let's go, Alexi." Buggy grabbed Alexi's arm. "Let's get far away from here!"

"Don't you touch me!" Alexi pulled her arm away. "When this shit is over. I'm gettn' lost, and you're not part of it."

"But, but..."

"You can go back to pimping your nasty ass hole for Jackson's for all I give a shit." Alexi pointed her finger into Buggy's chest.

"It was Bennies, you Bitch," Buggy screamed and started crying. "The devaluing of my service hurts and you know that."

Jillette simply put his forehead on his desk after watching the two human trafficking stooges banter about such disgusting things.

***

Buggy rolled a joint and reclined his seat in his Lexus LX SUV. His eyes were still filled with tears and Alexi knew he was still emotional about her cheapening his skills. Buggy wasn't exactly proud of his past days as a rent boy or male escort, but he never wanted to be referenced with low-grade prostitutes. His specialty was blowjobs and he claimed to have sucked a president and a few star athletes.

"You didn't mean it did you baby? You're not leaving me." Buggy handed the joint to Alexi after taking a long drag from it.

"I'm not leaving you, Sugar Pie. And I know it was Bennies."

"Really." Buggy's smile was large. He got pleasure from showing off his gold caps.

"We need to get on the move, though. We need to set up shop some where's else." Alexi took a drag. "Get far away from these so called law abiding motherfuckers." She paused to let the smoke drift away. "Jillette was right about being lucky last time."

"We have to..."

"We have to make some collections. I know." She passed the joint back to Buggy. "We make the collections and then we get on the move."

"What about the other shipment with Vargas?"

"We'll take that."

"What about these so called law types who want information?" Buggy was at ease when Alexi made all the decisions. "They're going to want something. Got to give..."

"We'll give up the Cowboy." Alexi grinned.

"Someone has to go down so why not that pig of a man?" Buggy took a long drag from the joint and handed it to Alexi. "He's been stomping on us long enough." He coughed.

"We'll make our move when they start putting the screws to him." Alexi took a hit from the joint.

Buggy continued to cough. "That shit's a little rough."

"It's that shit we got from Gene."

"All the zipper-heads we provide that motherfucker." Buggy coughed. "You would think he would give us the good shit."

I wish you all the best of luck

The five-ton military truck seemed to lumber through the Sierra Leone forest. The driver did his best to keep from hitting the many different potholes or large rocks but there was so many that it was impossible to miss them all. The drive from Monrovia, Liberia was a slow and methodical process for anyone who used the forest roads instead of the West African Coastal Highway; although some would disagree since the highway was in such deterioration because of lack of maintenance and heavy rains. The miles covered from Monrovia were a painful and rewarding trip for the owner of the truck, Bodhan Nesterenko. Painful in that the roads were tough to negotiate and the threat of ambush from any number of warring groups was always present. It was rewarding in that the payload of weapons, to help feed the Revolutionary United Front's (RUF) war making machine, was very profitable. The RUF was a group favored by Liberian President Charles Taylor in his effort to topple the government of Sierra Leone. Trucks filled with weapons crossed the boarder between the two countries on a daily basis. The weapons transported in the

142

trucks would be traded for diamonds and the diamonds would be funneled to western countries where people could decorate themselves with as fine a diamond as anyone could find in the world.

"Take this dog leg left and the gate should be in our view." Bodhan Nesterenko spoke to the driver as he looked at the map. "There will be a couple guards if I remember right."

"I'll be ready to get off this road." The driver slowed the vehicle almost to a complete stop so that he could evade a large hole in the road.

Nesterenko was tossed forward and into the steel dash when the passenger side front wheel fell into a hole.

"Sorry. Sorry about that, Snake." The driver called Nesterenko by his call sign, Snake, the only name he knew him by. He cringed as he gave the vehicle gas, which made the vehicle lurch forward, freeing them from the hole and tossing Nesterenko back.

"No worries." Nesterenko pushed himself back into his seat and noticed two guards holding their weapons in the air. "We better stop."

The driver brought the vehicle to a stop and turned the engine off.

"I know these guys. They're Mende but they speak good English." Nesterenko smiled as he jumped from the vehicle. "What'z up?" He held his hand out for a handshake.

"Stop right there." One of the Mende guards demanded. "I need for the driver to get out of the vehicle and come forward." He waved for the driver to join him at the front of the large five-ton truck.

"What's the matter? We have a delivery for Rashid." Nesterenko was stunned by the welcome the two Mende guards provided. He looked toward his driver who was moving to the front of the vehicle.

The driver raised his eyebrows and then shrugged his shoulders.

"We have been asked to hold you here until further notice." One of the guards spoke up as the other spoke on the phone in the guard shack.

"Don't you remember me?" Nesterenko questioned, but the guard made no gesture one way or the other.

The guard from the shack deliberately moved toward Nesterenko and his driver while drawing his pistol from his holster.

"Wait a second. Just wait...." The driver spoke his last words before the Mende guard fired a bullet into his face.

"Jesus! What the..." Nesterenko stood stunned. "Why did you do that," He shouted.

"The man you are working with is a government agent." Rashid, President Taylor's deputy, explained as he and his personal bodyguards exited the nearby forest and joined the fracas in front of the vehicle.

"Rashid, Tango is no government agent. He..."

"You need to do a better job of picking your friends." Rashid pointed to the dead man and made eye contact with his bodyguards. He made a gesture that told his guards to move the dead man from the road and they did.

"Rashid, what government are you talking about? President Taylor would nev..."

"He is an agent from the United States." Rashid interrupted Nesterenko. "He is here to spy on us. And it was President Taylor who gave us the order to kill this man. This spy."

"President Taylor ordered his killing? I just spoke with President Taylor yesterday." Nesterenko was still stunned by the killing of his driver.

Nesterenko had no connection with his driver other than the business of moving weapons from Liberia to Sierra Leone in an effort to help the RUF overthrow a government that President Charles Taylor felt threatened by. He only knew the driver by his call sign, Tango; after all, everyone in the mercenary business went by a call sign instead of their birth name. He went by the call sign Snake and was sure Tango knew nothing about his true identity.

The killing of Tango is not what stunned Nesterenko, mostly. He came to accept the loss of life due to murder and war, and he knew the part of the world he stood in dealt plenty of anything to do with death. What stunned him was the fact that he could have been working with someone who may have provided information about him that could put him behind bars for a very long time. He hoped that Rashid was wrong about Tango being an agent for the United States.

"Well my truck is still filled with what you need." Nesterenko nervously stated. He only hoped that Tango would be the only one killed before the day ended. He remained standing and breathing so he was encouraged, but cautious.

The thought of the driver being an agent weighed heavy on Nesterenko's mind. If the driver he knew as Tango was truly an agent of some sort, he would be missed sooner or later, and the search for answers would begin. Depending on the agency, department, or bureau, the search for those answers would be merciless.

***

The plane Bodhan Nesterenko landed in was late so he hustled to gather his carry-on bags from the overhead storage bin above his seat. The flight from Morocco was just one of a few connections he would have to make before he arrived at his final destination, Billings Montana. His plane landed at Heathrow airport, London England, an airport he knew well because of the many years of international travel. He had a little over an hour to make his next connection, a flight leaving terminal three with a destination of JFK airport, New York City. He looked at his watch and visualized and thought about what he had to accomplish before getting on the plane - *get off plane, make way to Heathrow Express, train ride to terminal three, bite to eat, etc....*

As Nesterenko left the aircraft he looked up to orient himself to the airport. He noticed a sign that pointed left for the Express so he briefly dropped his head and shuffled in that direction. He felt a tug on his elbow so he turned to see a couple men wearing nice suits, walking with him, and holding badges.

"Mr. Nesterenko, may we have a moment of your time?" The shorter of the two men questioned before he tugged a little harder on the elbow, which brought all three of the men to a stop.

"I've really got to get a move on if I want to catch my flight." Nesterenko knew by the looks of the two men that he might not be catching a flight anytime soon. "A moment?" He tried to lighten the mood with a smile.

"It depends on you," the shorter man said as he nudged Nesterenko toward a small room located not far from the aircraft he just exited. "Just need a few answers that we believe only you can help us answer."

Nesterenko entered the small room to find a different man who seemed a little more important than the two he initially met after leaving his plane. The man didn't rise from his seat or make any kind of facial gesture that encouraged a pleasant meeting. He only looked at the two men who escorted Nesterenko to the room and nodded his head up and down. The taller man nudged Nesterenko into the room farther and then shut the door once all three men had entered.

"Mr. Nesterenko? Bodhan Nesterenko?" The man sitting asked. "You are Bodhan Nesterenko?"

"Who are you?" Nesterenko asked sharply.

"My name is FBI agent Dawson. Kent Dawson, and I was sent here from Washington to meet with you." The agent opened a file he had laying on a table in front of him.

"I am Bodhan Nest..."

"We know who you are." Agent Dawson interrupted Nesterenko. "I need to know about this man." He pulled a picture of the driver Nesterenko only knew as, Tango. "You ever met this man? His name is Agent Dennis Hanley."

"Never met him." Nesterenko shook his head.

"We think you have." Dawson leaned back in his chair and put his hands behind his head.

"No, I really don't..."

"Agent Hanley is missing, Mr. Nesterenko. He was working in Liberia." Agent Dawson leaned forward and looked at the open file. "Says here, he was reporting on arms sales between the government of Sierra Leone and the Revolutionary United Front."

"Why would I know any..."

"You were just in Liberia. Is that right?" Agent Dawson stared into Nesterenko's eyes. "You work for President Charles Taylor. Is that right?"

"I just came from Morocco and I work for any number of people. I worked for Merchant Security as a Consult..."

"You work for the highest bidder." Agent Dawson interrupted Nesterenko again. "You are in with some dirty people, Mr. Nesterenko." He paused to close the file. "Some of these people, like Taylor, are considered not friendly to United States efforts in that region of the world."

"I really have no idea what you are talking about." Nesterenko sighed out loud.

"I really don't have anything to hold you on right now, Bodhan Nesterenko." Agent Dawson signaled for one of the other agents to open the door. "But understand that we will climb any mountain. We will search the deepest part of the oceans. We will find out what happened to Agent Hanley."

"I wish you all the best of luck." Nesterenko remained collected. He didn't want to irritate the agents more than they already were. "I'm sure you will find him."

"You are everything that is wrong with our well trained armed forces, Mr. Nesterenko." Dawson stood. "You go through the training and allow the pests of the world to benefit from it."

"I'm just trying to make a living." Nesterenko stood and walked toward the door. The taller agent stood holding the door closed.

Agent Dawson opened the file again, scanned it, and then pointed at something within it. "Mercenary work can be dangerous, don't you think...says here...Snake?" He looked at Nesterenko and smiled. "No real alliance or allegiance and all." He nodded toward the tall agent, which was a gesture for the door to be opened.

"Yeah, something like that." Nesterenko was stunned by the use of his code name, Snake, as he walked out the door and then hurried to catch his flight. The meeting with the FBI agents startled him. He had not even placed a foot in the United States and he was already being questioned about his driver's death.

I can trust you

"I'll have two more beers," Merrell said to the bartender, knowing she was busy with the regular Sunday crowd, gathered to watch the pivotal Redskins' game. The game was in its final minutes and the Redskins were down. Fans from the circular table and bar yelled in unison as the kick faded right of the goal post, missing the points to tie the game and allowing their opponent to take possession of the ball with less than four minutes remaining in the game.

Merrell had been waiting for McCreiess to get to the small bar for over an hour. He was more than a little upset when McCreiess arrived smelling as if he already had a few drinks in him. After all, it was McCreiess' idea to try the little dive. Merrell never would have noticed the place because he enjoyed places that were a little more upscale.

This is a shitty little hole of a place, Merrell thought to himself.

Football was a game that both Merrell and McCreiess played when they were younger. The sport was something they were both good at and it provided them a way to release pent up youthful energies. Merrell played outside linebacker for a small college in southern Indiana. McCreiess was an All-State fullback in Florida. Both realized early that football was only something that provided that early yearning for discipline and camaraderie. Both men used it as, what they considered a natural step toward the military and some of the rigorous training it would provide. Neither McCreiess nor Merrell could care less if the Redskins won or loss, the crowd surrounding them cared a great deal.

"Damn! Get rid of that son of a bitch," yelled a large man as he paced around a table directly behind McCreiess, and obviously upset with the kicker.

The large man was belligerent as he stormed around the bar.

"Get us a few more pitchers, Cindy," another man from the table yelled at the bartender.

Cindy glanced over and shook her head, knowing the men at the table were already drunk and becoming more cantankerous with each round of beers.

"Carl, please let Gill know they're cut off," Cindy informed the waiter working the small number of people in the establishment. "He's running people off."

"Thanks, Cindy," Carl murmured under his breath. "You know there's going to be a scene."

"Here you go guys. That'll be four dollars." Cindy glanced at McCreiess who had just moments before stepped up to the bar. "He's a quiet one, isn't he?" Cindy asked Merrell as she handed him two mugs of beer.

"You know him?" Merrell handed her plenty of money to cover the beer and tip.

"Know him. No. He's been in here the last couple Sundays."

Merrell moved down the bar and handed McCreiess his beer, not thinking much of the conversation he had with the bartender, Cindy.

"Let me know if you need anything else, pool tables are in the back and I make a mean ham sandwich," Cindy said with a smile her customers had grown accustomed to.

"Bullshit!" Cindy's smile was interrupted by, Gill, the large man with a loud voice. "We asked for a few more pitchers. Now bring us a few more pitchers." Gill grabbed Carl by the face with one hand and by his shirt with the other.

"Beat his ass, Gill," said Sal who was a man much smaller than Gill and sitting behind a table when he yelled. Sal smiled as he watched Carl be humiliated. "Good ass beatn' would be good for old Carl."

"Get your hands off of him, Gill," Cindy screamed from behind the bar. "I'm the one that cut you off. Not Carl!"

"Get me another pitcher," Sal hollered back at Cindy and then threw an empty pitcher at her. The suds in the bottom sprayed those in the direction of the thrown pitcher, barely missing Merrell.

"Gill's at it again. Let's get the hell out of here." Merrell heard the few customers from the small bar say as they were leaving.

"Nice place, Drake." Merrell provided his friend a stern stare.

"You want another pitcher God damn you! Here," Cindy said with a clenched jaw as she moved from behind the bar, slamming the pitcher on the table.

"That's all we wanted. Why you making such a big fucking deal?" Gill calmly asked as he poured himself a drink. "Gimmie your mug, Sal," he said to his smaller friend."Beer's on the house today."

"Again with the on the house crap." Cindy stormed away.

"We asked for a few more," Sal yelled and threw another pitcher at Cindy who made her way behind the bar.

"Look, you're making us miss the game," Gill explained as he sat down and crossed his stretched out legs. He locked eyes with the only two patrons left, McCreiess and Merrell. "What the fuck you looking at?" Gill questioned them.

McCreiess remained stoic as he kept eye contact with the large man people called Gill. He sipped from his beer calmly. Merrell turned away from the action.

Son-of-a-bitch. That's why, Merrell thought to himself as he took a large gulp of beer.

"Now, now, now. We don't need any more problems." Carl hurried to McCreiess and Merrell, gently placing his hands on their backs to try and lift them from their seats and guide them to the door. "Gill likes his beer and Redskins, and gets a little moody sometimes. Especially when things aren't going well."

"Yeah. I get a little moody." Gill agreed with Carl's assessment as he broke eye contact with McCreiess, turning his attention back to the game.

"We will finish our beers," McCreiess said calmly.

"We don't need the trouble, Drake," Merrell whispered to his friend.

"Damn right. You don't need the trouble," laughed Sal as he looked toward Gill and then back at Merrell. "You boys would be in a world of..."

"Cindy, fill that other pitcher up. I think our friends want to drink with us." Gill cut the little man off and smiled as he stood and walked toward the bar. He looked both Merrell and McCreiess over more carefully as he moved.

"Don't you think you have caused enough problems," Cindy shot back. "You've bullied everyone out the door again. It's no wonder we can't get a steady crowd..."

"Fill another God damn pitcher," Gill hollered as he shot a nasty and cold stare at Cindy. "I want to meet these crazy bastards."

"Cindy, don't worry about that other pitcher. We've had enough. We've all had enough." Merrell turned toward McCreiess who was still sipping from his beer.

"What I would do if it were Abby behind the bar." McCreiess chuckled. "Cindy seems to be a nice person."

"Drake, let's not...

"Fill that pitcher." Gill interrupted Merrell and kept an eye on McCreiess as he walked toward him, getting within arm's length before he stopped.

Don't do it, Merrell thought as Gill closed in on his friend.

"I was trying to be your friend." Gill stood looking down at McCreiess, now "brow beating" him. "I've seen you in here before. Never acknowledging..."

"We are not friends, and we're not leaving until you and your friend personally apologize to both Cindy and the waiter, Carl," said McCreiess as he stared into Gill's eyes.

"No, no, no. No one has to apologize. Gill sometimes gets..."

"Shut up, Carl," Cindy said as she stared at McCreiess.

Gill was a very large man at 6 feet, 3 inches, and weighing over 300 pounds. She could see that McCreiess could take care of himself. At 6 feet and weighing 200 pounds of nothing but muscle, McCreiess looked to Cindy as a person who backed down from not much, especially a man like Gill.

"You don't have to do this," Merrell whispered to his friend.

"Slap the shit out of him, Gill." Sal had not moved from the table.

Stupid friends, thought Merrell as he shook his head. He figured Sal to be the idiot friend who enjoyed watching his large friend bully others. He had never met Sal before but he could tell that the small man enjoyed encouraging Gill with stupid remarks, not understanding he left his large and dumb friend very little room to back away from a fight without losing pride.

"You boys ever been here before?" Gill questioned McCreiess.

"Tell them you're sorry and we will never return," McCreiess replied.

Merrell was relieved that Gill flinched by asking a stupid question. He could see the large mans eyes lose interest in fighting.

"I don't think you understand. You see, I own this shit hole of a place and that bitch behind the bar is my wife. That asshole over there is my employee and Sal... well he's my brother-in-law." Gill grinned as he looked at both McCreiess and Merrell. "I think I have had enough fun with you now, so I want you both to turn around and get the fuck out of here." Gill raised his voice.

"Another time," Merrell said under his breath, hoping McCreiess would turn and walk. He had no doubt his friend would be able to beat a man like Gill in a fight but he didn't want the unnecessary attention a fight might bring upon himself or his friend.

"Bye, bye, dick wads," Sal said with a laugh as he waved good-bye.

Merrell saw McCreiess glance at Cindy, who was now behind the bar cleaning the mess Gill and Sal created.

"I still want that beer Cindy, and throw me a ham and cheese in the microwave." Gill was still looking down at McCreiess.

It seemed to Merrell that Gill was gaining guts with each word he spoke.

The quick and straight jab McCreiess threw landed precisely where he intended, directly below Gill's left breast with a thud. The jab landed with a corkscrew type motion, allowing it to snap with full force. Gill was stunned as the air left his lung. McCreiess immediately followed the jab with an overhand right, crushing his beer mug into Gill's chin and mouth. Gill's head jolted back and fell forward before he dropped to his knees. Gill faded in and out of consciences after receiving the quick powerful hits.

Merrell noticed teeth falling out of Gill's mouth.

McCreiess immediately took a step back and loaded for a sidekick. He brought his right knee up and then twisted his body sideways and prepared to thrust his leg forward at Gill's head while rotating his body on the supporting leg.

Gill struggled to regain full consciousness, now holding his mouth with one hand and grasping on to a bar stool with the other.

"You're going to kill him," Sal yelled. He stepped forward but kept his distance by keeping a table between him and the action.

"Drake," Merrell hollered, "That's enough!"

McCreiess did not kick the man, but instead, he calmly dropped his leg and moved quickly to the door. Merrell placed his mug on the table before following his friend toward the door. Sal moved to help his friend, Gill, up and to a chair. McCreiess turned to see if Merrell was following.

"Move!" Merrell grabbed McCreiess by the elbow and pushed him as they moved through the doorway. "Let's go to the car!"

"I didn't see anything," Cindy yelled toward Merrell and McCreiess as they exited.

"Cindy, we're going to need some clean towels," Sal screamed as he held Gill's face.

"We! Gill knows where they are," Cindy said with a grin as she moved from out behind the bar, gathering her coat and purse. "When that fat ass comes through, tell him not to find me."

"Jesus!" Sal stood wiping his hands off on Gill's pants as Cindy ran for the door. "What the hell am I suppose to do with this?"

"The fat bastard asked for it and he finally got it!" Cindy laughed as she fled the scene.

***

Merrell and McCreiess walked to the car as if nothing out of the ordinary happened.

"Let's go to O'Hickey's," McCreiess quipped with a grin.

"I think you've had enough. I think we should get you home."

"Home! What the..." McCreiess jumped into the car and slammed the door.

Merrell looked around to see if they attracted attention to themselves before he got into the car. He made eye contact with Cindy after noticing that she was the only person staring at himself and McCreiess. The thought of her going with him and McCreiess filled his thoughts for a moment. She smiled as if to say thanks. He smiled but he didn't know why. She waved and hurried away. His smile faded.

***

Merrell was able to pull out of the parallel position and merge into traffic without distractions.

"What the hell are you thinking Drake? You asked for that. You..."

"Are you going to O'Hickey's or not?" McCreiess interrupted.

Merrell looked at his best friend and shook his head as he turned the car toward the Bar.

"You've been plotting all that out. Why bring me in to see it?"

"I can't stand a surly Redskin fan." McCreiess leaned back in the car seat. "I thought you might want to see something funny. That's all."

"Funny! That fat ass is going to be lucky if he ever..."

"Fuck him and people like him," McCreiess yelled. "You got any Elvis?" He calmly asked. "What's with this country..."

"That's nice." Merrell interrupted. "That's real nice about me thinking it would be funny." Merrell raised his voice louder than McCreiess expected. "And no, I don't have any Elvis," he yelled.

"Calm down. Jeeeshhh...it was just some idiot who needed to get throttled a little." McCreiess smiled. "No big deal if you ask me. And Elvis calms me."

***

Merrell and McCreiess were in a comfortable setting at O'Hickey's Irish Pub. They were able to sit without worry of anyone bothering them. It was a favorite of McCreiess'. Merrell preferred it to places like Gill's but he would still rather be sitting somewhere a little more upscale. McCreiess would often talk about how he enjoyed the long walnut and red oak bar and the many different beers on draft that O'Hickey's offered. Most beer connoisseurs in the area knew of O'Hickey's. McCreiess' name was etched in a large bronze cup as someone who drank a certain amount of different beers from around the world. He had a favorite booth and knew most of the regulars.

"Kip, we need a couple beers."

"I'll be right there, Drake," Kip yelled as he started drawing the beer from the tap.

Kip was the long time bartender of O'Hickey's. In a field where people jumped from one bar to another, Kip was a steady tender to O'Hickey's for over twelve years.

"I enjoy knowing that a friend will always be here for me when I get here," McCreiess said, as he looked the place over.

"Saw your name on the bronze cup. Quite the accomplishment," Merrell said with a smirk. "What is it, German beer now?"

"Couldn't get to Germany because I was in Iraq so I thought I would..."

"Drake, you were out of line." Merrell was disgusted by McCreiess' fight with Gill.

"Did you hear the Redskins lost," Kip said as he delivered the beers. "Spider IPA came in and I knew you'd want it, Drake."

"I hope it's as good as the last keg." McCreiess paid for the beers before Kip hustled away to serve other patrons.

"That's too bad. I bet Gill is going to be upset about those Redskins." McCreiess grinned before he took a long draw from his beer. "Now that is a good fucking beer."

160

"What's the matter with you? Why did you need to do that?"

"Do what?" McCreiess laughed.

"You know God damn good and..."

"So I punched some fat ass Redskin fan...bar owning type."

"So," Merrell snapped. Keeping his voice low.

"Yeah, so. With all the shit we have done to people, you're going to get upset over some lame dick that gets drunk and treats people like shit." McCreiess shrugged. "As if that is important."

"Hey Drake," the waitress Jenny said as she rushed by.

"Hey Jenny." McCreiess took a deep breath and let it out. He made sure Jenny was out of earshot. "We have friends overseas doing things shit heads like Gill would never do. We have friends overseas because assholes like those in that bar never seem to man up. Oh they talk about going to war, but they never seem to step forward when it's time to go...and guys like us seem to never miss the bus to the shitty little parts of this world that people hate to hear about." McCreiess raised his voice a little.

"You talk about the guy like you know him." Merrell's face turned red. "You set it all up. You cased the place. Got to hear his loud ass mouth over the last few Sundays. Had me come over to watch you close it." He sat back in his seat. "Why did I need to see it? You could have just beaten his ass and ..."

"You didn't want to see it? I thought you wanted to see everything, right?" McCreiess paused for a moment. "You're right. He'll remember me."

"I definitely don't think he will forget you." Merrell tried to lighten the mood by grinning. "It's not for everyone, Drake." He sighed. "Is that what it's about? It's about setting things straight?"

McCreiess took another drink and waited to hear more.

"I know what you have done Drake, and I've seen the things that you have, and I know Abby and Kevin being gone is eating away at you." Merrell paused. "It eats at me."

McCreiess turned away from his friend. "Don't bring them into this."

"If you need a break or if you need to talk with someone, let me know. I am sure Judge Carson can help us."

"Carson!" McCreiess laughed.

"Yes, Carson." Merrell moved McCreiess' beer out of his reach. "What's the matter with you?"

"You know. Put a bullet through a man's head and everyone pats me on the back and says great job troop." McCreiess grabbed his beer and took a large gulp. "And I have been shooting fuckers for a long time." He signaled Kip for another beer. "I kick the shit out of Gill the loud mouth bar owner and you ask me what's wrong."

"You have been a great warrior for this country and The System, Drake, and there is nothing wrong with what you are feeling."

"Really," McCreiess shot back with a low but stern tone. "I can't even watch the news without the feeling of kicking the screen in. Did you know that seventy percent of the people were for war when the towers fell?" He paused. "Enemy starts fighting back and seventy percent want to tuck tail and run home. Leaving guys like Kevin and many others to spend their lives for nothing." He looked around to make sure he didn't bring attention to himself and Merrell. "I sometimes feel like I am going to go off like a hand grenade."

"Drake, we can..."

"His wife and children found him. I made his wife a widow and his children orphans." McCreiess' mood seemed to move from anger to somber.

"Are you talking about that environmentalist nut bag that killed lumber jacks for the fun of it?" Merrell looked around the bar, making sure no one was paying special attention to his table. "Screw him, Drake. He had blood all over his hands."

"It's not right. What we are doing is not..."

"Jesus, Drake. With the wars and all the other shit we've been doing." Merrell began to smile. "You've probably made lots of women and children widows and orphans. And if you ask me, they all had it coming to them."

"I want out," McCreiess blurted it out. He sighed as if what he said lightened a heavy rucksack he had been carrying.

Merrell sat stunned by his friends comment. He tried to read his friend's facial expression, wondering if the comment was based on a serious thought or too much alcohol.

"That's right. I want out. The 'Old Man' got out. Why not me?" McCreiess leaned back in his seat. "We've paid up Max. I've paid up."

"Drake. Drake. What you are saying. Are you serious?"

"Very." McCreiess stared at Merrell.

"The 'Old Man' is being succeeded by Ellenberg. We give him a chance. We give him a chance...out of respect for the 'Old Man'..." Merrell sat stunned. "I need you, Drake. I...I don't trust anyone else."

Merrell wondered how long his trusted friend had wanted out. He wondered if it was truly his friend speaking or was it the alcohol playing with his thought process. He questioned if McCreiess could have a good night sleep and wake up willing to drive on.

"I need out. I owe no one anything after the 'Old Man'. I just feel..."

"We'll make it happen. I just ask that you sleep on these thoughts that you are having."

"Really? Out?" McCreiess looked into Merrell's eyes. Tears formed and he wiped his eyes. "I can trust you. Out."

"The members don't meet for a little while." Merrell searched for something to say. "I'll need your help for the next round, but other... I'll get you out. I'll start talking to people." He paused. "What about Matamoros and the vengeance for my brother? What about all the scum we took off of the streets of Miami? What about..."

McCreiess sat silent, spinning the sixteen-ounce glass of beer in his hand as if he was in deep thought. "I never really wanted to be part of a secret society and the only reason I became part of it was because I trusted you."

"You ever think about going to see a professional. Maybe a PTSD doc or..."

"You mean talk about troubles I might be having with war experience?" McCreiess chuckled. "All while I'm blowing the heart out of some ex-politician that some secret society has a problem with?"

Merrell sat silent. He knew neither McCreiess nor Kevin Halcot were given much of a choice in regards to joining The System, but he was never led to believe that either of them would have preferred jail.

"So why do you do it, Drake?" Merrell broke the silence. "I mean why do you still wear the uniform. Why do you still drill once a month and deploy to the far ends of the world." He looked to the ceiling for a moment and then toward his friend. "Haven't you given enough?"

McCreiess stood and took a large drink of his beer.

"If it's not for God or country?" Merrell was curious.

"It's always about the men with me. I'll never let them down. They showed up just like I did. I owe them that." McCreiess paused. "It beats wearing a suit and tie and sitting in an office." He finished his beer. "And it's pretty fun shit we do." He turned and walked away.

Merrell allowed a distant memory to enter his mind as he watched his friend walk toward the door.

:-

Judge Stephen Carson sat on the park bench and watched as the children played on the various swings, slides, and merry-go-rounds. The sun was setting so the heat of the day had passed, which allowed families to take advantage of the city park. He sat silent and took in the sounds that children created as they shrieked, laughed, and cried. He watched as parents coaxed their children to do one thing or the other. He looked to his right to see that his driver remained in the car. He looked to his left to notice the man he was waiting for finally arrived and sat at the other end of the bench. He glanced at the man, the man made eye contact and then scooted closer.

"An apple pie would be good right about now." Max Merrell used the password, apple pie, in a sentence. Not knowing if the person next to him sent him the anonymous letter or not.

"Only if you are finished driving a little red corvette." Carson responded with his password, corvette, allowing Merrell to breathe a sigh of relief.

"Why are we here?" Merrell asked after an uncomfortable moment passed.

"It's really in your best interest to hear me out Mr. Merrell. It is also in your best interest to never speak about this meeting." Carson looked toward Merrell. "Do you understand?"

"I do," Merrell responded with caution. "You have my attention."

"Mr. Merrell, would you like to spend the rest of your life behind bars?" Carson asked as he glanced toward the children climbing the jungle gym. "A lifetime in prison for a cop is not a long life at all."

"I think we both know the answer to your question," Merrell quipped. "I'm guessing there is an alternative to prison or you wouldn't have asked?"

"Mr. Merrell, you and your friends...a Mr. McCreiess, and Mr. Halcot, have been very bad men lately."

Merrell sat silently. He allowed his attention to drift toward a mother pulling her son away from the swing set. The young boy was crying because he was not happy about being told it was time to go home.

"You don't have children, but you had a brother. Is that right?" Carson knew the answer to his question.

Merrell remained watching the boy struggle to get back to the swing set.

"It's funny how known drug dealers and the likes just start falling over dead with gunshot wounds after your brother was killed by a known dealer, and..."

"My little brother was a great cop with a bright future. There are lots of people who wanted vengeance for his murder." Merrell interrupted Carson. "Known drug dealers and the like probably needed to start falling over dead long ago."

"I think you can help me Mr. Merrell." Carson smiled. "I believe you are the man I'm looking for, you and your friends."

"What is it that you need Judge?" Merrell leaned forward and placed his elbows on his knees. "You spoke about prison. You have anything else you want to say about that?"

"Not if you want to come work for me." Carson looked at his driver and nodded his head. The driver started the car. "Good pay and no bars to look through."

"You have nothing on me or I would already be behind bars." Merrell sat back and stared at the Judge.

"You may be right about that, but I know someone who is in deep when it comes to investigating you and your friends. I can get that investigation to go away."

Merrell was more curious than shocked after being told he was on someone's radar. "What do they have on us?"

"It's not what we have on you, Mr. Merrell. It is what we will pin on you." Carson stood and looked down at Max Merrell. "Believe me, Max, once you are in with me and my friends you will find that it is right." Carson walked toward his car and turned for a parting comment. "We can do a lot for you and your friends."

"Yeah, I bet you can." Merrell stood.

Judge Carson looked Merrell over.

"You hear what happened in Matamoros, Mexico a few weeks ago?" Merrell smiled.

"Who hasn't?" Judge Carson smiled. "Cartels have it out..."

"Let's talk soon. I would like to hear what you have." Merrell turned and walked away.

McCreiess turned toward Max and gave a farewell gesture and a halfhearted smile before he left the establishment. Merrell waved goodbye and gestured for Kip to bring him a drink.

Coincidence?

Working behind the five feet tall partition that separated her from neighboring agent's workspaces seemed odd to SueAnn. She hated being in any office environment, let alone one that was so uniform and bland. She understood the idea of cubicles. They do provide some privacy, which allows the occupant to concentrate without distractions, but the personalization of the space was something SueAnn just couldn't do. Cubicles beat the alternative, which were desks lined up in rows allowing everyone to sit and make faces at each other.

SueAnn's area would never show her private side. She would never put a picture on the wall or some motivational saying from some past coach. She never viewed herself as someone who needed to inspire others. In her mind, you either took the extra steps to do something different, or you didn't. The thought of a run in with her late father, Paul English, flashed into her mind.

:-

The chair SueAnn threw clanged off the brick wall as people watched with dismay. The folding chair didn't stand a chance against the brick wall building she threw it against. People continued to walk past, heads down, looking forward, acting as if they witnessed nothing. What they witnessed was a tantrum thrown by a talented runner who just moments before failed to qualify for the 1987 National Cross Country Championship to be held the following weekend. The event would host over 1000 runners from over 100 different organizations. Qualifying for the event was supposed to be nothing more than just another run for SueAnn English. Finishing in 12th place was something that never entered into the equation for her, but her father, Paul English, saw it coming.

SueAnn moved toward the chair and bent to pick it up again. She was hoping to bang it against the wall until it fell apart. Her anger grew with each step toward the chair. The warm moist air from her lungs could be seen as she released it into the cool air.

"That is enough," SueAnn's father yelled as he rushed toward her. He didn't care who heard him.

"I am so..."

"You are an embarrassment," SueAnn's father shouted.

"Yes! I know that. I..."

"You will get over here, right now." Her father pointed to a space directly in front of himself. "Now!"

SueAnn moved to where her father demanded she stand. Her face was red with anger. She prepared for her father to unleash a calm but aimed fury on her.

"Walk with me," He said as he turned to walk.

SueAnn immediately began to follow. She knew not to piss him off any further.

"Just what the hell are you doing?" His voice was raised but controlled.

"Twelfth place! I'm better than that," SueAnn screamed.

"I guess you're not, are you?" SueAnn's father stopped and turned to get into her face. "So you put yourself in the arena when others didn't. Doesn't mean shit. I guess it's better than those that don't, but that's about it."

SueAnn was stunned by what her father just said. She knew he was referencing Teddy Roosevelt's *"Man in the Arena"* speech. She had heard it many times. She had it posted on her college dorm wall. She looked at it often; it brought her inspiration for each day. She knew she did more than most people. She was not a normal student; participating in the ROTC, difficult classes, volunteer at the local Veterans Center, cross-country team. She took solace in the fact that she did what many others would not do.

"You said..."

"What I have consistently said is that I am proud of you. I know you do a lot. I know you work hard." Her father paused. "I never promised you anything. I never said you were going to win anything. On the contrary, I have always told you that nothing is granted or given."

SueAnn stared at the ground as tears formed in her eyes.

"This is a different league." Her father continued. "In high school you didn't have to work as hard to get a victory. This is division one!" He paused. "You have to work harder if you want to compete at an elite level."

"I am doing all I can do," SueAnn yelled.

"I wouldn't even put myself in the arena if mediocrity is my best effort," her father said in a soft and deliberate tone.

"Mediocrity! That's what you are saying. I'm mediocre!"

"I'm saying consequences," her father yelled. "There has to be consequences to any risk taken or there is no risk involved. Negative consequences, as well as positive consequences will keep your efforts balanced." He grabbed her face so he could look her in the eye. "There are few sure things in life. When entering the arena of any competitive event...it would be nice to know that victory was a sure thing. It is the consequence of losing that makes your efforts prior to entering the arena all the more important."

"What are you saying? I didn't work hard enough?"

"You either didn't work hard enough, or twelfth place is the best you can do."

"I'm better than that!"

"Not today you're not!" Her father stepped back and pointed to a young cross-country runner who finished third. "You see her."

"Yeah."

"You've beaten her so many times in the past that she probably never thought she could beat you. She was resigned to finishing behind you."

"Yeah, so?"

"You've given her hope. She's rebounded and now thinks she can beat you. I bet she really starts training now. You should've beaten her today and drained every ounce of hope from her."

SueAnn looked away from the third place finisher.

"It's not about any award. You don't do this for ribbons or trophies. You know those things are only incidental benefits. You know you're not entitled to any victory. Any award granted as a result of entitlement is never worth an award achieved through hard work and personal sacrifice." Her father put his arm around her. "I'm not saying you didn't work hard or sacrifice. I'm saying that twelfth place is ..."

"I'm going to kick her ass the next time I race her. I'll kick them all." SueAnn cut her father off.

"Remember. Always compete at a level you are capable of competing. Compete at a level your opponent won't compete at." Her father looked at the third place finisher. "And. Vision, ambition, and a well thought out planning sequence are always the ingredients for success."

"I'm sorry, Dad."

"Don't tell me you're sorry. Beat the piss out of them!" Her father hugged her...

i

SueAnn was brought back from her thought about her father by the movement of Jennifer Rizzoli and other agents arriving to their cubicles to start the day of work. SueAnn started to scan the Internet news sites, trying to get a train of thought on what the different news organizations think are important topics of the day. She heard Jennifer shuffling through the drawers of her desk so she arose from her seat to look over the partition.

"Jennifer, where were you yesterday?"

"Carmen and I had to sit through a briefing on harassment or some stupid shit like that. How did you get out of it? Or was it just for us lowly admin assistants?"

"I've got to go next week."

"I wish I could have gone with you. I had to sit and listen to Carmon talk about how the instructor was gawking at her tits."

"Was he?" SueAnn's jaw dropped.

"He looked at her name tag once." Jennifer laughed. "The stupid ho." She continued to laugh as she walked toward SueAnn's cube. "Anything good in the news?"

"Clown Face Murders." SueAnn sat back in her chair as she scanned the article.

"What kind of crazy shit is that?"

"It has to do with interstate sixty-five and the murders that take place within that corridor." SueAnn paused and continued to scan. "It seems that many of the people killed have things in common. They're young men and they are found in the river. It was thought these men were out partying. Get drunk. Fall in the river and drown."

"Was thought?"

"Yeah. This news source says that the other thing these dead people have in common is a clown face. It seems that where these young men were found to enter the river. There is always a clown face pin." SueAnn scanned the site. "Several murders had taken place before some genius decided it was too much of a coincidence and started looking around."

"I think that is some spooky shit." Jennifer paused. "At least it's men this time. Usually young women who become floaters." Jennifer's phone rang. "Gotta go!"

Jennifer hurried to her cubicle to answer her ringing phone.

"Coincidence," SueAnn blurted the word out for only her to hear. "Whatever. Nothing is ever a coincidence."

The thought of a clown face pin being found at the known entrance of the river was more than a coincidence. Officials knew of at least seven different points of where victims entered the river only to drown, and at each position a clown face was placed near the point. There was probably more, but it's hard to find an exact spot where someone enters a river.

SueAnn scanned the computer screen one more time before turning her attention to the files on her desk. She took a deep breath and picked up a handful of the files. The first two files she would open would be the files of Michael Henshaw and Ross Evans. The names meant nothing to her. If pressed she may be able to recollect why she had heard of the two men before, but no one was pressing her.

This cannot happen

Professor Jim Brannon sat at his desk reading an Internet story about how Tommy Mill was being released from prison. He felt the burning of acid reflux in his throat. He quickly reached in his top desk drawer for the bottle of anti-acid medicine. He hurried to twist the top off and take a long drink of the chalky liquid. It gave him relief. He rubbed his large belly and burped loud. He licked his lips and wiped what was left of the chalky stuff from his mouth with his sleeve.

"Damn it. No. This cannot happen." Brannon spoke to the computer screen as if it understood him.

Tears started to form in his eyes and roll down his cheek. He grasped a couple handfuls of hair from his balding head and pulled it straight up. He quickly stood, pushing the chair to the wall behind him with his legs. The chair made a loud crash as it hit the wall and toppled over. He began to pace behind his desk. He punched at nothing but air.

"God! I want you...."

"Is everything alright, Professor Brannon?" Millie, the administrative assistant peaked in the office.

"Is everything fine, Professor?" Brannon mocked the question. "Everything is peaches and fucking cream, Millie. How do you think it is?"

"Well the sun is shi..."

"Just shut the fucking door, Millie!"

"Yes, Profes..."

"And how about turning down the heat in this place. Why does it have to be so God damn hot in this building?"

"University rules. Can't turn on the air until..."

"Just shut the fucking door. Will you please," Brannon screamed. "Just shut the door and go about doing whatever it is you do."

Millie closed the door without adding another attempt of kindness.

Brannon picked up his chair and sat it upright behind his desk. He slowly sat down in the chair and slouched. He began to cry and speak softly to himself as he became animated with his hands. If anyone could see him, it would look as if he were truly having a conversation with nothing more than a desk.

Professor Brannon leaned back in his chair. A wave of fear hit him. Anxiety set in. He suddenly felt nauseous. He lunged for the wastebasket next to his desk and dragged it closer to him. Thoughts entered his head at a pace that made his head spin. The thought of him reaching out to his mother was the one thought more than any other that made his anxiety reach a peak level. He quickly plunged his face into the wastebasket and threw-up. His breakfast filled the bottom of the basket. The smell of his vomit made him heave more into the basket. He pushed the basket away and fell to the floor. The cool tile floor brought him some relief.

Brannon pushed himself to his knees. He waited a moment before he moved to a standing position. His knees were weak and his footing was not steady. He leaned on his desk and wiped the slobber from his mouth and the sweat from his face. He moved to the window and opened it. The fresh air gave him strength. *I can do this*, he thought as he saw a bird perched on a tree fly away.

He moved to his desk and pushed some papers around until he found his phone. The door cracked and a wave of sound and light entered his office.

"Get the hell out of here, Millie."

The door quickly closed and Brannon began to pace. Thoughts of what he would say to his mother entered into his thought process. His heart began to beat slower as his anxiety subsided. He pushed some buttons on his phone and placed it to his ear. The sound of the phone ringing broke his thoughts up. He had a moment of confusion. He suddenly wished he wouldn't have pushed the send button.

"How are you doing, Professor?" The voice on the other end rang in Jimmy's ear. "I thought I would be hearing from you."

"I didn't want to bother you, Mommy."

"Jimmy, you are not bothering me. Mommy knows why you are calling and I assure you that things have been set in motion to deal with your problem."

"Our problem, Mommy."

"Jimmy." The voice was stern.

"Mommy. Please don't get upset. I don't like it when you are upset."

We have fulfilled all obligations

McCreiess moved swiftly through a pop-up-target obstacle course. His pace was one that allowed him to keep his breathing under control as his heart rate increased. He understood that targets don't shoot back so he didn't have that hair-raising feeling that one gets when mistakes and bullets are the difference between life and death. What drove him on the range is the competition of topping his best time recorded.

McCreiess moved around a concrete barrier and noticed a window to his left and a doorway to his right. A lady holding a bag in her left hand and a pistol pointing at him in her right hand popped up in the doorway. In the window a man popped up with nothing more than binoculars held to his eyes, behind him was a man holding a sniper rifle. McCreiess immediately hit the woman with two shots to the chest. He turned to the window and hit the man in the background with the rifle with a shot to the face. The slide of his Colt .45 1911 pistol locked to the rear, signaling his weapon was empty. McCreiess moved to a wooden structure and took a knee as he held the weapon close to his face with his dominate-hand. With his non-dominate hand he retrieved another full magazine from his pistol belt. With movement that was smooth and deliberate he was able to drop the old magazine from the weapon and feed the weapon with a new full magazine. He allowed a past experience into his thought progression prior to punching the slide release to load the weapon.

:-

Kneeling behind a wooden barricade, Corporal Drake McCreiess received heavy automatic machine gun fire from hardened members of the Islamic Jihad. Beirut, Lebanon in the year 1983 was a dangerous place for Marines. McCreiess was a good thirty meters detached from his squad who were in retreat mode after being ambushed in an alley less than two blocks south of the building known as the Drakkar building, which housed French paratroopers. Between McCreiess and his squad were two Marines who were bleeding profusely from gunshot wounds they received before they knew an ambush was initiated. The effective fire that the Jihadists were able to muster overwhelmed the squad. A few other Marines were wounded but were able to retreat safely behind sand bags that French paratroopers discarded. The Marines started to return fire once they established cover. The volume of bullets the squad returned was at a high rate but the fire was more "contagious" instead of directed at anything specific.

McCreiess took a deep breath as he pulled two grenades from a pouch on his load bearing harness. He looked down the alley to make eye contact with his squad leader who was searching for an enemy force to fire at. He showed the two grenades to his squad leader and moved his head in a way that explained he was going to toss the grenades in the direction of the Jihadist. The squad leader gave a thumbs-up and turned toward the squad to explain what was going to happen. The fire from the Marines became more sporadic and less intense.

McCreiess knew the weapon used by the Jihadist was more than just small arms fire so he suspected a confrontation with more than one man. He pulled the pin from one of the grenades and tossed it where he suspected the fire came from. He heard it hit the ground and then pulled the pin from the second grenade and tossed it toward the fire but away from the first grenade. The first explosion shook the ground and tossed debris. Firing from the Jihadist and the Marines fell silent. The second explosion shook the ground again. McCreiess timed his movement with the second explosion. He stood as soon as the shock wave passed him and quickly moved around the barricade and toward the Jihadist in a disciplined manner. He noticed one of the Jihadists raising his chest from the ground and ready to push from the ground off of his knees. The Jihadist was missing his right foot and bleeding badly from his wound, but he still held a rocket launcher in his hand so McCreiess quickly fired a bullet into the man's face and watched him fall to the ground. McCreiess' weapon jammed. He heard a sound from behind him so he quickly turned to notice two men suspended in the air by scaffolding. The scaffolding was attached to a Greek Orthodox Cathedral and the men frantically struggled to put a belt fed machine gun into operation. One of the men noticed McCreiess raise his weapon so he reached for a rifle. McCreiess simply slapped his weapon's magazine in an upward motion, cleared the weapon by pulling the charging handle and releasing it, and fired a bullet into the man's chest. *Slap, wrack, attack,* he thought as he watched the man fall twelve feet from the scaffolding, hitting the pavement headfirst. The second man stopped fumbling with the belt fed weapon and simply remained kneeling and staring at McCreiess. McCreiess stared back at the man and then turned to find that his fellow Marines were rushing toward him. McCreiess turned back toward the Jihadist just in time to watch bullets rip through his chest, shoulders, and head. The Jihadist's upper left frontal and sphenoid bones lifted from his skull and bounced off of the Cathedral wall. He seemed to be frozen in place for a second, and then he simply slumped forward and draped himself over the weapon he so frantically tried to put into operation. McCreiess watched as the matter inside of the Jihadist's head spilled onto the wooden scaffolding before turning back to watch as his friends laughed and high-fived each other.

McCreiess was brought back to his task after hearing targets pop up so he pushed the slide release, which loaded the weapon. He learned early that it was most often the person who moved first after a shock that had the advantage. He understood that those who remain calm during disarray most likely defeat those who panic. He understood that accurate fire combined with a violent and methodical behavior is most often a better defense than hunkering down and hoping.

He rose from a kneeling position and in a disciplined fashion he went on to engage the rest of the pop-up targets. He knew he was accurate, but slow. He knew that accuracy on the battlefield was important but slow on the range would only piss his friend Max Merrell off.

"Done!" McCreiess shouted after two bullets hit the last silhouette in the chest and one hit the head.

"Done! Damn right you're done. You're dead, done," Merrell shouted back. "You're not only a few seconds off your mark. You're almost a full minute off."

"Set'em' up again."

"Why waste our time! I could be out flying today." Merrell paused to watch McCreiess slowly walk back to the loading table. "Hot ass day to watch your ass stumble over this range as if you're in some sort of stupor or something."

"Go flying if you want. I'll set them up myself."

"If your best effort is mediocrity, like I said, why waste our time?" Merrell paused again to gauge his friend's reaction.

"Ellenberg will be getting with us soon." Merrell changed the subject.

"Yeah." McCreiess could care less.

"Yeah. The members are meeting and we will have some missions that need to be accomplished."

"Ellenberg! How many more Ellenberg's do we have to work for? I agreed to work for Judge Carson. I didn't sign on for life."

"Give me time. I'll talk to him. This isn't something that will happen overnight."

McCreiess placed his weapon on the loading table and stepped back as he looked over the range.

"Is this what's going on? This getting out thing affecting your work?" Merrell rolled his eyes and put his hands on his hips. "You know we haven't even replaced Kevin yet."

McCreiess shot Merrell a glare that expressed his displeasure at his last comment.

"Listen. It's going to take me some time to find someone that I can trust. And right now we have no one in mind. Plus, it sure beats the shit out of a jail cell."

"Max. Max, you know you need to be looking to get out of this as well. I say we tell Ellenberg we're out." McCreiess moved to pick up the weapon, load it, and holster it. "He can find some other rogue cop types. We have fulfilled all obligations that Judge Carson and the others..."

"I love this Drake," Merrell yelled. "This is me! It's where I want to be. It's what I want to do! We're part of something bigger...something right."

"We're better than this. We are more than this. The System has paid us very well over the years. With Judge Mader dead and now Carson..." McCreiess shrugged his shoulders, unable to finish his thought. "We have no protection."

"Protection! Protection from what?"

"From what! You can't see?" McCreiess stepped toward Merrell and pointed at him. "You know as well as I do that this stuff always ends. And when it does, guys like us get shit on." McCreiess put his finger down and became more relaxed. "I trusted Judge Mader. I don't know his daughter. I trusted Carson, but for all I know, the others will roll all over each other to point fingers at us when this thing unravels." McCreiess stepped back toward the loading table. "People like them always do. And it will unravel."

"Unravel? How?" Merrell sneered.

"I don't know. But it will. It's a different age...I guess. People like them just do stupid things. And then act as if the who, what's, and when belong to everyone but them."

"I'm asking you to hang with me, Drake. Things are in the works. There are things I have kept from you out of...things that are bigger. Things you can walk from."

"You kept me out. Since when did you..."

"You're not listening! Okay, Okay, Drake. Maybe you are better than this." Merrell paused to look his friend over. "You are better than this. And maybe I was in a past life, but now, now I'm The System."

The two men stood silent for a moment. McCreiess loaded and holstered his weapon.

"Drake, I tell you things I would only trust my dog with. You know that. I trusted the Judges." Merrell allowed his shoulders to slump. "Dogs can always be trusted. And I trust you."

"Max?"

"You had someone. You had Abby and she showed you what you could become. I was never that lucky. All I had was the Army, a police department, and now this. It's what I am, and I'm proud of it."

McCreiess turned and walked away shaking his head. He turned to look Merrell in the eye one more time. "I only started this so that I could get out of it. It was a start to a new life...it was a prison sentence that had a time serve limit." McCreiess paused and stepped closer to his friend. "You won't see me chronicling all the different kills in some book. You won't see me on some off TV channel trying to get someone to listen to a story that is...just worn out." He turned again to walk away but held. "Do you know how many people I have killed while wearing a uniform? The so-called good kills. Do you think I give a shit if some military channel dreamer ever gets to jerk off to what I've done?" He spoke while keeping his lips tight and his jaw clenched. "I either dispose of the people that some society deems no longer worth having the right to live or I go sit in a cage." He shrugged his shoulders. "You think I like killing some fat politician or some radical environmentalist? Hell, most politicians are fat lying pieces of shit who will suck or fuck each other like billy goats depending on the vote they need. And radical environmentalists are what they are...radical. I get that they were not good people, but there is no honor in this."

"Drake, please..."

"I kill because it is a requirement to stay out of jail and I try and justify it by..."

"Time, Drake. I just need more time." Merrell pleaded as he interrupted.

"You really don't care, do you?" McCreiess stood stunned for a moment. "Time on this earth is finite. There is a set number of days and I am wasting mine." He turned to walk away with the understanding that no one was any longer willing to listen.

Are you kidding me?

Judge Michael Stallings walked the busy morning streets of Richmond every morning. He would often take a street that was out of the way of anything to do with his final destination, the courthouse, just so that he could enjoy something he hadn't enjoyed in a while. He wasn't a face in the crowd that anyone that didn't know him would notice. After all, how many people could recognize a federal judge if they never stood before him or her?

Stallings was taking no side streets on this journey to the courthouse. He walked south on Eighth Street in a pace that would have most people jogging to keep up. He would nod his head or give a quick wave to people he knew or recognized. His thoughts wondered between his wife and family, to his last conversation with Cynthia Mader. The thought of sitting on the federal bench and the cases before him never crossed his mind.

The phone in his pocket vibrated as he began to cross Broad Street. Pulling the phone from his pocket he immediately realized it was Cynthia who was calling him. *You've got to be kidding me*, Stallings thought to himself. The screeching of tires from cars traveling on Broad Street made him snap from his trance. The obligatory calls of ass-hole, moron, and stupid jerk could be heard coming from the cars as he hurried to cross the street.

Stallings made no eye contact with anyone as he stepped up on the curb. He moved to lean up against a building wall as he flipped his phone to answer it.

"Hello." Stallings' voice trembled from the anxiety he felt.

"Michael. Michael, how are you?" Cynthia's voice bubbled with excitement.

"I'm actually running late, Cynthia."

"This won't take long, Michael. Michael, as you know we will be meeting soon."

"I am aware, Cynthia."

"Well I haven't seen the final draft of your presentation. I haven't seen..."

"I wasn't aware you wanted to see it. You said call if I needed help. I am fully capable of putting together a presentation."

"Michael, I do not doubt your capabilities." Cynthia giggled. "Remember, I have photos of you and your young mistress enjoying the hump machine." She laughed out loud. "I just want to make sure the presentation is...well... persuasive." Cynthia paused as she heard Stallings sigh. "It didn't seem like your heart was really into it the last time we spoke."

"Jesus! Cynthia." Stallings made eye contact with a lady who looked his way. He smiled and nodded his head as she continued to walk.

"Michael."

"Isn't this case in the bag?" Stallings gave the phone the finger.

"Yes. Yes it is. But you know how important it is to get a unanimous..."

"Unanimous? Are you kidding me?" Stallings was both angry and drained. "Tommy Mill did not beat the justice system. He served his time. We should not be dealing with him."

"Michael!"

"I've looked into Mr. Mill, Cynthia. He was some misguided left wing nut bag who had a beef with Reagan and his fight against communism."

"Michael!"

"I don't know why you want this guy...I don't know the connection, but there is..."

"Michael," Cynthia raised her voice.

"Mill didn't beat the justice system. He served his time. The General will never go for it, and Ellenberg... he may be new. But he's a Carson guy...he...he will have some pride, honor...he will..."

"Michael. Michael. Calm please, Michael."

"Don't you understand what this will do?"

"Michael. Calm down God damn it! Act like a man, Michael," Cynthia screamed.

"What Cynthia?" Stallings leaned against the wall and looked at his watch. He wished he were anywhere but on the phone with Cynthia Mader. "Please just let me know what you want me to do."

"Michael, I am forwarding you the presentation that I would make if I were you. You don't have to use it. You understand."

"Yes Cynthia. Forward it. I would be happy to take a look at it."

"Will you? Really?" Cynthia's tone of voice became calm.

"Send it Cynthia." Stallings hung up the phone. He turned and caught a reflection of himself in a window.

"Jesus! What did you get yourself into?" Stallings was amazed at how irate Cynthia had become and how sudden calmness could overtake her mood.

So the plot thickens?

McCreiess sat alone at O'Hickey's and drank a fine craft beer that Kip suggested he try. The beer was dark, a little bitter, and strong, just the way McCreiess liked it. He looked over the establishment and found there were very few people enjoying O'Hickey's and that was fine by him. He didn't mind the alone time. He looked up at the TV and watched as a news anchor talked about a new rifle the army was investing in. It was called a "smart rifle" because anyone who fired it could be as accurate as a well-trained sniper at distances of up to twelve hundred yards. With only minutes of instruction a correspondent was able to hit her target of over one thousand yards. The anchor went on to explain that the new "game changing" technology could make years of sniper training obsolete. McCreiess shook his head in disbelief. *Fuck. Now they have corrupted the art of killing. Is there anything that is off limits? Godfather three, and now this. There is no honor in killing if there is no art behind it. The honing of the craft is the art. The splat after the trigger pull is the show,* he thought before a familiar laugh coming from the billiard room made him sit up and take note.

He had heard the deep-guttural laugh before but knew it couldn't be who he thought it was. The man he knew who had that laugh, Tim "The Brain" Wilson, was killed in Afghanistan. He took a large drink from his stout beer and thought back to a time he and Brain served in combat while in Afghanistan together.

:-

"We have a Forward Operating Base that is under heavy attack in a tier one Taliban stronghold." Major Aubrey stared at McCreiess. "The base is getting low on ammunition and water."

"What's the mission Major?" McCreiess continued to fill his canteen with water from the water buffalo trailer. "What needs to be done?"

"There is also a squad, part of a Marine patrol that got separated, that has been cut off from the base and we will lose them if they don't get armed on the quick."

McCreiess took a long pull from the canteen. He drank some water and then swirled some in his mouth and spit it out. "The dust in this place sucks," he said as he took another drink. "I'll take Mac and The Brain. We will fill our rucksacks with bullets and grenades." He sipped from the canteen and started to refill it. "Drop us a half klick off their location, if feasible, and we will get it to them. Once we link up, we'll make sure we get back to the forward operating base. If it's still there."

"It will be there. We will do a resupply for them soon, and we have Apache gunships on the way to help with support." The Major paused. "I wish we could just do a fly by and kick out for that squad, it's just that we're afraid the supply will fall into Taliban hands, or the Blackhawk would be shot to shit, or both." The Major crossed his arms and shook his head, knowing he had no other options that were better. "With all the shit going down in Iraq, we just don't have a lot of assets. Afghanistan is the red headed step child when it comes to equipment and manpower."

"Give me about fifteen minutes and we'll be ready. What about commo with the squad?"

"Commo is sketchy at best. We haven't heard much from them, but bullets are still flying in and out of their known position, so we know someone is still there." The Major paused. "We'll drop you off south of their position. There seems to be a trail that will lead you north so you can link with them."

"Why not have them retreat south?" McCreiess knew the answer before he asked, but he wanted to hear it.

"Communication is worse than sketchy. We haven't raised them on the proper frequency in quite awhile. Can't get a message out to tell them to do anything."

"And?" McCreiess knew there was more.

"And, the terrain is tough, and there seems to be a fuck load of Taliban heading north on that trail. About an hour or more away from the fight," the Major said hesitantly. "That's why we need to get you out there, soon." He dropped his head as if he was sorry about providing that news. "Lack of assets, terrain is tough, and lots of bad guys."

"Awesome," McCreiess said with a fake smile.

The Major looked up. "We'll lose them if this doesn't work. The squad will be lost." He paused. "If anyone is still alive when you get there you will have to head west of their current position. East is too rugged of terrain and ..."

"And lots of Taliban." McCreiess interrupted. "Well I guess it better work since I'll be out there as well."

"If it doesn't we'll just call in air strikes and other types of ordinance and take out the whole area, and just hope our boys get enough cover to survive."

"Why not call in air strikes now?" McCreiess asked.

"We don't have the assets in place right now to take out the advancing Taliban...and..."

"What?" McCreiess was curious. "And what?"

"That squad was led out there by some young Lieutenant, who happens to be the son of some friend of a General."

"So the friend of a general gets special treatment?" McCreiess halfheartedly smiled as he questioned.

"The friend is a female staff member and..." The Major didn't want to tell McCreiess the whole story but he continued. "The General is having an affair with this staff member and it seems he wants to do all he can to see that this young Lieutenant is found and led to safety if possible."

"How did you get this information?"

"The General convened a conference. Didn't come out and say he was screwing this staff member, the young Lieutenant's mom, but the young Lieutenant Keagan sent a letter that seems to have detailed information about what his mom and the General are up to. The General asked us to keep it on the down low, but you're the one who will be putting life on the line, so I thought I'd let you know."

"So the plot thickens." McCreiess halfheartedly smiled. "You know if I had a dime for all the dirty ass affairs going on around here, all the different deployment time marriage and romance." McCreiess laughed.

"You don't have to volunteer for this."

"I'm not going to do it for the general, God, or country." McCreiess turned to walk away.

"Then why would you do it?"

McCreiess stopped and slowly turned back. "Oh, I'm sure there is some private in that squad who is mixed up in this thing and paying a price."

***

"Indian, one, eight. Indian, one, eight, this is friendly's to your south. How copy?" Brain tried to raise the separated squad on the radio soon after the three-man team was dropped into the darkness and made contact with their command element to inform they were safely inserted. "Indian, one, eight. Come in, over."

"Friendly's, this is Indian, one, eight. Over." The voice that cracked over the radio was faint and garbled, but audible.

McCreiess, Mac, and Brain were huddled together in the dark. All three wore night vision headgear and carried heavy rucksacks filled with needed supply for the squad; each of them carried their personal weapons and supply that would be needed for the mission.

"Indian, one, eight, friendly's are coming from your south. Identify with IR as we approach, over."

"Roger that, hurry." The faint and garbled voice cracked over the radio for McCreiess and the two other men to hear.

"Sounds like that forward operating base is getting that gunship support the Major talked about." McCreiess looked to the north as the sounds of the Apache helicopters engaged in battle could be heard in the distance.

"That squad should be right up here." Mac pointed in the north direction and winced as he spoke.

"You all right?" McCreiess questioned Mac. "Don't tell me ..."

"I'm good," Mac said quietly. "I just twisted my ankle coming out of the bird." He complained about making the three-foot jump from the Blackhawk helicopter just minutes before raising command on the radio. "I thought he was going to land the thing."

"That pilot isn't as stupid as he looked. He knows what's coming from the south." Brain stood. "He wasn't going to fuck around."

"Neither are we." McCreiess stood and adjusted his heavy rucksack. "Mac, you're on the point. Turn the IR on and head north."

The men picked up a quick pace as they hurried to link up with the squad. In the distance the Apache gunships could be heard as they supported the forward operating base with relentless 30-mm chain gunfire and 70-mm rockets. The fire was continues and the sky lit up with overhead flares and tracers.

What concerned McCreiess was that the fire was distant front and not where he thought the squad should be. He was informed the squad was actively engaged with the enemy so the lack of fire from his immediate front puzzled him. He hoped the Taliban pulled from the engagement with the squad and went to support their brothers with the battle at the forward operating base, where they would most likely be cut to pieces with what the Apaches were spitting out. The thought of the squad being overrun also crossed his mind.

"Brain, raise that squad again. We should be coming upon..."

Mac holding up his fist to signal an immediate halt to their movement silenced McCreiess. The men quickly took a knee. Mac signaled for the men to rally.

McCreiess moved forward. "What's up, Mac?" He could already see that Mac had already run into the squad because dead Marines and Taliban fighters lay just a couple feet away to the front. "Get the IR off," he quickly said to Mac. "Looks like we're here and it's not good."

"We're too late," Brain said as he jettisoned his large and heavy rucksack. "What now?" He questioned McCreiess.

"Let's see if any of them are alive and we have to hurry up about it because we got bad guys coming from the south." McCreiess paused to jettison his heavy rucksack and look around his immediate surrounding area. "And, I don't know what is just over these rocks to our east."

McCreiess and his men found eight members of the twelve-man squad, plus the Lieutenant who led them away from their platoon patrol; one Marine from the squad was barely alive with injuries that needed immediate attention, seven members and the Lieutenant were dead. All members of the squad had combat wounds that signified the wounds that caused injury and death most likely came during a firefight. However, the young Lieutenant Keagan was found sitting up straight and leaning against a large rock with one of his wrists slit; a massive amount of blood pooled in the lap of the Lieutenant. It seemed to McCreiess and his men that the Lieutenant didn't want to finish the fight so he took matters into his own hands. McCreiess presumed the other four men had either headed west like he and his team would do, or they were taken prisoners by the Taliban.

After quickly tending to the severely wounded Marine's injuries, stacking the dead and camouflaging them, McCreiess raised command on the radio to inform them where the dead Marines could be found when the Taliban threat was eliminated. He then asked Mac to take the point and head west to the pick-up zone where he and his team would be air lifted to safety. The three men would alternate in carrying the wounded Marine; one man would jettison his rucksack and carry the wounded Marine while the two others would carry the extra rucksack.

Within 200 meters of the spot where the dead Marines were left the team found the remaining four Marines. The Marines they had come across were all found with their hands tied behind their backs and dead from gunshot wounds to the backs of their heads. McCreiess assumed the Taliban were taking them prisoner until the fighting around the forward operating base picked up. The Taliban probably executed the Marines before rushing off to help their brothers.

McCreiess and his men stacked and camouflaged the four Marines after informing their command of their situation. McCreiess knew the mission could end any number of ways. He hoped for the best, but assumed the risk for the worse.

As the Blackhawk helicopter lifted off from the pick-up zone McCreiess and his men could see that the trail they had followed was now being pummeled with all sorts of ordinance, destroying the Taliban using it to link up with their brothers at the FOB. To the north they could see that the fire around the FOB had intensified.

***

McCreiess drove the desert highway of 29 Palms a little slower than most behind him wanted. Every so often a car would pass him and he would look at its driver to receive the inevitable "stink eye." There were not too many places of business in the small town which was most known for the Marine base located nearby, but he didn't want to have to turn around because he missed the building he was looking for. Noticing Ben's place to his left he made a sharp turn and parked the jeep he was driving directly in front of the well-known bar and restaurant. He looked around to make sure the sound of the tires screeching while he made the sharp turn did not bring unwanted attention. Once satisfied he was not a spectacle he exited the jeep and entered the restaurant.

McCreiess looked over the establishment before moving to the bar where one man sat by himself drinking from a coffee cup.

"You're late," said the young man as he turned to look at McCreiess.

"Yeah and I'm sorry about that. I…"

"I don't have long." The young man held his cup up for a refill. "You asked to see me. I didn't ask to see you."

"I get that and this won't take long. I just need to know what happened out there."

"You and your buddies saved me. That's what happened out there. Thanks a fucking lot." The young man poured a large amount of sugar into his cup. "Hope you don't mind if I'm not real thrilled about being alive."

McCreiess looked at the young man's prosthetic left arm and legs.

"You can't see my shit bag hanging under my shirt." The young man lifted his shirt to show McCreiess his colostomy bag.

McCreiess waved off the bar tender who gave him a look that asked if he wanted anything. "Yeah, I'm sorry about how it ended up for you."

"You think it was hard for me to get pussy before going to Afghanistan? Now it's virtually impossible."

McCreiess had no response to the young man's condition.

"I get a bullet to my stomach and some shrapnel to my legs and..." The young man shook his head as if he were confused. "What do you want Sergeant McCreiess? You want me to cry and hug you? Slobber all over you about how thankful I am for you and your buddies for saving me?" He paused for thought. "It's not going to happen."

"I want to know what really happened."

"I told them what happened. I told them everything." The young man became angry as he turned toward McCreiess. "You were there. What more do you want?"

"I read the report. You went after a small element of Taliban and got cut off from the main element." McCreiess paused. "Tell me why the report never said anything about the Lieutenant cutting his own wrists."

"Oh, you want the real truth." The young man grinned. "The shit they kept out of the 'official' report."

"That might help me sleep a little better."

"I assure you, it won't." The young man turned back to face the bar.

"What happened? Why would a Lieutenant be out there with one squad?" McCreiess sighed deeply. "Why would he take his own life?"

"We were out there to rescue Lieutenant Keagan. He left the platoon with no weapon, no water, no nothing." The young man turned back to McCreiess. "He wasn't being real tactical either. He was shouting crazy shit and crying out loud."

"What was he saying?"

"When we caught up to him he told us about how his mother, who is an officer and on General Taylor's staff, was fucking some General. He said he went to surprise visit her in Kandahar, but when he got there, he could see her getting bent over the Generals desk and getting fucked from behind by the General, and she wanted it."

McCreiess sat stunned.

"When the Taliban engaged us he said he was sorry for getting us into the jam and then he calmly sat down and opened himself up." The young man shrugged his shoulders. "Before he did that he talked about how his mother brought him up on shit like courage, honor, duty, service, and commitment." The young man tried to smile but couldn't. "His father was home taking care of his two sisters and his mother was taking care of the General."

"I could tell that the fighting was brutal and..."

"We were out of ammunition. It became close quarter combat."

The loud deep-guttural laughter brought McCreiess back from his thought about Brain and the separated squad. He took a large drink from his beer and finished it off. The thought of the Lieutenant calmly taking a seat and opening himself up, all while his squad was actively engaged in combat flashed into his thoughts. He wondered how calming it could be and quickly let that thought go.

PART 3

Will you please?

Miami, Florida - 1978

Veteran police officer Amadeus Pagunus sat in his police cruiser and looked his young partner over as the young cop ordered pastalitos from the Little Havana food truck located near Domino Park. He knew the young officers background as far as being a Marine and he was impressed that the young officer attended law school at night, but he didn't understand the cop aspect for the young man. *What is this kid's angle*, he thought to himself. In the past six months of patrolling with the young officer, he noticed that the young man never seemed to be real interested in policing. The kid was smart, good looking, and in shape, but he never seemed interested in the culture of Little Havana. The kid never took the time to learn the Hispanic language or Latino culture, or immerse himself into the Latin flavor. To Pagunus, learning the culture in the area in which you patrol is the most important thing in becoming a good police officer.

The young officer, Ronald Ellenberg, paid the young woman who hung out the window of the truck and then moved to the wrought iron fence that separated the park from the streets. He stood and watched two older men play a game of dominos as they sat on milk crates at a portable table and studied each other's moves. He took a bite from the pastalito and then turned to walk toward the cruiser, continuing to eat the Cuban pastry as he moved.

"Ah man, I asked her for one with no raisins." Ellenberg shook his head and tried to pick some of the dried grapes from the pastry as he got into the cruiser.

"With an abundance of local owned shops and restaurants, you always choose that same truck and order the same thing, pastalitos. And you always ask for no raisins and you always act pissed when you get one with raisins."

"Where are you going with this line of questioning, Sarge?" Ellenberg asked as he continued to pick at the pastry.

"I've known you for more than half a year and you are not a bit inter..."

"What's with the gold bust over there?" Ellenberg cut Pagunus off.

Pagunus sighed. "It's a monument to Maxino Gomez, a famous general who led troops during the Cuban war of Independence. You might want to learn..."

"Castro. I thought he led the war of indepen..."

"Car Eighteen, Car Eighteen." A voice cracked from the cruisers radio and interrupted Ellenberg's question.

"This is Car Eighteen." Pagunus spoke into the microphone.

"Car Eighteen we received a call of a suspicious car on the corner of eighth and thirteenth. It is a white sedan and the complaint is that there is suspicious activity taking place around the white sedan. We need you to check it out."

"Car Eighteen in route." Pagunus spoke into the microphone and then hung it up.

"Should be a couple blocks to our left Sarge." Ellenberg finished his pastry.

***

Officer Pagunus noticed the white sedan parked near the Cuban Memorial Plaza so he pulled his cruiser directly behind it and stopped. He put the cruisers gear in park and left it running as he exited the vehicle and walked toward the sedan. Ellenberg picked up the radio microphone and then turned to look at a street performance, a young Hispanic man break dancing in front of a crowd of people, taking place within twenty feet of his position.

Pagunus stopped after noticing two men sit up in the front seat of the sedan. He sidestepped to position himself to the driver's side of the sedan. The man sitting on the passenger side quickly exited the vehicle as the man on the driver's side started the sedan. Pagunus stopped sidestepping and quickly moved to draw his service revolver after noticing the man exiting the sedan raise his pistol.

Pagunus dropped to his knees after a bullet entered his shoulder. He fired his revolver, hitting the man in the throat and forehead. The man fell over dead.

Ellenberg, startled after hearing shots fired, jumped from the police cruiser and drew his service revolver, accidently dropping the revolver to the ground and kicking it toward the street performer and the cowering people. Ellenberg stood stunned and embarrassed as he watched the performer pick up his revolver.

"You, in the vehicle. Keep your hands on the wheel where I can see them," Pagunus yelled. "Do not move!"

Pagunus looked toward Ellenberg. "You, get your service revolver from the street performer and give me a hand. Will you, please?"

Ellenberg stepped toward the street performer and met him half way. The street performer handed Ellenberg his revolver and then smiled as he shrugged his shoulders.

Ellenberg turned to look at Pagunus. "You alright?"

"Now just what the fuck do you think," Pagunus said as he grimaced.

Where did I go wrong?

Present Day

Judge Ronald Ellenberg had a mixture of different feelings pulsating through his body and mind as he steered his vehicle through the national forest linked to Cynthia Mader's family property. The road he traveled was a mixture of paved and gravel so he alternated his speed accordingly. Judge Carson warned him against speeding through the national forest. Carson explained that you never knew what could be around the next corner, anything from bears to hikers. The canopy of the forest was more beautiful than any painting of such forest could describe. The fall colors of gold, orange, and red were vibrant as they bounced around the scenic route. The understory of the forest of shrubs, herbs, and moss could still be seen so the leaves were at their peak. The view of the understory settled Ellenberg and allowed his thoughts to drift to a very different time in his life. :-

"Get your ass over here Officer Candidate Ellenberg," a burly Staff Sergeant yelled as he moved down a line of candidates who were hoping to one day become Marine Corp officers. The candidates were tired after a long movement through the North Carolina forest.

"Officer Candidate Ellenberg is using a tree as a head, sir," one of the candidates responded.

"Ellenberg," the Staff Sergeant yelled.

"Yes sir!" Ellenberg could be heard responding from a distance.

"Cut it short and wipe it deep! We gotta move."

"Yes sir," Ellenberg yelled.

The order from the sergeant brought laughter from the candidates.

"Shut that shit up," the Staff Sergeant screamed. "We need to move so ruck up."

The candidates started rising from the ground. They were tired and dirty so their movement created some moans and groans.

"Shut that moaning bullshit up," the Staff Sergeant ordered. "Ellenberg better have his ass steady on the map or it will be another long night. And I don't look forward to spending another night trampling..."

"Sir!" Ellenberg interrupted the sergeant.

"What?"

"Sir. I'm ready."

"You better have your shit wired tight, Ellenberg." The sergeant moved close to Ellenberg. "I want your map. I want to see your route. You're leading this cluster fuck."

"Yes, sir." Ellenberg handed over his map.

The sergeant paused for a moment as he looked over the map.

"I figured we'd..." Ellenberg was tired.

"What the fuck." The sergeant shook his head. "Candidate Ellenberg, you are as fucked up as a football bat."

"Sir?"

"You have us all moving off a big ass cliff."

"Sir?"

"See those brown contour lines on the map? See how they all come together? See how they all come together as one and then you see those tick lines along that single brown line?"

"Yes, Sir." Ellenberg felt small as the sergeant berated him in front of the others.

"You have us all marching off a thirty foot cliff."

A deer crossing the road ahead brought Ellenberg back from his flashback. He noticed the large lake ahead that signaled he would be turning onto Cynthia's property soon. He took a deep breath and let out a big sigh.

***

General Hathaway leaned on a large wooden support post. He admired the large porch he stood on. The porch was attached to a beautiful log cabin that over looked a lake and pasture. He noticed a car traveling the lake road. He unzipped his leather jacket that barely fit his large strong torso. He pulled a cigar from his jacket pocket and bit the end of it off and spit it out. He struck a match on the wooden post and held it to his cigar as he took shallow draws and rotated the cigar around until it was evenly lit. He took a deep breath and let it out. The smoke lingered in the air in front of him. The General was now in his late sixties; he had blown a lot of smoke over the years.

***

Ellenberg pulled the car into the parking space in front of the large log cabin. He opened the door thinking of the fresh air the great outdoors would provide, but the smell of cigar smoke and fungi-like bacteria in the dirt filled the air.

"You like that smell?" General Hathaway caught Ellenberg with a question as he came out of the car. "Streptomyces is what it is called." The General paused for a moment. "That earthy smell that makes you feel the need to defecate when you first enter the woods."

"Yeah. So that's what that smell is." Ellenberg moved toward the General in a hesitant manner.

"Ellenberg?" Hathaway asked.

"Yes, sir. General Hathaway?"

"Yep. We were beginning to wonder if you would make it."

"I'm on time. You must be early. How are you General?" Ellenberg reached to shake the Generals hand.

"I'm fine." The General looked at his hand as he pulled it away. "You might want to work on that handshake for future first impressions. I won't judge..."

"The scenery is beautiful." Ellenberg cut the General off. "It reminds me of the cabin Judge Carson and I would go to for our annual fishing trip." Ellenberg paused to take in the view of the cabin, lake, and surrounding forest. "When did you arrive?"

"I got in a few days ago. A friend of mine is stationed at a small base near here so I thought I would spend some time with him while I'm up this way. We like to..."

"I think I passed the base on the way in." Ellenberg cut the General off again.

"How is Judge Carson?" The General bit his lip.

"He is fine. Harriet, his wife, is making him comfortable."

"I should call him."

"I didn't know you two communicated outside of..."

"We don't." The General cut Ellenberg off. "Come on in. She wants to get started." He took a finale drag from his cigar before stomping it out.

***

Ellenberg and the General entered the large log cabin with smiles as the others continued with their small talk around the bar. Cynthia's butler, Bully, moved behind Ellenberg and helped him remove his coat.

"Your bags, sir?" Bully asked with a slow draw.

"In the car...and..."

"Bully. My name is Bully, sir." Bully put his hand on the suitcase Ellenberg carried into the room.

"I'll keep hold of this one if you don't mind."

"That would be fine, Sir."

"Bully is someone you will not remember." The General smiled as he gently grabbed Ellenberg's elbow and pulled him forward.

The others in the room started to gather around Ellenberg and the General to introduce them. Cynthia moved herself to the forefront by bumping elbows and sliding sideways through the men. She enjoyed being the center of attention.

"Mr. Ellenberg!" Cynthia proclaimed as she grabbed his hand for a greeting.

"Cynthia?" Ellenberg had never met the woman. He only knew that Cynthia was the name of the only woman in the group. His first impression of her was that she might be a little too forward.

"Bully, after you hang his coat and gather his bags, you can make sure his suitcase makes it to his chair." Cynthia looked at Ellenberg as she talked to Bully. "Your suitcase, Mr. Ellenberg."

"Yes. I will hand it over to Bully." Ellenberg nodded in agreement.

"And then please bring in the hor d'oeuvres, Bully."

"Yes. Hor d'oeuvres." Bully moved slowly.

Ellenberg continued to meet and make small talk with the other members.

***

In the middle of the room set a pentagon shaped mahogany table. Leather chairs surrounded the table, one for each member. On the table a pen and pad of paper set in front of each chair. Along the wall a table filled with hor d'oeuvres and drink was almost ready for the members to enjoy.

The members stood making small talk as Bully put the finishing touches on the food and drink table.

Russ Porter, obese and ungracious, looked over the bar. He moved closer to the table, prompting Bully to turn and stare him back so that he could finish.

Stallings moved to look over the table of hor d'oeuvres and drink. He gave it a once over before turning to make eye contact with Porter.

"See anything you like Mr. Porter?" Stallings broke eye contact and moved to the table. He picked up a deviled egg type dish. "What do you think of this Porter?"

"I think it is..."

"What it, is, does not matter." Stallings stuffed the egg in his mouth and swallowed it. "I particularly like the tuna on top. Don't you?"

"I haven't..."

"You should have it all, Mr. Porter. Get all you can." Stallings walked away as Porter stood stunned by the conversation, not understanding what happened.

"Gentlemen, it is time we take our seats. Bully will bring in more hor d'oeuvres as needed." Cynthia raised her hand as she spoke and snapped her fingers.

"What about the scotch?"

"Yes, Mr. Porter. There is plenty of scotch. I would suggest the Vueve Clicquot, but in your case...water is best served with scotch." Cynthia looked toward Bully. "Bully. Bully."

"Yes, Ma'am. More scotch and water."

The members moved to take their seats.

"Why, Mr. Ellenberg, how did you know which chair was yours?" Cynthia tried to make her question genuine. She knew that Judge Carson prepped his protégé.

"Judge Carson said it is the one situated right of the largest chair...or your chair." Ellenberg understood her question was more about propping herself up than actually understanding how he knew where to sit.

The members were now situated. Judge Cynthia Mader seated in the large chair. From her left and rounding clockwise were seated Judge Michael Stallings, General Hathaway, Mayor Russ Porter, and Judge Ronald Ellenberg.

"Gentlemen we have a new member this year so we should start with introductions." Cynthia stood as she turned on a recording device. "We should start with the oldest member, to my left, and follow to our newest member, Mr. Ellenberg, to my right." Cynthia paused. "Mr. Stallings, if you don't mind?"

Stallings stood and cleared his throat. He looked down the line of men and made eye contact with each and then made eye contact with Cynthia.

"My name is Michael Stallings. Judge Michael Stallings to be more specific." Stallings paused for a moment. The thought of his swearing in crossed his mind. Taking the oath in front of his family as he affirmed his obligation to the duties of Federal Judge weighed heavy on him. He allowed his thoughts to drift to that day for a moment.

:-

Michael Stallings stood as tall as he ever had with his wife by his side as she held the infant child and held the toddler's hand. His mother and father looked on from the front row seats. The President of the United States entered the room. Stallings made eye contact with him as the President strolled over to shake his hand and get introductory pictures. The President shook the hand of his wife and patted the children and gave them smiles. The President quickly began by holding his hand out to a staff member. The staff member handed the President the Bible.

"Are we ready, Judge Stallings?"

"I am, Mr. President." Stallings looked to his father, who had tears in his eyes.

"Repeat after me." The President locked eye contact with Stallings.

Stallings quickly glanced at his wife and then locked eyes with the President.

"I, Michael Aaron Stallings, do solemnly swear that I will administer justice without respect to persons, and do equal right to the poor and the rich..."

The President went on to administer the complete oath, "and that I will faithfully and impartially discharge and perform all the duties incumbent upon me as under the Constitution and laws of the United States. So help me God." Stallings repeated every word. He believed in the oath, every word of it.

§

What happened? Stallings questioned himself as he returned to his present situation. *Where did I go wrong? Where did this go wrong?* Stallings held eye contact with Cynthia for a moment longer. Cynthia remained smiling.

"I am an appellate judge with the Fourth Circuit of the United States Federal Court system. President George W. Bush nominated me to the bench in two thousand seven. Prior to the appellate nomination I served as an assistant to the attorney general." Stallings looked at the men. "I have been a proud member of this society. The society we call The System. For the past nine years."

"Thank you, Mr. Stallings." Cynthia smiled.

"I want to welcome Mr. Ellenberg," Stallings said before he sat. "I am sure he will serve our system well and use Judge Carson as an example. Always!"

"Yes. Thank you, Mr. Stallings." Cynthia looked at the General.

"My name is General James Hathaway." The General rose from his seat. "I am retired from the Marine Corps and my current position is instructor at the Naval Academy." The General sat down and looked straight ahead.

"You are too modest, general." Cynthia broke the silence in the room. "You forget to mention two purple hearts and a silver star you've accumulated during your three tours in Vietnam. And other escapades." Cynthia smiled.

"No. No, I didn't forget." The General remained looking straight ahead as the other members locked on to him.

Cynthia's smile diminished as she looked at Porter.

"My name is Russ Porter and I am the former mayor of New York." Porter remained seated. He leaned back in his seat and sipped from his glass. "I am currently working as the managing editor for the American Philosopher, a conservative blog. I am also an associate with the Traditional Foundation. I was elected mayor because I was known for going after drug dealers and criminals who commit violent crimes. I ended up at the foundation after I lost my re-election bid to a big government lefty." Porter saw that Cynthia rolled her eyes. "It seems the people of New York were not all that big on independence from government!" Porter raised his voice.

"Yes Mr. Porter." Cynthia leaned forward in her seat. "Some would say it was your connection to well-known gangsters that brought your political career to an abrupt halt."

Porter smiled. "The guy representing our nation's capitol gets caught smoking crack with a prostitute and becomes a hero. I invite a guy with union connections to my house and I get shit canned." Porter leaned back in his chair. "Go figure!"

"Your language, Mr. Porter."

"Yes, ma'am." Porter turned to look at Ellenberg, as did Cynthia.

"My name is Ronald Sam Ellenberg." Ellenberg stood and made eye contact with all members. "I currently serve on Florida's Superior Court. Prior to my service on the bench I served as a Marine platoon leader in the First Infantry. After leaving the Corps, I joined the Miami Police Department as a patrol officer and worked my way through law school." Ellenberg noticed the General lean back in his seat. "I worked my way into prosecution and eventually onto the bench."

"Any combat?" The General asked.

"No, sir. When I joined the First Division, they had already returned from Vietnam. My platoon did help with support during the evacuation of Saigon by providing comfort to refugees as they arrived in the States."

"Your service to our great nation is appreciated, Mr. Ellenberg. I am sure your selection by Judge Carson will pay dividends." Cynthia looked at Ellenberg and then smiled at the General.

"Cynthia, I believe it is your turn." Porter interrupted.

"Yes. Thank you Mr. Porter." Cynthia stood and looked over the men and made eye contact with each, although Stallings looked away. "As you know I don't really like talking about myself." Cynthia laughed as she noticed Stallings look to the ceiling. "But since we have to be formal, my name is Cynthia Mader and I currently serve on the Tenth Circuit of Appeals. Nominated by President Clinton, I started out as a prosecutor for the US Attorney General's Office." Cynthia paused to assure the members were with her. She continued regardless. "After several years of outstanding service, I was appointed to the New Mexico State Senate and subsequently re-elected." Cynthia paused for some sort of effect, hoping the men were hanging on every word. "In my last term, I was tapped by the Governor to serve on the New Mexico Court of Appeals."

"Some would say you are a breath away from..."

"I really have no idea what you are talking about."

An awkward pause was caused by Porter's interruption and Cynthia's answer.

"Gentlemen, let's take a break and refresh." Cynthia turned off the recorder and looked toward Ellenberg. "Mr. Ellenberg can I have a word with you?"

"Yes." Ellenberg was hesitant.

***

Cynthia caught up with Ellenberg standing by himself in the corner of the room. He watched the others mingle around the food and drink. Porter had the others laughing about something political. Even Hathaway was laughing. That surprised Ellenberg.

"Mr. Ellenberg, I want to personally welcome you to this long established occasion." Cynthia reached out with both arms and placed her hands on his shoulders. Ellenberg was taken aback at how personal Cynthia was. "I am certain Judge Carson has explained the procedures." Cynthia dropped her hands by her side.

"He has." Ellenberg looked over the other members. "Me being the new member, I will bring my case to the members first. I can have no association, connection, affiliation, or relationship with people involved in the case I bring forth. A vote will be held and a simple majority is needed for a pass." Ellenberg paused for a moment to ensure Cynthia and the other members who gathered closer were listening. "At no time shall one member interrupt another while the case is being presented."

"One more thing." Cynthia pressed Ellenberg.

"Yes and one more very important thing. A case can never be brought against a sitting elected official."

"Yes. Yes. And that is important." Cynthia grabbed Ellenberg's elbow and pulled him closer. "Politicians are a little skuzzy. As we know." Both Cynthia and Ellenberg looked toward Porter as he poured himself another scotch on the rocks as his mouth was filled with some sort of egg and cheese thing. "Wealth and power should never keep us away from anyone, but sitting elected officials... well they're a little different. Don't you think?"

"I think the devil will deal with them soon enough."

"The devil works closely with them, Mr. Ellenberg." Cynthia stared at Porter as he stood by himself eating and drinking all he could. "Think about all those hypocrites in Washington. Either the people are truly represented by people who are like them or the devil lives in that town." Cynthia stared at Ellenberg. "I'd like to think that the people are better than that town."

"I believe the people are generally lost sheep looking for their leader. And will follow anyone who has some sort of rhyme or rhythm."

"I'm looking forward to hearing your first case."

"I'm looking forward to presenting my first case." Ellenberg's voice cracked.

"You are nervous. There is no need to worry Mr. Ellenberg." Cynthia folded her arms. "What we do here is right, just, and honorable."

"Yes, ma'am."

"You should be proud to be part of this society."

Ellenberg looked to the floor and pulled on his ear.

"You are nervous? There is no need to worry, Mr. Ellenberg." Cynthia put her arm around him and walked him toward the large stain glass window that was the centerpiece of the room. "What we do here is right, just, and honorable. You should be proud to be part of this organization...this society." Cynthia looked up at the centerpiece of the room as if she was in awe. "Mr. Ellenberg, this secret society and its history date back many years. Remember! We are the check and balance to the United States justice system. We are the thin gray line, which separates our society from the vigilante. We have rules!"

"I assure you, Cynthia. I am well versed in the lineage of this society. Judge Carson and I..."

"You, Sir, are one of the few who have been trusted to provide an over watch of our justice system." Cynthia cut Ellenberg off. "It should never be taken flippantly."

Both Cynthia and Ellenberg stood looking at the window. A tear formed in one of Cynthia's eyes. She wiped the tear from her cheek and sniffed. Ellenberg was taken aback by her outward emotion.

"My father had this window before this cabin was built. He knew one day he would build a home around this beautiful piece." Cynthia turned to face Ellenberg. "This two hundred year old window sat in storage for over twenty years, until my father could finalize his plans. The walls that would support this fine piece." She sighed. "Committed."

"May be the most beau..."

"Ten minutes, Gentlemen. Ten minutes." Cynthia interrupted Ellenberg as she walked away. "Ten."

* * *

Cynthia stood at the pentagon shaped table as the men were seated. She slowly sat and turned on the recorder as she cleared her throat. She made eye contact with each of the members, holding her stare with Ellenberg a little longer than she did with anyone else.

"Gentlemen we will start with execution of orders. Mr. Ellenberg, being nominated as successor to Judge Carson has the task of operations. He will inform us on success or failure of the last orders." Cynthia turned her attention to Ellenberg.

"Cynthia. Gentlemen. I state that all orders of execution were carried out successfully. Both former banking executive, Michael Henshaw, and the radical environmentalist, Ross Evans have been terminated." Ellenberg looked over the members. "Both Max Merrell and Drake McCreiess have served this society, The System, with honor."

At the mention of Max Merrell, Cynthia leaned back in her chair and held eye contact with Ellenberg. Ellenberg broke eye contact and placed newspaper clippings related to the deaths of the condemned men on the table. Cynthia picked them up and briefly looked them over before she passed them to her left.

"Gentlemen, it is now time for new cases." Cynthia smiled as she put giddiness to her voice. "Mr. Ellenberg being the newest member will start. Mr. Ellenberg, please feel free to stand or sit when presenting. Whatever makes you comfortable."

"I will remain seated." Ellenberg cleared his throat. "Cynthia. Gentlemen. The case I bring forward today is one that I am confident will be approved by everyone. This case involves a former CEO of a now defunct energy company. The energy company I am talking about is Copen Energy and the CEO is Bernard Benny Shills." Ellenberg paused.

"Copen Energy was one of the world's leading energy companies and claimed over one hundred billion in revenue in the year nineteen ninety-eight. Copen employed over twenty thousand people and was recognized by the leading financial institutions as one of the most innovative companies in the world. We now know that Copen's financial condition was built on fraud." Ellenberg noticed Porter stuffing his face with food. "Accounting fraud that was premeditated, universal, and institutionalized. The leader of its downfall was Benny Shills." Ellenberg held up a picture of Shills.

"Copen is now an asset-less corporation more known for willful corruption and fraud than anything else. Benny Shills understood more than anyone that Copen was on the verge of bankruptcy." Ellenberg passed the picture of Shills to his right. "Shills ordered the sale of all Copen securities. Copen's stock was at its highest value of hundred twenty per share. Shills encouraged investors to purchase Copen or hold steady...all while he sold. Knowing the share price would soon be worth pennies on the dollar. Benny Shills was indicted for insider trading and numerous counts of fraud." Ellenberg sighed. He noticed Cynthia staring toward the ceiling.

"Because of incompetence within the judicial system, incompetent prosecutor, lost evidence, etcetera, investors who trusted Shills lost billions. Thousands of employees lost jobs and savings. Families were lost. Trust in our judicial system, trust in our corporations, were lost." Ellenberg held up another picture of Benny Shills. "I ask the members of this society, The System, to unanimously approve my case. Approve the execution of Bernard Benny Shills."

"Gentlemen. Mr. Ellenberg asks for the execution of Bernard Benny Shills to be approved. It is noted and will be voted on." Cynthia turned her attention to Porter. "Mr. Porter do you have a case for this year?"

"I do not." Porter slouched in his chair and swirled the ice in his glass.

"It is noted that Mr. Porter does not have a case for this year." Cynthia looked at the General. "General Hathaway, do you have a case for this year?"

"Yes, Ms., Judge Mader. I do have a case." The General moved some papers on the table and found the file he needed.

"Human trafficking victimizes society's most vulnerable individuals." The General stood. "I'm not talking about a governor transporting prostitutes across state lines for his pleasure. I'm not talking about a congressman who runs an adult prostitution ring out of his basement." The General looked toward Porter. "These are cases of adults making choices and decisions. I'm not saying they're not scum, because they are. But! What I'm talking about is the trafficking of children for the purpose of sexual exploitation." The General turned his attention to Cynthia and the others.

"Frightened runaways and immigrants who become trapped in a cycle of violence, prostitution, and forced labor." The General remained confident. "As one of our leading newspapers points out, human trafficking is an atrocious crime where victims, often times children! Are forced, or coerced into prostitution or other forms of sexual exploitation." The General shook his head in disagreement.

"Each year an estimated six to eight hundred thousand people are trafficked against their will." The General leaned on the table with his fists clenched. "More than fourteen thousand here in the United States." General Hathaway paused to allow his last statement to sink in.

"I ask the members of this society...this society that dates back to men such as Thomas Jefferson. A society of chosen people, The System!" The General pounded the table. "To unanimously approve the execution of Carlos 'Buggy' Brown and his partner Alexi Lelaage." General Hathaway held up pictures of Buggy and Alexi.

"These two disgusting excuses for human beings enticed a twelve year old little girl away from her house." The General paused to look over the group. "Once away from her home, the girl was thrown into a prostitution ring." He shrugged his shoulders. "According to documents filed in US District Court...Buggy and Alexi smuggled as many as ten children a month into North Carolina. Buggy and Alexi have become wealthy by practicing their disgusting trade. They were able to hire a smooth talking attorney. That combined with a smart ass overzealous prosecutor...the case was thrown out on technicalities." The General became emotional and he slammed his fist on the table.

"Crackville! Two dead crack heads in Crackville... should be a slam dunk." The General took his seat. "Again, I ask the members of this society, The System, to unanimously approve the execution of Carlos Buggy Brown and Alexi Lelaage."

"Gentlemen. General Hathaway asks for the execution of Carlos Boogy..."

The men interrupted Cynthia in Unison with "Buggy."

"Yes. General Hathaway asks for the execution of Carlos Buggy Brown and Alexi Lelaage to be approved. It is noted and will be voted on." Cynthia took a moment to shuffle over some paperwork.

"Mr. Stallings, do you have a case for this year?" Cynthia held her eye contact with Stallings.

"I do have a case." Stallings looked only at his file. "The case I bring forward today is one that I am confident... confident." He turned his attention to Porter for a moment. He opened his file and took a deep breath.

"I am confident the other members will agree unanimously that orders of execution should be ordered and acted on." Stallings remained seated. "The case I bring forward today is against Tommy Mill. You may not remember Tommy Mill, but I assure you...the families of the loved ones he destroyed will never forget him." He adjusted in his seat and paused to look at Cynthia who had her arms crossed and head down as if she was in deep thought.

"October, nineteen eighty-five, Colorado State College, ROTC program." Stallings continued. "The ROTC program provided our military with intelligent, competent, motivated, and enthusiastic young leaders." He paused again to look at Porter who was fiddling with a quiche cup.

"The ROTC building was not only a place where future military leaders could assemble and focus on leadership development, strategic planning, problem solving, and professional ethics." Stallings was stern. "The building also housed a Department of Defense funded think-tank, which provided research for many of the missiles being used by the US Navy and Air Force." Stallings looked through a file. "The think tank employed over fifty mathematicians that were required to spend at least two thirds of their time on military projects. The school newspaper, *The Daily Goat*, published monthly reports that were submitted to the Department of Defense on behalf of the think-tank, justifying its existence. Through undercover reports *The Goat* was able to convince many at the state college that the think-tank was providing the military, under the Reagan Administration leadership, with weapons that could be used in Central America." He noticed Cynthia yawn and look at her watch. He turned to see Porter take a long drink from his highball glass.

"The building became a lure for anti-war and American protesters, communist, and generally any anti-US cause." Stallings showed no emotion. "Protesters gathered often to chant. No bombs for Central America." He paused. "Tommy Mill was one of those protesters that were supposedly lured there. He was hate filled and he used the very freedoms this country is sworn to provide to spew his hatred." Stallings pulled a picture from the file. "Tommy Mill planned and carried out the bombing of the

Colorado State College ROTC building. A bombing that was so powerful that it leveled a wing of the building and left three people dead." Stallings remained calm. "People that had nothing to do with a military think tank or missiles that were allegedly designed there. Two of the people killed were cadets in their fourth year and the other was a female cadet in her second year that starred in basketball and softball." Stallings paused. "All three had bright futures." He closed the file.

"Mr. Mill has served time for the crime I mentioned. But an attack on our military is a unique circumstance and an example needs to be made." Stallings looked over the people sitting at the table. "I ask the members of The System to unanimously approve the execution of Tommy Mill."

"Thank you. Thank you, Judge Stallings." Cynthia placed her hands on the table.

"Gentlemen, I do not bring a case forward this year. But, we have three strong cases to vote on." Cynthia rose from her seat. "The presentations made today were both heartfelt and convincing. Our meeting is coming to a close for today, but, before we adjourn, I ask that each of us think of the power that our forefathers have endowed us. Not to be taken lightly and never to be used senselessly. We will meet again two days from now. We will cast our votes on the cases made this Thursday, at three thirty." She sat back down. "Today's meeting is adjourned."

***

Ellenberg was drained. The meeting around the pentagon table wasn't exactly what he had envisioned. He thought it would be empowering. Instead he felt nothing. He wasn't thrilled, happy, or sad. He just felt drained. The thought of sanctioning someone else to take another human's life seemed inapt. It was something he had fought against his whole adult life. Even though he accepted his role in the secret society, The System, he never really connected the dots. The dots that led directly to another human being losing his or her life based on a vote he cast; a vote that had no legal standing or Constitutional backing.

Ellenberg sat in a rocking chair looking out his bedroom window. The other members were in rooms spread throughout the large immaculate log cabin. He felt secure and alone. The moon shined bright and reflected off the lake his window overlooked. He took a deep sigh and reached for the telephone located on an end table next to his bed, but felt different about that decision when the phone was held to his ear. He placed the phone down and pulled his cell phone from his pocket, searched the directory, pushed a button and waited for the phone to ring.

* * *

Judge Carson slouched in his comfortable porch chair with his feet propped up on the railing. He slowly sipped a fine scotch from his favorite highball glass as he listened to the Gulf ocean waves crash the beach below. He felt the vibration of his cell phone in his jacket. He pulled it and looked to see who was calling. The name Ellenberg was on the phone LCD. He let the phone continue to vibrate until it stopped. He took a large gulp from the highball glass, which finished the scotch. He stared up at the moon, held the glass up, and shook the ice so that Harriet could hear the ring that the ice and glass made.

"That's number four," Harriet yelled from the kitchen.

"I could use another four fingers. No ice." Carson's voice was weak.

***

Ellenberg punched end on the cell phone once he realized there would be no one answer his call. He threw the phone to his bed and took a deep breath and let it out. He leaned forward in his chair and felt a presence before he heard the bedroom door creak. He quickly turned to see who entered his room.

"Not easy is it?" The General questioned. "We all come here with our experience of this or that. Hoping that something from our past will help us while we are here." The General stepped into the room.

"What helps you?" Ellenberg questioned. "What helps you sleep after you leave here?"

"Sleep? I don't have a problem sleeping." The General looked at his watch.

Ellenberg looked perplexed.

"I had to put my dog down." The General paused and crossed his arms. "I had this dog for twelve years. He

was in pain, but his mind and energy seemed good."
He spoke softly. "I lost sleep wondering if I could have
given him more time." The General stepped closer to
Ellenberg and pointed at him. "I won't lose one second of
sleep over Buggy, Alexi, or Shills. They can go eat shit
in hell for all I care."

"Mill?" Ellenberg looked toward the moon.

"Mill won't make it through." The General pulled a
cigar from his jacket pocket and put it to his nose for
a smell. "Stallings put him up and that surprises me. I
have never known him to be so careless when it comes
to making a case." The General sat on the bed. "That
case is something shit for brains Porter would bring
forward. He never gets anything through."

"Mill has paid his debt to society. The justice system
properly dealt with him. No tricks." Ellenberg turned
to look at the General. "People like Mill. I was told. No
chance of getting involved with what we do here."

"Yeah. I've spent the last day looking over the case.
Won't make it through. You're not going to approve.
I'm not going to approve. And Cynthia? I may not care
for the woman, but she is her father's daughter." The
General put his cigar in his mouth for a taste. "She
won't approve."

"Porter?" Ellenberg asked.

"Politician. No principles. Consensus rules him." The
General shrugged his shoulders. "I am surprised with
Stallings though. He is usually more conscientious."

***

Russ Porter stumbled a bit as he turned the corner, which placed him in the hallway where the bar was located. In one hand was paperwork related to the cases he had heard the day before. In the other hand was an empty wine glass. He wanted more wine. Porter was like many other alcoholics. His drinking was something his body craved and it was constant throughout the day. He preferred wine in the evening before bed.

Porter was relieved to see the door to the bar was open. He put his head down to glance over the paperwork. He felt the presence and heard the footsteps of someone else in the hall so he looked up. It was Stallings. He noticed that Stallings' eyes were locked on him and that his facial expression was one of anger.

"Need a nightcap, Michael?" Porter held his glass up.

Porter barley got his glass raised before it was knocked out of his hand and he was shoved to the wall. He let loose of the papers and they scattered over the floor. He was lifted off his feet as Stallings shoved his forearm into his throat and lifted.

"Jesus," Porter chocked. "Michael, stop. Please."

"God damn it." Stallings cried as he pulled him from the wall and slammed him up against it again. "Fuck you, Porter. You...you son of a...you son of a bitch. Fuck you!"

Stallings let Porter go and he suddenly walked away as Porter fell to his knees stunned.

"We're fucked," Stallings yelled as he rounded the corner. "We are fucked!"

Porter remained on his knees. He quickly crawled around the floor collecting the papers. He gathered the last piece of paper and he started to cry. He lifted to one knee, preparing to lift his large overweight frame. A memory from his past quickly crept into his mind.

:-

"You will pick Richard Hastert as the city's housing and development..."

"Richard Hastert?" Porter interrupted Sells, the single largest donor of his campaign for mayor. "Hastert is a well-known slum lord."

"Richard Hastert is an associate of mine. I wouldn't consider him a friend, but since he provides me with..."

"You make a lot of money from Hastert and off of his dirty dealings." Porter was frustrated. "If you're associated with him. That means I'm associated with him." Porter stepped closer to Sells to show his authority. "I am the mayor of one of the ..."

"You are what I say you are," Sells yelled and pointed his finger into Porter's chest. "Do you understand me? You are what I say you are!"

Porter sighed and stepped back.

"That's right you fat ass." Sells stepped forward and kept his finger in Porter's chest. "Don't ever think you can do anything without my approval. Got me!"

Porter lowered his head and started to whimper.

"You can sob all you want, but by the end of the day I will see Hastert where I want him." Sells lifted Porter's head by placing his fingers under his chin and quickly pushing up. "Got it!"

"Yes. Got it." Porter continued to whimper.

"And another thing, don't you ever interrupt me again!" Sells turned to walk away.

Cynthia's laugh from down stairs brought Porter back to his current situation. He remained kneeling on one knee and began to sob. He looked for the wine glass and saw that it was still intact. He crawled toward it.

***

Bully was finishing up with the breakfast setting as the members gathered around. The members made small talk as they waited for Cynthia to enter and announce, "Breakfast served."

"Bully, do you have any tomato juice this year?" The General asked as he pulled an unlit cigar from his jacket to chew on.

"Yes sir. I do. I will have it on the table soon." Bully smiled. "As I remember, you are the only one that enjoys a glass of tomato juice."

"Keeps the scurvy away ya know." The General looked toward the others.

"Didn't know scurvy was an issue these days, General Hathaway?" Bully walked away.

"Scurvy is caused by a lack of vitamin C and use to be common among sailors and pirates." The General looked toward Porter who seemed to lack very little in the ways of provisions.

"You were a Marine, General." Cynthia entered into the conversation. "Bully will bring the tomato juice."

Cynthia turned to face the group.

"Gentlemen, let's take the next half hour to have our breakfast before we settle around the table."

Cynthia noticed Porter was sitting by himself.

"Mr. Porter, no blueberry muffins this year?" Cynthia acted overly surprised.

Porter shook his head no.

"That is not like you Mr. Porter. Now you go get some," Cynthia demanded. "Bully made them especially for you. Added extra blueberries just like you like."

"Extra blueberries? Sounds about like you, Porter," Stallings said more for himself to hear, but the others overheard. He and Porter made eye contact for a brief moment.

"Bully. Bully," Cynthia called out.

"Ma'am?" Bully slowly turned.

"Bully, please hurry along with the coffee, orange juice, and the tomato juice to prevent scurvy for the General." Cynthia turned to the men. "We have work to finish, gentlemen."

***

All members except Cynthia were seated at the pentagon shaped table. In front of each of them was a bible. The Bibles were all very old. The Bibles were used each year since the year 1890 for the same reason, the voting held at the pentagon table. The men remained silent as Cynthia situated herself in her chair. She placed her Bible in front of her. She scooted her chair forward and looked each man in the eye individually.

"Gentlemen, I am sure all of you used your time wisely and studied each case thoroughly." Cynthia crossed her arms on the table.

The men nodded in unison.

"Does anyone need more time?" Cynthia asked.

The men replied "no" in unison.

Cynthia turned the recorder on.

"Gentlemen, we will now vote on the cases presented. We all understand the rules." Cynthia paused. "Although a unanimous decision is preferred, a simple majority is all that is needed for approval."

Cynthia pushed her Bible out in front of her.

"We shall begin." Cynthia looked toward Ellenberg. "In the case of Bernard Shills? Those that approve will place their left hand on the Bible and say, aye. Those that oppose will remain silent." Cynthia paused for a brief moment.

"Approve?" Cynthia questioned.

All members approved by placing their left hands on their Bibles and in unison said, "Aye."

"Oppose?" Cynthia quickly questioned.

The room remained silent.

"The ayes have it. The execution of Bernard Benny Shills has been ordered." Cynthia smiled at Ellenberg.

Cynthia turned her attention to General Hathaway who did not acknowledge her look. He remained stoic, looking forward, looking through Cynthia.

"In the case of Carlos Buggy Brown and Alexi LeLaage." Cynthia paused for a moment. "Approve?"

All members approved by placing their hands on their Bibles and saying "aye."

"Oppose?" Cynthia was only going through the motion, as no one answered. "The ayes have it. The execution of Carlos Buggy Brown and Alexi LeLaage has been ordered."

Cynthia made eye contact with Stallings. Ellenberg had a moment of discomfort. He inconspicuously took a deep breath and let it out.

"In the case of Tommy Mill. Approve?" Cynthia asked with a smile on her face.

Cynthia, Stallings, and Porter approved by placing their left hands on their Bibles and then said "aye."

"Oppose?" Cynthia knew deep down she wouldn't get a majority but she was hoping for the approval of at least Ellenberg. Knowing Ellenberg would oppose only confirmed to her that he was a Carson man, part of the old school. He could be changed she thought, but it would take time. After all, with the proper persuasion, Stallings could be made to change.

"Oppose!" Both the General and Ellenberg sounded off in unison as they sat staring at Cynthia.

Cynthia only looked forward, knowing that both Ellenberg and the General were staring at her.

"The ayes have it." Cynthia allowed a smile to be seen. "The ayes have it. The execution of Tommy Mill has been ordered."

Ellenberg sat stunned by the order. He never imagined that he would be part of something that would allow Tommy Mill to be executed. If Mill laid on a gurney and took a lethal injection provided by the State, Ellenberg would have never thought about it. But this is not what Judge Carson promised. The line that separated him from the vigilante, the thin gray line, was crossed and he was not comfortable.

***

Both Ellenberg and the General stood near Ellenberg's car. Ellenberg finished packing his luggage in the trunk. The General leaned on Ellenberg's car and pulled a cigar from his jacket. He offered Ellenberg one and was turned down. The General was careful to bite only the first ring of the cigar off. He lit the cigar and let out a sigh. He enjoyed the outdoors, and he enjoyed a good cigar.

"You're stunned by the Mill case. I can tell," the General stated.

"You're not," Ellenberg quickly shot back.

"I won't lose any sleep." The General moved from the car, allowing Ellenberg to get to the driver's side door.

"Listen. A few years back there was a retired judge. A judge...Judge Carter was his name. While Carter was on the bench he presided over domestic violence." The General pulled a nice long drag from the cigar and let it out. "So a wife is standing in front of this judge because the husband attacked her. The husband crushed her voice box. The wife begins to testify but she can't speak all that well. She speaks softly." The General looked out toward the lake. "The shit bag, Carter, tells her she's going to have to speak up." He looked into the eyes of Ellenberg. "That same judge, Carter, dismissed a protective order against a man with a well-known violent past. Few weeks later the man walks into his wife's place of work, douses her with gasoline, and sets her on fire. She survived. Third degree burns over ninety percent of her body, but she survived."

"General Hathaway, you are..."

"My point is that your idol, Carson, didn't approve the case against Judge Carter. Carson felt it was out of our reach. The justice system didn't have a crack at him first." The General paused to take another long drag. "The judge, Judge Carter, didn't do anything illegal. Betrayed the public trust. Sure he did. Carson didn't approve, but he carried out the order. And I bet he didn't lose a second's sleep."

"What are you saying, General Hathaway?" Ellenberg felt queasy asking the question.

"Well. Sometimes. Sometimes..."

"I'll be fine, General." Ellenberg interrupted the General. "My obligations will be fulfilled. We're judged by that you know?"

Well, you thought wrong

Jimmy Brannon lay on his couch in his apartment in front of the T.V. and passively watched a rerun of one of his favorite sitcoms, Friends. It was an evening like most for Jimmy. He was alone with his T.V. and wearing boxer shorts and a tee shirt. He changed into his nightwear as soon as he got home from the university and he stayed in them until he had to change for work the next day. He loved his Lassie tee shirts. One of his favorite memories was of when he was a child watching the television show Lassie. The shirt he wore was one that depicted Lassie jumping over a log.

Jimmy slowly ate his favorite cereal, Tony the Tiger. The bowl of milk and cereal lay on his stomach and he would slowly lift the spoon filled with cereal from the bowl and into his mouth. He would spill some in route to his mouth, but it never concerned him. He would just pick the dropping with his fingers from his shirt and plop them into his mouth. The milk would dry.

Jimmy was upset and stewing over Tommy Mill. He was sure he had rid himself of that part of his past that Tommy Mill represented. The thought of Mill breathing fresh and free air had never crossed his mind. His mother had assured him that the prison system would swallow young Tommy Mill up.

Jimmy began to get angry as Jennifer Anniston and Brad Pitt shared a table together.

"Why would you leave Jen for Angie," Jimmy yelled at the television.

In a fit, he threw the bowl onto the floor, splashing milk and cereal.

"Shit. Shit. Shit!" Jimmy sat up.

He picked the box of Tony the Tiger up from the coffee table in front of him and cradled it tightly. The cereal box allowed a distant memory of his late grandfather and his mother to enter his mind.

:-

The office Cynthia and Jimmy were in was made dim by the dark wood that permeated the room. The bookshelves were from floor to ceiling and they housed many years worth of law and history books. The room was lit mostly by sunshine and stained leaded glass lamps that were as dated as the office itself. The law office was separated from the main house to allow privacy for both the clients and the owner, Judge George Mader.

Jimmy sat in the rocking chair that decorated one side of the desk while Cynthia slowly walked the room, studying the many books and explaining the story about how her son was involved with others who created a large explosion that brought down part of an ROTC building on a college campus. Judge George Mader sat silent behind his desk, becoming more irritated with each word his daughter spoke.

"It is true. He is associated with these men, but I think..."

"Stop," Judge George Mader shouted. "Stop right there and say no more. God damn it!"

"Daddy. I really don't believe..."

"Believe!" The Judge cut his daughter off. "You better believe he is neck deep in it. He planned it. He had a part in it." He smiled. "He just didn't have the guts to honor his role in it. He left his friends hanging. The gutless little bastard."

"Hey." Jimmy leaped from his chair.

Judge George Mader leaped from his chair and slapped his grandson. Jimmy absorbed the slap and fell face first into the sofa crying.

"Daddy!" Cynthia cried.

The Judge stepped toward his daughter. "Don't you say a God damn thing. I don't want to hear from you or him." He looked at his grandson and then kicked him in the ass. "You think he has always been this screwed up? Hell no he hasn't! There was an evolution to this."

"What are you say..."

"What I'm saying is that you are a miserable excuse for a grandson." Judge George Mader stood over his grandson. "You will say anything you have to say to get out of the moment you're in." He paused. "You cover your lies later if you can. You..."

"He was only trying to explain..."

"No!" The Judge silenced the room by shouting. "Let me think."

Judge George Mader stood in the middle of the room and pondered his next thought and moves.

"I've worked too hard. I have done my best to make you something." George looked at his daughter. "I won't let this half-wit son of yours get in the way."

"What will you do?" Cynthia stood in front of her father.

"You make a mistake and the family conspires to compound the problem by becoming enablers." Judge George Mader turned to look at his grandson. "I'm not an enabler," he shouted and then moved to sit in the rocking chair. "You are out young man. Out! I will not hear of you again."

"What will you do?" Cynthia demanded as her son cried out loud.

"I have a friend who owes me and I will cash in. I hate cashing this chip in on this, but I have no choice." The Judge rocked back and forth. "His daughter got entangled with a man. Before you know it. She's hooked on heroine and becoming the newest porn star on the big screen."

"What did you do?" Jimmy asked as he sobbed.

"Well. She is now an anchor on one of the national news networks." The Judge stopped rocking and stared at his grandson.

"And what about her boyfriend?" Jimmy sobbed.

"The man she was entangled with became shark shit." The Judge grinned.

Jimmy lay on the couch clutching the cereal box and crying. He twisted to get comfortable and noticed some flakes fall from the box. He slowly picked the flakes up and placed them in his mouth and cried as a memory of a conversation he overheard his grandfather have with his universities chancellor crept into his mind.

:-

Judge George Mader sat in the office of the chancellor and waited until his friend arrived. The chancellor, Dev Bruce, was in charge of one of the largest multi-campus state university systems in the country and Judge George Mader needed a favor.

Judge Mader heard his friend Dev speak with his administrative assistant from behind the closed door. The conversation Dev was having with the assistant was a little longer than he expected so Judge Mader rose from his seat and looked out the window. He took note of the students playing the game hacky sack in a court yard. He heard the door to the office open so he turned to greet Chancellor Bruce.

"Judge George Mader." Chancellor Bruce beat the Judge to the greeting. "To what do I owe the pleasure of this visit?"

"Cut the crap, Chancellor." The Judge was in no mood for pleasantries. "You know why I'm here."

"Yes. Yes. I guess I do." Chancellor Bruce understood the meeting was strictly oriented toward business. "What do you want from me, or what is it I can do for you?"

Chancellor Bruce knew that Judge George Mader would one day be coming to cash in a favor; he only wished it was something he could accommodate.

"I have a half witted grandson and I need you..."

"The young man who is outside the door?" The Chancellor pointed toward the door. "Well I'm quite certain we could get him into a developmental..."

"He's not mentally handicapped you idiot. He's just a fucking screwball." The Judge became irritated. "No more of a screwball than anyone else in this place though."

"So he needs to take classes. I'm sure we can..."

"He needs a job. I want him to be a professor of someth...."

"A professor?" Chancellor Bruce acted shocked. "But Judge. I thought you said he is half witted?"

"He is a very stupid person but that doesn't mean he's disqualified to be a professor." The Judge looked out the window. "He can teach hacky sack or some stupid shit like that."

"But Judge Mader, I've..."

"You going to fight with me on this?" The Judge removed a disk from his suit pocket and tossed it on the desk. "After receiving the help I provided. The help that your daughter needed."

"And what would that be?" Chancellor Bruce asked as he pointed toward the disk while moving to sit behind his desk.

"That would be your daughter taking it in the ass." Judge Mader shook his head in disgust.

"I thought all of that was destroyed?"

"Well, you thought wrong." Judge Mader moved to stand in front of Chancellor Bruce's desk and looked down on him. "I was hoping you wouldn't argue with me over the favor."

"George. George. You know I will help you any way I can, but why professor? This is the finest academic..."

"His mother." The Judge paused for a sigh. "My daughter says that it will help him with his esteem issues." Judge Mader rolled his eyes and looked to the ceiling. "Esteem. Narcissism. Whatever the fuck you want to call it...she believes..."

"I can help." The Chancellor interrupted.

"That's what I thought." Judge Mader crossed his arms.

"I would bet we can get him something in the next..."

"Now! He needs a position now." Judge Mader demanded.

"All we have is a history position avail..."

"He's a historian then. Good." The Judge smiled and walked toward the door.

"But I have highly qualified people who are lined up and waiting to be interviewed for that position." Chancellor Bruce pleaded.

"You also have a daughter who has been filmed sucking lots of different dick." The Judge opened the door.

"May I ask what is behind this?" Chancellor Bruce picked up the disk, broke it, and threw it in the trashcan, understanding that it was not the last disk with his daughter on it. "What is behind all this?"

"Nope." Judge Mader stood at the door. "Just get it done." The Judge held the door open. He made eye contact with his grandson and then Chancellor Bruce. His name is now Brannon. Not Mader." He closed the door behind him.

Chancellor Bruce put his hands behind his head and leaned back in his seat. He looked at a picture of his daughter and her family. He looked at the picture of his daughter receiving an Emmy for the best documentary. He sighed and picked up the phone. The need to tell his daughter how much he loved her overwhelmed him.

Jimmy continued to cry as he slowly picked flakes from his shirt and ate them. He slowly fell asleep with his box of Tony the tiger clutched in his arms.

SueAnn smiled

SueAnn English and Branch Stevens sat before their boss, Carl Brenner. The large oak table was way too big for what they needed but the conference room was Brenner's favorite. He enjoyed sitting at the end of the table and receiving or disseminating information. Many of the meetings he sat in were formal and central to the department's goals. The weekly meetings he held with SueAnn and Stevens was anything but essential to the department's overall scope, but he did enjoy the time at the end of the table. SueAnn felt no need for the meetings and she was sure Stevens felt as she did, but he always used the meetings to get his nose as close to Brenner's ass as he could.

"Sir, I'm going to move forward with this little girl found in South Bend, Indiana," Stevens reported.

"Remind me again," Brenner requested.

"It's been all over the news, sir." Stevens gloated. "Little girl kidnapped by her mom's boyfriend in Michigan. He crossed state line. Check that. He actually crossed several state lines." Stevens looked at both SueAnn and Brenner. "We have evidence that he moved from Michigan to Iowa, and then into Indiana. He feels the pressure so he offs the little girl and then himself."

"Yeah, that one, ended, not good." Brenner cringed. "You'll present that one to the Senior Agent, Kelly."

"Yes Sir." Stevens puffed out his chest.

SueAnn kept her head down reading over her notes as Brenner and Stevens discussed their case. She was never one to care about the responsibilities of others unless it directly impacted her.

"Agent English, what do you have for us today?" Brenner asked. "How about some good news?" Brenner paused for a reaction from SueAnn, but she kept to her notes. "Just kidding. If there was good news there would be no need for the Federal Criminal Investigative Command Unit." Brenner chuckled to himself.

"Sir, I am actually working on something I think is exciting. I am working with a data specialist to confirm some numbers and I ..."

"Data specialist." Stevens interrupted while laughing. "That sounds exciting. I'm so glad I didn't purchase this chair because I'm only using the edge of it."

"I do think it's a little more exciting than tracking the last known sites of the latest little white girl to go missing." SueAnn held her look into the eyes of Stevens until he looked away.

"Go on Agent English," Brenner jumped in, "fill me. I mean us in."

"Sir, I have been running data on missing people." SueAnn started.

"We do that here? Who knew?" Stevens felt the need to say something sarcastic.

Brenner silenced Stevens with a hand gesture and looked at SueAnn as if to tell her to continue.

"There have been some high profile people that have ended up dead over the years and their murders still remain unsolved." SueAnn looked through some of her paperwork. "When I say high profile. I am suggesting that these people are not movie or sports stars. They are people that make the news for going on trial for a crime and then they are let off because of a judicial technicality. The thing is..." SueAnn paused to look at some data. "These people are scattered all over the States. For example, take this banking exec Henshaw. He met his demise in Florida. This radical environmentalist, Ross Evans, California." SueAnn looked toward both Brenner and Stevens. "What they have in common is that they made the news for a crime, got off, and ended up dead years later." She sighed. "Coincidence? Maybe."

"Are you saying..." Stevens tried to interject.

"What I'm saying is that the deaths of these people are not natural causes. They meet an early and untimely death." SueAnn stopped Stevens. "What I'm saying is that there are several of these cases that are similar. It looks like anywhere from two to four a year. Dating back to...well...we have only run the numbers back to nineteen eighty-nine." SueAnn sighed. "Sir, a lot of these people, but not all, end up dead, anywhere from seven to ten years after they have been let go or have fallen out of the news. They end up dead and they get very little national news, if any at all."

"You are thinking..." Brenner tried to question.

"I think someone didn't forget. The news media may have let it go." SueAnn smiled. "But someone, or something, has a hard time letting it go."

"Are you working on anything else?" Brenner leaned back in his chair.

"Softball, Sir." SueAnn sighed. "I have been tasked with getting the softball league up and running this year."

"FBI's Health Care Fraud Division always wins it." Stevens shook his head. "They're tough."

"Agent Stevens, you will present your report to the Senior Agent on Friday." Brenner announced. "Let's get together next Wednesday at the same time." Brenner paused to rise from his seat. "Agent English, the Senior Agent might want to speak with you." Brenner looked at Stevens. "Something about what fields he would prefer to play on this year."

***

SueAnn and Stevens walked a crowded hall toward an elevator that would take them to their floor. SueAnn didn't think much of her co-worker. She didn't dislike him, but she didn't like him either. She never thought of him unless he was in her path. Stevens seemed to her as a person who always had something to say, regardless of the situation. It appeared to her that he could not be quiet, but never said anything that was important.

Stevens purposely bumped into a female co-worker as she walked toward him and SueAnn. The co-workers papers fell to the floor. Stevens turned to watch the coworker bend over to pick up the paperwork. He giggled. The female coworker turned to Stevens and gave an expression of anger.

"Really?" Stevens laughed. "Act mad if you want. Love to see you bend," Stevens said under his breath as he elbowed SueAnn in the ribs to get a reaction.

SueAnn never reacted to antics such as the one Stevens just demonstrated. Her mission for that day was to get on an elevator and go sift through data.

"So are you going to play on the softball team this year or are you just setting it up?" Stevens pushed the elevators down button. "Love to go down." He smiled large after that comment. "We can always use more girls on the team."

SueAnn quickly had a daydream pass through as she waited for the elevator.

⁂

SueAnn turned and faced Stevens while they stood alone in an elevator. SueAnn hit Stevens with a quick jab to the chest and immediately followed the jab up with an overhand right to Stevens' mouth. Stevens dropped to his knees and began to spit out blood and teeth as he struggled to remain conscience. SueAnn delivered four vicious kicks to his head.

"Grow." SueAnn delivered a kick. "Some." Another kick. "Fucking." Another kick. "Balls." SueAnn threw a

final kick that pushed Stevens' head through the wall
of the elevator.

The elevator door opened for SueAnn and Stevens,
and the elevator was empty.

"I tell you." Stevens continued on with his conversation
about softball, unaware that SueAnn had a daydream.
"She sure could play. No one would have ever guessed that
that chubby little girl was so athletic." SueAnn entered
the elevator and Stevens followed. "She could pitch too."
Stevens looked around. "Alone on an elevator."

SueAnn smiled.

Three orders...

Standing atop a six-story parking garage made Ellenberg feel a little weird. He stayed near his car. The thought of looking over the edge never crossed his mind. He knew what was below; he was just down there a few minutes before. He could see the skyline of Miami so he understood he wasn't alone. It was just the thought of meeting a man like Max Merrell that scared him. When he was a police officer in southern Florida he witnessed the after effects of what a man like Max Merrell and a six-story parking garage could do to people who knew too much. Carson assured him that Merrell was nothing like some gangster, but he knew what happened to people who pissed Max Merrell off. He knew the story about how the southern Florida drug trade killed Merrell's younger brother, and how Merrell and his cohorts dropped a very large homemade explosive device on a textile factory in Matamoros, Mexico.

Ellenberg heard a vehicle coming up the ramp from the fifth floor. He looked at his watch (11:22 pm) and then toward the entrance to the sixth floor. He was told to meet with Merrell at 11:30 p.m. He knew Merrell wouldn't be late but he didn't know what to expect as far as a vehicle he might drive. The vehicle that turned the corner was a current year Volkswagen Jetta. He didn't take Merrell for a sedan type guy. He looked on as the vehicle parked.

He was dumbfounded when a woman rose from the vehicle.

"Boo," Said Merrell as he stood behind Ellenberg.

"What the..." Ellenberg jumped.

"The meeting is here. Doesn't mean I have to park here." Merrell circled Ellenberg.

"You...you startled me." Ellenberg laughed nervously.

"Yeah, I have that way about me, I guess." Merrell held out his hand. "What do you have for us?"

"Three different orders or missions." Ellenberg handed Merrell three different envelopes and held onto the fourth. "Three different sets of orders. One order will have two different elements." He paused as Merrell opened one. "The General says that his informant believes that the two hang close so..."

"So it should be easy?" Merrell was stern.

"Well I wouldn't think it would be as complicated as two separate missions." Ellenberg handed Merrell the forth envelope.

"You ever accomplished such a mission?" Merrell smiled as he asked the question. "No. I doubt there is any blood on your hands."

"The envelope is payment for the three orders and a bonus for an outstanding job last year. If you need more funds for expenses just give me a call." Ellenberg crossed his arms and disregarded Merrell's last question and statement.

"I'm sure there will be plenty as always and anything I don't use I'll return." Merrell looked in the envelope.

"I'll be waiting ..."

"Drake wants out." Merrell interrupted Ellenberg.

"Drake wants out? When? Why?" Ellenberg became nervous.

"I've discussed this with Judge Carson. He wants out." Merrell stepped toward Ellenberg. "He feels that he has fulfilled all obligations. He will work these last orders, but he wants us to start looking at getting him out."

"I wouldn't know where to start." Ellenberg stepped back.

"Don't worry about it. I'll start looking for a replacement for him and Kevin." Merrell softened at the thought of Kevin.

"I'm sorry about Kevin. I heard a lot about him from Judge Carson and I'm just sorry I didn't know him." Ellenberg looked toward the Miami skyline.

"You knew him. You just never met him. You investigated us for a couple years. You had to know him."

"I guess what I meant was..."

"You know I have an Army SF background. SF has some real degenerate social misfits." Merrell paused. "But there are some real good dudes there as well."

"Let's talk when...you..."

"Sure." Merrell turned and walked away.

Ellenberg stood stunned. He watched Merrell disappear into the stairway and into the darkness. A quick glance back allowed him to pause and think about how he knew Max Merrell.

:-

"Young man, you need to let this one go. There are plenty of others that you can be putting your cross-hairs on." Judge Carson sat behind his desk.

"Let it go, your honor?" Ellenberg stood before the judge, flabbergasted. "Sir, they are cops who have been on a killing spree. They are dirty cops."

"Dirty!" Carson sat forward and pounded his desk with an open hand. "Those men are doing this area a great service if you ask me." He paused to rise from his seat. "The people they kill are poison."

"Yes, but they are acting like vigilantes. No better than the drug lords they're killing. And I'm sure they're behind that military style assault at the Opalaka airfield." Ellenberg pleaded.

"Yes. Go on." Carson smirked.

"Go on? What do you mean?" Ellenberg questioned.

"Tell me what you know." Carson moved from around his desk.

"I know both Max Merrell and Drake McCreiess are Dade County cops who also serve in the Army Guard... in a Special Forces unit." Ellenberg sat in a nice leather chair that Judge Carson provided those that came to his chambers. "Kevin Halcot is just a young man in the guard unit who fell in with them. He goes to school at UM when he's not wearing a uniform."

"What else do you know?" Carson asked.

"Merrell's brother Mike was a rookie cop who was gunned down by some low level whacked out drug pusher." Ellenberg paused. "Merrell and McCreiess went on their rampage soon after, and they have racked up a lot of..."

"A lot of trash." Judge Carson interrupted. "They take out the trash. And I need them. I need them more than they need the prison system."

"Sir?" Ellenberg needed more information.

í

Ellenberg stood for a moment looking at the Miami skyline, not really sure where he should go or what he should do.

Like we matter

Retired Senator Russell Fellow slouched in one of Senator Claire Miller's sofas, which were positioned in front of her solid walnut desk. The desk represented her attitude when it came to what she believed. She could be soft and congenial when she needed compromise, but she was as hard as the desk she sat behind when she was not willing to budge, and that seemed to be most of the time, late in her career.

"Oh Claire, I don't know. I was excited when the President asked me to head this committee." Fellow sighed. "Now I just don't know. I just wish he never had asked me. I was happy being retired. I have my own think tank. I..."

"Russell. Russell. Why put yourself through this? Being a retired Senator should be about writing books and speeches. Okay, okay, in your case, the think tank you...you...conjured up..."

"Oh hell. You'll be conjuring up some worthless think tank one day. It's what people like us do. We win and lose elections. Then we want to feel relevant so we create a think tank that produces the information that helps our cause or causes." Fellow loosened his tie. "It's what we do to feel..."

"Like we matter." Claire interrupted. "We don't." Claire paused. "We just hope to get on some sympathetic cable network so we can feel useful." Claire looked at Fellow's and felt remorse. "I wish there were only four channels on the television like there use to be." She paused again. "More channels equal more opportunity for people like us to look foolish."

"It's not that easy anymore." Fellow shook his head and cringed.

"No it's not." Claire shrugged her shoulders.

"The President wants this next justice nominee to be agreeable, or at least tolerable to the other side of the aisle. He really doesn't have it in him to fight this out in the media." Fellow sat up straight in his chair.

"Agreeable? Tolerable?" Claire smiled.

"As agreeable or as tolerable as we can get, Claire." Fellow rose from his seat. "The President doesn't want to sell his soul here, but he also understands what he is up against."

"Russell, you know as well as I that regardless of the pick, left or right. Or center for that matter. They will scream. We are talking about picking a judge for the highest court in the land with a life time appointment." Claire leaned back in her chair.

"Judge Cynthia Mader. You submitted her name." Fellow stepped closer to Claire's desk. "You are the ranking member. Why Judge Mader?"

"I have spoken to the Chairman of the Judicial Committee about Judge Mader and he seems open. He likes the female part, and far as anyone knows, she has no writings on record that the fringe groups can nail him down on." Claire let her hair down. "She has been a federal judge for a short time and her past...well there is not much to crow about." She looked Fellow in the eyes. "With Judge Mader, the President wouldn't have to sell his soul and I doubt he would get much of a fight."

"No fight." Fellow's eyebrows lifted and he grinned.

"There is always someone who will raise a stink. It would be strictly partisan though, and seen as that." Claire shook her head in disagreement. "There is always some group out there. Some fly by night groups. Here today gone tomorrow. Hit and run politics."

"Her late father, Judge George Mader wrote..."

"Judge George Mader is dead. Why would you check into his leanings?"

"Well I ..."

"Judge Cynthia Mader is not her father, Senator Fellow." Claire interrupted. "She is no romantic. She understands that both political parties have wiped their Asses with the Constitution long ago."

"Claire!" Fellow left his mouth open.

"What?" Claire would hear no argument.

"The other members of the Judicial Committee?" Fellow went back to the task at hand.

"She will get through the process. I know her. She is strong and charming. She can stand up to any scrutiny."

Benny grinned

Ted Fienberg loved the city of Chicago. He loved his corner office that allowed him to look over the city and the great lake. He always dreamed of sailing the great lake but he never had time. He rarely left his office; sleeping and showering at his office had become common over the years. He walked to the large window to get a look before his next appointment. He looked at his watch. His client was late, but his next client was always late. Fienberg always built in time for his next client's tardiness. Of course he would collect for the time. His next client understood the value of a fine attorney, and Ted Fienberg was one of the best.

Fienberg turned when he heard the phone ring. He knew Benny Shills had arrived. He answered the phone and asked his administrative assistant to send Benny in. He quickly glanced at a picture on his desk, the picture of his deceased wife. He wished he had taken her last wishes to heart; the wishes for him to get out of law and take time to do anything other than work. The door quickly opened and in rushed his client.

"What's up, Ted. You fat bastard." Benny grinned at his verbal slap.

"Well. Benny. I have actually lost forty-three pounds since I last saw you." Ted answered with a sigh and a shrug.

"Really." Benny laughed. "Ted, when you're five foot ten and weigh three hundred twenty pounds, it takes more than forty to make a splash." Benny walked to the window to take in the city. "Call me if you take off sixty more and I might...I'm not real sure, but I might be able to get you laid."

"Benny..."

"What a suck ass of a place." Benny interrupted Ted. "Cubs still suck. Usually mathematically out of the playoffs three weeks into the season."

"Benny, you never stop amazing me." Ted sat behind his desk and turned to look in Benny's direction.

"Lots of people say that." Benny walked to sit in a love seat in the middle of the room.

"What are you doing?" Ted turned again to keep his focus on his sycophantic client.

"You know I'm here to settle this thing with the ex-bitch." Benny paused. "What, you not buying it? I want those kids, Ted."

"That's not what I mean, Benny." Ted opened the newspaper on his desk. "I'm looking at page two of the life section and guess what I see?"

"Gee, Ted. What do you see?" Benny leaned back and crossed his legs. "I bet...."

"I see four large breasts with you in the middle of them." Ted stood. "Another wild night I'm sure."

"Let me see that." Benny stood and walked to Ted's desk to get a look at what his attorney was worried about. "Oh that." Benny kept looking at the picture. "One got a way. Damn," he murmured under his breath.

The picture was one that had Benny standing between two large breasted blondes. He looked drunk as he held a champagne bottle in one hand and a glass in the other. His arms were wrapped around the waists of the women.

"We can't afford stuff like this Benny." Ted shook his head. "We don't need you in the press." He looked at Benny. "And I don't want to know about how fantastic the party was."

"No. Not even a little?" Benny grinned.

"We're damn lucky you're not sitting behind bars right now." Ted sighed. "We don't..."

"Did you invite me here to shovel sand in my face or what?" Benny scowled. "I'm sure the bill is already in the mail for this meeting." Benny rolled his eyes. "You Jew bastard, you."

"The Congressmen want their money. They say you promised them." Ted held some remorse for his client.

"Like I would promise blood to a tick," Benny hollered. "I owe them nothing."

"They stepped up to squash the Congressional hearings, Benny. They..."

"They stopped the hearings because I had information that would have implicated a whole bunch of those cocksuckers." Benny walked back to his seat. "They get nothing."

"Benny." Ted pleaded.

"Listen to me. Just listen for a moment. We will do what we did last year with those two bloodsuckers." Benny's tone of voice was calm. "We'll start another charity for some shitty little African country. This time we'll help the children of Mozam what the hell ever."

"Mozambique." Ted shook his head no.

"That's it. Stop shaking your head until I tell you how we can help the little niggers."

"Good God Benny." Ted new that his client was generally not a good person, but he always seemed stunned by how low Benny would sink.

"Just listen, Fienberg, you Hebrew, fat ass, blood sucker." Benny shouted. "You know I am genuinely frustrated at how forthright your fat ass can be."

"I'm sorry, but I..."

"Invite the normal do-gooder crowd." Benny crossed his legs. "You know. The people who think they're someone they're not." He put his hands behind his head and looked to the ceiling. "With the money we raise. We give point zero two five on the dollar to the little niggers." He noticed Ted's uneasiness. "Okay the little African Mozambiqueians." He looked away. "We take our normal cut and the ticks get the rest."

"Benny. I don't want..." Ted tried to get a word in.

"It'll be fine, Ted. Tell them that's the best deal they're getting."

Ted leaned back in his chair; knowing he would not be able to persuade his client to do anything other than what his client wanted to do. He knew Bernard Benny Shills better than anyone, better than Benny knew himself.

You two drive hard...

Dion Vargas paced back and forth beside his van. It was a hot Florida day and the dark van, parked near a swamp with no overhead tree cover, soaked up the sun. The vegetation was overgrown and other than the dirt fire break, there was no other manmade object to be seen.

Vargas wiped the sweat from his forehead and looked down the road and then at his watch. The vehicle shook, and pounding from the inside could be heard.

"Shut up!" Vargas yelled as if there was no one for miles that could hear him, and he was right.

The vehicle shook again.

"I said shut the fuck up or I'll just shoot you and leave you for the fucking gators." Vargas pounded on the vehicle hard.

The sound of a vehicle coming toward his position had Vargas turn from the van and look. He saw a silver Lexus DS Sedan speeding toward him. He stepped away from the van and walked toward the oncoming car. The sedan came to a slow halt behind the van and Vargas was there to greet Buggy and Alexi as the driver side window rolled down.

"Hey, hey, hey." Vargas worked up a big smile.

"This better be good, Vargas." Buggy put his sunglasses on as he opened the door to get out.

"Yeah Vargas. I want to see money." Alexi stepped out of the car and walked toward the van.

"It's Dion, guys." Vargas opened his arms. "Aren't we there yet? First names. You know."

"You sell..."

"Damn, girl you look good." Vargas cut Alexi off.

"Yeah. Yeah. I bet I lost weight too," Alexi chuckled. "I'm in no mood for meaningless shit-chat, Vargas. Just open the doors."

Vargas frowned.

"OK. Dion." Alexi gave in.

"Just open the doors, Vargas." Buggy broke into the conversation.

"Better be good, Dion," Alexi snapped, "drag my ass out here in this swampy looking shit."

"Only thing that should be out here is gator's." Buggy looked around.

"This is special shit just for you. Because I know you like special shit." Vargas flashed a smile and opened the rear compartment to the van. "What do you think, Buggy?"

Buggy and Alexi looked in the van and saw five young women staring at them. Three of the women were Hispanic and the other two were Asian. The women were dirty and looked as if they were physically roughed up. They were definitely in need of water and food.

"What the fuck is this, Vargas," Buggy shouted. "What the hell are we…"

"All right, all right." Vargas interrupted. "I cut the price by six points."

"Ten points!" Alexi turned to walk to the car. "Or you can shoot them bitches in the head and leave them for the gators." Alexi stood by the passenger door. "Then what good are they?"

"Shootm' my ass. I'll takem' to the Cowboy." Vargas looked at the girls in the van and snarled.

"That inbred is out of business." Buggy moved to the car as well.

"Out of business?" Vargas questioned.

"He's a fly by night operation at best. Probably strung out on meth." Alexi laughed. "Take our offer or leave it. Now!"

"Damn, Buggy. I'm just tryn'…"

Buggy looked toward Alexi who had an uncompromising look.

"Ten points." Alexi demanded.

"Yeah. Ten." Vargas gave up.

"Those three Beaners can go to the fields, but those zipper-heads, people will pay good money for that pussy." Buggy got into the car. "So stop beating on them bitches and feed them a little."

"Damn. You two drive hard." Vargas shut the van doors.

"Getm' to the ranch. I'll make calls and get some interest cooked up." Alexi smiled. "Don't be sad, Dion, we all make out."

We all make out, Vargas thought to himself as Buggy and Alexi drove away. The van shook and sounds of thumping could be heard coming from the women kicking inside.

"Fuck!" Vargas slammed the van with a fist. "Shut the fuck up!"

It's okay...

The Indiana summer was hot and dry. More dry than usual. The crops and farmers that tended the harvest suffered. Many of the farmers would meet at the local coffee shops in the morning and talk about the need for rain and the hope for something in the fall. Jamie Towns was not one of those farmers. She tended to the flower garden in her back yard. She enjoyed growth and if the corn wasn't going to thrive, the flowers would with the proper care. She knew that meeting with a bunch of elderly men to discuss the newest pesticide or the obvious need for rain did not make the flowers grow.

Jamie Towns walked her backyard garden. She was amazed at how well her roses were able to thrive. She raised her garden to help with the soil drainage and she watered regularly. She stepped between the rose line and the shrubs. She mentally measured the distance between the two lines. The thought of moving the roses a tad bit farther from the shrub line crossed her mind; she was concerned about her roses getting to much shade throughout the day. She looked out behind her backyard to the six hundred acres of corn that was struggling. She shrugged her shoulders and looked down on her roses.

"What are you doing over there," Jamie spoke to a weed as if she knew it. She kneeled down to pick the weed. "Oh," she spoke to herself. She put on some weight over the years and her left knee popped more often than not when she kneeled.

"You darn weeds drink more water than my..." Jamie stopped her conversations with the plants as she felt a presence behind her and a shade was suddenly cast over her and the plants. She turned around to look behind her and up. "Who is it?" Jamie couldn't see the person who was behind her because of the bright sunrays that peaked over the person's shoulders. "Who is it?" Jamie slowly stood. She was able to bring the person's face into focus. "Can I help you?"

"Jamie? Jamie Towns?" The person stepped forward.

"Yes. My name is..." Jamie moved so she could get out of the direct sun. "My name is Jamie Towns. Do I know you?"

"No. No. You don't know me. But you may remember me." The man's shoulders slouched and he put his hands in his pockets. "I know you're Jamie Towns."

"You don't look familiar. Why would I remember you?" Jamie smiled to make the man feel comfortable, trying to lighten the tension that was building.

"My name is Tommy Mill." Mill stepped back.

"Are you supposed to be...out? I mean are you..."

"It's okay, Jamie. I've been released. I didn't escape or anything like that." Mill smiled and put his hands in his pockets.

"I thought you were never to be released. Why would you come here?" Jamie asked.

"To tell you the truth, I didn't think I would ever be released." Mill looked out over the cornfield. "It looks like you got quite a place, Jamie."

"It's something my late husband and I built." Jamie looked toward the cornfield. "He built it. I worked for the Department of Resources and retired."

"You did well." Tommy looked toward the ground.

"Why, Tommy? Why are you here?" Jamie didn't feel fear. She didn't know what to feel.

"To tell you I'm sorry. I've wanted to tell you that for so long." A tear formed and fell down the cheek of Tommy Mill.

PART 4

Esteva Ruiz

Year 2000

Drake McCreiess steered the Sundancer 300 cabin cruiser out of the port of Brownsville, Texas. He enjoyed the Sundancer. He enjoyed the water. He enjoyed everything there was about putting a boat in water and pulling out of port. Behind him was land with so much going on while in front of him was nothing but water. He looked at his watch (1620). He thought of his friends who would be meeting him soon.

"Good luck, boys, without a hitch," he said aloud as he turned up the volume of the CD player that was playing one of his favorite Elvis Presley CD's.

McCreiess was a little late, but he wasn't concerned. It wasn't anything he couldn't make up. He knew that getting out of the port could delay him because numerous boats moved through the area and everyone seemed to be cautious with their large expensive craft. He didn't want to be the boat that everyone noticed, the captain that became "That Guy." He would just have to push the large two hundred and sixty horse powered Mercury engines a little more. He loved pushing the Mercury engine to its max. His destination was prescribed, but how he got there and the fun he had between there and the port of Brownville, Texas was all up to him. He planned on fishing anyway. Meeting his friends was part of the mission and he would not be late, but until then, fishing was what concerned him at the moment.

***

Max Merrell flew the Fokker 50 cargo twin prop engine aircraft low over the Mexican desert toward its destination, Matamoros, Mexico. The aircraft was not unique. It was just over 82 feet in length with a wingspan of approximately 95 feet. The aircraft was not large or extremely fast, but it was durable, and its type could be seen flying in and out of the Matamoros airport often, which would allow Merrell to blend in, a desirable feature for the day. Merrell had his route memorized. It was approximately twenty minutes prior to sunset with low covering clouds. He had the mission down to every turn and elevation.

Matamoros, a city located on the southern bank of the Rio Grande, and directly across from Brownsville, Texas, was a populated area with over five hundred thousand inhabitants. The economy was largely based on its proximity to the United States and foreign investment. Factories setup to take advantage of the cheap Mexican labor force and international bridges create a thriving city.

The city also had a dark side. It was run by the Gulf Cartel, one of the most powerful Mexican drug cartels, which took advantage of the different industries to launder its drugs and money through established factories.

Merrell knew where the populated areas below his aircraft would be, and the approximate number of people in those areas. He stayed clear of the densely populated areas but knew it was impossible to steer clear of everyone. Cargo aircraft flying around the Gulf were not unusual, so he knew he would never be suspected of anything other than enjoying a flight near the coast.

Kevin Halcot loved flying, especially when Merrell was the pilot. He and Merrell would often find time to fly during any spare time available. Aircraft such as the Fokker are capable of taking off and landing from short strips of asphalt, packed dirt or sand. Both Halcot and Merrell enjoyed flying similar aircraft low over the Gulf of Mexico, most often near Tampa Bay; landing most anywhere near the coast.

Halcot, sitting in the rear compartment, felt the plane bank to the left and go into a steep climb. He looked toward the front of the aircraft to make eye contact with Merrell. Merrell flashed five fingers on his right hand twice for ten minutes. He then straightened the Fokker out and leveled at four hundred feet, heading north. He slowed the aircraft to one hundred and twenty miles per hour. Halcot moved toward the package in the middle of the rear compartment. The package was taped to a four-wheel dolly and tied to the side of the aircraft directly in front of the side door of the rear compartment. The package was stuffed with over fifteen hundred pounds of plastic explosives, ball bearings, gasoline, and a flammable liquid viscous substance. Attached to the package were two military reserve parachutes.

"Five minutes," Merrell yelled as he looked toward the rear compartment and flashed five fingers.

Halcot hooked the eight-foot strap connected to his body harness to a D-ring hanging from the ceiling of the aircraft. The strap was one safety precaution that both McCreiess and Merrell demanded he use. He then opened the side door and secured it so that it wouldn't have a chance of getting in the way of anything exiting the aircraft. Looking out the door and feeling the Fokker bounce around from minimal turbulence was enough to remind Halcot why a safety strap was needed. The thought of tumbling out of an aircraft without a parachute while in flight was not a pleasant visual for him. He then moved to the package and cut the ropes securing it to the inside of the aircraft. The dolly was on tracks leading to the door to make sure the package remained on a one-way course out the aircraft. Halcot unlocked the wheels and inched it toward the door. He ensured that the static lines, leading directly to the parachutes and secured to a D-ring mounted near the floor and close to the exit, remained untangled. The static lines would pull the ripcords of the two military personnel reserve parachutes as the package exited the aircraft. Within four seconds of exiting the plane the chutes would be fully deployed.

Merrell remained on course. He could see the southern outskirts of Matamoros growing in his view. He could now make the outline of a textile factory that he was especially interested in, his target. He flew over a two hundred and fifty foot radio antenna, his one-minute reference point.

"One minute," Merrell shouted.

Halcot's heart raced as he inched the package closer to the door. The wheels of the dolly were well greased and the track was smooth. The pushing of the dolly out the door had been rehearsed many times before. There would be no hitch when the command of "Go" was given.

***

Esteva Ruiz dreaded getting to the top of the hill. She had been pedaling her bike up the same hill for the last few years. It wasn't the bike ride she dreaded so much, it was getting to the top and having the view of Vargas Textiles Factory. She hated working for the factory. The pay was good and the work was fine, and she enjoyed knowing that people were getting use out of the clothing she made. What she hated was twofold. She hated knowing that the textile factory she worked for was only a front for a major drug distribution center and she hated being groped by Castel, her boss, and others like him. She knew that drugs from the textile factory made their way to areas of the US to feed habits and she knew it was only a matter of time before the groping led to something far more than a cheap feel.

Esteva was running late. She knew it would cost her in unwanted Castel touches and kisses. As she reached the top of the hill she noticed something out of the ordinary, two parachutes with something dangling from beneath them. She had seen parachutist before, but this was no parachutist. She stopped pedaling her bike and came to a stop to watch where the parachutes would land. She was amazed to see that they landed on top of the building she worked in.

"That is odd," Esteva, stated to no one in particular.

There were a few people on top of the hill interested in watching where the parachutes would land.

"I think..." The child next to her was cutoff due to a very large explosion that came from the building she should be working.

Esteva was in shock. The explosion was so powerful that the building collapsed on itself. The remains of the building were totally engulfed in flames. She was sure whoever was in the building was no longer living. She hoped the only two other people who hated working for Vargas Textiles, her friends, were late for work as well. She knew that most likely was not the case so she said a quick prayer for them. Her thoughts then went to Castel and her hope was that he made it to work on time. She felt bad for that thought so she quickly asked God for forgiveness, but quickly went back to hoping Castel was in the crumpled burning building.

***

Moments after the package was pushed from the aircraft Merrell pulled up hard on the Fokker's yoke, which allowed him to gain altitude. He wanted to get above the clouds and turn east so that he could get over the Gulf and ultimately over international waters. The sun hung low over the water, just a thin red sliver that would disappear within a minute or two, so he turned all lights on the Fokker off. Except for a green glow inside the aircraft, it was now dark. Once he was sure the aircraft was over water he made eye contact with Halcot, who was now standing in the door of the cockpit, and nodded. Halcot moved to the rear of the aircraft and pitched the cell phone used to detonate the explosion out the door and returned to the cockpit.

"Take a seat and buckle up," Merrell commanded. "Get on the Sat with Drake!"

Halcot pulled the satellite phone from a compartment behind his seat, turned it on, and waited for a signal. Then he pushed the buttons on the phone and listened for a ring. Merrell put on a night vision headset.

"I got a ring." Halcot was excited. The call had been made a few times before during rehearsals so he never doubted he would get a signal, but to have it happen during a real time event was exciting.

"Thanks for calling Holiday Inn, Panama City," said the voice on the other end of the phone.

"Quit screwing around. This is serious." Halcot smiled at McCreiess' jest.

Merrell started cursing and mumbling, exasperated by McCreiess' nonchalant attitude about the mission.

"Hilton Panama or some crap like that." Halcot smiled at Merrell.

Merrell rolled his eyes.

"Where are you?" McCreiess asked.

"We are about fifteen minutes out." Halcot responded calmly.

"I'm waiting. All clear on this end." McCreiess remained composed.

"Good. We'll be there soon." Halcot turned the phone off.

***

McCreiess floated in international waters. All lights on the cruiser that made it legal were on. Nothing would look out of the ordinary. If the US Coast Guard looked to the cruiser - and they would - they would see an anchored ship with fishing lines. They would record the cruiser's name, as they did all ships in international waters. If and when the cruiser crossed the US border, the ships name would be recorded again. If anything seemed suspicious about the cruiser, it would be boarded. Lights from the city of Brownsville could be seen in the far distance, west of his position. Far to the north of him, lights from oilrigs glared in the dark.

McCreiess had anchored the Sundancer just an hour before he received Halcot's call. His predetermined position was well north of the Mexican border and directly north east of Brownsville, Texas. Not really expecting to catch anything, he baited three different rod and reels and let the hooks with shrimp drop to the bottom. Once he received Halcot's call he waited ten minutes and turned on the infrared light attached to the uncovered helm of the Sundancer.

McCreiess moved to the mid-cabin of the cruiser and retrieved his night vision headgear. Moving to the bow, he glanced at his fishing poles and found that nothing was biting on the shrimp. He scanned the area and saw nothing that would give him concern. It was very dark and the Gulf was calm, just what he and his friends hoped for. He sat alone on a starless night, nothing to comfort him other than the natural sounds that came from being on a large body of water, Elvis Presley tunes, and the thoughts of his wife, Abby. Abby was rarely far from his thoughts. He looked forward to being with her. Just the thought of holding her hand as they sat at a restaurant brought him comfort. After losing so many friends and comrades in Beirut, and the feeling of despair took hold after the Marines were ordered to withdrawal, Abby had helped fill the hole that such events created in his heart.

As a Marine and a soldier, before there was an Abby, he had spent many nights in the dark. The thought of what was past the stars was what had interested him then. He often found time to contemplate such things when he felt alone. The questions about God, sin, and redemption were things that weighed heavy on his mind and the thought of an infinite amount of space, stars, and planets fascinated him. He knew everything came together, somehow. He just didn't know how.

***

Merrell dropped below the clouds and immediately was able to pick up the infrared light from McCreiess' boat with his night vision goggles. From his view he could see that no other watercraft was nearby.

"I got him." Merrell smiled.

"What, those lights?" Halcot sounded concerned.

"I got the infrared, that's him." Merrell banked the Fokker hard right and then straightened it out, continuing to lose altitude.

"He's probably a good hundred meters closer to the shore than he should be." Merrell sounded pissed.

"How can you tell?" Holcot was confused.

Merrell smiled at Halcot's question, knowing his friend didn't get the sarcasm; a hundred feet in one direction or the other would make no difference. He had the Fokker closing on two hundred feet. He knew that McCreiess would now be able to pick him up by sound and with the night vision. Another bank hard left swung the Fokker to a position prepared to land. He hit a switch on the console that lowered the ramp at the rear of the aircraft. Once the ramp was lowered he cut the engines and allowed the plane to smoothly splash into the Gulf. The Fokker would quickly fill with water so Merrell looked at Holcot and made a hand gesture that suggested he move toward the rear of the aircraft and exit.

*　*　*

McCreiess heard the sound of a turboprop aircraft before he saw it so he looked to the sky and picked the

Fokker up moments after it broke from the clouds. He was always amazed at the vision the goggles provided. Looking up at the aircraft when it was directly above and maneuvering to land he could actually see the pilot, Merrell. The Fokker was two hundred feet off the bow of the Sundancer when it splashed into the water. It slowed quickly and eerily stabilized on the surface. He knew his friends should have plenty of time to make a safe exit before the aircraft sank, but his gut twisted until he saw Merrell and Halcot emerge from the sinking Fokker and jump into the water. McCreiess remained vigilant as his friends began to swim toward the Sundancer. He scanned the area, making sure nothing was out of the ordinary. He was not spooked.

"Little help?" Merrell asked as he closed in on the cruiser.

McCreiess threw a stepladder over the bow and secured it.

"Thanks. How is everything?" Merrell asked.

"All is good." McCreiess stuck his hand out to help the two men join him in the cruiser. "How'd it go Kev?"

"Without a hitch," Halcot chuckled as he handed a burlap sack filled with all equipment used during the in-flight mission. "It looks like we're all good on this end."

"Clockwork my man, clockwork." McCreiess filled the burlap sack with his night vision goggles, satellite phone, and walked to the front to collect the infrared light. "Did you toss the cell phone after you got over water?"

"Yep." Halcot quickly answered.

"Let's get out of here." Merrell scanned the area as he and Halcot undressed and put the wet clothes in the burlap sack with the equipment.

McCreiess counted what was in the sack. "We're missing something. There should be five, six, seven, no...it's here."

McCreiess tied off the burlap sack to an unsecured anchor and pitched it overboard. All evidence would soon rest at the bottom of the Gulf, unreachable by anyone.

Suddenly, the fishing pole leaning over the back of the cruiser twitched.

"Oh! I might have something," McCreiess whispered as if the fish below might hear him and swim away from the tempting shrimp.

"Seriously?" Merrell asked while Halcot grinned.

"I'll pull it in while you get dressed." McCreiess grabbed the pole that was twitching. "Hurry up. Get dressed." He flashed a smile at Halcot.

* * *

Once McCreiess reeled in the 40 pound Red fish and showed it off to his friends, he unhooked the large fish and returned it to the Gulf. Reds were protected outside the US boundary and since they floated in international waters, it was illegal to keep it. He pulled the other lines from the water and fired up the Sundancer. He turned the cruiser to face the Fokker, which was steadily sinking.

"She was a good machine. I enjoyed her while we had her," Merrell said as he nodded his head and smiled.

The men watched as the aircraft slipped well below the water line. McCreiess throttled the large mercury engines and pushed forward over the aircraft as it slowly faded out of site beneath the dark waters of the Gulf at night. The under current and other forces would pull it farther out and eventually to the bottom of the Gulf of Mexico. The authorities may find it but the men doubted anyone with law enforcement authority would search hard for a sunken aircraft that was used to destroy illegal drugs and the men who peddled such things. After all, there were hundreds of aircraft at the bottom of the Gulf, so who would really care? The aircraft was stolen, and there was nothing left behind that could be traced to anyone, much less to them.

McCreiess pushed the Mercury engines to get the cruiser north of Brownsville, away from any shore lights and into US territory. Once there they anchored and the remaining night vision headgear was thrown overboard. Fishing lines were also dropped to the bottom of the Gulf. If they were going to be approached by law enforcement, it would be there. Each man was well aware of what could happen if anything went wrong with the mission. They were prepared.

The whole mission was a ballsy move, but revenge for a brother's life was considered worth it. Death would have been worth it. Any number of things could have gone wrong, but nothing did, mostly because the mission planning was realistic, meticulous, and concentrated. Not one of the men had a criminal record. Each man had a distinguished military career. Two of the men were well-known and celebrated police officers. The other was just a great young man with a great life ahead of him. Authorities on both sides of the boarder would assume it was one cartel taking out a grievance on another – happens all the time.

***

Esteva Ruiz would never dread anything else again. She would never put herself in a position to work for such a place like Vargas Textiles again. She knew that her tardiness combined with tardiness of her two friends was more than a coincidence. She believed it was a sign from God. The prayers she said for her friends as she overlooked the burning factory worked so she took her mother's advice and did something that would honor God. She moved to the local Catholic Church and helped with raising orphans. Her wishes for Castel were answered as well. Castel was not late to work. He and many men like him perished in the flames created by a very large explosion. An explosion produced by men with vengeance in their hearts.

Esteva believed like most everyone else that the bombing of the textile factory was carried out by another cartel. She prayed that such violence would stop and she did all she could to ensure that the orphans she was charged with raising would stay away from the culture that created such destruction. She sought the council of her priest for visions she had as she slept. The vision of a lost man who wandered through life came to her periodically. She believed that the man was in a constant struggle with good and evil and she wished that she could help free him from his suffering. Her priest only suggested that she would one-day encounter the wandering man and that she should prepare herself for that meeting. Esteva and the priest knelt and prayed for the man. They asked God to send angels to help the man as he wandered. They prayed that God would relieve the wandering man of the agony and that the angels would provide a lighted path for the man to recognize and follow. She went on to pray each day after that she would have the encounter her priest talked about.

There is a king by your side

Present Day

Drake McCreiess walked up the steps of the cathedral, stopping half way to admire the details of the building. Even when he was a child, he had appreciated the detailed neo-gothic exterior. The crafted masonry was both intricate and elegant. Noticing the pinnacles, buttresses, and gargoyles, he remembered as a child how scared he used to be walking the steps, how his father would have to coax him into the cathedral with empathy at first and eventually with threats of spanking if he didn't move his ass toward the huge oak doors.

McCreiess turned to notice his childhood school across the street. The Catholic school, known for discipline, faith based instruction, and cultural experiences, was where McCreiess found his support early in life. It was how he defined himself. It was where he received his first kiss and where he learned that he could defend himself with fists if the situation called for it.

His first kiss was Becky Stone. Her tongue was in his mouth before he knew what to do or think. She had obviously had some experience. She was after all two years ahead of him. He left the kiss wondering what just happened. Not really knowing if he ever wanted to experience such a thing again. Instincts eventually kicked in and he soon had more girls to kiss than was good for him. He found out quickly that sexual encounters should be discreet and meaningful.

His first punch was thrown in sixth grade. It was an over hand right that connected with Brian Farley's nose. He quickly followed it up with a left to the chin. Farley landed on his back and was quick to ask for a stop in the fighting. McCreiess realized quickly that his tolerance for rude behavior was not much.

The young Brian Farley announced that McCreiess' mother was a pole smoker to everyone in gym class. McCreiess leaped into action even though he didn't understand what the young Farley meant by calling his mother such a thing. Before he knew it, he was being dragged to the principal's office. Brian Farley was scooped up and given ice for his bleeding nose. To McCreiess, Farley was cradled like a puppy while he was on his way to a good paddling. He would take that paddling and a few more before he left middle school, but his peers understood he was one who would not tolerate disrespectful behavior directed toward him or his loved ones.

On the fields behind the school was where he tackled running backs and hit a few homeruns. The fields represented hard work and effort, something his father explained was worth more than ten college degrees. *I am a Saint George Warrior,* he thought as he turned to open one of the large oak doors. While opening the door he was caught by surprise when a small Hispanic woman ran into him as she was trying to exit the cathedral. He looked down on the woman as she looked up. Their eyes locked for a brief moment before the woman suddenly stepped back. McCreiess remained holding the door open, expecting the woman to continue moving through the doorway. The woman stepped forward and had a look as if she was in the presence of something sacred. She remained silent and looked as if she was searching for something to say.

"Ma'am, is everything alright?" McCreiess asked cautiously.

"There is a king by your side." The woman spoke Spanish, as she looked McCreiess up and down. "You are struggling but your struggles will not last. You will be free and I will continue to pray for you. The King will provide."

McCreiess nodded and smiled, not knowing what to say because his second language was German and not Spanish.

The small Hispanic woman moved swiftly outside and then grabbed McCreiess' hand and held it tightly for a moment. "The King will provide," she said before hustling away.

McCreiess cocked his head and smiled as he crossed the threshold and didn't think much more of the brief encounter he just had. He was more aware of how the overwhelming feeling of God's presence no longer filled him as it used to when he entered the cathedral. Noticing the baptismal font fixed in the rear of the church,

McCreiess was reminded of the many times he dipped his fingers into the holy water before making the sign of the crucifixion to remind him of his baptism. Without dipping his fingers McCreiess turned from the font to walk down the long aisle leading to the Alter. Noticing the many pews on each side of the aisle, he allowed his thoughts to wander through the many good memories he associated with the church, and the understanding of the seven sacraments. It also brought sadness, thinking about the many times Abby and the rest of his family sat in the pews without him because of his absence. Being a police officer and a soldier in the National Guard was time consuming and required him to be away from his family. Time he wished he had spent differently.

Standing in front of the Alter, his thoughts immediately went to Abby. The sacrament of marriage defined his faith in the church. *She was beautiful*, he thought, as he looked down the aisle she walked to receive his hand in marriage. Abby's death on top of his experience with war now undermined his faith. Abby was the one thing that he could cling to when his faith would wane. It was Abby who insisted that they return to church at least once a week. Without Abby, he no longer felt the need to return. He would not be standing in front of the Alter now if it were not for her memory. "We always have the church. We can always depend on the church," explained Abby when tough times would arise.

"Drake! Drake McCreiess, it is great to see you," Father Kross spoke enthusiastically as he walked into the sanctuary. "Drake, how good it is to see you. How long has it been?" The smaller man asked as he reached out to grab McCreiess' hand. Knowing it had been two years since he presided over Abby's burial service.

"It has been a while I'm sorry to say."

"I can remember you planting running backs and receivers with thunderous hits. Hitting homeruns just right across the street. Some of my Sunday sermons were inspired by some of your hits." Father Kross laughed.

McCreiess pulled Father Kross closer for a hug. "How are you, Father?"

"Oh tending to the flock and making sure the Sister of Matamoros is taken care of." Father Kross shrugged his shoulders.

"Matamoros, Father?" McCreiess hesitantly asked.

"Matamoros, Mexico. We have an exchange program and this year we are working with an orphanage out of Matamoros, Mexico." Father Kross scratched his head. "Our exchange student doesn't speak much English so my Spanish seems to be getting better as the weeks go by." He crossed his arms and rocked back on his heels. "You ever heard or been to Matamoros, Mexico?"

"No," McCreiess said and looked away toward the large display of the crucifixion. He hated starting the conversation with a lie but he reverted to what he knew and that was to lie when anyone outside of The System brought up anything in regards to a mission. "I might have met the Sister." McCreiess smiled.

"Probably did. She just went to lunch not too long ago." Father Kross rocked on his heels. "What-da-ya say we move to the sacristy, Drake?"

"Sounds good, Father."

The two men moved from the sanctuary to the sacristy; a room in which McCreiess helped Father Kross prepare liturgical services as an alter server while a youth.

"I was so happy to see your name on the list of persons seeking council. It brings back so many good memories."

"Good memories, Father."

"How is your mother doing? I have not seen her since she moved farther south to live with your aunt. She writes me, but that is not as good as seeing her."

"She's well. She's keeping her new priest honest I think."

"Yes, I bet she is." Father Kross massaged his graying beard. "It was tough on all of us when Abby passed. She was such a presence in the church."

"Yes she was, Father." McCreiess answered as he sat on the old wooden chair he used many years before in service of the church.

"But we are not here to talk about your mother or Abby, are we, Drake?"

"I don't know what to say, think, or believe anymore, Father." McCreiess cleared his throat. "Since Abby's death, well even before her death, I have been losing faith. It is not that I don't believe in a higher being, Father. It is more that I believe that things have been created and put in motion with no direction from a creator."

Father Kross grunted and massaged his beard.

"I would explain to Abby that no one but ourselves is responsible for our wellbeing, but she insisted that I return to Mass each Sunday when I was not busy doing..."

Father Kross interrupted by pulling a chair over and sitting down, directly in front of McCreiess.

McCreiess rose to his feet.

"Please sit, Drake. I am sorry for the interruption."

"Father, when Abby was dying of breast cancer I prayed with her and assured her that I was a believer only to comfort her during her last days. Her death only solidifies my disbelief of a guiding force." McCreiess sat back down, elbows on his knees, his head resting in his hands.

"Why the disbelief, Drake? When and where? Can you put your finger on a specific instance, is it Abby's death, or is it something else?" Father Kross now leaned forward placing his left hand on McCreiess' shoulder.

"It is years of instances Father." McCreiess sat back in his chair.

"In Acts, five, seventeen, eighteen, the Bible tells us that not even the most faithful are exempt from suffering. The apostles were jailed and beaten. Faith does not make troubles go away. It only makes troubles less frightening."

"Troubles, Father! I am not talking about losing work and having my house foreclosed on." McCreiess rose to his feet to be able to speak in a more adamant fashion, taking steps backward to create distance from his old mentor and friend.

"A car explodes next to a market and several people are killed. The people don't die quick and painlessly. No, they cry out in agony, watching their insides spill out all over the street before their souls are allowed to leave their bodies. In Africa I saw the bodies of soldiers who were so sick and weak with dysentery that they fell into trenches and drowned in their own shit and piss. I'm not talking about troubles Father." McCreiess noticed his voice getting louder so he clenched his jaw to muffle his tone.

"I was at a firing range many years ago. I watched a beautiful winged creature, one of God's creatures." McCreiess rolled his eyes and paused as he permitted his thoughts to drift to the moment he talked about.

:-

Soldiers stood at the loading table and filled magazines with bullets they would soon fire on the range they looked over. Men gathered in three's and joked and laughed as McCreiess and another sergeant stapled targets to the range backboards. The soldiers were part of an elite Special Forces group who was use to handling all sorts of weapons, so range rules were more relaxed than what the regular army would call for.

Coming off the loading table the soldiers locked and loaded one full magazine into their weapon and placed the weapon on safe. Most men slung the weapon over their shoulders but a few were more relaxed, carrying the weapon by the rear slip ring.

"Men, we need to spread out and align with a target. There should be one target per man, so spread out." McCreiess stood in front of the men and raised his voice. "One hundred meter zero..."

McCreiess was interrupted as a red-winged black bird landed 25 meters to his left. He was caught off guard by its beauty. He watched as the bird flared its wings. He flinched at the sound of a sudden gunshot and looked to see a soldier pointing a weapon in the direction of the bird. He followed the muzzle of the weapon the soldier was holding to where the beautiful winged creature lay dead.

"What the...Why did you do that?" McCreiess stood stunned as some of the men laughed and moved toward the bird. "Sergeant Hunt! Why?"

"I was just having a theological discussion with Kit and..."

"He was telling me about how there is no God." Kit interrupted Sergeant Hunt as they stood over the bird. "He said if there was a God, God would surely make the bird fly away before he pulled the trigger."

"There is no God." Sergeant Hunt bent over and picked up the bird as some of the men laughed.

"Stop the laughing!" McCreiess shouted.

McCreiess stood in shock for a moment. He moved to where the men were holding the bird.

"It's just a bird, Drake." One soldier laughed as he watched McCreiess hold his hand out.

"It's a life. A precious life." McCreiess had the image of his good friend Kevin Halcot lying dead flash through his mind. "It's not to be taken for granted."

Most of the men put their heads down and scattered.

"Give me the bird, Hunt." McCreiess demanded as he stood staring at Sergeant Hunt. "Place him in my hand."

Sergeant Hunt realized that McCreiess was in no mood to be played with so he gently placed the bird in his hand.

"Get on the line and align yourselves with a target." McCreiess demanded as he placed the bird in his pants cargo pocket. A tear rolled down his cheek.

"With all the shit we've seen and done in the sand box, Drake. You're going to..."

"Get on the line!" McCreiess interrupted Sergeant Hunt.

"You have got to be kidding me...

"Hunt," McCreiess spoke so only Hunt could hear, "I make no idle threats. What I'm about to tell you is a fact. One more word and I will shove the butt of my weapon through your warped fucking head." McCreiess gritted his teeth and stepped so close to Hunt that the bill of his cap touched the bill of Hunt's cap. The two men stood toe to toe.

Sergeant Hunt knew that it was best he kept his mouth shut. He stepped back, quickly turned, and jogged to align himself with a target.

"I watched it land a few feet from a group of men. One of the men pointed his weapon at the bird and shot it as the others laughed." McCreiess broke from his thought.

Father Kross allowed his head to drop. He looked at the floor as he listened.

"I asked the man why he did that. He said it proved to the others that there was no guiding force like God. He explained that if there was a guiding force, the force would have surely stopped him." McCreiess paused, took a deep breath and let it out. "Abby was beautiful. We were planning on having a family."

"Drake. Drake, please listen. Please sit down and listen. I know you have witnessed the evils of this world. In this country we are protected from the real evils of the world because of people like you. You help provide a blanket of security. That blanket is good for us, but it also shelters us from witnessing those evils." Father Kross moved to McCreiess so that he could put an arm around him. "I sometimes wish people in this country could witness those evils. They might appreciate what they have here a little more." Father Kross took a deep breath and let it out. "Remember, if God always rescued the faithful, there would be no need for faith."

McCreiess looked at his old friend inquisitively.

"Think about the selfishness that would arise if God intervened every time we faced evil. Our eternal reward is worth any suffering we first have to endure. My son, you have been tested like many before you. Some are tested more often than others and I don't know why that is. In my experience God gives people only what they can handle. I don't think you are any different. Am I wrong?"

McCreiess frowned at the thought of not being able to handle the evils he may have participated in or witnessed.

"Whether he intervenes on our behalf or not, we should be faithful. Go home and think, Drake. Think about the significant events that you have witnessed. Think about how a particular set of circumstances came together. Think about certain people who entered your life, when they entered your life, and why."

McCreiess walked away from Father Kross.

"You want to believe, Drake, or you would not be here. There is something pulling you here. I think for many the church represents answers. They are not always the clear easy answers we want, but they are answers." Father Kross leaned against the limestone wall of the sacristy. "Confession, Drake, is one part of the sacrament of penance. That combined with contrition, satisfaction, and absolution will free you." He stepped toward McCreiess. "Is there something you would like to get off your chest? Something that may free you?"

"I have killed, Father. I have..."

"Many soldiers before you have worried about Gods law and the struggles of mankind." Father Kross interrupted McCreiess.

McCreiess was relieved that his old friend stopped him from going farther into a confession he really didn't want to make. He knew the difference between the death and mayhem soldiers create compared to the curse attached to an assassin. He felt there was nothing that Father Kross could say that would redress any action in which the church considered a mortal sin. *I'm on the doorstep of Hell*, he thought as he slumped his shoulders and looked down.

"Go home, Drake. Look through the pages of your life. I think if you look hard enough you will find those significant events, particular circumstances, and people that give hope and create faith."

"Abby..." McCreiess spoke softly.

"It's not about Abby, Drake." Father Kross put his hands in his pockets and rocked back and forth on his heels. "I'm sorry to say, but, Abby was there for only a moment. And in the grand scheme of things, it's only a brief moment. There is much more out there for you, Drake."

I did not know him...

The lamp on the desk was brightly lit. Ellenberg looked over paperwork that had to do with an upcoming case to be presented before him. The thought of two attorneys standing before him, and using the actual Constitution as a guide, provided him some relief. His log cabin experience left him drained of willingness to hand down decisions that would have a great impact on anyone. He hoped the embezzlement case before him would get him into the spirit of rendering judgment again. The case seemed to be a slam-dunk. The prosecution had more than enough evidence, but the defense was still hanging their hope on entrapment. Ellenberg didn't see the entrapment part of the case but he believed everyone deserved the opportunity to be heard, especially when the judgment could mean many years behind bars for a person who was once thought to be a leader within his community.

The background noise of dishes clanging and the television comforted Ellenberg. He enjoyed knowing that his wife was close by. The picture of himself and Judge Carson got his attention. It was a picture of the two men standing in front of the Jefferson Memorial in

D.C. It was that D.C. trip that solidified his friendship with Judge Carson. The two were able to put away the leader and subordinate roles long enough to get a personal understanding of each other's beliefs.

Ellenberg looked up from the picture when he heard the phone ring.

"Hello." He heard his wife Cindy answer the phone. "Yes he is." Cindy walked into the office. "Hold for a second."

"Who is it?" Ellenberg questioned.

"It's a man but I've never heard the voice before. He asked if this was the home of Judge Ron Ellenberg." Cindy handed the phone to her husband.

"This is Judge Ron Ellenberg." Ellenberg listened for a moment. "Yes I will and please tell her I'm sorry and I will call her later." He hung up the phone.

Cindy noticed the somber mood her husband suddenly took. "What is it?"

"That was Judge Carson's nephew. Judge Carson passed away this afternoon." Ellenberg looked again upon the picture of himself and Judge Carson.

*　*　*

The funeral home parking lot was filled and the line to get into the funeral home was long. People patiently waited to show their respect to a man who touched so many citizens. Most of the people in line never really knew the man personally, but they were all well aware of his work as a Judge, his World War Two and Korean

War service, and his charitable work for wounded vets and the local children's hospital.

McCreiess worked his way through the line and into the home. He made his way to the viewing room where he could see Judge Carson laying peacefully. He scanned the room and noticed Merrell standing in line to greet Harriet. He turned to notice Cynthia Mader enter the room. She smiled as she shook the hands of the different politicians and elite people who flew in to be part of the spectacle. Ronald Ellenberg stood in the center of the room with his arms crossed, taking in the surrealism of it all.

McCreiess noticed Merrell standing by himself so he made his way across the room to meet with him.

"When did you get here?" Merrell asked.

"Just got in." McCreiess looked around the room. "He knew lots of people."

"Lots of people knew of him. He accomplished a lot and there were many who jumped on his coat tail." Merrell looked toward Cynthia and saw that she was laughing with others in the rear area of the viewing room. "I see she arrived."

"You didn't think she would come?" McCreiess knew the answer to his question.

"Yeah. I knew she wouldn't miss it." Merrell looked toward the body of Judge Carson. "You going up to see him?"

McCreiess moved toward the body without answering. He never got to know Judge Carson as well as Merrell did, but he knew he should pay his proper respect for the man who kept him from behind walls and bars; not free, but not prison.

Standing by the body, McCreiess looked down on Judge Carson with a bit of awkwardness. He didn't know what to do with the moment.

"Did you know the Judge?" An older gentleman asked McCreiess as he moved to stand side by side with him.

"I knew him," the old man somberly said.

"I did not know him. Well, I mean. I did not know him well." McCreiess felt uneasy answering a question about his association with Judge Carson, but he could tell the older gentleman was no threat.

"I parachuted into Saint Mere with Steven. He and I marched all across Europe together." The older gentleman smiled. "He was as fine a soldier as you would ever know."

"Silver Cross awarded him." McCreiess looked over the Judge. "Korean War he earned two purple hearts. Killed a lot of Chinese."

"The man was a real leader." The older gentleman walked away and then turned back. "We lost a good one."

***

The funeral home seemed a little raucous at times. Some were somber as others were laughing. Ellenberg remained at a distance from the body of Judge Carson. He met with Harriet for a few minutes; she was busy greeting all that stood in line to visit the Judge for that last time so he moved on quickly. People surrounded him but he felt alone. He looked around and saw Merrell keeping a vigilant eye on everyone, especially Cynthia who seemed to speak with anyone who would listen to her. He turned as a gigantic looking man entered the room; he had no idea who the man was but the man had a presence about himself. He turned away and noticed that Merrell was no longer in the room.

"Mr. Ellenberg." Cynthia snuck up from behind and startled Ellenberg.

"Cynthia." Ellenberg cleared his throat.

"Did I scare you?" Cynthia smiled.

"Well. Sneaking up behind me seems to be what people like to do."

"When will Mr. Merrell move on Tommy Mill," Cynthia spoke soft but stern.

"Not here. Please." Ellenberg made quick eye contact and moved to exit the viewing room. Cynthia followed.

***

Ellenberg paced the prayer room knowing that Cynthia would soon make an entrance. She enjoyed making entrances and Ellenberg knew her next entrance would be no different. Her entrance in rooms at the cabin, her entrance just an hour before into the viewing room at the funeral home, all had something to do with the way she wanted people to know her; as a person everyone in the room should know and respect.

"Mr. Ellenberg." Cynthia entered and seemed to parade around the small side prayer room. She looked over the place as if she were truly interested in the pictures of Jesus and the portrayal of his last days.

"Is this why you came here? You want to talk shop?" Ellenberg cut Cynthia off by moving to the center of the small room.

"I always liked this one. The one where he is struggling on his knees with this large wooden cross on his back." Cynthia stopped, stood, and stared at the picture. She smiled as she turned toward Ellenberg. "Do you really believe he..."

"Stop right there. I will not get into a theological discussion with you. What do you..."

"I want to know when Tommy Mill will be dealt with. He has been released from prison and he is getting further from our grasp." Cynthia's smile vanished as she interrupted.

"Merrell and McCreiess will carry out the orders. They will carry them out as soon as they see fit." Ellenberg sighed. "They are competent men who need no instruction from me or anyone else."

"That's good. That's what I want to hear." Cynthia kept a stern voice. "I just want to make sure things aren't slipping now that Judge Carson is no longer with us." Cynthia looked toward the picture of Jesus nailed to the cross. "I understand power, and now that Judge Carson has gone to join my father in the world after, well...Mr. Merrell, he might want to take advantage of the current situation. Power grab if you know what I mean."

Ellenberg had never met Cynthia's father, Judge George Mader, but he had heard a great deal about the man. The only real thing that he knew about Cynthia was that her father groomed her for the positions in her life and that he thought she should sit in the big chair at a pentagon shaped table.

"From what I have been told, and personally seen, Max Merrell is a professional who understands his role within our society, The System. He will act as a professional whether Judge Carson or your father is alive or not."

"Good. Good. I will inform the other members that things are on the smooth." Cynthia smiled and turned toward the door.

"Yes inform the others that everything is on the smooth or whatever you want to call it." Ellenberg's shoulders slouched and his head fell.

Cynthia opened the door. She turned to see Ellenberg look as if he were about to cry. "And, Mr. Ellenberg, watch the tone you take in the future when talking about my father." She quickly closed the door behind her as she left.

Ellenberg moved to take a seat and contemplate what he had gotten himself involved in. He realized that the only one who could protect him was lying dead in the other room.

***

The funeral home parking lot was not as full as it was a few hours before but there were still people flowing in to pay their final respects to a man who many thought deserved more of tribute than what was being mentioned in the press, which was very little.

Cynthia was happy with herself. She was able to pay respects to an associate and long time family friend without talking to anyone about her father, a subject that could go a couple different ways with her. It could be a conversation that brought her great pride or a conversation that could drive her to madness.

"Cynthia. Cynthia." A voice from behind a car could be heard.

Cynthia looked toward the direction the voice came. She waited for someone to come out of the darkness.

"Cynthia." Senator Claire Miller waved as she made it into the light from a parking post lamp.

"Claire. Claire. I didn't know that you knew Judge..."

"Who didn't know Judge Carson? The man was a legend in many different arenas." Claire smiled.

"He was a judge you know?" Cynthia felt foolish with her last statement.

"Yeah, here in Florida." Claire smiled and hugged her friend.

"And how were you and Judge Carson acquainted?" Cynthia was surprised with having an unexpected meeting.

"As you have probably witnessed, there are lots of political people in there. He was a man that had more than judicial influence." Claire noticed a gigantic man looking at her and Cynthia. "Who is that?"

"I don't know. Don't know that we've ever met." Cynthia made eye contact with the gigantic man and then quickly looked away.

"Is everything alright, Cynthia?" Claire asked.

"Oh I'm fine. Just a little tired." Cynthia turned from Claire. Her heart seemed to skip a beat but she controlled the anxiety that quickly overwhelmed her. "I think I better get back to the hotel. I have a flight in the morning I have to catch."

"We need to get together soon. The process of getting your name circulating within the right circles started long ago."

Cynthia turned back and hugged Claire tight. Claire was surprised by the hug, but went with it. They both stood back from each other. Claire smiled. Cynthia stood stoic. For the first time Cynthia realized that the death of Judge Carson was a turning point for many people.

* * *

Merrell approached McCreiess as he started his A6 Audi and put it in reverse. McCreiess looked over his right shoulder to back the car out but held when he saw Merrell standing behind the car.

"What the," McCreiess said to himself as Merrell walked around to the driver side. He rolled down his window and Merrell leaned in.

"Good news," Merrell pronounced.

"Yeah. What's that? Did the 'Old Man' jump out of the casket?" McCreiess put the car in park.

"You're out. Just confirmed it." Merrell looked around the funeral home parking lot. "You good with that?"

"How? When?" McCreiess grinned.

"Finish the new orders and you can part ways." Merrell paused. "Just do what we've got planned and all will be good."

"Cynthia and the rest of the judges give the okay?" McCreiess smiled.

"Something like that." Merrell hesitated as he made eye contact with the gigantic man across the lot.

"Well I'll say I didn't see that coming." McCreiess leaned his head back.

Merrell thought about the meeting that just took place moments before.

:-

Max Merrell stood in the middle of the funeral parlor prayer room as if he were a child waiting for his father to walk in with the paddle. The man he was waiting for was known for fairness but he was also a man who wanted little if any contact from a man like Merrell.

The door to the prayer room opened and Merrell was surprised by the size of Ben Kelly. It seemed as if Kelly filled the door way as he entered and closed the door behind him.

"Let's make this quick, Mr. Merrell." Kelly had a calm demeanor but he made it clear that the meeting had a limit.

"Drake McCreiess wants out." Merrell didn't hesitate.

"Reason?" Kelly quickly responded.

"Because Judge Carson is now out." Merrell nodded his head toward the room that Judge Carson laid peacefully.

"Judge Carson is dead." Kelly stepped closer to Merrell and looked down on him.

"Drake feels he has done enough and he doesn't want to serve another..."

"He feels strongly about this?" Kelly interrupted Merrell.

"He does." Merrell spoke with confidence.

"And you?" Kelly questioned.

"I want nothing more than to continue to serve The System." Merrell put his hand out as a faith gesture.

"It's done. Have him finish up the outstanding orders and he's out." Kelly took Merrell's hand as a gesture of faith and the men exchanged a strong handshake. "You will meet his replacement soon."

Merrell stood stunned.

"I will let you know when." Kelly released Merrell's hand and turned to exit the room. "As always. Keep doing what you are doing." Kelly opened the door to exit and then quickly closed it. "Judge Carson gave me his blessing. Drake McCreiess has done plenty." Kelly opened the door and disappeared.

Meet his replacement soon? Judge Carson gave his blessing? When? Merrell had so many thoughts running through his head.

i

"You better get going. We have to hook up soon." Merrell remained looking toward the gigantic man as he snapped back to the conversation he was having with his friend.

"What are you thinking? Is everything good?" McCreiess quietly asked. "You seem a little concerned."

"I don't know that anyone is thinking." Merrell paused. "Everything is good. You better get going." He stepped back and watched his friend drive away. He allowed his thoughts to drift back to another time when he realized that questions had to be answered.

:-

The distinct sound of AK47 fire was heard long before anyone could be seen firing the weapons. The sound of explosions created by rocket-propelled grenades got McCreiess' attention. Sounds of war were common in Karbala Iraq. If it were not for the sounds of the grenades, McCreiess would have kept his attention on planning his next mission and studying the topographic map that he held. Automatic gunfire was common but gunfire mixed with explosions created by rocket-propelled grenades usually meant a battle was ensuing. The sounds of war, that was once a half kilometer to his south, were now within eyesight. McCreiess folded his map and placed it in his pant cargo pocket. Men from his operational detachment team gathered on the government center rooftop in which they operated. The men watched as soldiers from the Mahdi army engaged in combat with Iraqi police and a squad of soldiers from an Iraqi commando team. It seemed as if both sides' maneuvers created a battle that was continuously moving, encapsulating anyone in the area. The combat seemed to roll into a market where civilians struggled to seek cover and remove themselves from the intense fire that seemed to come from all directions. Men from both sides of the fight fell to the ground as they became dead or wounded.

McCreiess noticed a woman wearing a burka run from a house and move toward a Humvee that was stalled in the middle of the market. On top of the Humvee was a commando who indiscriminately fired a belt fed weapon into crowds of people, vehicles, and buildings. The woman wearing the burka fell to the ground after being hit by several bullets. She struggled to her feet. McCreiess first noticed a flash and then came the sound of a very large explosion followed by a fireball with heavy black smoke. The person wearing the burka vanished into thin air, leaving only her right foot and ankle on the ground. The inevitable screams of the victims followed the large explosion that sent nuts, bolts, glass, and nails in all directions. The battle that once raged was now silent. It seemed to McCreiess as if the Mahdi army took advantage of the diversion created by the suicide bomber and escaped from the battle, leaving dozens of men women and children dead or clinging to life.

"Jesus," Brain said as he used binoculars to survey the market. "That little cocksucker became atoms in the wind."

"Holy shit!" One soldier chuckled. "That's one way to get the momentum."

"What do you think, Sergeant McCreiess?" Another soldier asked, as he stood stunned. "Should we provide some sort of support?"

"I don't think anyone is thinking anymore." McCreiess watched as one of the Iraqi police officers struggled to prevent his guts from falling to the ground as he limped toward nothing in particular. McCreiess turned to look at his friend Captain Max Merrell who was also surveying the market. "What do you think, Sir?"

"It looks like we probably need to recruit and train some new commandos."

A honk from a car brought Merrell back from his flashback. He looked around and noticed that the gigantic man had disappeared. He put his hands into his pockets, lowered his head, and made his way back into the funeral home. He wanted another moment with Judge Carson's remains.

Hot dog he is born again

The targets popped up quick. They were up for a second or less. The individual running the range tested his ability to quickly cipher information because of the shoot/no shoot targets. A woman holding a remote control devise compared to a man holding a revolver popped up. Targets with such comparisons and split second cipher time tested the most elite master gun handlers.

A target of a woman holding a log was bypassed. A man holding a semiautomatic pistol was shot twice in the chest. A man holding a baby was bypassed. A woman holding a knife in a threatening manner and wearing a pistol holstered in her belt was hit square in the forehead with a bullet.

McCreiess moved over the range at a steady pace. He understood that slow and steady could be quicker and more accurate than fast and erratic. He had practiced handling weapons most of his adult life. Turning to face a target never seemed to be contemplated. It was muscle memory that took over his range response. The trigger of the pistol was methodically squeezed, never jerked.

Merrell worked the targets from the watchtower that over looked the range. He didn't let up with the speed of the targets. Providing McCreiess as little time as possible to react to targets was his plan. He knew the competitive spirit his friend had when his mind was right; thinking about nothing but mission success. He knew McCreiess was in need of a magazine change but he wasn't going to let up.

McCreiess moved to a knee position behind a wall. He was aware that his Colt 1911 .45 caliber pistol was getting light. The targets were still popping quickly. Two no shoot targets popped so he advanced toward a pile of wooden debris that acted as cover. Two shoot targets quickly popped to his left so he turned and fired. Bullets hit both targets squarely in the chest. His magazine was empty so he pushed the magazine release button and continued to the debris as the magazine fell from the weapon. Two shoot targets popped in front of him as he was reaching for a new magazine with his left hand. He quickly adjusted by moving his left hand to his reserve pistol stored on his left side belt holster. He was able to pull the pistol with his left hand and get two quick kill shots off; one bullet for each target.

"Done!" Merrell yelled from the watchtower. He was excited.

"Thought you had me?"

"Hot dog he is born again. You are born again you ambidextrous son of a gun." Merrell laughed. "I thought I had you."

"Set them up again!" McCreiess turned to walk to the reload table. "I can do better."

"No. Let's stop here," Merrell said as he climbed down from the tower. "That was a great run, Drake. Best time by five seconds. Let's hold here." Merrell was happy about his friend's ability to come back strong after his last range experience. "We got a lot to get done. Three separate orders. This weekend we'll start planning for the first order. Go into isolation sometime early next month."

"What's up?" McCreiess asked.

"Guy named Shills." Merrell reached the bottom of the tower and walked with his friend to the reload table. "Benny Shills. Remember him?"

"Name rings a bell but it doesn't mean anything." McCreiess placed his weapons on the table and started breaking them down.

"Probably wouldn't unless you were one of the people he financially fucked over." Merrell started helping with the cleaning of the weapons.

"What about an Army gig sometime soon?" McCreiess questioned. Bringing up the Army allowed a distant conversation he had with Kevin enter into his thoughts.

:-

Drake McCreiess noticed his friend, Kevin Halcot, sitting at a lunch table by himself. He could tell his friend was in deep thought so he didn't say anything as he sat across from him. The two sat in silence as they ate the beef stew the Army cooks stirred up.

"Good stuff don't you think Kev?" McCreiess wanted to break the silence after a few minutes.

"When do you think we will get our chance to get over there, Drake?" Kevin disregarded the question about the stew. Since the twin towers fell in New York, by the hands of terrorist, he was more interested in a war that was brewing.

"Oh I'm sure we'll get our shot shortly. The people are demanding something be done." McCreiess took a bite from his stew.

"What about you, Drake. You want to..."

"Kevin, we will get our share of the fight. Just beware of your investment into the people who are calling for war." McCreiess continued to chew the tough meat. "They will turn on you in a heartbeat."

"But this was an attack on the homeland. Something has to be done." Kevin put his utensils down and stared at his older friend. "A response is right and called for."

"I agree. A response is right and called for." McCreiess sighed. "There is going to be a lot of killing that needs to get done and the people that call for war now will not have the stomach for it. More than seventy percent of the people want war, now. Wait until bullets start flying." McCreiess leaned back in his seat. "And then you throw in all the people who will want to make money off this thing and the Flag Officers who want to make this a defining mark on their careers?"

"What do you mean?" Kevin sat up. "What are you saying?"

"All I'm saying is...just don't buy into all the heroic shit people are going to pump into your head, Kevin." McCreiess paused. "The talking heads, the politicians,

Wall Street, and the officers, all have an interest in this thing. They will pump you up just to get you to do something they won't let their own children do."

Kevin stared at his friend.

"Just go into this knowing that you do this because of who you are, Kevin. You are a warrior who wants and needs this. Nothing more or less." McCreiess looked around the lunchroom. "If anyone is here for the heroics, or if they believe they will be owed something, their energy will be crushed when it is all said and done."

McCreiess took another bite of the stew as Kevin continued to look at his friend with curiosity.

"You don't believe me?" McCreiess asked Kevin. "You watch. When soldiers fill body bags, and they will." McCreiess paused. "The politicians will squabble and blame each other. The talking heads will go for ratings by creating stories that their viewers want to see. If their viewers are against the war we will be the poor uneducated souls who just didn't know better. To some we will be the Devil. If their viewers slant for the war we will be heroes, made to be bigger than life. It's propaganda to get the next generation to fight the next war. It will have everything to do with ratings and nothing to do with the soldier." McCreiess continued to eat stew. "Wall Street will make tons of money because they will invest in the war machine." McCreiess paused. "Not one Flag officer will die in this war going toe to toe with some misguided, malcontent, Jihadist."

"I guess..."

"The catch is." McCreiess cut Kevin off. "Not one of their kids will spill blood over this." McCreiess pushed his bowl of stew away. "There will be plenty of us, and men like us, who will spill blood. We will make others spill lots of blood and we will see and do things that will keep us up at night." McCreiess sighed. "But we'll be some poor dumb bastard Devil heroes."

"Think we will win?" Kevin asked in a voice that wasn't as confident as it once was.

"Win what?" McCreiess stood. "We'll kill lots of them and we'll break their machine apart. The politicians will keep getting elected. The talking heads, for ratings, will move to the next crisis. Wall Street will make money on the next big thing. The officers will pitch the next big war because they won't get this one right. But we." McCreiess paused. "The soldier who will stand on the battlefield and go toe to toe, the guys that do the door kicking." McCreiess looked over the lunchroom. "We'll win nothing."

"Damn, Drake. Why?" Kevin stood and walked with his friend.

"Why what?"

"Why do you continue to do this stuff if you have that outlook? The country..."

McCreiess stopped and turned to look his very good friend in the eye. "Country," he said in a low and stern voice. He clenched his jaw and continued, "I'm not putting my life on the line for Democrats and Republicans. Fuck that. They use us as some sort of political weapon to beat each other up with." He looked over the lunchroom and calmed himself by taking a breath and letting it out. "I just know who I am." McCreiess stared into his friend's eyes. "I know you, Kevin Halcot."

"Couple training spots opened up at Camp McCall." Merrell's answer interrupted McCreiess' thought. "'Q' Course starts soon and I think we can help push some want-a-bees through it." Merrell paused. "I was thinking we take care of Shills and a couple human traffickers before we put the uniform on and get out of 'Dodge' for awhile."

"Yeah." McCreiess stood silent. "Back to work."

This is wrong

Nighttime Bethesda, Maryland was quiet for a summer Saturday. People meandered up and down Woodmont avenue in search of drink, eat, and shopping. The people who walked the avenue were some of the best-educated and wealthy people in America so Cynthia did not feel out of place as she peered through the windows of luxury stores. Bethesda is the home of some of the most successful corporate offices and government agencies so it was not uncommon to see powerful people dining at upscale restaurants. No one who saw Cynthia walking the streets would recognize her as powerful. They might assume she is a person of great financial means because of the clothes that she wore, but other than a judicial scholar, who could recognize a federal judge being considered for the highest court in the land?

The DC area was nothing new for Cynthia. Her father traveled to DC often when she was a child and he would allow her to accompany him as he visited powerful people who held powerful positions. As a teenager she stood in the oval office as her father and President Ford discussed legal issues in regards to easing the controls exercised by the regulatory agencies. As an adult she stood in the oval office again with her father as he and President Clinton shook hands after the two finished legal discussions on the subject of perjury and what the word "is" really meant. Her father, the late Judge George Mader, was a well-known attorney on both sides of the political isle and he had good friends from both of the major political parties. Thanksgiving dinner with Speaker of The House Tip O'Neil happened annually up in till the Speaker's death. A long time friendship with Secretary of Defense Casper Weinberger allowed her father to have conversations with him regularly, especially when the Defense Secretary needed legal advice regarding the Iran Contra Controversy. There were many politicians who sought out the friendship and advice from Cynthia's father.

The Bethesda Crab House was a unique place for the Bethesda area. To look at it, one might find that there is nothing upscale about the place. The establishment was quaint for anyone who sat at a booth and cracked into a hard-shell Maryland blue crab or had the opportunity to taste its famous succulent crab cakes. Over the years Cynthia had the opportunity to do both. She learned to crack crab from her father and the cake was pretty much self-explanatory; just dig in. Cynthia made her way down to the crab house with reservation. It had been a few years since she sat in one of the booths with her father. She tried to avoid the place since his passing. If it wasn't for Claire's insistence she would have never even thought about making a trek from main area Bethesda to the out of the way crab house.

The passing of Judge Carson weighed heavy on Cynthia. It was just another reminder of time. Time was not infinite and the generation before her was being introduced to that reality. Her father and Judge Carson were the old guard and now they were gone. She felt the need to make changes. Standing outside the crab house brought up a recollection that was seared in her mind.

:-

The two older men stood toe to toe in the light that a 200-year-old window provided. The anger could be felt more than it could be seen. Their arms were crossed and they stood straight up and walked around counter clockwise, creating a small circle footpath before they settled to confront each other.

"George this is wrong. It is not what this society is designed to do." Judge Carson stared into the eyes of his long time friend. "Why would you bring this case forward?"

"What do you mean, why?" Judge Mader asked sharply. "You have no reason to question me." Judge Mader stepped forward as if to show his long time friend that he would not waiver. "Don't you ever question me, God damn it!"

"Judge Carter has never been charged with anything." Judge Carson paused. "So he is a dreadful human being with power. I'm not saying the man isn't a stupid pig." He gritted his teeth and allowed a tear to run down his cheek. "I'm only saying that he is out of our reach! Or at least he should be."

"It's settled. The vote has been cast." Judge Mader stepped back to provide his friend space.

"It was a three-two vote." Judge Carson suddenly looked to his left to see Cynthia standing in the doorway. "How long have you been there?" Judge Carson looked back and forth at the two. "She was a yes. And so was the General. Am I missing something?" Judge Carson turned to walk away.

"Amendments have to be made." Judge Mader spoke to his friend and then turned toward his daughter.

Cynthia stood silent. She never knew the two wise men to disagree. Just moments before she sat stunned when she realized Judge Carson did not say "aye" in unison with her, her father, and the General.

I

Cynthia's phone vibrated. She woke from her deep thought and realized she was now inside the crab house and seated. She looked at the text message from Claire (COME OVER).

"Ma'am, can I help you?" A young waitress asked with a smile. "Are you waiting for others?"

"No." Cynthia stood. "I'm sorry but things have changed." Cynthia left the crab house and she didn't turn to look back. It was a part of her life that was gone forever.

***

The short cab ride from the crab house to Claire's house was uneventful. It gave Cynthia time to put her friendship with Claire into some perspective. *How well do I really know Claire Miller*, she thought. Claire knew Cynthia's father and Cynthia knew Claire's husband Jeffery before his untimely death due to a car accident. The two met twelve years before and they developed what some considered a close friendship.

Cynthia stepped out of the cab and looked over Claire's property. The estate was a magnificent piece of property even for Bethesda standards. The house was an exquisite country manor house located in a private enclave of several of the finest homes in the Bethesda area. It was a spectacular setting.

Her closing the door of the cab stirred interest. A large German shepherd dog pushed the curtain away in the large front window of Claire's home and started to bark, the barking was followed by more lights being turned on.

Cynthia sighed. It had been since Jeffrey's death since she had been inside the house. She gave herself a once over and walked toward the house.

Cynthia stood at the door as the large dog continued to bark on the other side.

"Ike. Move Ike." Claire's voice could be heard saying from inside the house. "Go on, Ike. Go to your bed." The dog's bark was not as loud now that Claire was involved.

"Thank you so much for coming over," Claire said as she opened the door.

Ike barked and growled as he peeked from around the corner.

"Now you go on and go to bed, Ike." Claire put some anger behind her voice.

Ike moved slowly toward another room as he moaned and groaned.

"So do you like my dog?" Claire smiled.

"A dog, Claire?" Cynthia stood shocked. "A big dog."

"Yeah. I never thought I had time for a pet. But since Jeffrey passed...well...you know. Company." Claire looked toward Ike lying on his bed. "He will keep us safe tonight." Her speech was slurred.

"I guess a Wild Turkey doesn't make a good pet." Cynthia was speaking about her friend's favorite drink.

"Don't you start with me," Claire said with a slur and stepped with a stumble. She then walked into her den and Cynthia followed.

"Now I know why we are here and not at our favorite crab house." Cynthia picked a bottle of Wild Turkey from the bar.

"I just couldn't do it, Cynthia." Claire sat in her leather sofa and pulled a blanket over her legs. "I just didn't feel like being seen."

Cynthia pulled two glasses from a liquor cabinet. She filled one of the glasses more than half way and the other only less than a quarter. She moved around the den slowly looking at pictures as if she cared.

"You look amazing." Claire admired her friend as she lay on the couch. "I mean it. You look amazing."

Cynthia smiled and continued to look over the pictures.

"Brooks Brothers, Pin-Dot three button jacket and matching skirt. And the alligator pumps to match just set you apart." Claire reached for what Cynthia was holding.

Cynthia handed her the glass that was more than half filled.

"We are almost there girl." Claire took a long drink. "Thank you for coming. Did I tell you that?"

"I love this picture of Jeffrey." Cynthia pointed to a picture on the wall.

"Yes. He enjoyed the outdoors, especially the national parks, like Yellow Stone." Claire squinted to see the picture. "Come and sit."

"I'm sorry. It's just been a while since I've been here. And Jeffrey looks so..." Cynthia's voice softened. She moved toward the sofa.

"Your name has been sent forward." Claire laid her head back after taking another long drink.

"Forward? Me? I never thought." Cynthia smiled.

"Well what the hell do you think we have been talking about all these months?" Claire giggled. "Did you ever think? What would your father think?" Claire's giggle was now a laugh. "Your name is on the President's desk with my endorsement. And that's a big stinking deal. Don't you know?"

"Claire. I honestly never thought our friendship would lead to this. I'm stunned." Cynthia held her glass, never taking a drink. "I'm stunned. I know we discussed it but I...I. I was just happy being there for you and Jeffery. Through the good times and the bad." Cynthia stared at the picture of Jeffrey.

"We did have our bad times and you were there for us. When we weren't speaking to each other we could always count on you to listen." Claire started to cry. "Jeffery thought the world of you."

Cynthia walked to the picture of Jeffery on the wall. She stared at the picture and started to cry.

The women continued to speak about everything from love to hate, as well as religion and politics. Cynthia never took a drink from her glass. Claire filled another glass and drank until she passed out on the sofa. Cynthia tucked Claire in and then called a cab. She reached the downtown DC hotel just in time to get a few hours of sleep before she was up and moving to Dulles International Airport to catch a mid-morning flight home. Her friendship and eventual nomination remained intact.

Elvis...

McCreiess was in a good mood. He stood in the parking lot stretching near his vehicle. The parking lot was a few miles away from the recreational area that he would use for trail running but he was good with that. The plan hatched in isolation called for him to park at a point that adjoined the woods he would eventually traverse so that he could avoid anyone that might be in the main vicinity of the recreational area. He would move through the woods until he found the trail his target would be running. He enjoyed trail running and the thought of running a new trail pumped him up, although he would probably only run a hundred yards of an actual trail. Merrell would be monitoring radios and scanners from a van at least ten miles away.

As usual, McCreiess' radio was tuned to the Sirius XM all Elvis station. He sang along with the tune "*Way Down.*"

McCreiess spun toward the trunk of his car as Elvis' voice peaked. He popped the trunk, opened his gun bag, and used the weapons silencer as a microphone. He did his best to mimic the voice of Elvis as he sang.

He grabbed the H&K USP sub compact .45 caliber pistol. He stepped back from the vehicle and danced to the chorus, doing his best to move the way he thought Elvis would have.

When the lyrics kicked in he stepped forward and grabbed a full magazine. He slapped it into the weapon and charged the pistol.

*** *

The single-track trail bounded toward the forest and left the marsh. With the forest came the hills and they were considerable. The hills were both up and down and they tested the most experienced trail runner. Benny Shills had traversed the trails around Chicago before and many others like them since moving to Europe. The trails allowed him to get away from the city and all that had to do with the hectic life of living in a major metropolitan area. It had been awhile since he was able to run this particular trail so he tried to remember the upcoming twists and turns.

The time was mid morning and on a weekday so the chance was remote that someone other than an enthusiast would be out on the trail with him. Benny passed ponds and crossed streams. His body was wet with sweat and his legs became caked with mud. He loved everything about getting out in the sunlight in the midst of a forest. The rolling terrain and the many different hills were a test for him; he pushed harder. He looked forward to the upcoming bend in the trail because it provided tree cover, which was usually accompanied by a cooler air than other parts of the trail.

***

McCreiess stood about ten meters from the trail waiting patiently for his target. From his vantage he could see a bend in the trail and his plan was to jump the trail before the target could make the turn. Merrell informed him by radio earlier when the target started the run and which trail he would be running, so he knew his target should be closing on his point soon.

***

Benny picked up the pace. He was making great time. He felt the vibration of his cell phone from his fanny pack. He kept running while he thought about whom it could be. If it was the ex-wife he didn't want to hear anything. If it were his attorney Ted Fienberg, he would only talk about the upcoming charity event that only he was interested in. He stopped and pulled the phone from his pack to look and see who was calling (Ted Fienberg).

"Ted. You fat piece of..." Benny answered the phone. He took a large breath and let it out. "Do you know where I am? What I'm doing?"

"It's morning. Mid-morning." Ted responded.

"That's right, shit for brains. It's morning and I'm getting a run in." Benny acted more upset with Ted than he actually was. He continued to catch his breath.

"Benny, the politicians don't want anything to do with a charity." Ted quickly got to the point.

"What do you mean they won't participate? They don't want anything to do with a charity?" Benny stretched as he spoke. "We have already set things in motion."

"Benny, they want cash. They said they spoke with you over a year ago and..."

"Bull shit, Ted!" Benny yelled. "You fat..."

"Benny they don't care. They feel ..."

"Oh no! I'm not giving them shit!" Benny cut Ted off by yelling. "They can go eat shit and spit corn."

"Benny they will get their money by..."

"They're going to do what? Those two little ..."

"Benny, please don't be that way." Ted pleaded.

"No! I will call them later and get this worked out." Benny took a deep breath.

"Benny. I want you to..."

"Blow me!" Benny hung up the phone and stuck it back in his pack.

Benny Shills looked around to get a view of the forest, thinking only the wildlife and he was around the trail. He took another deep breath and let it out. He looked at his watch and started running. His pace was quicker. He had lost run time because of his conversation with his attorney and he wanted to make it up. He was also anxious that the two politicians did not want to participate in his scheme. He rounded a bend in the trail and saw an oncoming runner. The cooler air felt good but he was unable to take advantage of it because he was still steamed by his last conversation. He continued to run, hoping the man coming his way would give a little space and pull to the side so he could get past on the single lane trail. Seeing the man closing quickly, Benny slowed.

"Hey dick head! One of us is going to have to give way," Benny shouted at the oncoming man.

The man pulled a weapon from behind his back.

"That was quick." Benny choked on his last words. The thought he had was that the politicians who felt cheated by him took a very drastic measure. He stopped running because of the acute stress response that overwhelmed him. His sympathetic nervous system kicked in as he momentarily struggled with the urge to engage the man before his bowels loosened and he messed himself. His last thought was to flee.

***

McCreiess stopped within ten feet of the man he was tasked to kill, Benny Shills, and stared into his eyes. He broke eye contact after noticing the involuntary shaking that overcame Benny's body. He let his eyes drift down to the mess that Benny created; excrement seeped out of Benny's shorts and crept down his leg. McCreiess cocked his head, shrugged his shoulders, and grimaced. He felt some sympathy for the man he was commissioned to kill, and he knew a man much stronger than Benny Shills lose control of his bowels when immediate future moments meant death for the man if good things didn't happen. There wasn't anything good going to happen to Bernard Benny Shills in the next few moments.

"I can get you the money." Shills' voice quivered. "No charity scheme. No..."

McCreiess methodically pulled the trigger of his pistol twice and quieted Benny Shills. The two bullets fired from McCreiess' silenced pistol hit shills in the chest like a sledgehammer. McCreiess watched as Benny stumbled back and stood stunned. He watched as Benny gasped for air, while a sucking sound came from one of the holes in Benny's chest. He heard gurgling sounds as Benny's lungs filled with blood. He calmly stepped to his left when Benny took a slight step forward and stumbled but somehow remained standing. McCreiess felt as if they could have danced around the trail all day together but the internal clock inside of him said, "Get a move on." He made a few steps forward and placed the barrel of the weapon within an inch of Benny's forehead.

Benny looked into the eyes of the man who would kill him. He tried to speak but his mouth was filled with blood so he chocked and then spit the fluid. His eyes glazed over and tears rolled down his cheeks. He looked down and away.

McCreiess pulled the trigger. A mist of red and grey formed around the back of Benny's head as he remained standing for a split second, and then collapsed to the ground. McCreiess was sure the third bullet put Benny out of any misery he was experiencing before he hit soil. Benny's body lay crumbled and contorted in a manner that left his feet underneath his body. McCreiess stepped forward to look over the body. He thought about firing another volley of bullets but decided against it after noticing the brains of Benny Shills spread out on the trail. He holstered his weapon, and looked at his watch.

"You had to answer to someone, Mr. Shills. Nothing personal," McCreiess murmured. *Few more and I'm out.* He looked around the immediate area to ensure there was no one around.

"Lights are out," McCreiess spoke into his radio. "Route Alpha."

"Roger that. Lights out," Merrell responded. "Route Alpha and I've got it from here. I'll keep you informed of Blue Falcon movement." He used the call sign Blue Falcon when speaking about law enforcement.

"It is a beautiful day for a run," McCreiess said as he quickly jumped from the trail into the woods.

This just in...

The FCICU lounge was filled with people for lunchtime. Most people used their time to get a quick bite before returning to an office or cube. It was a great place for agents, analysts, and techs to get face time with each other where they otherwise wouldn't see each other. The lounge was filled with several microwaves, vending machines, and a few televisions. People who didn't bring their lunch pail mingled about as they made their decisions as to what noxious food would pervade their bodies.

SueAnn sat in one of the hard plastic chairs and enjoyed the tuna salad that she prepared the evening before. The salad was missing something and she couldn't quite put her finger on what the ingredient might be. On the television was a commercial about the latest spicy mustard to hit the market. The powdered mustard she worked into the tuna was exactly what her father put in.

Jennifer sat at SueAnn's table and prepared to eat a chili cheese dog she purchased from one of the vending machines. Prior to sitting down she used one of the tattered microwaves to heat it.

"What'cha got there, Agent English?" Jennifer smiled. "Let me guess, something healthy."

"Well I assure you, you won't find it in one of those machines." SueAnn took a bite and thought about what her salad might be missing. "It's missing something and I just don't know what."

"Onion." Jennifer took a huge bite from her chili cheese dog.

"No. I think I'm good on that." SueAnn pondered the onion ingredient.

"No. I mean I love these little onion sprinkles they put on these dogs." Jennifer picked onions from the table that fell from her hotdog and licked them from her fingers. "Yummy."

"How can you eat anything from a machine and heated in one of these break room microwaves?" SueAnn grimaced as she watched her friend enjoy the hotdog.

"What do you mean? This is great American..."

"I mean the germ payload on a microwave door is more than you would find on a typical toilet seat." SueAnn interrupted Jennifer before she could demonize American cuisine.

"Well aint that nice." Jennifer smirked and looked at one of the heavyset analyst eating a chili cheese dog. "I guess as long as it's not his toilet seat."

"Well isn't that nice." SueAnn faked a gag and then turned her attention to breaking news on the television.

"This just in," the news anchor said. "The body found the other day on a running trail outside of Chicago was none other than the former C.E.O. of the now defunct energy giant, Copen Energy. You may remember Benny Shills. Eight years ago he was the face of evil for many people. He took Copen stock from over a hundred dollars a share to pennies and walked away with millions..."

SueAnn continued to watch as the anchor elegantly switched the topic from death to weather.

"Good riddance." Jennifer took another large bite from her hotdog.

Would she think he was sexier?

The law chamber was unusually hot as Judge Ellenberg looked over notes from the case before him. The thought of the jury coming back with anything other than a guilty verdict made Ellenberg contemplate the reliability of eyewitness accounts. How reliable can a well-known heroin addict be? He considered the defense position in regards to the fact that the addict owed the defendant money and hoped that prison bars would protect the addict from the defendant recouping his money by using any means necessary, including violence. He chuckled at the thought of telling the jury they couldn't use the threat of future violence the defendant threatened to use against the addict if he didn't pay up in a timely manner.

The cell phone on his desk vibrated. Ellenberg loosened his tie and sighed before he picked it up. The text message was from a number he didn't recognize so he was hesitant to read it. He pushed a couple buttons and the message popped up (HOCKEY TICKETS?).

The message was a preplanned simple question that confirmed the termination of Benny Shills.

Ellenberg quickly searched the Internet for any story that might relate to Benny Shills. The search wasn't long. The story wasn't a lead headline but it was noted on many different national news networks. Many of the stories briefly mentioned that he was once in charge of an energy company that failed, and that his bullet-riddled body was found on a running trail in Chicago. Some of the articles flirted with editorializing by suggesting that not many would care that Benny Shills met an early demise and that there would be any number of people who had the motive to see him not reach an old age.

Ellenberg suddenly felt ill. He felt the urge to vomit but was able to allay the feeling by leaning back in his chair and taking a deep breath. He felt nauseous again so he quickly bent over and put his face in a waste can. Nothing came up but the metal from the can felt good on his forehead. He remained clutching to the wastebasket for what seemed like hours but was really only minutes. He took a deep breath and sat up, pushing the wastebasket under the desk with his feet. The realization that he had a hand in the death of Shills struck him like a bolt of lightning and guilt overwhelmed him. He thought about just running far away but where would he go and what would his family think? He thought about Judge Carson and anger swept over him. He was angry that he allowed Judge Carson to get him involved in something as evil as The System. He thought about why he allowed the judge to talk him into it. Was it simply because he wanted to be close to a man like Judge Carson and people like Max Merrell and Drake McCreiess? Regardless of what he wanted, he now realized he was very close to the men who dealt death. His thoughts moved to whom he could speak with about what he was involved in. He quickly realized that Merrell and McCreiess were two people he would not speak with. He knew they could care less about what he was feeling. He thought of his wife and how she would react to such news. Would she think he was sexier for being part of such an organization, a secret society that set justice straight? Or would she think he was crazy for getting involved? He would not present the case to his wife for judgment. The only thing he did know was that he had to get out. McCreiess wanted out so why couldn't he? He quickly felt the wave of nausea hit him again so he lunged for the wastebasket.

Your daughter is unique.

Senior Agent Ben Kelly looked over paperwork that piled on his desk; reports that someone thought was important enough to be reviewed by the person in charge of stuff the FBI no longer wanted to look at. The files were unsolved murders, kidnappings, bank robberies, and anything else that went unsolved over a period of time. The FCICU seemed to be the place where the FBI could dump cases, yet claim they were still working even though they were no longer interested in whether or not the case was solved or not. If a mother wanted to know if her missing daughter would be found soon, the FBI sent her to Ben Kelly and his crew. The FCICU became the graveyard of FBI agents who were too stupid to realize they weren't going anywhere with their careers, at least that's what Ben Kelly thought. SueAnn English was that FBI agent. She created a stir by doing the things some thought women shouldn't do. When Agent Bear froze, she advanced and went guns blazing. The FBI silenced those that wanted the true story told about how she took out two bank robbers who were dead set on going out in a blaze of glory. She provided the blaze, but the glory never seemed to mount for them. Those in charge of the FBI wanted to credit the agent who gave the coup de grace to Marcwell. They never wanted to mention the fact that more FBI agents would represent notches on Marcwell's pistol grip if it were not for SueAnn English. Others in the FBI wanted to credit Agent Bear for listening to orders, especially his uncle, Assistant Director of the FBI, Derrick Bear.

Kelly knew the truth about SueAnn English and he knew her father, the late Senior Agent Paul English. SueAnn's father spoke out against Bear and people who promoted him. He didn't promote his daughter because he understood she would succeed on her own merits, but people like Bear created chaos when they reached levels where decisions were made.

Senior Agent Kelly placed a file on his desk and remembered one of the last conversations he had with his great friend Paul English.

:-

Kelly stood and looked up at the monument that honored a man who was fast becoming just another figure in a history book that only historians read about. The General William Tecumseh Sherman Monument was placed in President's Park and was dedicated by President Theodore Roosevelt. It stood at the site of the reviewing stand for the Grand Review of the Armies, where General Sherman, President Andrew Johnson, and General Ulysses S. Grant reviewed the Army of the Potomac after the defeat of the Confederacy and the tragic murder of President Lincoln.

B E L F O R D   S C O T T

Thousands of people walked by the monument on a daily basis, but most, if not all, failed to realize the significance of the man memorialized on the horse or the spot the monument rested on. It was not lost with Kelly. He asked his friend Paul English to join him because of the significance.

"Great man," Paul English said after he walked up from behind and stood next to his friend, looking up at the monument, "His march to the sea destroyed the will of his enemies."

"The man was a leader." Kelly turned to look at his friend. "You know what made him a great leader?"

"I would say it was that after all his success, he still only wanted to be remembered as a simple soldier." English paused. "He was a man that understood it was about doing something and not being a somebody."

"Yes. Yes." Kelly turned to stare at the monument again. "I know someone else like that."

"My daughter is not to be used." English was stern. "I don't want her anywhere near..."

"Your daughter is unique." Kelly smiled.

"What happened to Judge Carter was an awful display of power run amuck." English's shoulders slouched and he pulled his trench coat up around his neck to help keep the warmth from leaving his body.

"It's a cold ass day." Kelly wiped his nose.

"It's real cold for people who see what they've worked so hard to protect disappear like the stench of New Orleans during a hurricane." English stood stoic. "George, his daughter Cynthia, and the General have strayed from the path set forth by our forefathers."

"There was so much power that stood here. So much change going on." Kelly searched for his next words. "Reunification of a country and death of a leader. Two great powerful men standing next to a scummy politician." He diverted the conversation away from current members of The System.

"What if it were Lincoln instead of Johnson standing here?" English asked, understanding his friend didn't want any part of what he wanted to talk about.

"By all accounts Lincoln was a fine man. Fine leader." Kelly shrugged his large shoulders. "Still just a politician."

"Things change and I get that, but my daughter, as tough as she is." English paused. "She is not what The System is becoming."

"Judge Carter was the beginning and it won't stop there." Kelly shrugged his shoulders. "I just hope..."

"I don't want SueAnn involved. She isn't what you are looking for." English grabbed Kelly's elbow and gripped hard as he interrupted his longtime friend. "I don't have long. I need you to promise me that she doesn't get involved."

i

A knock on the door interrupted Kelly. He looked up to find SueAnn English staring at him. He leaned back in his chair.

"Come in." Kelly smiled as SueAnn entered.

"Do you have a minute sir?" SueAnn stood before him.

"I do. I do. As a matter of fact, I have been expecting you to drop by." Kelly remained seated and motioned for SueAnn to sit.

"Sir?" SueAnn cocked her head.

"Oh yeah. Agent Brenner and I have been talking about your thought process."

"My thought process, sir?" SueAnn sat forward in her seat.

"Lead investigator Brenner talked to me about what you are thinking. And I'm not talking about softball." Kelly smiled.

"Yes, sir. I have been running data and I was really hoping..."

"You know." Kelly interrupted SueAnn. "I have been doing this for a few years now. Some would say too long." Kelly sat forward in his chair, hands clasped on the desk. "What you are thinking has been thought before. Investigated even. Some even thought this small detachment, the bureau as a whole, or another agency, may even be behind what you are thinking." Kelly paused. "If not behind it. Condone such behavior."

"Sir. My father explain..."

"Nothing has ever come of it." Kelly cut SueAnn off. "A report was even submitted discounting an organization or secret society that would be behind the activity you're looking into."

Kelly reached into his desk drawer and pulled out a report and handed it to SueAnn.

"Look it over." Kelly smiled. "You may be interested in the author."

"My father." SueAnn's voice made an unusually high pitch.

"You might want to look that document over carefully, SueAnn." Kelly leaned back in the chair again. "You might find something in there that can help you. Although I don't know what that would be."

"Thank you, Sir. Do you want me to report back?"

"Yeah, I do. I need to know if our home field will be Alpha or Bravo this year?" Kelly could see that his question drained the excitement from SueAnn. "I prefer Bravo field. It's closer to home. Maybe you can do something about that?"

"I'll get that, Sir." SueAnn halfheartedly grinned.

"Mrs. Kelly would appreciate that." Kelly smiled. "She doesn't like to drive that far into the city.

Held to his lie

The parking lot had few cars in it at 4:00 in the morning. Most who took their last shot, downed their last beer, or tucked their last buck left the Grape Garter Lounge when it closed an hour before. The "Grape" as most of the loyal patrons called it was a low rent strip club located on the south side of Daytona. The people who entered the place understood what they wanted; lots of ass, tits, and no penis tucked under the bikini bottoms. They wanted girls who would cross the line the State of Florida imposed on behavior at such establishments, and they could care less if any of the women who hung from a pole ever had dreams about using their tip money for a college degree.

Buggy was a different kind of patron though. He had both business and pleasure to tend when he visited the "Grape." The owner, Gene, was a client of Buggy's who purchased several illegal immigrants over the years. Gene enjoyed working with Buggy because he knew Buggy's weakness for young Asian women, and that Buggy would reduce rates for special favors. It was not uncommon to hear Asian women reciting certain passages of Sun Tzu's *"Art of War"* behind closed VIP room doors within the "Grape." Only Gene knew that the girls were sodomizing Buggy with plastic vibrators as they did their best to recite Tzu's masterpiece.

A breeze from the ocean hit Buggy as he opened the door and exited the "Grape." He stumbled and caught his step by grabbing the handrail. Alexi stepped out the door and noticed Buggy holding on to the rail. She slowly moved behind him and noticed he was sleeping as he stood.

"Boo," Alexi yelled.

"What the..." Buggy woke and then bent over and vomited.

"Jesus!" Alexi stepped back and gagged as she got a whiff of Buggy's lunch and breakfast. "What the fuck Buggy!"

"It must have been the cheese on that cheeseburger." Buggy mumbled and dry-heaved.

"Bullshit! It was fifteen beers and six shots of JW Red." Alexi bent under the rail and stepped into the parking lot so she wouldn't have to step in Buggy's puke.

"It was that fucking cheese they put on those burgers God damn it!" Buggy held to his lie.

***

The large cardboard box shuttered and out popped the head of a homeless man who lived in that same box for the last few days. The man knew it was early but didn't know the exact time. He never would have stirred if he didn't hear the sounds of someone throwing up across the alley and parking lot his box adjoined. He kept his eyes on the two people arguing near the entrance of the "Grape." He decided to settle back in until he heard a familiar tune coming from the window that overlooked his box and parking lot.

Elvis! Anne Margret, the homeless man thought to himself as he started humming along with the tune "*Viva Las Vegas.*"

***

Alexi stumbled as she simultaneously held Buggy up and opened the passenger side door to the silver Lexus. Buggy was starting to come around but his knees still felt weak. Buggy leaned onto the car and slid into the car seat.

"I saw the way you were looking at her ass," Alexi yelled as she shut the door and walked around to the driver side and jumped in.

"It's a fucking strip club, baby." Buggy tried to fight back.

"She's no fucking stripper, Buggy."

"Alexi, the bitch was wrapped around the pole just two fucking hours ago." Buggy slurred his speech.

"Two hours ago you were getting your ass pumped full of plastic by some..."

"What the hell are you talking about?" Buggy's voice rose.

"That's right. Gene told me..." Alexi stopped in mid-sentence when she felt a presence outside the car.

"Gene! We aint cutting you anymore deals on Asian ass and we don't need any more of your stinkweed," Alexi yelled as she rolled down the window.

"Who the...that's not Gene," Buggy said as he leaned over to look out Alexi's window.

"Oh no," Alexi yelled as she saw a pistol jammed into the open window.

***

McCreiess stood looking over Alexi and Buggy and he felt no remorse as he squeezed the trigger of his silenced weapon. Two bullets hit Alexi in her chest and her body convulsed. He saw that Buggy suddenly became sober and rushed to open his door, so he fired two bullets into his back and watched as his head slumped to the floor board. He could tell that Buggy was alive by way he labored to breath. He figured the bullets shattering his spinal cord either paralyzed him or he was faking death. McCreiess was not concerned as long as Buggy was not moving.

Alexi's gasp for air brought McCreiess back to the task at hand. She looked toward him. McCreiess pulled a thermite grenade from his pants cargo pocket. She looked up.

"God! Jesus! Why?" Alexi cried and gasped. "Buggy..."

"If you believe in God, you will have lots of explaining to do," McCreiess said before he pulled the pin of the grenade. "We all do," he said before tossing it between the two human traffickers.

With the sound of puff, the grenade started to burn from the inside out. The pyrotechnic composition of metal powder and a metal oxide produced a thermite reaction that burned at 1,665 degrees Fahrenheit. Commonly used to destroy heavy metal equipment in war, the thermite grenade could easily burn a Lexus sedan and the two crack heads inside.

McCreiess walked away as the car started to fill with smoke and fire. Hearing Alexi cry out in agony brought no feelings one-way or the other.

"Hey!" A voice came from a short rotund man running toward the burning car. "Alexi! Buggy!"

McCreiess turned and walked back to the burning car.

"What the fuck just happened," yelled the short rotund man.

"You Gene?" McCreiess asked.

"Yeah!" The short rotund man answered. "What happened?"

"Alexi mentioned you." McCreiess pulled his silenced pistol and fired two bullets into the head of Gene, the short rotund man who peddled human beings.

You're a Dragon, man

Judge Ellenberg stood in the locker room alone. He felt a little sore after completing an hour class of Krav Maga. The contusion on his chest made him wince as he removed his shirt. He moved toward the mirror to look at himself. He took a quick look at the bruise and then did a once over of himself. He was proud of hardening his body over the last year, and the dragon tattooed on his shoulder made him feel as if he was invincible. He was not happy about being involved in an organization such as The System, but the dragon tattoo comforted him. His father persuaded him to get the tattoo after law school. His father explained it was a message that he could overcome all obstacles.

The thought of his upcoming cage bout had him a little nervous but what else was he suppose to do after a year's worth of Krav lessons. He had never been in a fight and he wanted to test himself. Looking in the mirror he was attracted to the tattoo; he flexed his muscles and quickly stopped when the locker room door opened.

Ellenberg's cell phone rang so he quickly reached for his gym bag. He pulled the phone and realized it was a text message (BASEBALL TICKETS?).

Ellenberg sat on the bench and slumped over. He felt nauseated. He knew the crack heads in Crackville, which the General spoke about, had breathed their last breath.

"You ready?" The Krav Maga instructor asked.

"Ready?" Ellenberg replied meekly.

"Yeah. Your fight. There's nothing like it." The instructor danced and sparred with himself in the mirror. "You'll love it, man." The instructor paused to throw some punches at himself. "Going toe to toe. You're going to love it."

"Yeah." Ellenberg did his best to sound pumped.

"Dragon man! You're a Dragon, man."

Ellenberg dove face first into his gym bag and cried out loud.

"What the hell are you crying about, man?" The Krav instructor stepped back and crossed his arms. "I know you're nervous but what the fuck?"

Never solved...

Jennifer bound down the alley of cubicles. She was ecstatic about the big win her Yankees had the night before and she wanted to share it with the only other Yankee fan in the department, SueAnn. Rounding the corner she bumped into the cart Martin, the mail carrier, was pushing as he delivered computer hardware.

"C'mon, Marty." Jennifer smirked.

"It's Martin, Jennifer."

"Well move your Red Sox ass out of the way." Jennifer hurried past.

"I don't even like basketball." Martin kept pushing as Jennifer stopped in her tracks and turned.

"And you wonder why you're a virgin, Marty." Jennifer turned again and moved quickly toward her destination.

"I don't wonder," Martin said with a smirk. "I know."

Jennifer slid to a stop when she got to SueAnn's cube.

"Did you see Jeter last night?" Jennifer asked as she threw her hands in the air.

"Four for Five. Two dingers." SueAnn turned away from her computer. "Who said the man is done?"

"Done! I would let that man crunch crackers and pour them all over me while in bed." Jennifer laughed.

"Wow!" SueAnn leaned back in her chair. "That could have been a lot worse."

"Well I was going to say that I would crawl a mile through broken glass to lick the last pussy he fucked, but I figured that would be a little too much." Jennifer looked as if she was thinking about the decision she made.

"Yeah. I'm glad you went the cracker route." SueAnn grimaced and turned away.

"What the hell happened there?" Jennifer looked over SueAnn's shoulder.

"Excuse me?" SueAnn remained fixated on the Internet story she was reading.

"On your screen. Looks like a guy made enemies."

"Oh. That. Just a story I'm looking over. Seems this guy met a premature death. Murder. Never solved." SueAnn kept reading.

"And why are we interested?" Jennifer leaned over to see why her friend was so interested in the story.

"Attorney. Not a real nice guy, especially to women. Gets whacked nine years ago." SueAnn paused as she continued to read. "Eight years before bullets appeared in his skull and chest he was tried for murder of three women. Suspected of killing many more. He got off. His murder was never solved." SueAnn leaned back in her chair.

"I hope you find that some sister took a stand." Jennifer turned after she heard her phone ring. "That's my phone." She hurried back to her cube.

SueAnn stopped reading the story and picked up the document Senior Agent Ben Kelly gave her. She thumbed through the document; holding something her father created comforted her.

A note from the document fell to the floor after she bumped it on the desk as she was putting it down. She picked the document up and unfolded it. After reading it she jumped to her feet and looked over the cubes as if she was looking for a certain someone, but really didn't know whom.

Couple things to talk about

Alone in her chamber Judge Cynthia Mader read an
Internet news story. The headline of the story read "Three
killed in Strip Club Car Fire." The pictures of Buggy, Alexi,
and the owner of the club Gene were situated directly
under the headline.

Cynthia silently clasped her hands together and
smiled. She was giddy as she reached for her phone.

***

Ellenberg kissed his wife at the front door of his house
and walked to his car parked in the driveway. His cell
phone vibrated so he reached in his pocket, pulled it
out, and looked at it (Cynthia).

"Ahhhhh, come on." Ellenberg rolled his eyes and stood
silent for a moment. "Hello, Cynthia." He answered the phone.

"Mr. Ellenberg, I just got the good news. That is two
out of three." Cynthia's giddiness was obvious.

"Yes, Cynthia. What can I do for you? Talk about
something else?" Ellenberg knew she was angling for
the third and final order to be fulfilled.

"Couple things to talk about." Cynthia took a serious tone. "I'm wondering who the third person was in the last order, and when..."

"Stop there." Ellenberg leaned up against his car. "I don't know who the third person was. It definitely wasn't someone ordered. And the other order will take time."

"Time," Cynthia yelled.

"Yes. Time!" Ellenberg became angry enough to cry. "Our friends had to take a break."

"Let me guess. Africa! Or some other God forsaken place." Cynthia paused to collect herself. "They need to be here working for us. We pay them very well you know."

"Where ever they are is good with me. I think two out of three within four months after our..."

"You have him call me when he gets back from whatever waste land he is." Cynthia interrupted Ellenberg. "I want to..."

Ellenberg cut Cynthia off by hanging up the phone. He was stunned after hearing that a third person was killed.

"Two dead crack heads in Crackville," Ellenberg said to himself, as he stood stunned. "Where did the third one come from?"

Ellenberg thought about running to the house and telling his wife everything about what he was involved in. He felt if he just lay in her arms and told her, she would somehow have some magical plan that would make it all go away. He continued on to the car. The thought of telling her only worried him more than he already was. *She wouldn't understand*, he thought.

Too many fingers in the pie

The platoon size element struggled to get through the thick brush. The men carried heavy rucksacks, weapons of all sorts, and water. They were dirty and tired after six days of movement with little food and sleep. They were Special Forces recruits who were on their final patrol before finishing phase one of three phases of the most demanding school the Army offered. The men came to a halt and each of them took a knee. The student leader of the platoon, Sergeant Udall, moved to the point of the patrol to see why the movement stopped. He stumbled and fell face first into the North Carolina red and wet dirt. The men who saw the Sergeant fall giggled. Udall pushed himself from the ground and remained on both knees. He shook his head to clear his thoughts.

"Sergeant Udall. I'm right here," Sergeant Piper whispered, "Right here."

Two other members of the patrol helped Udall to his feet.

"It's alright, Udall," one of the men said. "We're almost there."

"It looks like we've come upon a danger area of some sort." The other man spit tobacco juice. "Better pull your map and get a check."

"What's the hold up?" Sergeant Panetta, the Special Forces instructor made his way to Udall. "Where are you Sergeant?"

"Right here. SF Recruit seven one four, Sergeant Panetta." Udall took a knee and held his hand up.

"No fucking shit, Sergeant." Panetta knelt down next to Udall. "Where are you on the map? Use one of your ball scratchers to point it out to me."

Sergeant Udall pulled his topographical map from his pants cargo pocket. He unfolded it and scanned it. His mind was foggy.

"I think we're right here, Sergeant." Udall pointed at the map. "Right here on this ridge line moving down into that flat open area."

Sergeant Piper moved back from the point to look over the map as well.

"That flat area is..."

"I'm asking Sergeant Udall, Sergeant Piper. He is the platoon leader." Panetta cut Piper off. "He will tell me where we are."

"Sergeant we are here." Udall pointed again at the map and then looked toward the open area ahead of them.

"It's zero six twenty two." Panetta looked at his watch. "Major Merrell and Sergeant McCreiess are waiting on us." Panetta paused to look the line of men over. "Day break. A hot breakfast is waiting on us. Let's get on the move."

"Roger that." Piper smiled and moved to the point.

"Sergeant Udall. How you planning to negotiate that open area?" Panetta asked with skepticism. "You going to skirt it?"

"Speed is our security," Udall blurted out. "We will blow right through it." Udall's empty belly and the thought of a hot breakfast allowed him to throw caution to the wind.

***

The field that lay ahead was flat and brown Army property. The trees that surrounded the field were typical North Carolina Pine trees. Camp McCall training facility was situated near the home of the Army Special Forces, Fort Bragg. The camp was small in comparison to Bragg but it was secluded and the terrain was tough. It tested many a man over the years that dared to wear the coveted Green Beret.

Both Merrell and McCreiess stood atop an Army Humvee vehicle. They provided a watchful eye over the flat field that lay ahead of them. They wore the Army wood fatigues. The patches on their uniforms recorded that they both attended the Army Airborne, Ranger, and Special Forces schools. Both were gold star parachutist with master blaster status. Their uniforms showed that they both were awarded combat infantry badges. Anyone that saw their uniforms would understand that they were well trained and hardened individuals.

"What happened with the crack heads?" Merrell asked McCreiess.

"They got what was ordered. Haven't you heard?" McCreiess continued to look through the binoculars.

"There was a third person. He was found half in and half out of a burning vehicle. How? Why?" Merrell acted as if he were mad.

"Do you know who it was?" McCreiess questioned.

"The owner of the place." Merrell turned to look at his friend. "You know who he was."

"Maybe he decided to commit suicide after discovering that his friends were burning in a car." McCreiess smiled.

"Suicide? By jumping in a burning car? I could think of better ways to go." Merrell paused to look over the field. "Oh. His brains were found on the pavement." Merrell looked again at his friend. "Hard to make such weighty decisions about life and suicide without your brains don't you think?"

"I haven't seen you since I departed for Daytona. You just got in here this morning. We have recruits in the field and you want to bust my balls about how I carry out my orders?" McCreiess stared at Merrell. "The fat fucker ended up dead with his crack head friends." He paused. "Order was fulfilled and no questions need to be asked."

"It looks like we will have to move on that Mill order soon after we get back." Merrell changed the subject. "Got a message from Ellenberg that he's getting pressure from some of the other members."

"Who?" McCreiess questioned.

"Stallings and Mader." Merrell looked over the open area. "I don't know why this one is any more important than the others. Mader has tried to make contact with me directly...and Judge Stallings, he's called me a couple times. He's never reached out to me in the past."

"Too many fingers in the pie." McCreiess shook his head.

"Yeah. I don't like it. Seems like the 'Old Men' die... and well." Merrell shrugged his shoulders.

"We've got less than two months left here. We'll get home and take some time to settle in and get started," Merrell was thinking out loud. "Shouldn't be hard, but I don't want to be rushed. Mistakes are made when we rush." Merrell looked at McCreiess. "Planning as you know is everything."

Merrell's attention was directed to the open area. Soldiers broke from the pine tree wood line and entered the field. Merrell and McCreiess watched carefully as the platoon element moved slowly into the field. The platoon had no defined movement. They grouped closely together.

"A Haji with an AK could take out the whole lot of them." McCreiess looked into the Binoculars.

"Sergeant Panetta. This is Major Merrell," Merrell spoke into the radio.

"Go ahead, Major," Panetta's voice cracked from the radio.

"Tell them to spread out, and send that team leader to me. Now!" Merrell's anger could be heard by anyone within earshot of Panetta's radio.

Troops in the field started to spread out immediately.

"Roger. Send team leader to you," Panetta's voice cracked.

One soldier left the platoon in the field and ran toward Merrell and McCreiess.

"Who's the platoon leader responsible for that mess?" Merrell asked.

"Sergeant Udall is platoon leader," McCreiess said as he jumped from the Humvee and Merrell followed.

It took a few minutes for SF Recruit 714, Sergeant Udall, to make the long trek from the open field to the Humvee that Merrell and McCreiess stood by.

"Sergeant Panetta. This is Major Merrell."

"Go ahead, Major Merrell. This is Sergeant Panetta."

"I have SF Recruit seven one four. Continue the mission." Merrell looked over the recruit that stood at attention before him.

"Roger. Continue the mission, out." Panetta took control of the platoon and moved out of the open area and into the tree line.

McCreiess moved between the recruit and Merrell. He stood face to face with a man who wanted more than anything to become an elite soldier, a Green Beret.

"Seven One Four, get in the front leaning rest," McCreiess calmly said.

The recruit fell to the ground and assumed the push up position with his rucksack still on his back and his M-4 rifle on top of his hands.

"Recruit seven one four, why would your men be bunched up as they came out of that tree line?"

"Sir! Sergeant McCreiess. I...I..."

"I've read your file Sergeant Udall. You've been in the sand box a couple different times with the hundred and first. You were awarded the Bronze Star for honorable actions in Najaf." McCreiess kneeled down to the level of Udall. "Have you ever seen what happens when an explosive goes off with a bunch of people standing near it? All bunched together."

"I...I..." Udall stuttered.

"Yeah, yeah, yeah. I.I.I." McCreiess paused.

Watching McCreiess lecture Sergeant Udall allowed Merrell to drift in thought.

:-

Asadabad, Afghanistan is a place where hills can rise to over nine thousand feet and the clouds can blot out the sun for weeks on end. The villagers who live in the steep hills are used to its narrow valleys and rugged terrain that is considered inaccessible land to most of the US Army and its allies.

The area of Asadabad, situated near the Afghanistan, Pakistan border, was important to US Special Forces as well as the Taliban and other foreign fighters. The Special Forces needed Asadabad for its people because they believed that the people in the area could play a significant role in defeating the flow of foreign fighters and the weapons they carried. The Taliban needed the area for its twisting mountain passes that provided them cover when moving arms, explosives, and fighters into Afghanistan from Pakistan.

As the Special Forces advance operational commander, Major Merrell was familiar with missions that would send his men hiking for several miles into areas that were inhabited by insurgent fighters. He was never reluctant to fight but the years of war seemed to eat at his spirit. The cost seemed high for what his men and the people of Asadabad were paying. It was clear to Merrell that indigenous forces would never be able to independently secure the area he operated in, let alone the country.

There was such a wide range of evil groups that aligned against the people of Afghanistan, he often times contemplated to himself. He took a moment to look over an Afghan Special Tactic Team making final adjustments to personal equipment before departing the camp. Sergeant Wilson, the American Special Forces team sergeant, inspected each Afghan soldier to ensure the team was prepared for its upcoming mission.

Merrell witnessed firsthand the brutality of the Taliban and the foreign fighters. On his first deployment he entered a town where the village leaders and their families were disemboweled and the thumb of any person who voted during Afghanistan's first NATO sponsored election was cut off. Scenes of brutality were just part of the world he operated in.

"Sir, we'll be moving out soon," Sergeant Wilson said as he left the Afghan soldiers and approached Merrell.

"They look good. You did a fine job with them Sergeant Wilson." Merrell paused to watch one of the Afghan soldiers pull a US issued satchel charge from his rucksack. "I don't even..."

An explosion launched Wilson forward and into Merrell, sending both men to the ground. The eight sticks of C-4 plastic explosives contained in the satchel caused and explosion that ripped through the ten Afghan soldiers making their last minute preparations. Body parts, equipment, and debris scattered the immediate area.

Did the Afghan soldier cause the explosion by committing suicide? Were the plastic explosives rigged improperly? Could it have been static electricity that caused the explosive devise to go off? No one would ever really know for sure, but as the war raged more and more Afghan soldiers would turn themselves into weapons for the Taliban.

Merrell felt the sense of certainty that the feeling of slow motion provided. He lay on the ground for what seemed like minutes but was really a second or two. He sat up quickly, shook what seemed like cobwebs from his head. Things moved in real time. He noticed McCreiess running toward him and Wilson lying close by, face down, but not moving. He pulled Wilson over and saw that his eyes were blank and empty of life, his head contorted in a manner not natural. He slowly let go of the team sergeant and attempted to stand, but he felt a sharp pain in his lower leg so he sat back down. He looked down to notice his leg bleeding profusely. He leaned over to get a closer look and found that another man's jaw bone was imbedded just below his left knee; teeth and flesh still attached to the bone.

"Well, isn't that fucked up," McCreiess said as he leaned over to look at the wound.

"Yeah. It hurts pretty bad." Merrell writhed in pain. "Wilson didn't make it."

"Yeah, I've seen The Brain look better." McCreiess bent over to dress the wound. "I wonder if you'll get to keep the gold in the teeth?"

"Yeah, yeah, yeah. I.I.I." McCreiess looked at Merrell and noticed he was in deep thought. "I assure you, Sergeant Udall. You won't forget it. Especially if it's your men who get the full impact of it."

"Over there mistakes are unforgiving, Seven One Four," Merrell chimed in, "they're like bullets, once fired, you'll never get them back. And they destroy whatever they hit."

The beer dulled his senses

"So the Kepler spacecraft confirmed the existence of the first alien world in its host star's habitable zone." Mill staggered a little as the beer started to take effect.

"Habitable what the...?" One student asked.

"Habitable zone is that just-right range of distance that could allow liquid water to exist." Mill paused for effect as everyone who was listening glared at him. "You know. Life!"

"So you're saying' we found...?"

"I'm saying we one day. I say we like it's me out there looking. I mean. One day a planet will be found...much like ours."

"So will there...?"

"Who the hell knows woman!" Mill cut the young drunk woman off. "What I'm saying is that we will screw it all up! Think about William Smith of the Pilgrims..."

"Who in the hell..." An older gentleman piped up.

"Ever read your history books you old puke? You know the Pilgrims? Left old world Europe for new world... Plymouth Rock."

"How do you know so much?" The young drunk woman sighed.

"I've had plenty of time to find out a bunch of shit." Mill lifted his beer as if to salute Warden Bean.

***

Mill stumbled from the bar. He smiled at the thought of his conversation about the spacecraft and William Smith. He learned so much by reading in prison. The Warden was good to him. He knew he was at a point in his life when there was few if anyone looking out for his best interests. Playing with the drunks at the bar was something to pass time, but he knew he had to get lost and start over.

The beer dulled his senses just enough to relieve the worry of being on his own. He stood in the middle of the road watching the late night drunks of Bourbon Street move from bar to bar. Beer was something he missed while in prison. The warden would get him some every now and again but never enough to make him get stupid enough to get anyone in trouble. The warden would often say, "Don't know that you're ever getting out of here. Beer doesn't do anyone any good in here."

Mill understood the concerns the warden had, but he wished the warden had provided some of the fine craft beers he was now able to get. Beers changed over the last few years and he wished the warden had showed him; light beer was now something in his past.

***

Tommy Mill walked the center of Bourbon Street listening to the sounds that live music bars produced; people yelling, laughing, and cursing. His smile was as big as it had ever been. He had always heard of Bourbon Street and the wild things that can happen on a street when drink, smoke, and anything else a person can imagine flows steady. Before he got caught up in the anti-Reagan Central American movement he was nothing more than a bright kid who wanted nothing more than to go to school, party, graduate, and possibly get a job protesting something in Denver. Things didn't work out that way. He was now a fifty-two year old man looking at things he only imagined. He moved to the curb and sat down. A tear formed in his eye and he wiped it away. He wished he never had met some of the people he met earlier in his life. "Hang with losers and you are a loser," the warden would say. He lost so much and for what? He thought about the many years that he wasted in the federal prison system. He cried.

I was instructed on what to do

The classic black leather club chair and its matching
ottoman were the only furniture that existed in SueAnn's
studio apartment. She had a pull out of the wall bed and
some kitchen utensils, but nothing she would consider
being attached to other than that leather chair and its
matching ottoman. The chair was a reminder of her
mother. Her mother use to sit in it and read, or mark
papers of the grade school children she taught. SueAnn
remembered sitting on the ottoman while her mother
braided her hair just like she asked; the way Gretel would
have her hair braided in the play Hansel and Gretel.
Her mother wouldn't hesitate when asked to braid, she
just started braiding and conversations about anything
and everything would start. The chair meant stability
and it made it through one marriage and a couple other
boyfriends that didn't hold the significance of an old
Oxford.

SueAnn pulled the note that fell out of the report that
her father wrote and looked at it (call 285.419.2865 –
tell him the Monitor sent you). She slowly sat in the
chair and thought about the meaning of the note. *Who*

am I calling? Who would know if I called? What will be said? Who is the Monitor? She was uneasy with dialing the number but she did. She went against her better judgment, hoping only good things would come from making the call. Sitting in the ottoman, reading a report created by her father, and making the call, somehow made her feel closer to her parents.

"I know what you want." A man's voice answered SueAnn's phone call.

"Yes my name is Sue..."

"Hold up. I was instructed on what to do. You only need to provide me with some information. Give me..."

"Give you..."

"Give me some information and I will get back with you in a few days with some name or names," the man said with authority. "I'm doing this as a favor to a friend so make sure what you give me is good stuff because you won't get another shot at this."

"At this? I really don't know what I'm looking for." SueAnn was stunned about how fast things were moving.

"Yeah well. What I will provide will make things more clear."

"Yes. I'm sure." SueAnn reached into her pocket for a list of names she jotted down over the last few months. "I have names, dates, and locations."

"That's good," the man said. "What we are doing is not..."

"Please just get me what you can, and remember, this is a favor." SueAnn became bold.

"Sure, get me what you can." The man on the other end of the phone paused for a moment. "You'll want more. They always do. It's addictive."

"Addictive?"

"Oh yeah it is," the man said with the hint of a laugh. "Just remember that anything out there in regards to information about someone is also out there in regards to you."

"Give me a second to get my list. I have several names with places of, times, and dates of death." SueAnn disregarded the man's last statement.

His name is Brannon for a reason

The picture on the wall crashed to the floor and broken glass scattered over the floor of the Chambers. Cynthia and her administrative assistant, Ginger, raised their heads to see the damage.

"Oh my." Ginger rose from the sofa. "What the..."

"Please keep thumbing through those files, Ginger." Cynthia left her desk to survey the destruction. "I need that Atkins file."

"Yes Ma'am. I'll find it." Ginger continued with her task.

Cynthia bent over to pick up the picture that crashed to the floor. It was a picture of her father. The picture was one where her father stood smiling with Mount Kilimanjaro in the background. Cynthia stood silent looking the picture over, as Ginger remained hard at work. She slowly walked to her desk and took a seat. She propped the picture up, leaned back in her chair and remembered taking the picture of her late father.

:-

Judge George Mader and his daughter Cynthia stood outside Moshi Town and looked toward the tallest

380

mountain in Africa, Mount Kilimanjaro. Judge Mader held out his hand and made a "V" shape with his thumb and index finger. He placed the symmetrical cone of the mountain within the "V" shape. Cynthia held the camera patiently, waiting until her father gave her the go ahead for a snap shot.

"Each time I climb her is just a renewal." Judge Mader continued to view the mountain through his hand shaped in a "V." "She stands over nineteen thousand feet and I have scaled every bit of her."

"I love the way the sun light is hitting it as the clouds cast a shadow on Mawenzi." Cynthia stepped back and aimed the camera at her father.

"Wait," Judge Mader whispered, "let's let the sun set a little more."

"Thanks for bringing me, Daddy." Cynthia smiled at her father.

"I wanted you to see it and to climb it. I want you to take it in." Judge Mader turned away from the mountain to look at his daughter.

"Next year can we bring..."

"No!" Judge Mader became stern. "He will never be part of this."

"He is your grandson." Cynthia's voice quivered.

"No. He is not! His name is Brannon for a reason. Because I want nothing to do with him." Judge Mader turned back to the mountain.

"He made a mistake a long time ago." Cynthia pleaded. "He has paid his..."

"He has paid nothing," Judge Mader shouted. "What he did could have ruined us." He paused. "Providing him a position at the University is all he gets from me." Judge Mader frowned. "And I'm sure he will eventually screw it up." He paused. "He is in a position where he does nothing and believe me, it's better for all of us."

"Daddy we..."

"He is not part of us," Judge Mader yelled. "He is a retard who has cost me far more chips than what he is worth. It cost me a lot to get him into that college professor position. A lot!"

i

"Got it." Ginger pulled the file from the pile. "Atkins file."

Cynthia remained silent as she studied the picture of her father.

"Ma'am. You wanted the Atkins file." Ginger held the file up.

"Is your father proud of you?" Cynthia slowly looked up and stared at her administrative assistant.

"My father is proud of all of his children. He worked..."

Cynthia's phone vibrated on her desk so she looked to see who was calling (Judge Stallings). She interrupted her assistant by holding up her hand to silence her. She pointed toward the door so her assistant placed the file on the desk and hustled toward the door. Cynthia answered the phone as the door closed.

"Why, Michael. This is a surprise." Cynthia faked excitement.

"Are you busy?" Michael Stallings asked.

"As busy as a federal judge can expect to be, Michael. If there is anyone who knows how busy a federal judge can be. It would be you."

Stallings sipped from a glass of scotch as he paced his bedroom. He threw a picture of his wife and daughters on the bed.

"Okay, Cynthia. We have established that federal judges can be busy people." Stallings voice trembled. "That is not the reason for my call."

"Why are you calling, Michael?" Cynthia questioned.

"We can stop the order. We have time, Cynthia," Stallings cried. "Cynthia, please." He poured more scotch into his glass and took a large gulp. "We have not gone too far."

"Wait right there, Michael!" Cynthia yelled as she leaped from her chair.

"I don't know what you have gotten me involved with, but I want out." Stallings pleaded. "My weakness as a man allowed for your incursion. It allowed for you to be able to bend and twist me...to make me do something I would have never thought of doing." He finished his glass of scotch. "I am sickened by the whole damn thing."

"Michael! You need to pull your balls from your wife's lock box and start wearing them." Cynthia was calm but stern. "Stop acting like a God damn coward." Her calmness turned to anger. "Mr. Merrell has returned from the army thing he does, so I am sure things are in motion," She yelled. "I wouldn't know. He never seems to be able to return my phone calls. He..."

"Cynthia!" Stallings interrupted. "Why! Why does it have to be this way?" He picked up the picture of his family.

"Oh, act like a man, Michael," Cynthia screamed.

Stallings hung up the phone. He sat on the bed looking at the picture of his family. He lay back on the bed and cried.

King of Rock and Roll

Tommy Mill walked up the outdoor stairwell with caution. He had been out of prison for months and things seemed to be going too smooth for him, he felt. He had it better than most people released from prison and he knew it. The money his father left meant that he would never need a job if he made it last. Most of his urges had been satisfied since leaving the concrete walls the prison system offered. His visit to New Orleans saw to that. He felt something amiss though – everything seemed to be going too smooth. He just couldn't put his finger on what he was feeling. His visit with Jamie did a lot of good for his spirit. He was able to rid the demons of regret and doubt, at least for that part of his life, so he felt.

Reaching the top of the stairway, Mill looked right and left down the corridor. The sound of a woman shrieking with drunken laughter as her and a man entered their hotel room made the hair on his neck rise. He looked again both ways and noticed his room (206) three doors down to his left. He pulled the plastic card key from its holder and lightly stepped down the corridor.

"What are you doing Tommy, what the hell are you scared of," he whispered to himself after a few steps. He switched to a normal walk. "Quit freaking yourself out."

***

The corridor was dark. McCreiess stood for a moment and scanned the area. He looked down the open-air stairwell to ensure no one was stirring. He looked at his watch (0328 hrs). A dark van entered the hotel parking lot and parked exactly where he wanted it. He looked to his left at the door he would soon enter (206). He moved at a steady but cautious pace toward the door.

***

Tommy Mill suddenly woke from his dream. He sat up straight. Feeling panicked he scanned the dark hotel room; noticing light shining provided by the hotel sign beaming through the crack in the blinds. He looked at the clock (3:34). He took a deep breath and let it out as he kicked his covers off. His pillow was soaked with his perspiration. He swung his feet to the floor and sat silently for a moment. He was drenched in sweat so he took off his shirt.

"What a screwy ass dream that was," he said to himself as he sat and replayed it in his mind.

⁖

Mill ran through the forest as fast as he had ever run before in his life. He was amazed at how fast he was running. He was being chased. He was scared. His heart rate increased steadily. The crashing of trees and brush startled him so he turned to look. *Oh my God. What in the hell*, he thought to himself after noticing Tony the Tiger had joined the chase with Mighty Mouse.

"Why are you chasing me," he cried.

He turned to notice that Mighty Mouse split from Tony the Tiger and crashed through the trees and brush to the right. He noticed a tomato, and then a cantaloupe soar by his head. He breathed a sigh of relief; the two comic characters didn't have good throwing arms. It started to rain. He worried about keeping proper footing. He looked down to find that he was now wearing clown shoes.

"What in the hell can go wrong now," he yelled.

He noticed that the trail was bearing right. *Oh no. Mighty Mouse is to the right.* He felt Tony the Tiger closing in. A small tree was thrown in his path. *Mighty Mouse is strong but what the hell is it with Tony the Tiger?*

Mill was interrupted from reliving the dream as the hotel door suddenly burst open and the light turned on.

"Jesus! What the hell." Mill was startled. "How did you get in..."

McCreiess interrupted Mill by standing with his pistol pointing at him, and using his other hand to put his index finger to his mouth as a hush sign.

"You like Elvis?" McCreiess closed the door.

"What? Who?" Mill choked as he stood.

"You know. Elvis. King of Rock and Roll?" McCreiess questioned with a shrug of his shoulders.

"I...I..."

McCreiess started to do his best to mimic a young Elvis as he sang the song "*That's Alright Momma.*" He stepped closer. "I prefer his old stuff." McCreiess pointed his gun at Mill. "Now do you like Elvis?"

"I like Elvis." Mill stepped back into the telephone stand. "I guess. I mean it's been..."

"Young or old Elvis?" McCreiess questioned. "Well he died at forty-two, so old in Elvis years, I guess." McCreiess looked over Mill. "You need to get some clothes on."

"Yeah. Yeah. Clothes." Mill pulled his pants from the second bed and started putting them on.

"You know. They have a whole radio station dedicated to Elvis."

"Will you stop screwing around," Merrell's voice cracked through McCreiess' earpiece.

"I didn't know that." Mill started putting on his shoes. "I'm more of an ACDC fan."

"Oh yeah, Bon Scott or Brian Johnson? I'm more of a Bon guy myself." McCreiess answered. "Guy on the other side of this radio and in the dark van down stairs is an ABBA guy."

"Ha, ha." Merrell laughed. "We are all clear down here. Get a move on."

"Okay. Tommy Mill. That's your name." McCreiess became serious as he pointed the gun toward Mill's face.

"Yes. I'm Tommy Mill."

"We are going to head down stairs, Tommy Mill. You will follow a direct path to the dark van I spoke about and if you deviate. I kill you." McCreiess spoke nonchalantly.

"I...I..."

"You will not deviate from the path or I will kill you." McCreiess interrupted. "I have been tasked with killing you. Where, when, or if, may still be up in the air." He paused. "But as sure as the sun rises, and it has been rising for millions of years now. I will kill you if you don't do exactly what I say."

"Where are we going?" Mill took a deep breath and let it out.

"Be lucky it's not a body bag for you. At least not this day."

***

The room was silent and dark. Tommy Mill woke suddenly and panic-stricken. He tried to rise from his seat but found that his hands and feet were tied to a wooden chair. Frustrated he rocked back and forth until his chair tilted back, making him crash to the floor. He laid on the floor in silence. He looked for light, but could find none. He thought about what he last remembered. A tall man asking him questions about Elvis entered his mind. *What the hell? Elvis?* He remembered moving down a stairway and tumbling down a flight; the tall man helped him to his feet. He remembered a dark van and the slide door opening. *Who? What? How long? Where am I?*

"God damn it," Mill raised his head from the floor and yelled. "Jimmy Mader! You son-of-a-bitch!"

Mill heard the sound of keys clinging together. He laid his head on the floor and tried to remain silent. The cool concrete floor felt good against his skin. His hand was going numb so he tried to adjust to get the blood flowing to it again; his adjustment brought pain so he cried out.

"What the hell is going on in here," a man yelled as he opened the door; allowing light to shine into the room. "Didn't think you would ever wake." He turned on the light.

"What is going on?" Mill screamed. "Please help me."

"They didn't help Elvis." Another man entered the room.

"Jesus, what the hell is it with Elvis," Mill yelled, "I was twelve when he died for God sake."

The two men joined in laughter as they pulled a table and chair to the center of the room. The man who liked Elvis snatched up mill and set him up straight. He was then pushed in front of the table. The other man sat across from Mill at the table.

"Good. Good. Answers. You can tell me just what the hell is going on," Mill yelled. "It's Jimmy Mader. You're working for Jimmy Mader. Right?"

The man who liked Elvis tapped Mill in the head with the barrel of his pistol as he paced.

"God! Mother Mary! Come on, man." Mill twisted to view as much of the room as he could. "What is it with Elvis back here? Will someone please..."

"Easy, Tommy." The other man thumbed through a file in front of him. "We need you to calm down."

"Elvis has left the building," the man who liked Elvis whispered in Mill's ear.

"You know that man never wrote any of his own music." Mill did his best to look back.

"He was the King. All songs were his if he wanted them." The man who liked Elvis slapped Mill in the back of the head. "King of Rock and Roll."

"Is this really why I'm here? To discuss some fat dude who died on the shitter?" Mill laughed.

Mill was slapped hard in the back of the head. Mill's head went forward.

"What the fuck is it with this guy," Mill winced and yelled.

"He's happy," The other man calmly said. "He likes Elvis."

"I'm happy, Tommy," The man who liked Elvis whispered in Mill's ear. "I have either killed the last person I'm going to kill, or you will be the last person I kill."

"That's right, Tommy," the other man chimed in. "You have decisions, and we may have options."

"Jimmy Mader! Cocksucker. Jimmy Mader." Mill slouched. "What are you guys wanting from me?"

"Do you know me?" The other man asked.

"Know you? No. No. Fuck no," Mill yelled. "I have never met you." Mill paused and shook his head. "I just met the Elvis guy behind me. I guess. How long ago…"

"You're in a tough spot, Tommy." The other man interrupted.

"Ya think," Tommy Mill responded with a cry.

"My name is Max and my friend's name is not actually Elvis, his name is Drake. The reason I tell you our names is simple, because it probably won't matter."

Mill sat silent.

"It's very important that you tell me everything, Tommy Mill." Merrell continued to look over the file in front of him. "The truth will set you free." He paused to look over a picture. "I'm going to ask you some questions. Obviously, I don't know the answers to all the questions. I know some of the answers to some of the questions. The problem you have is that you don't know what I know or don't know."

"Who? What," Mill blurted out.

"All of that will come out. But you need only tell the truth, Tommy." Merrell leaned back in his chair and took a deep breath and let it out. "If I get so much as a hint of a lie."

Mill felt the barrel of a pistol nudge the back of his head.

"It won't be good for you," McCreiess spoke with confidence.

"Cynthia Mader?" Merrell placed a picture of Cynthia on the table. "Do you know her?"

"I knew it! That Bitch." Mill tried to get out of his chair but was held by the ropes restraining him. "I know her." He felt McCreiess' looming presence and he became frightened. "Can I have these ropes cut?"

Merrell nodded to McCreiess. McCreiess untied the ropes to Mill's hands.

"She's the mother of that idiot, Jimmy Mader." Mill rubbed his wrists and shook out his hands; trying to get blood flow. "I knew this had to do with those ass holes."

"The picture?" Merrell pointed to the photograph on the table.

"That is Cindy Mader." Mill looked closer. "Aged a little, but that's Cindy Mader."

"Judge Cynthia Mader?" Merrell leaned back in his chair. "Federal Jud..."

"Judge Cynthia Mader." Mill laughed. "I have no idea what she does for a living." He paused. "Her father was a big to do judge so it figures." He continued to chuckle.

"Get right." McCreiess tapped Mill's head with his pistol.

"If you know anything about me." Mill became angry. "And I'm sure you do or you wouldn't have a gun pointed at my head!"

Merrell leaned forward and stared at Mill. McCreiess acted as if he was hanging on Mill's every last word.

"Give me a break guys, I'm trying here. I really am." Mill sighed.

"Jimmy Mader? You mentioned the name Jimmy Mader before we came into the room?" Merrell asked.

"That must be what you don't know." Mill winced after receiving another slap in the back of his head. "Jimmy Mader is the son of Cindy Mader."

"I've made the Mader connection, Nimrod." Merrell sighed.

"Jimmy Mader is literally the shit that runs down the crack of a woman's ass." Mill pounded the desk.

"Why would Cynthia Mader want you dead?" Merrell calmly asked.

"You're not working for her?"

"Why?" Merrell pressed.

"It's her son, Jimmy Mader." Mill sighed and tilted his head to get a better view of McCreiess. "Jimmy Mader is her problem."

"Cynthia Mader has a son named Jimmy that is a problem. And that problem has something to do with why you were in prison?" Merrell looked at McCreiess. "I'm guessing out loud." He smiled.

"I'm glad this amuses you," Mill yelled. "I'm the one tied up with Elvis lover…" Mill was interrupted with a smack to the head.

"Watch it," McCreiess said.

"Give us the run down on how all this Mader stuff ties to you." Merrell leaned forward. "You were in prison for bombing an ROTC building in the eighties. Some anti-Reagan bull shit."

"I voted for Reagan." McCreiess announced.

"Yeah well. I guess you and Warden Bean would get along real well. I probably would have as well knowing what I know now." Tommy looked at McCreiess. "Twenty something years with Warden Bean and…"

"Let's get past our voting records for a minute." Merrell interrupted. "The news clippings from that time say that you were with a Gerald…"

"Cutter." Mill interrupted. "His name was Gerald Cutter and I can help you. It's making sense now."

"Explain." McCreiess prompted Tommy Mill to continue.

"Jimmy Mader. I don't know where he is now. But he had a huge part in the bombing of that building. He was up to his chin in planning and building the explosive device." Mill became angry.

"Article here says that Gerald committed suicide." Merrell holds up a newspaper article. "Says nothing about a Jimmy Mader."

"It wouldn't." Mill became somber. "Jimmy's mother Cindy, or Cynthia as you say, made him drop out of site. I'm sure she had help with her well connected father..."

"You're telling me that Judge Cynthia Mader has a son who helped you in the bombing of the Colorado State ROTC building?" Merrell paused. "She then whisked this son of hers away to where? What?"

"I don't know where he went. Dropped out of sight." Mill felt McCreiess' presence. "Do you have to be back there?"

"Did you know that Elvis was known worldwide? He sold millions of albums. He was bigger than big." McCreiess paced. "All without the Internet, CD's, DVD's..."

"What is it with this guy and Elvis," Mill yelled.

"Help us, Tommy." Merrell demanded as he laughed at his friend imitating Elvis Presley karate moves.

"Okay. Yeah. Yeah. You know what I did. Bombing the ROTC building, years back. I wasn't the only one as you know." Mill sighed.

"Articles mention no Jimmy Mader and they say your friend Gerald Cutter killed himself while in prison." Merrell held up a few articles.

"He didn't kill himself. He was killed, and she killed him." Mill pointed at Cynthia's picture. "She had him killed or they...."

"Yeah." Merrell leaned back in his chair.

"Yeah. You think he would have slit his own throat from ear to ear?" Mill paused. "Isn't it funny how Professor Shapiro ended up hanging himself and my lawyer ended up drowning during a fishing accident?"

"Go on." Merrell prompted Mill to tell more of his story.

"It's true. She had them all killed because they either knew her son was a nut or knew he had something to do with bringing that building down. And since she decided to protect her son...well...she is part of it all as well and she knows it." Mill paused. "Instead of handing her son over to authorities. She opted to get rid of everyone who knew her son's involvement in destroying the ROTC building."

"I like where this is going." McCreiess kneeled next to Mill.

"Shapiro wouldn't have killed himself." Mill chuckled. "He was a real commie who lived for the day that the Russians would cross the southern border, rescuing us all from the evils of capitalism. He lived for that day. He was real involved in the anti-Reagan Central American policy type stuff."

"Fucking communist." McCreiess quipped.

"Your lawyer?" Merrell interjected. "What about him?"

"After Gerald was found in his cell. My father made a deal with the warden. To protect me." Mill paused to control his anger. "He was able to protect me for years. But said he wouldn't be able to help me out here."

"Go on." Merrell pushed.

"My lawyer delivered a message to me. Sent from... he didn't know who. The message was a picture of my sister with drawn crosshairs on her head."

"Message is direct and to the point." McCreiess stood. "Maybe not my style, but effective."

"He was found floating in a river, my lawyer was." Mill sighed. "They couldn't get to me because my father paid a great deal of money for the warden to protect me in prison." He paused. "The message was clear. If I talk, my sister dies."

"Yeah. That's the way those things go." McCreiess massaged Mill's shoulders and gave him a gentle pat before he stepped back.

"Where's your father now?" McCreiess questioned.

"My father. He's dead." Mill seemed sadden by having to disclose that his father was no longer around to help him.

Merrell made eye contact with McCreiess.

"Oh no. My father passed away. Natural causes." Mill interjected.

"Anything else you want to let us know?" Merrell asked. "Anything that can help us? Anything that you think might help your situation?"

"There is another guy." Mill sighed. "Nesterenko is his name. Bodhan Nesterenko. Real mean fucker." Mill paused to remember.

:-

The three young men gathered at Jimmy Mader's low rent off campus apartment to brief each other on the status of their parts of the plan. Mader paced as Tommy Mill and Gerald Cutter sat on the couch.

"He will be here soon," Mader announced. "He is a friend of Mommy's."

Cutter and Mill looked at each other and rolled their eyes. A grown man calling his mother Mommy seemed a little weird to both, but they were willing to overlook such immaturity for the ultimate goal.

"How well do you know him?" Mill asked.

"Does Mommy know he's involved?" Cutter asked with a giggle.

Pinto, Mader's cat, jumped into Mill's lap and quickly fell asleep while his master continued his rant.

"I know him well enough, and no, Mommy is not aware of any of this. This will all be a surprise to her and the professor." Mader answered. "Pinto likes his belly rubbed, Tommy."

"What we are planning will make that half ass actor in Washington take note." Cutter pulled a joint from behind his ear and lit it. "The nuke marches your mom and the Professor attend are all well and good, but they are what they are. Marches."

"We will be seen as Gods...we will take those sons of..." Jimmy Mader was interrupted by a knock at the door. "We will have them..." He opened the door.

Suddenly a large man, Bodhan Nesterenko, kicked Mader in the chest and followed it up with a slap to his face. Mader stumbled back into the laps of Mill and Cutter, trying to catch his breath. Pinto jumped to the couch's armrest. Nesterenko chased Mader to the couch and continued to slap his face. He then grabbed Mader's left nipple and twisted hard.

"Listen you fat little Bastard." Nesterenko made eye contact with Mill and Cutter as Jimmy Mader screamed with pain. "From now on you don't answer the door without asking who the fuck is behind it."

"Yes. Yes." Jimmy Mader cried.

Nesterenko let up on twisting the nipple. He stepped back.

"You are now at a point of no return. No return!" Nesterenko was stern. "The van is packed. You will forget me. Understand!"

"Yes, Bodhan. Yes." Mader continued to cry.

Nesterenko quickly slapped Mader again. "Forget me you stupid bastard. You don't know my name!" He grabbed Pinto and ripped his head off. He threw the body of the cat to the floor and pitched the head into the lap of Jimmy Mader as the three young men screamed out loud. "Don't remember me." Nesterenko turned and stormed out the door, leaving the young men horrified.

"Who in the hell was that?" Mill quietly asked.

"That was Bodhan Nesterenko." Jimmy Mader sat stunned and crying as Pinto's head lay in his lap. "Pinto. Oh my poor beautiful Pinto."

"That was fucked up," Cutter said. "That was really...."

Mill crossed his arms and leaned back in his chair. He looked toward McCreiess and then toward Merrell.

"So, now what?" Mill took a deep breath and let it out.

Your weakness isn't chocolate...

Michael Stallings sat in the family room taking in the sounds of his family going about their daily routine. Mia, his eldest daughter, sat on the floor reading her favorite fashion magazine while Trinity, his youngest daughter, was deep into a game she played on a hand held device. His wife could be heard clanging dishes in the kitchen. A conversation he had with another judge crossed his mind.

:-

"Look, Michael." Judge Henry Fousset sat across the table from his friend. "This girl you are with."

"Girl?" Stallings questioned.

"Michael. You know damn good and well what I'm talking about." Fousset sipped from his double shot of whiskey on the rocks. "It's getting around that you two are more than friends. If you know what I mean."

"My friendships are of no concern of anyone..."

"Oh no?" Fousset interrupted. "You have a lot of people who ride your coat tails. People who are invested in you." He leaned back in his chair. "Anyone who mentions your name on a resume will be instantly tagged as a person who worked for the idiot who had it all, but fucked it all up over a piece of ass."

"Hold it right there." Stallings gritted his teeth. "You have no right to come here..."

"You have a wife. A beautiful family." Fousset interrupted. "What! Don't have the guts to confront the wife? Don't want to split the farm in half? Or are you stupid enough to believe it won't come crashing down on you?" He sipped from his glass. "And it will. Always does. Your enemies will discover your weakness and they will use it against you."

"I..."

"Michael! Good God, man. Your weakness is your enemy's avenue of approach. And your weakness isn't chocolate. It's ass that isn't your wife's."

"I have no enemies." Stallings sighed. "Who is my..."

"You are a federal judge who is aspiring to be more. You have enemies and they will make themselves known when the time is right for them." Fousset took a long drink that left only a little whiskey at the bottom of the glass. "Mark my word. You will lose it all if you don't end it now." He stood up.

"I appreciate your concern but...."

"Son." Fousset interrupted. "If you're not careful." He finished off the whiskey. "You will be in front of a crowd that's screaming Jerry, Jerry, Jerry." He turned and left.

Stallings stood from the couch and walked into the kitchen. He watched as his wife prepared dinner for the family.

"Making enough roast for an army," Stallings said as he moved to wrap his arms around his wife.

"No, just enough for your brother's family and us. He, Ellen, and the kids are stopping by."

"That's right. I forgot." Stallings hugged his wife tight. "You do know that I love you. Don't you?"

"Yes Michael." His wife leaned into him.

Dragon...

The two men circled each other. Both men were worn and tired. The crowd around the cage was energized after watching the men exchange brutal kicks and punches to each other. The referee encouraged the men to move forward and engage each other.

The man wearing blue trunks quickly took the initiative and stepped forward and delivered a flurry of punches to his opponent's head.

The man wearing red trunks received the blows and attempted an uppercut but missed. He was exposed and received a front kick to his chest. He staggered back into the cage and received a direct punch to his nose. Blood scattered the front row of the cheering crowd. He fell to the mat. His opponent, wearing blue trunks, moved forward and prepared to stomp him. He quickly raised his butt from the ground and delivered a powerful kick to his opponent's grounded leg. The leg hyper extended and buckled forward at the knee. His opponent fell to the mat, screaming in pain.

"Holy shit! Did you see that," the Krav Maga instructor yelled. "That's gotta fire you up, Dragon." He stood on a chair to watch the man in the red trunks deliver elbows to his opponents face; blood splashed from his opponents face with each blow. "You're up next, Dragon."

Judge Ellenberg stepped forward to survey the brutality and quickly fainted.

I'll be okay

Ronald Ellenberg twisted and turned in bed the night before. He lay staring at the ceiling or face down in the pillow, but his eyes never closed for more than a few seconds. His thoughts were of Benny Shills and others who had their lives cut short by a society who deemed them not worthy of living. He wondered how long such a society existed and how many people have been eliminated. He wondered if Shills ever knew who, what, or why he was being put to death. *Did McCreiess say anything to Shills*, he thought. *Did Shills have any last words?* His thoughts drifted to Judge Stephen Carson and how well he really knew the man, and he came to the conclusion that he didn't really know the man at all. *Did I really need something or was I just trying to be something I thought others wanted and needed.*

***

Ellenberg sat at a local diner having a cup of coffee that he really had no appetite for. He struggled to take sips as he waited for a phone call from his friend, Jack Daily.

Jack helped him in investigating both Max Merrell and Drake McCreiess before the investigation was suddenly closed. He knew the phone would ring any second so he mentally prepared himself for the conversation. *You can do this. This must be done*, he thought to himself over and over.

The phone rang and he quickly answered.

"Hello. Jack, hello." Ellenberg chocked on the coffee that went down the wrong pipe. He started to cough.

"Are you alright, Ron?"

"I'll be okay." Ellenberg coughed until he was able to breathe properly. "Thanks for calling me back."

"No worries. What can I help you with?"

"Jack, do you remember the names Max Merrell, Drake McCreiess, and Kevin Halcot?" Ellenberg wasted little time in getting to what he wanted to talk about.

"Uh, yeah." Jack paused. "I do remember those names. They've dropped off the grid, but I do remember them. We pulled the plug on investigating them."

"Yeah I know. Merrell and McCreiess quit the police department and..."

"Why are we interested in these guys?" Jack interrupted.

"I need to speak with someone and it is very important." Ellenberg held himself from crying. "It is very important."

"I'm here, Ron. What is it?"

"I can't speak over the phone. I will need to meet with you soon." Ellenberg's voice quivered.

"Is everything aright Ron?"

"Yes. Everything is fine. I just need to get with you when you return."

"It will have to wait a couple weeks because I'm here in North Dakota on a fishing trip with my family. Can it wait until then? Because it's been a long time since we have taken a vacation like this?"

"It will have to." Ellenberg sighed. "Please get with me as soon as you get back in town." He pleaded.

"Is everything alright, Ron?"

"I will be fine...it will be fine, but I need to get with you as soon as you get back."

"I'm assuming this has something to do with Merrell and McCreiess."

"It's more than that." Merrell sighed. "It is much more than that."

PART 5

Please help

Bedroom - Year 2005

Swoosh, swoosh, KABAM! KABAM! The ground shook underneath McCreiess as he ducked behind a HUMVEE vehicle for cover. The explosions brought immediate gunfire from, what seemed to McCreiess, all directions. The sounds from all sorts of weapons were loud and consistent. The smell of gunpowder filled the air. McCreiess elevated himself, just a little, to see what initiated the current battle, but saw no one he could identify as enemy. He could see a white Chevrolet Suburban vehicle engulfed in smoke and flames as security contractors across the road from him moved quickly to help their team members exit the suburban. He identified one of the contractors as an old Special Forces friend, Stan Brown, who left the army a few years earlier. He couldn't make out the faces of the other men. Two security team members were pulled from the suburban as two others sat burning in the front seats. A small vehicle being driven by an Iraqi shot through an intersection and slammed into a suburban parked behind the one currently burning. The small

411

vehicle exploded, sending security contractors flying through the air. The body of the men and vehicle debris scattered the area.

McCreiess stood up straight, trying to see if there were enemy to engage, as chaos ensued. The driver of the third suburban, parked behind the two currently burning, drove his vehicle into a storefront; doing anything he could to get out of the line of fire. McCreiess watched as the driver crushed anyone in his path; stunned civilians and wounded contractors were run over by the heavy vehicle. The enemy fighters honed in on the back-end of the vehicle that stuck out of the coffee shop. Bullets and rocket-propelled grenades rained down on the cafe.

"Over there," a soldier yelled. "Over there!"

McCreiess looked to see who yelled but he couldn't get a visual of the person. It seemed like those that moved around him had blank faces. He jumped to his left just in time to dodge a rocket-propelled grenade. The grenade went through the open door of the vehicle and out the window on the other side. The explosive slammed into a building across the street and made a large explosion. It seemed as if he was surrounded. Soldiers around him were falling dead and wounded from gunshot and shrapnel wounds. McCreiess kneeled on one knee to simply just take in a moment of thought before he made his next move. His body trembled from fear. He couldn't control the shaking.

"Help me," McCreiess screamed to anyone that would listen. "Please help..."

A large bright-lighted flash and powerful explosion silenced McCreiess' plea.

:-

Drake McCreiess suddenly sat up. His body was drenched from perspiration and he gasped for his next breath. He looked around in panic. He looked for anyone who could help, but soon realized he was by himself. He lay back in his sweat soaked bed and took in a deep breath. He inhaled through his nose for twenty seconds. He exhaled through his mouth for thirty seconds. He repeated the process of inhaling and exhaling until the anxiety subsided.

That was one scary ass dream

Present Day

Russ Porter lay on his couch watching his favorite news channel. Out of all the different news networks to choose from, he enjoyed the one where editorials slanted toward his views. He also enjoyed the fact that whoever did the hiring at the network, hired attractive women who if not intelligent, could at least read a prompter.

The story on the network had to do with another battle between Israel and Hamas. The narrative was the same. Hamas launched missiles into Israel, and the current US administration asked the Israeli leadership for caution and restraint. Israel expanded air assaults into Gaza, as Hamas, Syria, and Iran cried that Hell would soon be upon the Jewish State. Porter fell into sleep and allowed a dream to consume him.

⁙

Mortar rounds landed in threes. Three dull whomps at a time. The explosions kicked up dust, smoke, and debris. Porter leaned up against the wall as the rounds became relentless. The soldiers he was in command of fell to the ground, wounded, bleeding, dead, and dying. The smell of his mother's tuna casserole hung over the field of battle. He could hear the enemy voices on the other side of the wall. They were Vietnamese. *Why Vietnamese?* He thought that was odd. *Oh my God. The Vietnamese are working with Hamas.*

Porter grinned at the thought of knowing that he was the only one who knew that the Vietnamese and Hamas were working together. The thought of himself receiving the Medal of Honor from the President flashed in and out of his dream.

Surveying the battlefield he saw Michael Stallings wounded and bloodied; he had no legs. Stallings was crying out for help. Stallings crawled over to another soldier who was laying face down. He rolled him over. It was General Hathaway.

"Why? Why, General?" Stallings screamed.

"Join the fight God damn you," General Hathaway yelled to Porter.

Porter turned his attention toward the Vietnamese voices on the other side of the wall. He pulled a grenade from his vest. The volley of mortar rounds seemed to increase. He noticed he was wearing a tuxedo and bow tie. *Shit!* The explosions seemed to become louder and more intense. He looked toward Stallings and the General and found that the field was nothing but the carnage of bloodied corpses. He saw a female in the distance but couldn't make her out. The thought of Cynthia Mader consumed him for a moment. The smell of his mother's tuna casserole overwhelmed him. He felt the urge to do something. He pulled the grenade pin by placing the pin in his mouth and pulling. The grenade fell out of his hand and landed next to him. He jumped face first to the ground. The grenade exploded. He turned to look toward the sound of the explosion. The explosion created a hole in the wall and allowed a bright light to shine through. The mortars stopped raining down. He sat up. The explosion left him stunned. The light amazed him. He noticed that he was naked and that he felt no shame. He slowly reached for the light as he slowly walked toward it.

Porter woke to the sound of the stove alarm in the kitchen. The tuna casserole was done and he was hungry.

"That was one scary ass dream," Porter laughed and said to himself as he walked to the kitchen. "Casserole smells yummy." He smiled and rubbed his belly.

***

The hallway was long and the apartment Michael Stallings looked for was at the end of it. Stallings moved slowly down the hall, bumping off the wall occasionally as he went. He stumbled on a ruptured seam in the carpet so he looked down and was amused to find a ten-dollar bill lying on the floor. He picked the bill up, wadded it up, and threw it behind him as he giggled. He moved a little further toward the apartment and noticed that a picture on the wall, a Kincaid reprint of a grape garden, was hanging crooked. He straightened the picture and smiled. He then positioned the picture in the way he had found it and continued to move on with a smile.

Coming to the apartment he stood for a moment looking at the door. With his finger he traced the outline of the apartment number (810). He sighed and stepped back from the door. He giggled and then knocked on the door.

The door opened quickly and Russ Porter stood surprised with a bowl of tuna casserole in his hands.

"Michael. Michael, I'm surprised too..."

Stallings interrupted Porter by pulling a pistol from his waist.

"Michael! No, please," Porter cried.

Stallings fired a bullet into the face of Porter. The bullet hit Porter directly under his nose and lodged in the chair behind him. Stallings was stunned to see Porter still standing and that there was no blood coming from the hole that the bullet created in Porter's face. Porter dropped the bowl filled with tuna casserole and it crashed to the floor. Stallings fired another shot that hit Porter in the forehead. Porter fell to the ground on his back. *That should do it*, he thought after noticing brain matter scattered on the floor. Stallings stepped forward and noticed he had stepped in the tuna casserole.

"God damn it," Stallings cried as he fired twice more into the dead body of Porter. "You fat fuck!" He walked backward out of the apartment, surveying the damage as he backed away and doing all he could to wipe the casserole from his shoe.

"Oh no!" A woman down the hall screamed as she stopped in her tracks.

"Sorry," Stallings whispered to the woman. He held his hands up as if to show the woman he meant no harm to her.

Noticing that Stallings still had a gun in one of his hands, the woman screamed louder.

Stallings felt the urge to run but didn't because he realized there was no place to run or anyone to run to. He looked the woman in her eyes and a quick thought of his girlfriend Carmen entered his mind. The thought of his 9th Christmas and opening his only present to find that his mother got him cowboy boots flooded his thoughts. *Fucking cowboy boots, she got me cowboy boots,* he thought. *Who the fuck does that?* He shook his head and spit as an awful taste filled his mouth before he placed the barrel of the pistol under his chin and pulled the trigger.

The bullet exited the top of his head and lodged into the ceiling. His left eye fell from its socket and dangled. The woman screamed louder as other people opened their doors to find what the commotion was all about. Stallings pushed the barrel deeper under his chin and pulled the trigger.

Judge Stallings' body lay motionless on the floor. A few people slowly walked toward the dead body, while others quickly closed their doors.

Answers woman

The large oak stump towered over Cynthia Mader as she stood near it. It was eleven feet high and seventeen feet in diameter. She stood in awe of the large oak. Before its death, the tree was at least four hundred years in age.

"And though a tenth remains in it." Cynthia whispered one of her favorite Bible verses; Isaiah 6:13. "It will be burned again, like an oak, whose stump remains when it is felled." She continued to walk around the tree. "The Holy seed is its stump." She stopped as she noticed a large cluster black-staining polypore.

The large fungus only affirmed that it had been a long time since she had visited the large oak stump. The fungus was sixty inches in diameter. Cynthia kicked the fungus until it fell completely apart. She stepped a few feet back from the stump to get a complete view. She stuck her hand out and made a "V" shape with her index finger and thumb. She stepped back a few more feet until the huge stump fit within the "V" shape. The vibration of her phone interrupted her so she looked at it (GENERAL). She pushed a button to read the message (Richmond Sentential).

Cynthia went to the Safari browser on her phone and googled the Richmond Sentential. She hit the first link that popped up (Federal Judge and Ex-Mayor Involved in Murder Suicide). She quickly scanned the article and found that both Judge Stallings and Mayor Porter were the two people the article referred to.

"Oh my God," Cynthia said as she walked to the stump. "What? Why?" She leaned against the oak stump. She felt nauseated so she bent over and then collapsed to her knees. She felt faint but fought the feeling and rolled over to her backside and rested against the tree. She placed her head between her knees to fight the light-headedness.

Cynthia's phone vibrated again. It was an incoming call. She looked at her phone to see who was calling (GENERAL).

"General Hathaway." Cynthia answered.

"What the hell happened? Please tell me just what the hell happened." The General paused. "How in the hell..."

"I don't know. I. I. I wish..."

"Wish! Wish my ass, damn it. Answers woman," the General yelled.

You're late

The oldest masonry fort in the US is located in Saint Augustine, Florida. The Spanish felt the need to construct Castillo de San Marcos after the English sacked the tiny garrison town. The town was never sacked again after the fort was built. The fort was built by a shell stone indigenous to the area, coquina, which provided an impenetrable barrier to shells fired by all sorts of navy's.

Merrell enjoyed visiting the fort anytime he was in the area. He toured the fort every chance he could, hoping to learn something new with each visit, but the reason for this visit to the fort was not for learning, it was business. The only reason he chose to meet Ellenberg at the fort was because he felt comfortable in the setting.

Merrell stood atop a bastion that protected the sally port and provided a view of Matanzas Bay. He saw Ellenberg approaching so he looked at his watch. Ellenberg was late. He smiled as he noticed a piece of gauze taped over Ellenberg's eye.

"You're late." Merrell started the conversation.

"I had a hard time finding this place." Ellenberg sheepishly responded.

"You had a hard time finding this place in Saint Augustine, Florida." Merrell chuckled half-heartedly. "Why can't you just say I'm sorry, I'm late?"

Ellenberg looked out over the Bay. He turned to get a view of the fort.

"Lots of flags raised over this garrison." Merrell continued to view the Bay. "Spanish, English, Spanish, US, Confederates, US." Merrell paused. "Lots of changes, don't you think?"

"Yes. Yes I..."

"Mill explained everything." Merrell interrupted. "Cynthia Mader overstepped her bounds on this one. She had a personal grudge to settle and she was using Drake and me to settle it. The slippery slope, type thing, everyone talks about." He picked up a stone that separated from the wall. "And I must hand it to you. You sniffed it out."

"Judge Stallings contacted me." Ellenberg admitted. "He phoned me after he wasn't able to convince Cynthia to stop the order. Getting answers was the only thing I could think to do. That's why I asked you to question him first."

"He got a hold of me as well." Merrell shook his head in wonder. "I knew..."

"Did you complete the order?" Ellenberg interrupted.

"No." Merrell responded sternly.

"And why not. There was a Judge Carter that..."

"Yeah. Well there were also two 'Old Men' that were in control of this organization. This secret society we call The System." Merrell paused. "It may not be so secret anymore after what happened in..."

"I know. I have no idea what Judge Stallings was thinking. May God rest his soul." Ellenberg leaned against the bastion wall. "Where is Tommy Mill?"

"He's where ever he wants to be." Merrell leaned against the bastion wall next to Ellenberg. "Things are changing. You need to prepare for the changes." He held the stone up. "Coquina. Seashells made to solidify." He tossed the stone to the ground. "It absorbed cannon shell, didn't really repel." He stepped in front of Ellenberg. "Absorbing worked for this fort, but changes and shells are not the same."

"I don't know what you mean. What you are talking about. I...I...wouldn't even know where to start." Ellenberg dropped his hands to his sides and then dropped his head.

"I don't think..." Merrell stopped his thought process. "Don't worry about it."

"I wish I would never have..."

"You will have to meet with her." Merrell interrupted. "And the General."

"And say what?" Ellenberg asked. "What the hell else needs to be said or done?" He leaned against the wall and folded his arms. "Why can't we just all cut loose of this?"

"Cut loose." Merrell turned to face Ellenberg. "You want out?"

"I just think..."

"You need to think about what you are saying." Merrell interrupted. "From what I was told, you wanted this."

I knew he was corrupt

Newspapers covered Senior Agent Ben Kelly's desk. New York Times, Washington Post, Wall Street Journal, and the Washington Times were just a few of the media outlets that Kelly briefly scanned each morning he arrived to work. He was constantly amazed at how each paper covered different events. The Washington Times lead story had to do with American deaths in Libya. The New York Times highlighted another possible ground war between Israel and Hamas. The Journal's top story had to do with national debt. The Post led off with the Presidents overseas travel.

Kelly scanned the Post and found the story of how a federal judge murdered a politician and then turned the gun on himself. The story was on page ten of the first section. He leaned back and turned his chair so he could look out his window. The thought of media people from different news organizations on the payroll crossed his mind. He knew the Post didn't have anyone on the roll but he knew they would follow along with what the Times and Journal wanted to lead with, and the birth of a Royal from Great Britain was something everyone wanted to write about.

"Ben. Did you get a chance to speak with Agent English?" Special Agent Carl Brenner peeked in.

"Oh yeah. She stopped by and we talked." Kelly continued to look out the window. "No need to worry, Carl. She dropped that nonsense about..."

"Thanks, Ben. I appreciate you speaking with her." Brenner remained at the door.

"No problem, Carl." Kelly was a little irritated about being cut off but he let it go. "Hey, can you forward the status report?" Kelly turned toward Brenner. "I need to keep the big guy informed on what we actually do in this detachment."

"Sure thing, Ben. I will have it to you soon. I can get..."

"Did you hear about that nut job federal judge killing the politician?" Kelly interrupted.

"Yeah. I read a little bit about it. I just saw it as a news flash. So Mayor Porter was gay?" Brenner smiled. "I knew he was corrupt, but gay, I never would have guessed."

"I guess you really never know someone, huh." Kelly leaned back in his chair.

We have a bigger problem

Bodhan Nesterenko walked the hallway of the federal courthouse as if he walked it every day. He nodded and smiled at everyone he met. He bent and kneeled to help a heavyset woman pick up the paperwork she dropped. He touched her hand as he handed over the file. She blushed and he winked. A child bumped into his leg and became startled. The child held on to his pants. Nesterenko smiled, picked the child up and blew on his belly, making a loud suction sound. The mother of the child laughed as the child screamed with excitement. Nesterenko provided the child a friendly swat on the rump and watched him run to his mother.

The Administrative Assistant stood stunned as Bodhan Nesterenko presented himself. Nesterenko stood six foot two and was a large chiseled man. The clothes he wore highlighted the fact that he took care of himself.

"Can I help you sir?" The Assistant asked.

"I'm looking for Cynthia Mader." Nesterenko looked directly into the assistant's eyes. "She is expecting me."

"Yes sir. But I don't see..."

"Yes. I'm sure I'm not on the list, but I assure you, she needs to see me."

The Administrative Assistant picked up the phone and pushed a button.

"Judge Mader. Ma'am, there is a man here to see you." The Assistant paused to listen. "Your name, Sir?"

"My name is Bodhan Nesterenko."

"Ma'am, his name is Bodhan Nesterenko." The Assistant paused again. "Yes Ma'am I will." She looked up to see Nesterenko already opening the door.

***

Cynthia Mader stood stunned behind her desk as Bodhan Nesterenko entered her chambers.

"Bodhan," Cynthia said quietly.

"Yes, Cynthia, Yes." Nesterenko moved slowly as he scanned the wall filled with pictures, awards, and certificates. "It is me." He looked to see that the door behind him was closed.

"Please sit." Cynthia pointed toward the sofa in front of her desk. "It has been such a long time." She remained stunned. "I guess I ..."

Nesterenko sat but continued to scan the wall. "I notice your son's picture isn't on the wall."

"No. No it's not, is it?" Cynthia became stern.

"That kid always looked like he was ten pounds of shit stuffed in a five pound bag." Nesterenko smiled. "Probably good you left him off."

Nesterenko rose from his seat to get a better view of a picture on the wall.

"Is that..."

"Yes. That's Senator Claire Miller." Cynthia answered.

"Haven't I seen her on some of those Sunday morning talking head shows?" Nesterenko pulled the picture from the wall.

"I suppose you..."

"Weren't you fucking her husband?" Nesterenko interrupted his old friend as he hung the picture back on the wall and straightened it.

Cynthia was appalled by the question. She stood with her mouth open.

"You may not have been watching me over the many years since we last spoke. But I've been keeping an eye on you." Nesterenko laughed.

"Bodhan. Please sit..."

"So how's the Old Man?" Nesterenko paused to look at a photo of Cynthia's father, Judge George Mader.

"He's dead, Bodhan. He passed..."

"So he's been better." Nesterenko grinned.

"Bodhan, sit down," Cynthia yelled. "Please! I know it has been awhile since we have last spoken. But I'm sure you are not here to discuss family."

"Oh, but it is family." Nesterenko became less jovial. "I know what the problem is. I keep up on things. I read the news. Especially if I'm involved." He strolled to place himself in front of Cynthia's desk. "Tommy Mill." He paused to see that Cynthia seemed dumbfounded. "What? You don't think I know how to use the Internet. Little

Tommy Mill got out from behind bars so you and that fat ass son..." He smiled. "He's still fat right?"

Cynthia sat silent.

"With all these diets. You know the one. No carbs..."

"Bodhan, please!" Cynthia put a stop to Nesterenko's fun.

"You want me to do something about your problem?" Nesterenko became serious.

"He is a problem for us. Don't you think?" Cynthia stepped out from behind her desk. "Or don't you remember?"

"By the looks of this office. He is more of a problem for you." Nesterenko smiled. "Probably wouldn't be good to have your connection with Mill spilled out all over the news."

"You're right, Bodhan. It wouldn't be good to have Mr. Mill speaking about past connections to my family." Cynthia looked toward the picture of her father. "But you are up to your neck in Tommy Mill shit as well."

"Ahh, shit." Nesterenko scoffed.

"It was you who was able to get to that dope head friend of his." Cynthia stepped in front of her old friend. "And it was you who was able to..."

"The professor." Nesterenko smiled. "Don't forget the attorney. That was a little more challenging than you would think." He paused. "I was beginning to think that dude could breathe under water."

Nesterenko stepped back and turned to look at the pictures on the wall.

"Emotions," Nesterenko yelled. "It's all emotions with you. Kill the professor, kill the attorney, and kill the dope head!" He turned to stare Cynthia in the eye. "Now it's Mill."

"Well if we could..."

"If you would have thought it through. You would have thrown a plastic bag in your son's crib many years ago." Nesterenko held his stare. "Would have saved a lot of people from a lot of heart ache." He smiled and sat down. "Anyway, I could really give a dimes worth of shit about Mill. I could be in some turd world shit hole tomorrow if I want."

"How is the mercenary thing working for you, Bodhan?" Cynthia smiled.

"Mercenary! I'm offended. I prefer Security Consultant." Nesterenko sat, crossed his legs and stared into the eyes of Cynthia.

"Really. Then why are you..."

"I thought I would lend an old friend a hand." Nesterenko interrupted. "And when I finished helping you, maybe you can use some of your influences to help me." He paused to look at the wall filled with pictures. "By the looks of it, you do have some influential friends."

"I would be glad to hear about your problems, but I have a bigger problem than Tommy Mill, Bodhan. We have a bigger problem."

You saw it coming?

General Hathaway sat at the edge of his bed hoping the call he placed would be answered. He needed answers. The news of the judge killing a politician was buried news but he understood how it could become front-page news if things were not played carefully.

"Hello, General Hathaway." A man with a deep voice answered the phone.

"Yeah. Hello." The General was nervous. "What's your feeling on what is going on?"

"Oh. I think it has all been pretty predictable since the 'Old Men' are no longer in the picture." The deep voiced man replied. "What happened in that apartment was a little much, but some of the other stuff was predicted."

"Predicted!" The General became angry. "You saw this coming?"

"We saw..."

"Well if you saw it coming...there has to be a plan." The General cut the man off. "There has to be an end game of some sort."

"Just hold tight, General, and I will get with you," the deep voiced man said before the phone fell silent.

"Hello. Hello. You there." The General realized the phone went dead.

General Hathaway tossed the phone to the other side of the bed. He sat in silence as a thought back to a significant event entered his head.

:-

The cigar General Hathaway smoked was down to its last few draws. The General put the cigar out by mashing it into the dirt.

"You afraid those things will kill you?" Judge George Mader asked as he walked up from behind the General.

"No. I guess after beating all the bullets fired at me. I guess I never figured I would lose to a cigar." The General stepped back.

"You good with the Carter vote?" Judge Mader asked.

"No. No I'm not." The General paused. "I thought it would be unanimous."

"I never assured you of that." Judge Mader wrapped an arm around the General. "I only said that a change needed to be made."

"It feels like you had a personal grudge against Carter and..."

"You stop right there. You have no idea what..."

"No. You stop." The General interrupted Judge Mader. "Carter is out of our reach. Or at least he should be."

"Then why did you say 'aye'?" Judge Mader asked sharply.

"Because your daughter said it was a new direction that we were all taking." The General pulled another cigar

from his jacket. "I guess Judge Carson wasn't informed of the change. He and Stallings weren't for it."

"You let me handle Judge Carson." Judge Mader paused to allow the General to light his cigar. "Stephen and I go back a long way. He will come around."

"Stallings?" The General asked.

"Weak." Judge Mader answered sharply.

"This society was started long before us and I'm guessing the rules have been the same ever since..."

"The lineage of this society. This secret society we call The System has been written." Judge Mader walked away.

"Just some changes need to be made, I guess." The General watched as Judge Mader got in his car and drove away.

General Hathaway lay back on his bed and closed his eyes. He understood the part of battle where men fought with everything from their bare hands to tanks and aircraft, but he was never good at treachery and deception. While in Vietnam he was once asked by a subordinate about using a platoon to make a feint movement to distract the enemy from the main thrust of the attack. General Hathaway, who was then a Colonel, dismissed the idea as a waste of killers. He would rather use that platoon to be part of the main attack and flanking movements. "We need killers killing gooks," the General was heard to say in regards to using maneuvers that took men away from killing the enemy.

A dragon tattoo, really?

Merrell and Ellenberg stood in a large parking lot similar to any lot featured in every city where vehicles are the dominant means of transport. The lot was nearly empty and it was late. The Baltimore Orioles had lost another game to the Yankee's and many of the Oriole faithful had departed.

Merrell looked at his watch (0035) as Ellenberg pulled an envelope from his vehicle.

"She wants to meet. She wants to meet at the cabin." Ellenberg handed Merrell the envelope. "Says she can explain everything."

"Wants to meet who?" Merrell was angry. "And what the heck is this?"

Merrell stared at the band aide above Ellenberg's right eye but chose not to say anything.

"She wants to meet everyone. She says she can make it right." Ellenberg pleaded. "I think she's willing to step aside. I really don't think we have a choice."

"There are options. Believe me. We have options, and what is in this envelope?"

"Can we please shelve what you are thinking? I would rather not..."

"I don't trust her. Find it hard to trust anyone of you now that the 'Old Men' are gone." Merrell interrupted. "And for the last time. What is in this envelope?"

"It's money. Money, God damn it, money." Ellenberg cried. "I thought it might..."

"You thought wrong." Merrell stepped into Ellenberg's space. "You're just trying to buy your way out. I'm here to tell you, it's not happening, at least not yet."

"What are we waiting for? The whole thing has collapsed. There is virtually nothing left except a woman who wants to make amends and an old retired general..."

"Enough," Merrell said angrily as he looked around to see that he didn't bring attention from anyone still leaving the lot. "You really have no idea what you are involved in, do you?"

"Please just get McCreiess and ..."

"Drake McCreiess is out." Merrell pointed his finger in Ellenberg's chest.

"Out! How the hell can he just get out?" Ellenberg became angry. "He thinks he can just leave. Hell I want..."

"You have no authority to say who and when anyone can..."

"I stepped in for Judge Stephen Carson, and I ..."

"Listen. You have no idea who he is or what he's done." Merrell interrupted. "And I'm not just talking about the killing." He paused to control his anger. "You may find it hard to believe but the man has more education than you." Merrell began to smile. "You wear a robe to work and your ego tells you that you're smarter than most everyone you look at. Probably even treat your wife that way."

He read Ellenberg's face and saw disbelief in his eyes. "The man you look down your nose at is better than you and has done far more." Merrell stepped back. "You have done very little and know less."

A pause caused Ellenberg to shake his head as if to disagree.

"He has degrees in economics, history, and nutritional science. He is working towards a degree in English lit. We get paid well you know." Merrell laughed and held up the envelope. "He has a work ethic and he's creative. And he…"

"I didn't…"

"Yes you did." Merrell pointed the envelope into Ellenberg's chest. "You meant to suggest that because he pulls the trigger he is somehow the knuckle dragger on a leash." He stepped closer to Ellenberg. "You're too ignorant to know who is on the leash."

Merrell turned to walk to his car.

"You know. People in uniform are called the best and the brightest. We all know they're not. But we say it. We say it so they'll feel good about themselves for doing the stupid crap people like you demand." Merrell began to smile again. "He figured it out long ago. That's why he got away from those that believed the crap pumped into their heads." He laughed. "He could be a high ranking officer, but he chooses to be enlisted because he enjoys being a door kicker." His smile turned to a frown. "I fear it may get him one day."

"You and..."

"When I was a young soldier I had a private who didn't secure the firing pin in his weapon properly. His weapon didn't fire during an exercise." Merrell paused. "The command brought the kid up on UCMJ charges. The kid never recovered. Bureaucrats in the State Department lose a consulate and an ambassador in Libya and they shift left to a different assignment." Merrell ensured Ellenberg was following. "They must be part of a grand system where no one can fail." He smiled. "They call it the DC boogie."

"But!" Ellenberg tried to interrupt. "I have no..."

"Everyone has a specific place in your world," Merrell muffled his tone by clenching his jaw. "To you, they are what you and your talking head type friends were taught they are. Got news for you. People just do what they do. Sometimes just because. See a mountain. Climb it. See a broom and sweep the floor. Have kids and you keep sweeping the floors because it's what you know and it provides." Merrell paused. "The Janitor just hopes the kids become more. If that is what they're capable of... or...or if that is what they want."

"I..."

"You have no clue!" Merrell held his hand in the air to silence Ellenberg. He paused for reflection. "Drake McCreiess went off the reservation. Did something ballsy and without sanction from people like you. And you wanted to send him in with the idiots that stand in front of you. The people who..."

"I feel he and I have..."

"No way! You have nothing in common." Merrell turned toward Ellenberg and snickered. "You've learned some martial arts crap. Get a tattoo and think about getting in a cage but faint at the first site of someone getting their butt kicked in."

Ellenberg rubbed his shoulder, the area that had the dragon tattoo.

"He knows how to fight and would not hesitate to take down anyone who threatened him or a loved one. He doesn't have to jump in a ring or cage to prove anything to himself. Nothing against anyone that does, but if you go to the fight," Merrell said as he chuckled and shrugged his shoulders. "You might want to get in the ring."

"How did you..."

"You think about doing. He does. You'd hesitate. He won't." Merrell opened his car door. "While you are observing, he is deciding. While you are orienting yourself he is acting. He remains two steps ahead." Merrell paused and grinned. "And he has no tattoo to tell the world whatever a tat is supposed to tell the world." He paused. "He has a tattoo. It's something only those that are close to him know about. He's apathetic in regards to them, really. He doesn't use it to define him. He doesn't use it as a billboard of some sort. Just knows that what he was yesterday he isn't today. What he is today, he probably won't be tomorrow."

Merrell sat in the car, started it, and rolled down the window.

"A dragon tattoo, really?" Merrell smiled. "You're the master of all the elements of nature?" Merrell couldn't help but laugh.

Merrell shook his head as he slowly backed the car out, stopped, and put the gear in drive.

"He's not into self promotion because he prefers to be noticed by his work ethic and intelligence." Merrell shrugged his shoulders. "You won't find him in the night clubs, and you won't find guys like him on Face book. There is something to be said about not saying everything."

Merrell rolled the window up, but thought of something else to say so he rolled it back down.

"By the way. His dad was the best floor sweeper you would ever meet. He only asked his son to be the best at whatever it was he wanted to be. Your Dad probably told you to be a lawyer and that's what you did." The window was rolled back up and he sped away.

Ellenberg wondered how he knew about the dragon tattoo and the cage match. The tattoo was something he had inked after he graduated law school. A symbol of the emperor felt appropriate to him after completing law school. His father pumped so much shit into his head.

He saw Merrell's car in reverse coming toward him. Merrell's car stopped and the window was rolled down.

"Oh, and by the way," Merrell said with a grin, "If you want to try and prevent him from leaving, try and stop him." He paused. "He wants you to."

"I..I.I..."

"We have things to finish. Set it up." Merrell rolled the window up and sped away.

Ellenberg watched the car disappear and then took a moment to remember a moment with his wife.

:-

The bathroom was unusually clean. Ellenberg looked under the sink and then the drawers of the cabinets. *Where are the damn band aids, the fly ones?* He quickly rummaged. He had just used one for a cut on Trinity's knee after she cut herself climbing on the rocks near the bay. *Why the hell would she clean the bathroom today,* he wondered.

"Honey, what are you looking for?" His wife asked as she entered the bathroom.

"Oh." Ellenberg was startled. "I'm sorry if I woke you. I'm just looking for a band aid for this cut above my eye." He kept rummaging through the drawers.

"Let me see, Ron. Let me look at it." His wife removed the gauze his Krav instructor put on after his head bounced off a chair after he fainted.

"Oh my." She flinched. "That is deep."

"Yeah. Not as deep as the cuts I put on his head." Ellenberg's lie made him feel good. "He got me with a left hook and then I went off."

"Why do you keep getting in the cage with those..."

"I love it honey." He looked in the mirror. "It's just who I am."

"I used to think I wanted to come and watch you but..."

"No. It's best you stay at home." Ellenberg cut his wife off. "You wouldn't want to see it."

"You are a dragon, my love." His wife placed her hand on his tattoo.

ī

"Oh shit!" Ellenberg jumped after leaning on a car and setting its alarm off. He looked around to see if anyone noticed him and then crept away.

Our connection would be...

Diana's Diner's rush hour was long over. The regular patrons who stuffed themselves of the famous pancakes were long gone. A few clients remained but there was plenty of room for Merrell to sit and enjoy coffee and feel that he was alone with his own thoughts. He scanned the sports page until he found an article about his favorite baseball team, the Yankees.

"Pitching." A voice from over Merrell's shoulder sounded.

Merrell turned to see SueAnn English standing behind him.

"Yeah." Merrell turned back to the article. "Probably another year to flop in the post season."

"Well you know that Jeter..."

"Take a seat, SueAnn." Merrell pointed to a chair across the table.

"How do you know my name?" SueAnn questioned.

"That's a great question." Merrell leaned back in his seat and tossed the paper to the side. "How do I know your name? How do you know my name?" He sipped from his coffee. "Let's do a trifecta. What do we have in common, Agent SueAnn English?"

SueAnn sat down.

"Want some coffee? Diana makes some darn good coffee." Merrell sipped.

"Our connection would be..."

"So you make a call. You give a person names. You probably give the names, Shills, Evans, Henshaw, Carter, just to name a few." Merrell picked the paper back up. "Great job, Agent English. You're a real Sherlock Holmes."

"I called a man and..."

"You gave a person names, dates of death, and cities." Merrell interrupted. "The person checks data against data against data. The only name that comes up consistently is Matt Merrell." He opened the paper and went back to the article. "I must have been careless. Or was I?"

"I looked over your background." SueAnn took the paper from Merrell. She folded it and tossed it to another table. "Your military background and your service as a police officer were above and beyond."

"What you did was illegal." Merrell acted annoyed about his paper being taken. "Doesn't the Constitution mean anything to you? Where is your warrant? You know the Patriot Act isn't for guys like me. What gives you the right..."

"You're going to lecture me on the Constitution? Shills had his day in court. He walked with the blessing of the justice system." SueAnn leaned across the table. "And he is just one in a long line..."

"I guess someone felt there should be some balance to the system." Merrell interrupted and paused to look the diner over. "You need to be careful, Agent English. You still need to believe. You lose that something to believe in...well...then you venture into that gray area." He leaned across the table to stare into SueAnn's eyes. "It's that area where things can be justified, where ends justify the means."

"My father..."

"I know what your father did and who he worked for. Your father trained me."

***

Drake McCreiess listened to his favorite radio station, Elvis Sirius radio, as his friend Max Merrell and SueAnn English met at Diana's Diner. Sitting in his car and looking through the large diner window provided him a great view of his longtime friend and a person who he only knew from a conversation. He sang with Elvis as he put the meeting into some sort of perspective. The song "*Such a Night*" allowed him to stay up beat while thoughts of trust or the lack of trust entered into his thoughts.

No more Tony the Tiger for you

The apartment was dark so Nesterenko turned a lamp on to light the living room. He pulled the shades closed. He slowly looked over the books on the shelf and pulled one off – *"Crime and Punishment." Stupid fucker didn't read that,* he thought, as he looked it over. He placed the book back on the shelf and made his way to the kitchen where he noticed a sack filled with apples. He pulled one, wiped it off on his shirt and sat down on the couch. On the coffee table was a box of Tony the Tiger cereal. He picked it up and looked over the nutritional contents. *What a fat ass.* He placed the box back on the table.

Nesterenko looked at the clock (10:12 pm) and then turned on the television. His favorite show as a child, Gun smoke, was on. A young Bert Reynolds was a guest actor and played the part of an Indian. Matt Dillon and Chester were close to catching up to Bert. Nesterenko knew how it ended so he laid his head back and remembered a different time.

:-

Nesterenko scurried around his apartment looking for things he would need for a trip out of town. He grabbed a trash bag and emptied a drawer full of shirts into it. He did the same with drawers of pants and underclothes. He rushed to the bathroom and filled the bag with personal hygiene supplies. He quickly moved to the door leading outside. He went to open it but was surprised to see Cynthia Mader open the door and enter the apartment. She was angry and nervous.

"Where are you off to, Bodhan?" Cynthia demanded. "Do you know what happened?"

"Know what happened? The whole damn town shook. Everyone in this town knows what happened." Nesterenko stepped back.

"You were part of this." Cynthia stepped deeper into the apartment. "Blood is up to your neck."

"Your son is up to his neck. Him and those two idiots." Nesterenko stepped to the side of Cynthia and moved to exit the apartment.

Cynthia grabbed his arm and swung him around. She grabbed him by the collar and slapped his face.

"What did you pump their heads with?" Cynthia screamed.

"Me! Me! I filled their heads with nothing. I simply..."

"You are not going anywhere." Cynthia pushed Nesterenko against the wall. "There is a mess to clean and ..."

i

The door being opened startled Nesterenko so he jumped from the couch and stood in the dark of the kitchen. Standing behind the refrigerator he saw Jimmy

Brannon enter the apartment and stagger a bit before noticing that the lamp and television were on.

"Did I leave that on?" Jimmy questioned himself. "Gun smoke? Is that Bert Reynolds?" He staggered back and bumped into the coffee table.

Nesterenko pulled his gloves tight and then drew his pistol from inside his coat.

Hearing a noise Jimmy turned toward the kitchen. Noticing a shadow on the wall he stood stunned. Tears formed in his eyes and rolled down his cheeks.

Nesterenko stepped out from the shadow and smiled. "I was just telling your mother we could have saved a lot of people from heartache if we would have done this years ago."

"Mommy," Jimmy cried out loud before a bullet slammed into his head.

Jimmy Brannon's body crashed on top of the coffee table and shattered it.

Nesterenko stepped forward and stood over Jimmy's body.

"No more Tony the Tiger for you," Nesterenko said before he fired two more bullets into the back of Jimmy's head.

Nesterenko unscrewed the silencer from the pistol and holstered his weapon and silencer. He pulled an apple from his pocket and took a bite. He walked to the door and opened it slowly. He looked both left and right to ensure no one was interested in the sounds of a shattered coffee table and then closed the door behind him.

It's about assigning blame

General Hathaway opened the backdoor to his house and stepped into the covered patio. He turned on the lights, removed his jacket and hung it on a coat tree. He removed a cigar from the jacket pocket and bit the end from it. He turned to notice a corner of the patio that was normally lighted was not. He stared into the dark corner and watched as someone dressed in black stepped from the corner and into the partial light.

"It's about assigning blame is what Judge Carson told me." The General's voice was calm as he spit the end. "People want someone to pay a price. But for some reason the prosecution couldn't seal the deal or some defense lawyer was able to convince at least one juror that these people were something other than guilty." He rolled the cigar in his lips. "We are never adverted from the facts of the case. Facts have a funny way of making things black and white. Facts make that line between the two. There is no shade." He watched as the figure disappeared into the darkness of the corner.

"Is the line black or white?" The General stood confused. He hoped to get another glimpse of the figure.

"The line we talk about that separates the two." His voice rose. "It could be pink for all I give a shit." The General smiled. "The point is that there is no mixture. There is no gray...a confusion."

The person in black stepped out of the darkness and closer to the General. The General did his best to see if he could recognize the person but he couldn't.

"The trigger pulling side of things." The General took the cigar from his mouth and looked at it. "That way you never get confused."

The General was flung back into the coat tree by the two bullets that slammed into his chest. He fell to his knees. He held his chest and gasped for air. He knew the rest of his life was measured in seconds and not minutes, hours, or years. He thought about his wife who passed a little more than three years before his current predicament. The thought of her embracing him after he returned from one of his long tours of duty consumed him. He hoped she would be there to embrace him in the afterlife.

The third bullet fired split the General's heart in half and he slumped to the floor in a manner that left his feet underneath his buttocks.

The person in black pulled the General's feet out from underneath him and made sure his body lay in a natural state. She then said a quick prayer for the General, opened the back door, and disappeared into the night.

A meeting like this is unwise

The sofa was large and extended from one wall of the log cabin to the other. It was sixteen feet long and leather. The sofa was specially built with the leather used from the cattle that roamed the ranch Cynthia's father owned. Bodhan Nesterenko sat at one end of the sofa and Cynthia sat at the other. Cynthia worked frantically on the phone she held, pushing buttons and scrolling pages. Nesterenko was amazed to be in such a room. The room was filled with the heads of beast that Cynthia's father killed over the years, from the very woods the cabin stood.

"Is this a Grizzly head?" Nesterenko stood to look over the large bear head. "And is this a..."

"Yes Bodhan. They are very large and scary." Cynthia was annoyed. "I need for Mr. Ellenberg to answer his phone."

"I'm sure he will..."

Cynthia holding up her hand to signal that someone had answered her call interrupted Nesterenko.

"Yes, Mr. Ellenberg." Cynthia sighed. "I am so happy I was able to get a hold of you." She paused to listen. "Yes. Yes. I just want this to be over. I want to get past this."

She paused to listen again. "At this point I am willing to accept whatever you and the General propose. We will..."

***

Ellenberg and Merrell entered the room Cynthia and Nesterenko lounged in as if they knew exactly where they were going and what they were doing. Merrell was calm. Ellenberg would have jumped out of his skin at the sound of a mouse farting.

Cynthia sat with her mouth open as the two men entered a room her father crafted many years before. Ellenberg took his cell phone from his ear and held it up for Cynthia to see. He closed the phone and put it into his pocket.

Merrell pointed a silenced pistol at Nesterenko and guided him to sit next to Cynthia on the sofa. Nesterenko moved slowly to the sofa, not taking his eyes off of Merrell.

"I kind of like the Grizzly..."

"A meeting like this is unwise, Mr. Ellenberg." Cynthia interrupted Nesterenko's small talk and closed her phone.

"General Hathaway was a fine man, Cynthia. He was one of America's..."

"Was?" Cynthia questioned Ellenberg.

"Cynthia. Men. It looks as if you all have business here." Nesterenko interrupted. "I'll be..."

Nesterenko's dead body slumped in the couch after the first of three bullets entered his chest and head.

"Stop right there," Cynthia screamed at Merrell once she recognized the weapon he held was trained on her.

"We can work this out." She stood from the couch. "Think of the scrutiny, Mr. Ellenberg. Think of what will be said." She trembled with fear.

Ellenberg stood shocked after witnessing Nesterenko's body slump lifeless into the couch. He turned to stare at Merrell. His body trembled for a moment before he got control of himself.

"You had something you wanted to tell her." Merrell nodded toward Nesterenko's body. "I didn't think he needed to hear it."

Ellenberg turned toward Cynthia and stared as if he was looking through her. "What we do here is right, just, and honorable." He spoke softly. "We are the check and balance. Do you remember saying that," Ellenberg cleared his throat. "We have rules, a thin line that separates us from the vigilante. We are a select few. People like the General. Who have been trusted..."

Ellenberg was interrupted by a metallic sound made behind him so he turned to notice Ben Kelly and SueAnn English enter the room.

"Who are you?" Ellenberg asked nervously as he noticed Merrell step away from him.

"Ben," Cynthia cried.

Ellenberg looked at both Cynthia and Ben Kelly. "You know him?" Suddenly, the back of Judge Ellenberg's head exploded and his body fell to the floor.

Merrell and Cynthia looked at the woman, SueAnn English, as she held a smoldering silenced pistol.

Max Merrell remembered a conversation he had with Judge Carson.

:-

Judge Stephen Carson was alert and comfortable as he lay in his hospital bed. Harriet, who just moments before, helped him get down the bland mashed potatoes and carrots he was allowed to have for dinner had just left after giving him a longer than usual hug. Max Merrell slipped in his room after noticing the Judge was alone.

"Judge Carson." Merrell paused to take in the seriousness of the situation. "I need to speak with you."

Carson took a deep laboring breath and let it out. He then tilted his head so he could look into Merrell's eyes.

"It's about Drake, Judge." Merrell sat in a chair next to the bed. "Drake wants out."

Carson smiled.

"He feels..."

"He feels now that I'm on my way out...why should he have to stay." Carson spoke softly.

"Yes. He feels as if he has done enough." Merrell matched Judge Carson's tone. "He wants nothing to do with Judge Ellenberg."

"He has done enough. You both have." Carson coughed and choked and then regained composer. "Some things have been set in motion. Things you can't know about." Carson let out a sigh. "When I'm lying peacefully you will meet with a man. You will know him because he is a gigantic man who will be present. You will discuss this with him, but only at that time."

"I don't think The System is..."

"Hang in there, Max. Things are in motion. Things will happen, but The System will survive." Carson swallowed and coughed. "Ellenberg is the beginning of the end of an era. A cleansing of sorts."

"I don't believe he has the strength..."

"Trust me, Max." Carson took a deep breath and fell asleep.

Ï

"I don't think we have met," Cynthia said to SueAnn.

"I didn't want to go this route." Kelly stood in front of Cynthia. "But I was left no choice." He paused until Cynthia sat back down on the sofa. "Clean slate," he hollered. "You know we didn't really want partners, but we didn't want puppets either. Our leash was not short. But we can't let the dog run wild. When the 'Old Men' went to the way side..."

"Ben." Cynthia pleaded. "I can..."

"We didn't always agree with every order." Kelly held his hand up to silence Cynthia. "Thought Carter was way out of bounds. Mill would have been out of the box as well. But this merc, Nesterenko?" He took a deep breath and let it out. "We expected change. Sort of a new guard of sorts." Kelly looked at SueAnn. "But we never expected people like Nesterenko getting involved. Or that shit bag Porter for that matter." He stepped away from Cynthia. "We knew you would be a challenge, Cynthia. Especially when your father handed you the big chair, but we never expected...well we never expected this."

"I can make it work, Ben," Cynthia cried. "I will make this work." She dropped to her knees.

"Covering up your son, Cynthia." Kelly stared at Merrell. "Never knew you had a son. Especially some old commie professor type son." He laughed. "Never would have known you were a communist."

"I'm no..."

"Did you really believe you would get away with using The System to hide some past connection?" Kelly's voice boomed.

"Ben. I really didn't know..."

"Passion!" Kelly interrupted Cynthia's excuse. "Never underestimate illogical passion. You thought you would deal with the consequences of your irrational moment when and if you had to." Kelly glanced at SueAnn and then Cynthia. "Well now you have to." Kelly stepped back, looked at SueAnn and nodded.

"Ben please...I have..."

A bullet hitting Cynthia in the chest interrupted her. Cynthia's body fell back into the couch. SueAnn stepped forward and placed another bullet into Cynthia's head.

"Federal Judge kills a politician." Kelly smiled. "Must have been a love interest gone wrong is what our friends on the payroll will continue to write." He looked at Merrell. "A retired General gunned down as he enters his home." He paused to look at SueAnn and shrugged his gigantic shoulders. "Our friends in the press will write that he must have gotten involved with the undesirables."

"What will they say about two dead judges and a mercenary?" SueAnn asked. "This might be a little hard to explain."

"I'm sure we can think of something." Kelly made eye contact with both Merrell and SueAnn, and then all three turned to leave.

***

Ben Kelly never met his killer, Drake McCreiess, before he fell to the hard wooden floor after only catching a glimpse of him. The .45 caliber bullet hit Kelly in his right eye and exited the back of his head before any thought of what news organizations would ultimately say about judges and a mercenary being found murdered. If the gigantic man had life within him before he fell to the floor, he showed no actions that said he did. His body hit the floor with a thud and the inside of his head slowly drained, leaving a large pool of blood and matter to surround the feet of Merrell and SueAnn.

Both Merrell and SueAnn stood silent and stunned as they looked at Drake McCreiess standing in the foyer with a smoking gun trained on both of them.

"It's over Max. The System is over." McCreiess said as he closed the gap between himself and his friend. "For you SueAnn, it's not going to start." McCreiess kept his weapon trained on his friend. "Both of you drop the mags of your weapons, clear the pipes, and break them down."

Both Merrell and SueAnn dropped the magazines containing bullets from their weapons to the floor and cleared the pipes.

"Break them down. I want the pins." McCreiess wanted the cotter pins that held the upper and lower receivers of the weapons together.

"Drake! What is going on?" Merrell asked as he did what he was ordered.

"What is..."

"SueAnn, I promised your father I would keep you out of this. Max, you are better than this," McCreiess said as he allowed his thoughts to drift.

:-

McCreiess looked across the old dirty diner table at the man he would replace. The man he looked at was frail but proud. The man was so close to death that McCreiess actually thought Paul English was capable of placing his head on the table and expiring.

"You will be replacing me," said Paul English as he sat shaking. "You! My daughter is to never have anything to do with this."

"I understand I guess." McCreiess was confused.

"Ben Kelly will not listen to me."

i

"You knew my father?" SueAnn English tossed the cotter pin of her weapon next to the pin from Merrell's and interrupted McCreiess' thought. "Why..."

"Don't ask." Merrell interrupted.

"You both need to walk away from this." McCreiess picked up the pins and backed out of the door. "Do yourselves a favor and don't follow me." He disappeared.

What can you tell us about how our son was killed?

McCreiess drove the long driveway to the rustic home that he spent over two days of travel time to get to. The journey meant alone time, which meant any number of thoughts about his current situation could pop into his head. He was happy to be finally free of a secret society that used him for nothing more than creating misery for so many. He knew the people he killed were not good people, but he was sure most of them had a mother or father somewhere that loved them. His understanding of death was simple – death of friends was sad, but death of children could be crushing to the spirit. When he was in Beirut, Lebanon his commander said, "We are sad today because so many of our friends have fallen, but there will be someone who will get a visit sometime soon, and they will be given news about how their child paid the ultimate sacrifice, and they will be crushed. Some will never have a good day again." What his commander from Beirut said was what drove him to make the two-day trip to the rustic home that he was now parked in front of.

McCreiess walked the walkway with trepidation. He was still not sure he wanted to knock on the door. Standing at the door he took a deep breath and knocked. He heard someone moving behind the door so he prepared himself for the initial meeting, understanding it would be awkward.

"Hello. Can I help you?" The older gentleman asked as he answered the door.

"Mr. Keagan?" McCreiess asked quietly.

"Yes, my name is Darrell Keagan."

"Mr. Keagan, my name is Drake McCreiess and I served...I mean...I..."

Mr. Keagan opened the door and gestured McCreiess to enter and he did.

"You knew my son, Darrell?" Mr. Keagan gestured for McCreiess to sit and he did. "You knew Darrell?"

"I did not know Darrell, Sir." McCreiess sat forward in his seat. "I was one of three men tasked with finding your son. I can only say that I wish I could have gotten to him sooner."

"We were told that his squad ran out of ammunition and that the resupply was late." Mr. Keagan choked up. "We were told it became hand to hand. We were..."

Mrs. Keagan and one of the Keagan' daughters interrupted the conversation McCreiess and Mr. Keagan were having.

"Darrell, we're home," Mrs. Keagan said as she entered the living room from the kitchen. "You have a guest."

"Yes we do. His name is Drake McCreiess and he was one of the team members that were tasked with resupplying..."

Mrs. Keagan moved closer to her husband and they both put their arms around each other, both started to cry.

"What can you tell us about how our son was killed," Mrs. Keagan said as her and her husband slowly sat on the couch directly across from McCreiess, they were still embraced.

"You don't know ma'am? You're a Marine. I thought you were there in Afghanistan at the time." McCreiess was stunned. He thought for sure she understood what really happened to her son.

"I was only told that he engaged the enemy and he eventually succumbed to enemy fire," Mrs. Keagan said as her voice quivered. "His body was so badly damaged after all the ordinance they dropped…"

"My brother would fight as hard as anyone, and I know his men loved him for it." The Keagan' daughter entered into the conversation by interrupting her mother.

"We raised our son to be the man he was, a Marine," Mrs. Keagan said as she wept.

"He was as heroic as anyone I know, or ever knew." McCreiess paused for thought. "They all were courageous, committed, and honorable." He didn't know if he should believe what Mrs. Keagan said she knew about her son's death. The truth was not in the official report, but the truth was told.

McCreiess went to the Keagan home to tell the truth about how the young Lieutenant Keagan died. He was going to talk about how the young Lieutenant was so distraught over the actions of his mother that he simply sat down and slit his own wrist. He had a change of heart after looking into the eyes of the father and sister of the young man.

The daughter moved to the couch to share in the embrace of her mother and father. McCreiess remained silent, allowing the family a peaceful moment.

"Where are you staying?" Mr. Keagan asked.

"I'm heading east, sir. I guess I just wanted to see the young man's family."

What do you mean?

McCreiess remained guarded as he stood over his friend who was lying peacefully in his bed at home. His friend, Stan Brown, looked whole but he wasn't. His friend could not stand long before severe headaches, fatigue, and fainting spells would send him to the ground. Stan Brown was once a proud member of the US Army Special Forces. Many considered him near genius, with an IQ of over 150, before being struck in the head with a piece of shrapnel. Stan shocked many people when, after receiving his bachelor degree from Ohio State and then receiving his master's degree from Notre Dame, he joined the army infantry as an enlisted soldier. He wanted nothing to do with the officer corp. That was the type of person he was; he wanted to be where the action was and could care less about getting the credit. He would often say, "There were a lot of regular Joe's that had to do great things before Patton and others like him could be considered great leaders. Be the man doing something, and not the guy trying to be a 'somebody'."

Stan retired from the Army and did what many considered natural; he joined a security company that was contracted by the US government to help with the security of its diplomats. While serving in Iraq his vehicle drove over an IED that exploded, killing everyone in the vehicle except him. The doctors picked over 50 different pieces of metal from his body. He would have died if it were not for a Marine patrol that happened upon the situation. If it were not for his mother, he would have appreciated it if the Marines had left him alone.

Stan's mother entered the room and moved to stand next to McCreiess. She pulled the bedspread up to allow fresh air to circulate under the covers. Stan smiled at his mother.

"Where's Carla?" McCreiess asked about Stan's wife.

"She left soon after we got him home." The mother paused. "She didn't want any of this."

"Are you the only one taking care of him?" McCreiess sat on the bed.

"Yep."

"What about the security company, Greystroke?"

"They hired a law firm to fight the workers compensation benefits."

"What do you mean?" McCreiess was stunned.

"They are trying to fight paying any of the Defense Base Act claims that he was promised." The mother sat next to McCreiess. She looked tired and sad, but she was not going to cry about her son's situation anymore.

"I thought the Defense Base Act was specifically designed for guys like Stan, guys who act on their countries behalf in dangerous areas of the world."

"That's what he thought too." The mother stood. "They paid initially. Medical bills and compensation, but now they are trying to get out from under all of it."

"What do you mean?"

"We had to go to court and we're waiting on a Judge's decision. Greystroke and their workers comp insurance company argued that he was never an employee of Greystroke. They even claimed he was faking his injuries."

"I met Stan in Iraq while he was working for Greystroke."

"It doesn't matter. This has been going on for a couple years now. It has been a constant struggle to get the insurance company to pay the bills. They act as if they owe nothing and they only pay at the last moment." The mother sighed. "They know he can't work. They know he can't make payments on his home so they always float like two hundred and fifty thousand and say take it or leave it. They know that is nowhere near what he will need for a life time of coverage."

"Greystroke..."

"Greystroke paid workman's compensation premiums in access of six hundred dollars a day, per employee, to the insurance company. And the insurance company accepted every dime on behalf of thousands of employee's."

"How can this..."

"Greystroke and the insurance company are fighting every case that looks like it will be a lifelong complaint." The mother turned to walk from the room. "He told them to take the two hundred and fifty and pound it with a load of nails in their ass."

"When will you know? When will the judge..."

"The decision could come anytime now." The mother paused. "If it's in our favor he will stay with me. If Greystroke wins, I fear Stan will not want to be a burden. It would be his last straw."

McCreiess sat stunned. He was appalled that anyone would think that Stan Brown would fake anything. He witnessed his friend hobble miles with broken ribs just so he could be with his men, when he could have easily bowed out of the dangerous mission.

"After Carla left, it seemed the only thing he had to keep him going was the fight the worker's comp people picked."

"I never knew the struggles..."

"The Veterans Administration is no better when it comes to our soldiers." The mother interrupted. "They are doing everything they can to get out from under a wounded vet." The mother left the room. "I saw where some of the bureaucrats were getting five digit bonuses' to slow up the process. It's all a scam, it's a system based on corruption."

"A system." McCreiess stood and looked down on his friend. "I'll be there for you."

Before McCreiess left the home of Stan Brown, he wrote a check for just a little over three million dollars, a little less than one third of his savings, and gave it to Stan's mother. He explained it was for his future care regardless of what the court's decision was in regards to his compensation case. Stan's mother asked how he was able to afford so much and he explained that his curses have been as plentiful as his blessings and he was just able to save some of the blessings.

Stan's mother explained that she would help others with the generous gift. "I will say it was from the Drake McCreiess society," she said.

McCreiess explained to Stan's mother that the bureaucrats, politicians, and officers should never be trusted, and that it was up to people like Drake and Stan to protect each other. He explained that warriors look out for each other.

He stared...

Article 38 of the United Nations Convention on the Rights of the Child stipulates that countries shall take all measures to ensure that anyone who has yet to reach the age of eighteen should not take part in state sponsored hostilities. The article also states that countries take measures to prevent recruitment of children for the battlefields that consume the world. It is estimated that child soldiers engage as combatants in at least three quarters of the conflicts in the world.

The Lord's Resistance Army of Uganda abducted more than thirty thousand boys and girls as soldiers. The resistance army is known to spread violence throughout many countries of Northern Africa and they are accused of human rights violations to include murder, mutilation, and child sex slavery. The US designates the Lord's Resistance Army as a terrorist group and the International Criminal Court wants to hold its leadership responsible for crimes against humanity.

Namilyango College, located in Mukono Town, Uganda, is the oldest boy's boarding school in Uganda. It is one of the most prestigious schools in Uganda and children that attend the school can master any number of subjects ranging from Technical Drawing to Physics and Chemistry.

The Biermans House was one of ten residential houses located on the campus of Namilyango College. The house was air-conditioned and for Drake McCreiess that was priority. He had just finished a very long surveillance mission that had him trekking through the dense Maramagambo Forest.

McCreiess waited patiently for April Khol, the United Nations lead council for a commission tasked with reporting violations of Article 38. He smiled as April entered the room with three boys dressed in their school uniforms. The boys were smiling and laughing as April kicked a soccer ball toward a door that led outside. The boys got the hint and went outdoors to play.

"Have you been waiting long?" April asked.

"Not long." McCreiess jumped from his seat, a marble bench, and shook her hand. "I would have waited longer." He smiled.

"Yeah." April laughed.

"Yes." McCreiess sat back down and grabbed a file from his satchel. "Because I believe what is in this file is that important."

"I'm sure it is." April sat next to McCreiess and scanned the file. "You were highly recommended."

"From what I have seen. The LRA is operating in the Maramagambo Forest." McCreiess pointed at a picture from the file. "That is a camp and I believe it is being used to train children soldiers."

"How many?" April frowned as she asked.

"I would say no more than fifty." McCreiess paused. "We will have to act quickly if we want to save that bunch."

"Many of them are children from Christian families. Their parents were killed for being Christians and the children are converted at gunpoint. The girls will be sold as slaves and the boys will be converted to soldiers." April paused to look over the picture. "Two hundred and seventy eight girls were taken a few months ago. The girls that couldn't be sold were killed." She sighed. "What will you need?"

"You work for the United Nations. There are lots of people in the UN sympathetic to the groups who convert, sell, and kill the children. The silence on such an issue speaks loud and clear."

April cocked her head and slightly grinned. "What needs to be done will not be sanctioned by the United Nations. There are some private entities that are not so sympathetic when it comes to stealing children."

McCreiess took a deep breath and let it out. "I will need a squad of men and all the arms and equip..."

McCreiess was interrupted by April placing her hand on his arm. "Drake, please tell me about you. What do you know?"

McCreiess sat for a moment. He looked up and then down.

"I need to know more about you. I need to know why..."

"I know that life is a puzzle that can only be completed by fulfilling the allotted time God has provided us, and the time allotted is only known by our Creator." McCreiess gently interrupted April. "I believe that pieces of the puzzle are placed daily with or without our knowledge. We probably hold a piece or two in hand but don't know where to place them. It will only be when we drop something, forget something, run late, or see something...something will happen and another piece of the puzzle will fall into place, and they fall when least expected, and without notice in many instances." McCreiess leaned forward and remained looking down.

April remained holding onto McCreiess' arm. She was surprised by his willingness to open up about personal beliefs, but she was interested in what he had to say so she remained quiet.

"It's hard not knowing how it all works out in the end, but I know that it is known. I have to believe there is a Creator that knows. I pray that there is." McCreiess sighed. "People spend a lot of time searching, guessing, and wanting, only to miss the small fun stuff while fretting about something that may or may not ever come." McCreiess took a deep breath and let it out. "Something thought huge at a specific time, in the grand scheme of things is probably only one chip of wood from a large oak tree. The future has already been decided. I have to think or believe that. And we have to have the honor, strength, and courage to deal with anything that comes our way. I know this is easier said, but as each noticeable piece falls into place, we have to take the time, maybe for just a brief moment and smile, cry, laugh, sulk, shake with fear, or fight for life." He paused and looked up. "I believe it is the reaction to a specific event that allows us to move forward, onto the next piece of the puzzle. The moment to react should be brief because the next piece, probably in hand, needs to be positioned. Regardless of what we do, what reaction we have, the pieces of the life puzzle will fall in place."

April tightened her hold onto his arm.

"I'm sorry. I know I'm rambling on. I...."

"No. Please go on. I want to hear more." April scooted closer.

"Well I believe the puzzle of our life was created long ago and is known by the one who created our time. I just trust that it will all come together. Some pieces may not have as smooth as edge as other pieces so they may seem harder to fit. At least from our view, some pieces will be missing, lost and may never be found." He paused to reflect. "Regardless, the puzzle will be complete."

"Go on. Please," April encouraged.

"I think decisions we make may or may not affect our future. We make decisions based on the doors that are opened and closed. I know that none of the decisions made today will ever change actions or events of the past. The past is etched and the moment is free. I just keep with the journey. Keep trying to improve. Understanding that there is a plan." McCreiess sighed as a tear ran down his cheek. "There has to be."

"My mother," April chimed in as she gently wiped the tear from McCreiess' face. "Well, a person I thought of as a mother often said, know that you are loved. Know that there is a plan for you, a destination. And it is good." She paused for a moment. "She would say that what others want for you might not be what is in your heart. The journey of others is not your journey and their destination is not what is planned for you, and we have to accept the fact that others are not going to be pleased with our passage and ultimate purpose. She said that we shouldn't worry about what others think. She said we have to search our hearts and stay out of the mold others create for us."

"She sounds like a wise woman." McCreiess turned to look at April.

April stared into the eyes of McCreiess.

McCreiess returned the stare with a smile.

"You don't have to do this. The LRA will be dealt..."

"I want to do this." McCreiess remained staring into the eyes of April. It was the first time he stared into the eyes of a woman since he last stared into Abby's.

The End.